Wildrose

THE HISTORICAL COLLECTION
BOOK FIVE

KATIE CROSS

www.katiecrossbooks.com

A Note On The Timeline

WILDROSE takes place in the year 1481, which is approximately one hundred and twelve years before you meet Wildrose for the first time in the Sisterwitches Series (which occurs in the year 1593).

THE DAUPHIN FAMILY

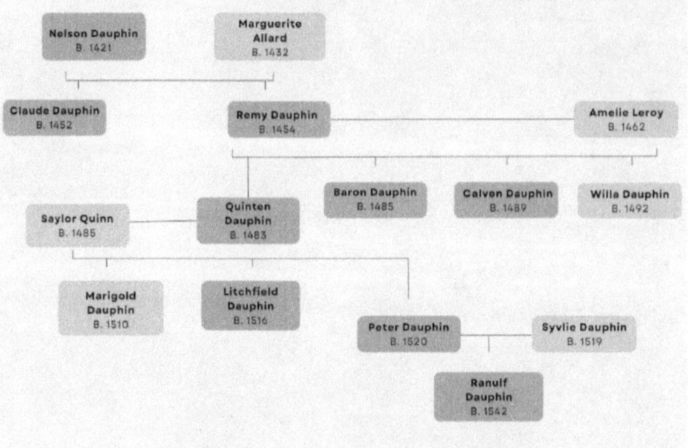

Chapter One

A banner, flapping in the wind, boldly stated, WELKUM BAK REMEE.

Remy Dauphin tilted his head, squinted one eye, and smiled. Must be from his neighbor, Caterina Leroy. She was seven years old and the youngest of nine daughters.

Delightful.

Remy peeled away from the window to leave the library of his family's ancestral estate. Two hundred years old, and counting. His older brother, Claude, would inherit it. A pity. Remy would love to grow old within these blessed walls.

Preparations for his welcome home party bustled in the stories below. The tantalizing smell of a hintaberry tart wafted up the stairs, teasing him.

Well.

He better check on those.

As he spun on his heel, a book leaped off the shelf and slammed into his chest. Taken aback, he coughed and grabbed it by the spine. Dust sprouted from the edges. The moment his right hand touched the leather, an unidentifiable pull gripped each finger, as if strings looped around his bones and drew them to the cover.

He shook his hand.

The hold didn't loosen.

Gripping his right wrist with his left hand, he attempted to fling the book free of his palm, to no avail. He grabbed each finger with his other hand and attempted to yank them off, but the magic clung tenaciously. No matter what he tried, invisible tension remained.

"I worked for a traveling book binder the last six years," he muttered, "and I've never seen book magic like this before. What strange magic is this?"

A mixture of fascination kept him focused on the grimoire. Nevermind the title, he'd figure that out in a moment. He may have flitted around Alkarra for years—and noted obvious changes in his family since he returned for good last week—but *this* was something else.

No book had ever thrown itself at him.

And so *boldly*.

"What do you want?" He turned his right hand to better view the front cover.

Wildrose
A grimoire.

Greater space existed below the word *grimoire*, as if more should have been there. A magical book of spells wasn't out of place—certainly not in his family. His father, Nelson, had a near tragic love of grimoires. He built a successful career and modest fortune on finding, rehabilitating, and selling rarely-used grimoires. This piece should have come with no shock. None of them had ever launched themselves, though.

"Wildrose," Remy murmured. "I haven't heard of *you*."

"Remy! Remy? Where are you?"

Mother's call rang through the Dauphin estate, nestled along the edge of the countryside on the far outskirts of Ashleigh city. Her dulcet tone was like music. He'd missed her.

"Here, Mother!"

"Come down! Some of the Leroys will arrive soon, and they want to welcome you back." After a pause, she added, "Amelie might be with them."

Her tone turned up at the end, setting his jaw on edge. He wrestled the urge to tell her to be quiet.

Amelie.

Really?

Could Mother be more conspicuous?

At twenty-seven, he was hardly ready to settle into courting and *real life* as Father called it. His employer had just died, the business dissolved, and he'd moved home in a bid to figure out some major life twists.

His nose wrinkled.

Also, Amelie Leroy?

Certainly not.

Amelie the Awkward, his friends always called her. The title had been well-earned. Seven years younger than him, she had gangly arms and a pimpled face. At least, she had six years ago.

She hid in the bushes to spy on him, sighed endlessly while reading romance novels when he had to endure dinner with her family—though, really, her parents weren't so bad—and stared at him with intense adoration every chance she had. The intensity of her affection had been daunting.

However, despite visiting twice a year, he couldn't recall seeing her.

The Leroy family lived next door all of Remy's life, forming a powerful bond between Remy's parents and James and Joyce Leroy. Handfasting a Leroy girl, and sharing grandchildren, would seal Mother's infinite joy.

"Come down, Remy!" she called. "We need to finalize a few

details on the guest list. I've invited several young women from the neighborhood." Her trilling voice was downright musical now. "Several of which you have yet to meet. We'll find a wife for you yet!"

His eyes rolled to the back of his head.

This would be agony. For Mother's sake, he brightened his tone.

"Be right there!"

The second his response finished, a potent force jerked him out of the room by his arm. The grimoire, still attached to his hand, elevated him into the air. With a shout, he attempted, unsuccessfully, to free himself. The book jerked forward, driving him out of the library.

"Whoa!" Remy cried.

He stumbled over his own feet, yanked into the hallway. He slammed into the balustrade with a shout and nearly cracked a decorative board in half. He flailed, attempting to reach for the book with his other hand.

"Let me go!"

The book led the way, zipping down the hall. Unable to keep up with the unnerving speed, Remy lifted his legs to avoid a chair. The grimoire swung his feet off the ground. He soared down the long hall, racing past rooms.

This must be a hallucination. Had he eaten a bad mushroom? Claude tried them before. His description of the experience resembled this quite closely.

No.

Impossible. He hadn't eaten yet today.

Two broad windows streamed sunlight into Mother's favorite tea room at the back of the Dauphin estate, which overlooked their orchard and the Leroy backyard. Beyond that, the rolling, thick forest of Letum Wood sprawled to endless horizons and vistas.

"Oh no!" he yelled. "Not the windows!"

He barely had time to wrench up his shoulders and curl into a ball, anticipating a painful shatter of glass over his shoulders, when the windows breezed open and he sailed through.

A scream blocked his throat as earth flew past his dangling legs three stories below. Hedges, trees, gardens, and high grasses proliferated in the early summer sunshine. Puffy white clouds studded a bluebird sky, defying the utter terror that rushed through him.

"Where are you taking me?" he shouted.

Past the estate, over the hedges into a wild field, and through the wood they raced. The book dodged around trees as if it had done this before, expertly avoided a gargantuan oak with a glaring eye knot, and kept him high enough off the ground that the tips of his shoes skimmed the tops of the grass. A gigantic tree, wide as a carriage, loomed ahead. His lodged scream broke free. At the last second, the book swung him to the right, wheeling him above and below several gargantuan branches, then winged into a field.

The grimoire dropped Remy in an open, grassy spot, tumbling free of his hand. They collapsed to the ground together. The elegant cover flopped open and shuffled to the first page.

Gasping, Remy braced his hands beneath him.

"Are you mad?" he cried. "What are you doing? How did you bring me here? What is going on?"

His head snapped from side to side, studying the quiet meadow. Forest hemmed in a wide, grassy lot that more than tripled their current estate. It was almost completely cut off from everything else, though the road hadn't been far away. He'd never been here before, that he could recall. A peaceful quiet reigned.

Not unpleasant.

The grimoire trembled, then settled with a sigh, reminding him why he was here in the first place. He peered at the words on the first page. Astonishment made him gasp. The title had changed!

Wildrose: The Manor.
A grimoire.

"You only said *Wildrose* before. Why should it change now?"

A table of contents trailed into a multitude of options. The thick book had pages upon pages upon pages of lists, blueprints, designs, descriptions of intricate details, all the way to shelf depth and crown molding. An entire house contained in a book the height of two fists stacked on top of each other. He'd never seen one quite this thick.

"My former boss would have something to say about your binding." He sent an errant gaze to the stitching. "Well . . . not so bad. Durable, certainly, if you're dragging unsuspecting witches all over the place."

Intrigue pushed him to return to the beginning of the grimoire and peruse it again, this time with greater attention to detail.

Remy turned page after page, muttering questions and exclamations under his breath. Different chapters appeared with an animation that bordered on emotional. He couldn't deny the value of such a find. Must be quite rare, too. Such a strange treasure. Father brought home peculiar magic often, but this beat all the others.

Was it a new acquisition?

From the far edge of the field floated a voice.

"Remy?"

He straightened and instantly replied, "Claude?"

His brother, almost a spitting image of Remy himself, stumbled into sight. Unlike Remy, whose blond hair lay on his shoulders, Claude kept his short. Remy had sky blue eyes; Claude had chocolate brown. Remy was always clean-shaven, but Claude kept a shimmer of stubble.

Claude staggered sideways, belched, waved a hand, and fell to one knee with a laugh. In less time than a heartbeat, he'd toppled all the way into the grass, disappearing behind the waist-high strands. Remy sighed.

Drunk again.

Of all the changes in his family since he'd returned, Claude had altered the most. The heady stench of ipsum stained Claude's breath as Remy approached. The sour smell hung in the air like invisible, limp clouds. Claude's ruddy face narrowed into a grimace meant to be a question.

"What're you doing out here, Remy?"

The slurred speech and drawling *e*'s testified to his drunkenness.

Before noon.

Rather unsavory.

"Is this a result of a late night, or an early morning?" Remy asked with forced wryness. It *could* be worse, he supposed. Claude responded as well to perceived judgment as one might a nest of angry bees, which meant he was sometimes easier to deal with when inebriated.

Claude blinked hard.

"What?"

Remy rolled his eyes. "Nothing. What are you doing out here, of all places?"

Claude stood, spun around, lost his balance, and landed on his bottom again. He scratched his head.

"Don't know."

Wandered into the forest after drinking all night, probably. This wouldn't be the first time, according to Father's most recent letters. Unfortunate. Now that Remy had returned home, it would be easier to help Claude through . . . whatever pained hm. Witches didn't drink into oblivion for no reason.

Claude, still blinking harder than made sense, broke into a chortle. His hand lifted, pointing to the book.

"I know that grimoire."

Too late, Remy realized that the Wildrose grimoire hovered above the field, tailing him like a puppy. He'd prefer not explaining to his family what just happened, but his curiosity won out. Instead of convincing Claude he imagined it, Remy asked, "You know this grimoire?"

"Sure. That's the house I tried to build."

"You tried to build a house?"

"Last year. Didn't I write to you about it?"

"No. I would have remembered that."

Claude chortled, then fell onto his back. "Waste of time!" He hacked up a cough and closed his eyes, humming in the sunshine. "Didn't do anything. Bought the stuff." He yawned. "It just . . . just sat there. Too many lists, if you ask me."

"Bought *what* stuff?" Remy asked, but Claude didn't answer. His hands twitched as he dove toward a ready sleep.

Remy tentatively brought the grimoire back into his arms and shuffled to the beginning. It required both hands to lift it. Pressure didn't hold his hand hostage, nor grasp him, which probably meant something. Whatever brought him here, this book or the magic within, placated at this spot. Clearly, it wanted him to see this empty field. He turned the book over, inspecting each part of the leather exterior.

Claude sat up all at once, eyes wide. "Cursed," he shouted, an arm in the air. "That bloody magic is cursed, I swear it!"

Remy startled, observed his delirious brother, and then calmed. Claude, not noticing Remy, hiccuped. He giggled and lay back down.

"It's a wretched book. Requires so much work and detail. Father says it's part of our inheritance. His grimoire collection is worth almost as much as the Dauphin estate. I think we should sell it."

"The estate?"

"No." Claude waved a hand. "The grimoire collection." He yawned and snuggled his face into the grass. Remy wished he'd go to sleep already. "Stupid books. Can't believe this is part of our inheritance."

Remy frowned. "The grimoire?"

"No!" Claude shook his head like an exaggerated toddler. He pressed a hand to his forehead and winced, slowing the intense motion. "No, no, no, Remy. Not the grimoire. The *land*. This plot." Eyes closed, he waved a hand in a maniacal circle. "Father bought *this*."

This spot of forest had always been wild. The neighborhood where they'd grown up pressed the boundaries of *civilized society*, according to Ashleigh city witches. Their home was on a road near a collection of six estates that formed a half circle, not far from the small village of Pershington, outside of Ashleigh city.

Growing up, it had been a delightful mix of sophistication and open space.

"I didn't know the lot was for sale," Remy said.

Claude shrugged. His breath elongated as he inched closer to sleep for a third time.

"Worthless." He turned onto his side, rested his cheek on top of a mossy rock, ignoring the sharp stalks of dried grasses in which he burrowed. "Just a buncha forest . . . wild creatures . . ." He yawned. "Worthless tract of . . ."

Claude dropped into a snore.

Unsurprising that Claude couldn't wrestle functionality from a grimoire this elaborate. Claude was more of an untamed investor. He threw currency at schemes, tested them, then backed out unless prodigious success resulted. Claude possessed no patience. He desired a quick return, easy for the taking.

A distant stirring of memory recalled Mother mentioning a house in one letter. Claude dove into the project with his usual gusto, desiring an estate in which to live, but abandoned the project after a month.

Too many details, she'd said.

Remy pressed both hands to either side of the cover, sandwiching the grimoire. Intrigue captured him as effectively as the magic stealing him to this spot. The elegant pictures, the depictions.

Understated brilliance awaited within.

In fact, it *called* to him.

Claude snorted and twitched, drawing Remy's attention. He shook his head, withdrawing from the siren song.

"Take a nap, Claude. No one will bother you in this field, and the sunshine might do you some good. You're pale, these days. Too much time in your taverns. I'll be at home, preparing to see the Leroy girls again." He groaned. "Mother is on a matchmaking bender and she's already mentioned Amelie. Can you imagine how awkward it will be? I want nothing less than a handfasting, though I do enjoy James Leroy."

Claude gave a light snore. With the grimoire tucked under his arm, Remy strode out of the field and into the forest, homeward bound.

Waiters slipped gracefully behind Remy's back that evening, a worker's anthem in their footsteps and the gentle clink of plates on trays. The soothing social lullaby was welcome amidst so many mingling bodies.

Mother hadn't exaggerated. She invited *all* the young women.

He recognized a Leroy face here and there, but they were the youngest girls. Caterina and Manon and Sophie. Too young to be any threat to him. Other ladies, clearly in their late teens and twenties, grinned from behind fans. Remy smiled weakly and tried to mean it, but longed to find his boyhood friends and escape outside.

Candles lent a stuffy perfume to the thick air, despite open windows trailing a light breeze. The room, overly bright thanks to the fully lit chandelier, glittered. Magic prevented the wax from dripping to the floor, thank heavens, or he would have had sizzling wax in his hair more than once.

Mother and Father stood on the other side of the room, smiling as they welcomed newcomers into the foyer and main hall. Mother wound her arm through Father's, gripping him with an affectionate squeeze and warm smile. Remy made a mental note to check on her in a bit. Her knee had been bothering her, and she couldn't stand for long.

An arm elevated, clutching a wine glass, as two familiar male voices rang out, "Remy has returned!"

His best friends from Mr. Riley's School for Boys slammed into him, sloshing their plum wine onto his frock coat, and patting him on the back. Concerns for his family faded to the back of his mind as they pulled him off to the side.

"My job is so boring," Allard said with a cluck and shake of his head. "This business of being a responsible adult is a mess, you know. No wonder Father always groaned over taxes. I'm working too much to court a pretty girl, even!"

"Not half as bad as what's going on with Jimmy." Bill nudged Allard in the ribs. "Tell Remy what happened."

Allard's thin mouth went slack. "You won't believe it, Remy," he breathed. "Not a word. You agree?"

"Sure."

"It's all because of Amelie Leroy."

Remy recoiled.

"Amelie?"

Sniggering, Bill asked, "Have you seen her yet?"

"No."

"Don't bother." Allard tossed back the last of his wine.

"She's a lost cause, and a cold-hearted witch. You'll never have a chance with her. No one else has, anyway."

"Sneaky little Amelie that used to spy on us through the hedges?" Remy asked in a low tone, glancing to the side to ensure James or Joyce weren't within earshot. They wouldn't appreciate gossip about their daughter. "What are you talking about?"

A shout came from the front door, only a few paces away. Claude stumbled through the doorway. Dried grass and twigs littered the back of his shirt. He hadn't changed, but he had restocked his ipsum. He clutched a half-empty bottle in one hand.

"Where's my brother?" he slurred.

Bill frowned.

Allard turned his back with a touch of cool hauteur. Remy clenched his teeth and sucked in a sharp breath. What a humiliating display.

"Later?" Remy asked.

They nodded, sending him away with vague nods. The wine had started to sink in, because their glazed eyes shone as they turned their attention to the sheer amount of dazzling girls.

Remy slid into the hallway as Claude bumbled in that direction. As Remy turned the corner to catch up with his brother, a body appeared. He avoided a collision by grasping the upper arms of the other witch.

A bitty gasp followed.

"Oh!"

"Forgive me!" he said. "I didn't see you. I—"

Remy paused, blinked. Quick as his horror over Claude and bowling into this girl occurred, astonishment followed.

He'd know that dark hair and that slightly-upturned, pert nose from anywhere. A Leroy daughter, but certainly *not* a younger one. The dumpy Leroy daughters, who had pretty enough faces but droll expressions and a lack of humor, typically shared flouncy, tightly-coiled tresses. This girl—no, woman—had no such awkwardness. Her locks flowed onto her shoulder with lazy curls.

This had to be Amelie.

But, no.

It *couldn't* be Amelie.

This woman was a delightful little vixen, and Amelie had been a blundering teenager with acne and a whisper. The smattering of freckles over her cheeks became more visible as her face lowered into surprise.

"Remy?" she breathed.

"A-amelie?"

A frosty smile graced her lips. Amelie curtsied and stepped to the side with polite, but vague, irritation. The response was as proper as one might expect. Apparently, the Network school system had been good to her.

She *had* attended, hadn't she?

The Leroys sent all their daughters to Network schools, as a point of pride. Remy side-stepped to block her path.

"You can't be Amelie."

Her cool smile turned frigid.

"Can't I?"

"That is . . . I haven't seen you in years."

"I'm aware."

"How have you . . . that is . . . how old are you now?"

Her hair shifted when she tilted her head to the side. "Is that really what you want to ask me?"

Horrified that *he* should be the awkward one, Remy stammered through an excuse that didn't form words. With painstaking tolerance and a waxen, charitable smile, she waited for him to finish.

"Ah," slurred a voice from behind, "so you've finally seen her, have you, my brother? Our ugly little Amelie has grown up at last."

Amelie's gaze tapered to slits.

Claude's voice sliced like a serpent, punctuated with a tint of wine. He dropped a hand on Remy's shoulder, then leaned so much of his weight onto Remy that he staggered to stay upright. The smell of a rancid belch floated with Claude. His forehead pressed to Remy's shoulder in a delirious giggle.

Disgust curled Amelie's upper lip. Before Remy could apologize, she recoiled another step.

"Ah," she slurred in return, perfectly mimicking his toneless words, "the pig of the neighborhood has returned from his slop to embarrass his parents yet again. Who here is the most surprised? Certainly not me."

Claude scowled.

Amelie's stoic indignation and firm response shocked Remy. Shy little Amelie! She had once adored him from a distance and could barely squeak out a word in his presence. Yet this . . . woman . . . nearly filled the room, and in opposition to a too-broad male personality?

Impressive.

A bit terrifying, too.

Claude moaned and nearly stumbled into the wall. Remy leaned to the side to pin his brother in place and prevent him from falling, then managed a sheepish smile that Amelie ignored.

"Unfortunately," Amelie glared at Claude, "this isn't even half as embarrassing as what he's done while you've been gone. Count yourself lucky for being spared the horror of other social events. Your parents weren't."

Claude slid down the wall, melting like a candle. She spun on her heels and left with the *tap-tap-tap* of departing shoes. Remy hesitated for a full ten seconds, torn between his desire to speak to Amelie—perhaps that was the first time he ever thought such a thing—and the obligation to help his brother.

Amelie vanished before he could conjure something to say.

Remy wheeled around, a tongue lashing at the edge of his

teeth, but Claude sat on the ground, gurgling small bubbles, and utterly oblivious in the worst way.

The Turners, who lived three doors down, strolled by. Their fixed smiles drooped when they caught sight of Claude, slumped on the floor. His ipsum bottle streamed a thin trickle of liquid to the marble floor. Mrs. Turner buttoned up her rampant disapproval with a slight widening of her eyes at her husband, who immediately steered them toward the doorway.

Remy shook his head.

"You're a bloody fool, Claude, and you always have been."

He cast a glance around, confirmed no one else entered the hallway, and spoke a quick spell. Claude levitated into the air, his body hanging like a slack jellyfish. He floated ahead of Remy's magical guidance all the way up the stairs and into his bedroom.

Remy settled his brother, but he thought of Amelie.

Gentle star shine beckoned Remy outside sometime past three in the morning. As always, Mother and Father continued, oblivious to the late hour, at the round table with their closest friends. The Leroys, as well as one other couple—but definitely *not* the Turners, thanks to Claude—tossed cards back and forth. Light ipsum followed. Every now and then, a hiccup and a giggle floated on the breeze.

Remy closed his eyes and relished the quiet.

He'd never seen so many available young women in his life, all of them wide-eyed curious about his time with the book binder, in the other Networks, and what his future plans might be. Of special emphasis was his next career move, whether he might be able to support a family, and if he had plans later that week.

Savage desert dogs, all of them. Was he a hunk of ham in a

meat market? Each young woman had approached him at one point, salivating in her own pretty way.

All except Amelie.

For hours, she skirted the edges of the house, speaking to her sisters, older matrons, or men that could be her grandfather. Her studious avoidance of anyone her age sent a rather clear signal.

Everyone left her alone.

Except Mother.

Something in the smell of fresh forest, or perhaps the whirling sensation of nearby magic, guided Remy's focus into the distance. He set aside the conundrum of Amelie Leroy and remembered that afternoon. His thoughts soared beyond home, beyond understood boundaries.

Beyond *here*.

To *there*.

The spot of land that Claude claimed was part of their inheritance was little more than a clearing in a gigantic, overgrown, dangerous forest. Naturally, Remy's thoughts popped to the grimoire that took him *there*. In his memory, the spot had a hallowed recollection, despite the fact it had been less than a day since he discovered its existence.

Soon as his attention turned to the grimoire, a heavy something landed in his hands. He reared back, shocked to find the book in his fingers. Had he summoned it? Perhaps it invited itself. It had proven to be rather pushy that afternoon.

"By the skeletons! Was it really just this afternoon that you yanked me away? It feels as if ages have passed since then."

The pages whirred, racing forward, until they stopped on the first chapter. A gigantic, curvaceous number one, written in the very middle of a page, shone with silver design. Remy ignored a few written instructions, then flipped the page. The next side dictated what to do next to start a project, it seemed. What the project led to, he wasn't certain, but later images revealed a clock face.

"You're bossy." He set it down on the balustrade. "No."

When he tried to close it, the book wouldn't budge. Applying all his strength—of which he once thought not insignificant—changed nothing. Mystified, and more than a little curious, he studied the words on the first page again. His bleary eyes and stifled yawn made it difficult to focus, but he persevered.

The grimoire wouldn't take no for an answer.

Remy skimmed the words again, intrigued by a list of supplies. Work tools, mostly. Hammers, chisels, saws, etc. Another page recited a list of nail widths and lengths. At least twenty of them. He hadn't realized such specificity existed.

"That's quite the grimoire you have there."

Remy nearly jumped out of his skin as he whirled around, clutching it to his middle.

"What?"

Amelie stood in the middle of the doorway. Hesitation lingered around her in an aura, as if she hadn't been sure whether she should interrupt him or not. One of her hands pressed to the doorframe, but she stood at a canted angle, as if ready to flee.

Remy smiled. To his consternation, the book closed with only the slightest pressure from his fingertips. He set it aside on the balustrade, and it allowed him.

"How'd you know it was a grimoire?" he asked.

"At this house, they're all grimoires."

Laughing, he said, "Touche," and beckoned her farther onto the porch.

Taking his response as an invitation, she lifted the corners of her mouth ever so slightly and advanced. Her tentative steps brought her outside, though it appeared a difficult decision to make. She chose to stand on the other side of the balcony, overlooking the gardens. She couldn't stand much farther away without jumping free. He tried not to take offense.

Finding it best to say nothing, he returned his attention to the yard. His diverted focus eased the strain. Out of the corner of his eye, he caught how the moonlight glimmered on her features. The faint glow highlighted the scoop of her loose curls and the long bow of her neck. The shoulders of a violin player.

One of the Leroy girls played beautifully.

Was it Amelie?

Shame that he didn't know which one crept up on him. Of course he didn't know. Time gave him the advantage of reality, and he understood what he had *really* been like six years ago: a self-absorbed wretch, focused on finishing the Network school system and leaving home at any cost.

Well, he'd received his dream, lived in the world, returned in dismay, and now he struggled to know what to say.

"How has it been?" she asked without facing him. He was glad. The conversation would be easier if he didn't have to look right at her. He saw Amelie and thought of hot summers and wispy music.

"How has what been?" he asked.

"Returning home."

"Oh. That. Ah . . . it's been . . . strange."

Surprise lilted her tone, softening her features for the first time. "How so?"

"It's good," he quickly amended, "I love being home again, but . . ."

"But it's been six years," she murmured knowingly. "And you can't ever go back home, can you?"

"Yes," he drawled. "That's it exactly. You really can't go back. I thought home would feel the same, but it doesn't. It's different. You know, I've struggled to put to words the . . . discontent . . . I've been feeling, but I think you just did. Thank you."

She shrugged. Her hands held onto the balustrade as she leaned back, studying the stars. Her dress clung to her legs as she tilted her attention higher.

"How did you know how many years I've been gone?" he asked.

A chuckle floated out of her, and the brief smile changed her expression utterly. "Marguerite."

"Ah. Mother."

Amelie faced him for the first time with a smile. "She's missed you very much."

"So I've heard," he said wryly.

"Did she write as often as I assume she did?"

"Constantly."

"I'm not surprised. Your mother and I have become quite close."

"Oh?"

Her voice softened. "She's a wonderful witch, and a good friend. We've had tea many afternoons together. Were you working all the time that you were gone?"

The rapid shift in topic, executed without even a hitch of breath, required a moment for Remy to follow.

"Oh, uh . . . yes. Mostly working." This time, he shrugged. "Traveling occupied a good amount of our work, depending on where we went. There's only so long a traveling book binder can stay in one place, because there are only so many books. Mr. Donaldsen hated cities, so we went to smaller communities, too, which further restricted us."

"Did you like an ever-changing environment?"

"I think so."

She sounded amused when she asked, "You're not sure?"

He hesitated. How to summarize six years and a botched career?

"I have no regrets."

"Will you continue with book binding?"

"No. Mr. Donaldsen did the book binding, and I ran the company, found the book owners, sometimes coordinated sales, etc. Now, I'm in the market for another company to run."

"Within the book binding market?"

"Not necessarily."

She took that in with little change in expression. "What did you do on your days off?" she asked.

Sheepishly, he admitted, "I traveled. Mr. Donaldsen was an old man and we had to move slowly. I'd keep a list of things I wanted to do or see and return when I could."

Amelie laughed. "Of course. I remember all your big ideas."

"Really?"

"Oh yes. So many of them."

How odd that she had paid attention.

Remy leaned against the railing and faced the Dauphin manor. The brick exterior hadn't changed, nor the ivy that crawled across it in the warm months. He thrilled to the sameness in his formerly ever-shifting world.

"And you?" he asked.

"What about me?"

"What have you been up to?"

"Finished schooling," she said nonchalantly. "Played the violin in several concerts, and loved it."

He snapped two fingers. "I knew it! I remembered one of the Leroy sisters playing the violin, and I thought it was you."

A new hesitation stole over her that he couldn't hope to read. She faced out again, her profile tense.

"I . . . don't play violin anymore." The hastily-spoken words rang with tension. Before he could ask, she plowed on. "Ever since I stopped, I've been teaching my younger sisters."

"You don't play?"

Her neck barely moved when she shook her head back and forth once. She stood tight as a bow, ready to snap. Her right hand had curled into a fist, but her left lay at her side, fingers twitching stiffly. Based on her body language, he knew better than to question her further, but the burning curiosity was hard to stifle.

"Do you like teaching?" he asked, opting for the safe route she offered. Her tautness ebbed at the shift in conversation.

"Ah, no."

"Really?"

A hint of a smile returned. "I don't have the patience for teaching younger girls, but it's helped my parents not to hire another tutor, and it's been . . . well, better. Teaching is preferable to being bored. Until I figure out something else, it's the best path for everyone."

He had a feeling that *figuring out something else* intersected directly with not playing the violin anymore, but had no clues to build assumptions.

"Which Network school did you attend?" he asked. "I vaguely remember hearing rumors that Miss Vee's School for Girls had a musical slant."

She smiled with a cheeky gleam that immediately caught his attention. Sensing something naughty about to reveal, he leaned closer.

"I didn't attend a Network school."

"No?" His jaw dropped. "A daughter of James Leroy did not attend the revered school system?"

She grinned.

"That is of greatest surprise," Remy whispered. "James constantly extolled the virtues of a Network education. I thought it was a standard expectation for your family."

She charmed him with a sly chuckle.

"I tried. Shall we say that it . . . wasn't a good fit. Structure, routine, ridiculous teachers . . . was more of Katriona's focus. She loved every second of the Network school system, and so did Mathilde."

"Katriona is your second oldest sister?"

"Well recalled," she drawled with a hint of appreciation. "She has since married and been blessed with too many children."

"Good for her, but why not the Network schools for you? You certainly present yourself as if you attended the Network schools. They pound etiquette and performance into each and every student," he added with a bitter aside.

Amelie didn't appear annoyed with his singular focus on the subject.

"It wasn't my style."

"What is your style?"

The ghost of a laugh lived in her eyes, but her voice held only sadness. "The violin," she whispered. "That was my style, until it wasn't. Anyway, I was glad to avoid the Network school system and haven't regretted it. Until, well, recently. It's hard to find a career path that doesn't involve babies or homemaking without a Network education."

"You don't want babies?"

The fire of a challenge fueled her response. "I didn't say that," she instantly countered.

He held up two hands in a gesture of peace, and she exhaled. The flare of heat fizzled. A contemplative silence allowed sounds from inside to drift to the patio. Mother's gentle laugh, followed by a high guffaw, signaled that both of his parents had too much wine.

"Claude," Remy stated. "I want to apologize for—"

She held up her hand.

"Don't. There is no apologizing for that lech."

The fire of her passion startled him, but he strove to hide it. He regretted the topic when distance glazed her eyes again. So far, she'd unwound from her careful cocoon in surprising and unexpected ways. He wasn't sure he'd ever get used to her speaking like a regular witch, instead of a shy, love-besotted teenager.

Remy hurriedly sought for a change in subject, eager to keep a conversation flowing, but she prevented it. Her stiff, "What of Claude?" snapped like the heart of a fire.

"How long has he been this drunk?"

"Forever."

"Not that long."

In her arched brow, tilted with judgment and colored by indignation, she carried shades of the eldest Leroy daughter, Mathilde, a dragon in her own right.

"You just didn't see it before you left," she drawled, "but he's always been a bit of a lech, Remy. You had stars in your eyes over your future, and Claude hid it better then."

"Still, he's my brother," he said with a hint of warning.

She ignored it.

Any hope of her looking directly at him had left with the topic shift, but he couldn't bring himself to turn away. This unpredictable woman, with all her changing temperatures, confused him.

With a resigned sigh, she continued.

"Claude has taken as freely of ipsum since you left as before, only there hasn't been anyone to hide his indiscretions or help him out of bad situations. You did more to cover up his rotten core than you might remember. There's been no one else for him. Not anyone worthy of calling a friend, anyway," she added with a careless flutter of fingers. "He doesn't associate with witches that your father feels any pride over, is the best way of saying it. That means he's embarrassing himself, your parents, and your family name. No one is stopping him, certainly not himself."

None of this came as any great surprise, though it made Remy sick to his stomach. Letters from home indicated a decline in Claude for months, but seeing it with his own eyes was an altogether different experience.

Sharply, she studied him.

"Do you care about Claude?"

Irritated by the nosy question, he retorted, "Of course I do."

"Hmm."

"Why do you ask?"

"Curious. The two of you were close for a long time. It seemed as if you drifted apart in the years before you left."

As astute an observation as one might have expected. Remy nodded, reluctantly. "We were close, once. As age claimed us, we had different ideas. Different paths."

She snorted.

"Very different."

Her angst against his brother tinted the entire evening with trouble. Remy wanted to cling to the earlier fun of rediscovering Amelie, but she'd already put the poison in the metaphorical wine.

He couldn't help wondering whether she was right.

Had Claude *always* been like this?

A little?

He regretted this choice of discussion, but he couldn't hide from Claude's reality forever.

"I see," he finally said, for lack of anything else.

"Not yet," she whispered. "No good will come of Claude anytime soon, Remy, unless you can engineer some change of heart. It would take a miracle. Maybe *you* are that miracle, but none of us are holding our breath."

Her hidden venom kept his hackles on edge. Something else must have put it there, for Amelie had a greater disdain than made sense. Thwarted love? Perhaps she once cared for Claude.

His nose wrinkled at the thought.

It didn't deliver any pleasant emotion to think about it, first of all, and secondly, would someone like Amelie care for Claude? Years ago, Remy had clearly been the object of her deep affections, which only confused him more.

He straightened, eager to leave this conversation on a better note. "Well, Amelie, it's late. I'm exhausted, and I think I better slow my parents down before there's no stopping them. It's been an unexpected delight to see you again. I . . . I hadn't known you'd appear so . . ."

A hint of her earlier vixen reappeared.

"Adult?"

His lips pressed into a subdued smile. "Adult," he repeated gently. "It's been a pleasure. When will I see you again?"

The dissonance of speaking about Claude melted into a slush of afterthought as they turned together toward the double doors, flung open to the cooler air and stepped inside. Heat thickened as they strolled toward the front of the house.

"Oh," she said airily, "probably soon. Our families rarely need an excuse to spend time together. We can hardly keep my father at home. He's always over here, examining new grimoires with Nelson or conspiring over clock faces."

Her voice turned droll as they rounded a corner to find both sets of parents cackling around a table blazing with candelabras.

"They're worse than children!" he said, laughing.

"Much has changed in the six years you have been gone, Remy." Amelie aimed an affectionate smile toward their parents. "The important things remain the same. For good or ill, our families will always be closely aligned, and we should do our part to keep it that way."

Chapter Two

In typical Claude fashion, piles of old resources lay forgotten in the fallow field, overrun with weeds and growth.

Their disorganized bulks, waiting for something to make them purposeful, struck Remy as oddly sad. He hadn't given much thought to these wasted planks and rusty nails when he visited last week. Bushes had overgrown most of the bricks and stones. Ivy snaked through them in a twisting hug.

Remy kicked a dirt clod away from warped wooden boards. Beneath those, the glint of a metal hammer shone in the muted sunlight. Clouds rolled over the sky, suffusing the day. He tilted his head, nudged a board aside with a toe.

"What a waste."

The same open pasture with surrounding forest stared at him, but this time, it felt different. Only a few days had passed since the grimoire brought him here, and he couldn't resist the insistent tugging that brought him back again. It satisfied only when he stepped on these grounds.

Magical insistence.

The grimoire appeared, floating. The first chapter opened, with its endless pages of lists. Somewhere behind them, into the thickness of the book, drawings of floors, rooms, staircases, and other oddities filled the pages. It included details like tapestries, carpet tacks, mirrors, and engraved crown molding. He'd never carried a book so massive.

"You have an extensive list, Wildrose. It seems you'd like me to obtain the items on that list and build this for you?"

The pages trembled in response.

He took the motion as an affirmative as he tapped a finger on his waist. His lips bunched up to the side in a wrinkled bow—a bad habit he acquired as a boy when thinking deeply. He had a hunch that the magic didn't care about currency all that much. What might happen if he *did* obtain these required supplies?

At the top of the first page was a list titled **Grandfather Clock.** Compared to the other chains of supplies, it was bitty, with only a handful of items. Most of which he couldn't fathom. *Dials* and *mounts* and *chime* and *tenon* and *mortises.* Half of the things he couldn't comprehend, but a few were easy enough.

With a spell, Remy summoned the first four items on the top list. Hammer. Wooden planks. Hinges. Nails. Father's workmen had hammers, boards, and other frivolities they left in the outer garden shed. The tools appeared on the soil at his feet, laying in the wide open sunshine.

He drummed his fingers on the book.

"There you are, Wildrose. The first four tools. What say you now?"

His jaw dropped as the words *hammer* and *nails* scrubbed free of the book, yet nothing else occurred. The pages shivered, drawing his attention to a specific size of nails listed at the bottom of the page. Somehow, he'd missed them. He frowned.

"Not sure we have that exact size of nail, but I'll try."

He summoned a hefty wooden bucket of odds-and-ends. Nails, mostly. Father kept it in the shed. Remy turned back to the grimoire.

"Well? Anything you can use in there?"

The pages flurried like bird wings. A zip of magic electrified his bones. The small pile of boards, the hammer, the lot of nails, and several thin planks rose into the air. They sped in a whirlwind around Remy. Nails raced this way and that. The hammer lifted. Boards came together. Two of them cracked in half with an ear-rending sound, tumbled upside down, and reassembled in a different formation.

Within five minutes, the oddities had assembled into a small, crooked box that settled on the ground at his feet.

Remy gaped.

"So that's how this works?"

The pages returned to the list, where ink whisked away, as if trailing around to find a new home. For a long, intangible moment, he forced himself to ask the obvious question.

Had he imagined it?

No.

Impossible. The bones of a grandfather clock stood before him, assembled on the spot.

Ye gods. He hadn't expected this.

Remy sucked in a breath and transported home. He rummaged through the dusty old shed, plucked out bits of wood and lumber, and tossed them into a pile on the ground. Next, he slipped over to the Leroy's shed, transported several cast-off pieces from there, then returned to the spot at the field.

Panting from the effort, he used magic to bring the whole lot of wood to the empty field.

"Can you use any of that?"

The grimoire rose, shaking two pages. *Saw* and *sandpaper* stood at the top of the second page. The first now lay blank.

"I don't have sandpaper, but Father has saws."

Another summoning spell brought three handsaws to the pile. Boards leaped into the air. Two saws went to work on a long plank, while nails drifted by. As quickly as the pieces arrived, they assembled into another box, similar to the first. The bottom, perhaps? Breathless, he watched as the ink twirled off the page and vanished.

"Hang on! Why else would you have . . . that is . . . did you have those items on there first for a reason?"

The ruffling pages led him to the start of the blueprints. The lists bled into images with measurements and specifications that made his eyes cross. The details of what the grimoire contained would be a good thing, or a bad thing, depending on the witch who had to bring this about.

He couldn't make heads or tails of it.

He eyed the clock.

Then again . . . maybe he wouldn't need to.

"You anticipated me? You somehow knew that I'd want to test it or see for myself perhaps?"

The book whirred to the beginning of the lists again. The empty space remained scrubbed free. When the list on the back side was gone, would the page disappear? A few loose, blank pages existed at the back, but nowhere else.

Remy swallowed long and hard. By the skeleton of Ignar, but what sort of magic system was this?

The book closed and disappeared, leaving no doubt it was finished with him. Whatever point it strove to make, it must have. Remy set his hands on his hips, overlooking the property. Persuasive sunshine warmed him through, revealing that more time had passed than he expected.

The lot itself wasn't much. Thick forest, more tangled vines than passable terrain, and a knobby field with too many rills and bumps to make building work easy.

Why *had* Father bought it?

Resolved to ask him, Remy turned to head toward home. A flutter of movement in the tree line caught his attention. He turned to see Claude leaning against a tree, a bottle in his left hand. From this distance, his eyes glittered.

A decidedly . . . dark . . . energy lingered about Claude.

Irrefutable since Amelie called it out. Remy no longer wondered *if* something egregious happened between Amelie and Claude, but wondered *what.* The question made him nervous. Whatever occurred, he wouldn't be likely to defend his brother. Not with the building reputation Claude had created for himself.

Claude lifted the hand with the bottle in a salute. He didn't appear inebriated, but if his habits were as steep as Amelie insinuated—not to mention the whispering servants—then Claude was more functional when drunk.

Claude disappeared as quickly as he came, leaving Remy alone in the field with his thoughts and empty hands.

Wrinkles lined Father's face when Remy sat next to him that night, near the fire in the sitting room. Paintings cluttered the wall. Ancestors from ages past, peering down with tight-lipped judgment or merry approval. Remy knew them as names. Vague faces. All of them had some sort of story.

Sometime in the future, he planned to sit down with Father and hear each story out.

"Mind if I join you?" he asked.

Father stirred out of reveries and managed a tired smile. His drawn eyes worried Remy. Advancing age hit harder with each passing year, like a cudgel that gained power as time passed. Father's blonde hair had long since turned to snow. He wore it in a braid at the back of his head. Strands shifted loose around his temples, glimmering in the low light.

"Merry meet, son. You're always welcome to sit with me. I've missed our fireside chats since you've been gone."

"Me too."

"How is it being home?"

With a chuckle, Remy picked up the poker and stabbed the flames. They sprayed cinders, spreading a burst of heat the house didn't need. Mother opened windows in other parts of the house to counter the heat. Father became cold quite easily these days, and found comfort in the fire.

"Overwhelming," Remy admitted. "I didn't expect it to be."

"Change always is."

Father's easy agreement soothed Remy. Returning home had been more fraught than he expected. Claude's obvious changes, Amelie's vague insinuations, the onslaught of the grimoire.

With the welcome home party behind them, big decisions lurked. Questions of careers, inheritance, the estate, and Claude.

Remy wouldn't live at home forever, but had nowhere to go. He might find an apartment in Ashleigh to rent, but reluctance kept him at the estate. Claude had lived at home since Remy departed years ago, so he knew his parents wouldn't mind.

"James popped by tonight." Father met Remy's gaze. "Asked if you were searching for a job now that you're back."

"What did you tell him?"

"That you were."

"And?"

"He's interested."

Remy leaned against the divan. "In hiring me?"

"In retiring."

"Oh."

The idea of working for James Leroy had instant appeal. The messenger paper business had been James' whole life, and Remy knew him well. His detailed mind and business savvy meant the business would be clean. Mr. Donaldsen had been a mess.

"With no son to take it over," Father continued, "and reputedly none of his nine daughters or son-in-laws interested, James is worried about what will happen to it. I can understand the stress. We spend all of our lives building up a career that enables us to feed our children, and we end up loving it. Legacy is . . . everything to old men like us, my boy."

The long lick of flames drew Remy's gaze to the fire. Somehow, in the folds of life, he'd never considered the idea of legacy.

"He loves you like a son, you know."

"James is a good man."

"Always has been," he said softly.

"Are you saying that he wants me to take over the company?"

Father shook his head. "I'm saying he wants to interview you about taking over the company, that's all. You may not want it, and that's fine too. It's not much different than what you did with Donaldsen. Business management, mostly. Relationship with vendors, employees, sources, etc."

"Familiar."

Thanks to his messenger paper company, James Leroy raised nine daughters, maintained his estate, and lived a full, if not somewhat currency-stretched, life. The warehouse and headquarters were part of Ashleigh city not far away.

The Leroy name had a powerful reputation and a long vendor list across many Networks. With eleven mouths to feed, an estate to run, and servants to pay, currency had always been tight. The Leroy girls were known to wear second-hand clothes, forage for berries instead of paying for them, and kept cows and chickens for many years.

Yet, they were a happy, delightful family, and no one cared how much currency they had. If it had been a problem, the Leroys never noted it.

"The factory would make enough currency to care for a small family," Remy mused, "if it fed the Leroys. Don't you agree?"

Father's lips twitched. "Something you haven't told us?"

Laughing, Remy shook his head. "No. Nothing like that. I'm not hiding a wife and children. I'm just . . . thinking ahead."

"Are you really?"

"I suppose so."

Father leaned an elbow on the arm rest and said, "I've never heard you speak of children."

Remy shrugged. "Haven't thought much about it."

"What about handfasting?"

"What about it?"

"Have you thought of that? Usually, it's the first step in the process."

"A little," Remy admitted. "Not because any woman has inspired the thought, unfortunately."

"But you're interested in a woman who *did* inspire the thought?"

Slowly, he said, "Yes, I think so."

Father smiled with great affection. "Handfasting your mother was the greatest decision I ever made, Remy. There's a bliss that comes from sharing life with another soul. A sort of . . . contentment that makes everything in the world worth it. I want that for you, my boy."

"I know."

Slyly, Father added, "Your mother loves Amelie, you know. Says she has spunk and wit."

"Father—"

Father held up two hands. "That's all I'll say. I'm fond of her myself. Some of the Leroy girls live with their heads in the clouds, but Amelie is grounded. She's bold, too. Maybe she wasn't always, but now? She holds a lot of room for love in her heart."

"Amelie doesn't seem to love anyone." Remy stabbed at the burning logs in the hearth. After his party, he'd sent her a message, to which she never responded. The perceived friendship he thought existed clearly didn't.

At least, not on her side.

It stung.

Wrinkles lined Father's brow. "She's . . . changed."

"You think?" Remy cried, incredulous. "I've never met a witch more altered than Amelie Leroy. After six years, I didn't recognize her."

Father waved a hand. "No, no. Of course she's *changed*, as she grew up. She's a beautiful and successful young woman. But something else caused her to be different. When she stopped playing violin, it seemed . . . I don't know. It was very hard for her. James was quite worried for a long time. She's pulling through, of course, but it cost her. She doesn't trust easily."

I noticed, Remy almost said, but it didn't seem fair. What reason did Amelie have to trust him? He'd been an aloof neighbor that didn't give her the time of day. Perhaps snubbing him was her way of reminding him where they stood.

An earned position, really.

Father shook his head and straightened in his chair. "I'm tired and plan to go to bed, but before I do that, might we schedule a time to chat in the morning? I need to discuss matters of home and business with you. Basic stuff." He yawned, lips stretching wide. "Inheritance and the estate. Those sorts of things. My legal witch is coming in the morning to help me finalize everything, and I wanted to sit down with you and Claude."

"Anything you need, Father. I have no plans, so I can be available whenever you require."

He smiled, patted Remy's hand, and fought another yawn. The low surges of heat from the fire began to ebb, burning to coals.

"After breakfast is soon enough, if Claude is awake. Claude won't like the topic or the timing of it," Father said with a mournful wince, "but we do what we must. We'll talk more in the morning, after a good night's sleep. I love you, son. Sleep well."

Vague dreams stirred Remy that night.

His throat burned, as if he'd swallowed a live poker. When he coughed to clear it, ebony smoke built inside a glass bottle in his chest. The cork prevented him from exhaling. In the bottle, lightning cracked. It zapped outside the confines, splitting Remy in half. A percussive *thud* rocked through his head in painful spasms. The burning persisted until it turned into a scent.

The *crack* of a hand hitting his cheek brought him out of the dream.

"Remy!" Claude screamed. "Wake up!"

Remy bolted upright so quickly he almost hit Claude in the forehead. The near-miss sent Claude wheeling away. Arms flailing, he landed on his backside with a groan and a shout.

"What's wrong with you?" Remy demanded.

Dumbly, he blinked away the tendrils of half-formed dreams. Why did the room appear so hazy? He could barely see Claude on the ground.

Was that . . . smoke?

His eyes burned, just like in the dream. Smoke crawled across the room, seeping in from the hallways. It rose from the stairs, visible through his open door. In the distance, a crash. Claude struggled to his hands and knees as Remy threw his covers off.

"Where's the fire?"

"Don't know . . ." Claude heaved, sputtering through the thickening air. "Downstairs . . . somewhere. We gotta go."

Remy hauled his brother up by the arm. Claude's bloodshot eyes spoke to terror and desperation, but no ipsum that Remy could smell through the smoke.

"Transport!" Remy called. "I'll go after Mother and Father."

"No!" Claude clutched both his arms. "Don't go there! They're already gone."

"What?"

Claude doubled over, barking a cough so hard he spit up.

"Just . . . went . . ." He panted, hands braced on his bent thighs. "It's gone. The whole first floor is . . . crumbling."

A spray of sparks ascended up the staircase, twirling. Something else collapsed. Remy's fluttering breath ached with each attempt. Another minute in this room and they'd die.

Claude attempted to stand on his own, but swayed. Remy hooked an arm around his brother's shoulders and transported them out. Within a blink, night surrounded them. The cool kiss of fresh air, untainted by noxious smoke, rushed through Remy's nose. Chilly grass blades anchored him to the ground.

They stood in the front yard, staring at a horrifying sight.

Fire concentrated on the first floor, near the front and south side, facing the Leroys. His parents' bedroom was on the second floor, directly above. Flames plumed from their windows. Heat billowed with stupefying intensity, radiating. Black smoke belched overhead. The cries of neighbors exiting their home and racing past barely registered over the roar of the flames.

Claude collapsed in a heaving mess. He lay on his side, eyes closed, a cheek pressed to the ground. Every breath whistled through his narrowed airways while Remy stumbled toward the front porch.

"Father!" he screamed. "Mother!"

Shock propelled him toward the house. He trod over the spongy grass in nothing more than a pair of breeches. The air felt oddly cold on his skin compared to the sweltering heat. Windowpanes shattered. A roar bellowed from within.

Hoarse, he yelled, "Mother!"

His first step gained the stairs, but he hesitated. Such terrifying power rolled out in heat waves, rushing toward him. The flames couldn't touch him here—not yet—but he felt their presence like a deep pressure.

No one could survive it.

No one.

Throat thick, he cried, "Father!"

A cool hand grabbed his wrist, jolting him out of the disbelieving tunnel.

"Remy!" Amelie cried. "No! You'll die yourself if you go in there. It's all going to fall any minute now!"

Her touch unlocked the haze. As the roof of the porch crumbled to cinders, he curled away. His arm wrapped around Amelie, escorting her out of the way as smoke, ash, and flames spurted in a molten waterfall.

They raced away from the inferno. Embers burned his bare back. A thousand crashing memories issued as the estate shattered from the inside out. Where the flames hadn't touched, smoke spewed in rounded tufts.

At the edge of the lawn, Remy spun. Amelie held onto his waist, but coughed into her elbow. She wore a shabby robe over the top of a cream-colored nightgown. Her bare feet sank into the grass as she gripped his arms. Tears coursed down her cheeks.

Remy couldn't move. Terror and disbelief claimed him in a paralysis. Somewhere in that awful, white-hot center lay his parents. Crimson spirals and flames surged with irreverent pulses. Wooden boards toppled.

His world collapsed.

Chapter Three

Gentle rain poured the next day, coating the soggy remains in waves. The house burned for hours. Through the rest of the night, the morning. After noon, it settled into a smolder.

Thankfully, no other homes suffered. Sprawling lawns and rapid incantations protected the Leroy home from sharing the same fate.

Smoke steamed from the ruins. Toppled walls spilled. Hints of a half-standing hearth, a jagged plate, the old oven from the kitchens. Little survived. Remy itched to sort through it.

The raindrops, surprisingly soft, swept by in a warm caress again and again. They coated the world in waves. Remy stood in the midst of the storm and stared at the charred ashes. He had to see it through to the end. To stand stalwart next to the remains, to his parents, until all lay in the past.

He couldn't reconcile.

How had it happened so quickly?

An umbrella appeared at his side. He expected to see Amelie, because she hadn't left his side. James Leroy stood there, his aged face deepened with sorrow. Shock permeated his loose lips, which hung half open. He walked around in disbelief. James put a trembling hand on Remy's arm.

"My boy, I am so sorry."

Tears gummed up Remy's throat, but he'd already cried so much. When the Apothecary told him that Claude had a broken clavicle and burned lungs—though how the clavicle had happened was anyone's guess—he'd hardly experienced any surprise. To aid Claude's recovery and set the bone, the Apothecary gave him a potion to sleep through the night. He hadn't awoken.

Remy put his hand over Mr. Leroy's. He squeezed it. They stood in the downfall together. Through a thickened throat, he asked, "Do you think they suffered?"

"No," James said immediately. "I don't."

"Why did it happen?"

"A mistake, probably. Missplaced candle, perhaps?"

"My parents weren't forgetful witches, James."

"I agree."

"Claude might know more."

Hesitantly, James said, "He might. But he might not. He was in bad shape. The Apothecary was worried about his lungs. Claude had a small burn on his fingers and hand, but nothing serious. It seemed he was in the fire and smoke far longer than you."

"I don't think he was drunk."

James said nothing for a long time. The wash of rain eased in the intervening moments.

"Someone may have left a candle burning that fell," James offered, a tremor in his voice. "A servant. James. Joyce. Claude, even. A spark might have leaped from the hearth. The possibilities are endless, dear Remy. With devastation this complete, we won't know. We can't pick through the remains to figure it out."

Remy shook his head, thinking of Mother's injured knee, Father's deep sleeps. Any number of factors might have conspired. It boggled the mind to attempt comprehension, but he couldn't help it.

"I know."

James put his hand on Remy's shoulder. "Some questions are not to be answered, son. Some things are not to know. They just . . . are. You can agonize over the *what ifs* and *whys* and *hows* forever, or you can accept that you'll never know. It will be hard, but we will work through this together."

To Remy's surprise, the permission quelled a rising storm. He didn't know why Mother and Father didn't transport out of the fire, or why they couldn't escape. Where had it started? Why had it started? Unlikely they'd ever know the answers. The fire swept secrets and truth to the sky.

All whisked away.

His parents, his inheritance, his planned future.

Gone.

In a night.

"You will always have the Leroys, Remy." James removed his hand from Remy's shoulder and patted his arm, as if he found soothing from the gesture as much as he meant to impart it. Remy pulled James closer out of concern for the old man. The shock of losing his best friend gave him a frail appearance.

"Thank you, James."

With a teary sigh, James whispered, "I'll leave you to your family. I'm going to miss your parents . . ."

James shuffled away. The soft scuff of another pair of shoes joined Remy minutes later. Amelie. Nothing but the swash of rain across his shoulders could be heard. He half expected Amelie to leave, too.

She didn't.

Out of the corner of his eye, Remy tracked her silent form. She folded her hands in front of her, gaze trained on the rubble. Regret and shock permeated every well-wisher that came from the neighborhood and nearby covens, but Amelie's emotions pierced with an unusually canny depth.

He had an idea she'd been very good friends with his mother.

Remy drew in a breath, let it back out, and bolstered himself for what lay ahead. Claude, for one. Soon enough, he'd wake up. Existence, for another. They'd have to find an inn to stay at until they could figure something out. Eventually, they might recover objects. After the weather turned, Remy would sort through the wreckage with a shovel and attempt to discover remnants. Grimoires were normally protected from fire by their own magic.

As Remy turned to leave, he paused. His heart arrested with a thought.

Wildrose.

No sooner had it entered his mind than a heavy thud landed against his chest. The grimoire appeared, unstained, unsoiled, unbothered. It endured the flames without a speck of abuse. Water pooled on top of the cover, beaded up, and slipped down the sides. The paper within remained utterly dry and flat.

Remy stroked the tips of his fingers along the leather bound edges. It felt more like a weight than a world of magic within pages and ink. He tucked it under his left arm, in the crook of his elbow, and faced Amelie.

She stared at the grimoire with mild surprise, but asked nothing.

He didn't know why she stood there. He didn't deserve her loyal display of friendship, no matter how deep the relationship between their parents. Yet, he didn't have the heart to question. He needed someone. If Amelie was willing to stand in the rain with him, he'd accept her solidarity with gratitude.

"Remy?"

Her breath misted in the rain. He returned from his dazed thoughts with rapid blinking and the intrusive thought of, *I'll never see my parents again.* How odd that his witches simply . . . didn't exist anymore.

Was death really so simple?

Could the same happen to him?

"I'm ready to go inside," he said. "I think . . . that is . . . Claude and I will have to start over. It might as well be now. I'll check on him and then . . . find a place to stay."

"You already have a place to stay."

Her gentle tone rang with a hint of chiding. With several of her sisters living elsewhere, the Leroy mansion had rooms enough.

"I—"

"Father will insist." Her stubborn flair spoke like a commander, a woman in charge. With a backbone like that, she reminded him of Mother. "So will Mother, and so will I," Amelie continued firmly, as if he needed more convincing than the hearth of beloved friends. Gratefully, he accepted the offer with a nod.

With tenderness, she said, "The next couple of months might be very challenging, but you're never alone. My family already plans on you staying with us for however long it takes." She raised her chin and added in a whisper, "Claude, too."

"Thank you. You'll never know what that means."

He extended an arm. She stepped up to his side, put her arm through his, and followed him through the rain across the lawn and toward the Leroy home.

Something in the tug, jerk, and yank of physical labor set Remy's bottled grief free.

Sweat trickled down his back as he groped along a line of ivy grown into the soil. Sun bore on his shoulders, heating him. He ignored his saturated shirt.

"You're a madman, Remy," Claude cried.

Remy ignored him.

Claude sat with his back against a tree, legs sprawled wide. The last week without ipsum had either saved Claude's life, or broken him beyond measure. The lost child wandering in Claude's glazed eyes peeked in and out, peering through livid flames. Occasionally, Claude would cry in painful bursts, then dwindle to silence. The tremors ceased yesterday, but he still looked a shade away from death.

The broken clavicle heightened Claude's weakened state. He couldn't transport, and could barely walk. Dragging him outside and carefully navigating to the field had been an agonizing process, but Remy held to his belief that the sun would help.

Claude didn't have any fight left in him by the time they arrived. He sank to the ground, wincing, and didn't move except to draw cool water from his canteen and quip something sarcastic.

When Remy jerked the final vine from the earth, he tossed it onto the ever-growing burn pile and stepped back. The cleared earth was a rectangle bigger than expected.

"You're mad," Claude insisted. His eyes were closed, head tipped back, throat bobbing as he swallowed. The rising heat created ripples in the ground. Soon, Remy would have to take him inside. Claude's penchant to retreat to dark places—metaphorically and physically—left his skin sensitive and pale.

"Not mad," Remy countered, breathless. "We need somewhere to live. We can't stay with the Leroys forever."

"Got that right," Claude muttered.

Remy reached for his canteen. *We're desperate,* he almost added. Pointing out their current predicament wouldn't help. They knew they were desperate. The fire destroyed everything. Their parents, their inheritance, and possibly the grimoires Father meant to sell. The legal witch would be coming over soon to discuss ramifications.

Claude scoffed.

"We can't live *here*. Wildrose won't work. You'll see. You're wasting your time."

"I don't know that we are living here," Remy shot back. "I'm just . . . testing it. If the magic works the way I think it does, it might be our best chance."

"This is cursed ground, Remy. We should build where we used to live. With the right application of spells, we can have the rubble cleaned up soon. Might be able to use it to our advantage somehow."

Claude's voice brightened around the edges. What was in that pain potion the Apothecary gave him? Or had Claude found ipsum after all? A slight spike in energy left Remy crawling with suspicion.

The Leroy family drank ipsum only during social gatherings and didn't allow it in their house in between events. Surely, Claude wouldn't be so rude as to imbibe in their home while they were being so generous?

The question hovered on the tip of Remy's tongue, ready to ask, but he shoved it away.

Here wasn't the place, or the time. Claude carried the burden of emotional and physical pain. Plus, Remy didn't want to deal with the inevitable argument. As long as Claude didn't get wildly drunk, he'd hold off.

Besides, their list populated with plenty of other tasks to focus on. The open house and memorial for his parents would be next week. Joyce hired a chanter of blessings to come, and a memorial constructed for Mother and Father.

In anticipation of life moving forward again, Remy had sent job applications out already. Two had returned, requesting interviews. Another application went to James, who chortled when he learned Remy actually submitted instead of voicing interest.

Far as he could tell, Claude didn't currently have a job. He mumbled something about *in-between work* when asked.

At this moment, the best Remy could do was lean into something. That *something* was creating a space to live.

Remy crouched down, ran his hand through the dirt. Good soil. Black with nutrients, and slightly wet. It would produce a powerful garden. He tipped his head back to drink from a cool glass of water he conjured from the Leroys. The liquid slid down his throat, quenching his overheated thirst.

When he finished, swiped his forearm across his mouth, and straightened, he studied the cleared rectangle with a profound sense of satisfaction. Technically, the grimoire hadn't asked him to clear the giant space in the middle of the field. Wildrose had requested an army of shovels and pickaxes, but Remy craved the sunshine, the workload, an escape for building steam.

Every other moment, the realization that Mother and Father wouldn't return haunted him. He wouldn't walk into Mother's warm arms and chiding smile, tsking and asking when he would provide her with grandchildren.

Never again would Father tut as he considered life advice, or build a fire when it was clearly too hot.

The welling pain threatened to be too much, so Remy worked. Extrication from the intense emotions followed the labor, for now. Eventually, he wouldn't be able to stem the tide. It would rush and flow.

Today, he could.

"All right," he sang. "I'm done."

He knew what to expect. The grimoire appeared, hovering above his sweaty arms, with the rosy foil of *Wildrose* across the front. The pages shuffled open, sprawled to the original plans. An amalgamation of measurements, rocks, squares, lay before him. For all it encompassed, it might have been a different language.

He frowned.

"I don't know what that means. What list should I put together?"

The pages riffled backward, ending on the next list. Several grandfather clock supplies remained, packed with words and items he couldn't fathom. To finish that one, he'd have to visit a clockmaker.

He'd do that tomorrow. Seemed odd to complete a clock first, but he wasn't sure he cared about the order of operations enough to argue it. Besides, who would reply? For now, his attention rooted into the list that followed the clock, which remained the same as before.

Shovels of all sizes. Pickaxes. Rakes.

"You want fifty shovels?"

The list remained unchanged in the wake of his astonishment. Where would he find fifty shovels?

"I don't know if I can find that many. Nor do I know how much it would cost to buy fifty. Currency is a problem."

The book vibrated. Remy felt deepening displeasure from the tome, as if he annoyed it with reality.

"Father's solicitor will be coming over this week. I'll ask what our options are with . . . the old house. Until then, forgive me, but I won't buy fifty shovels. I can leave three, but that's it. I don't even know . . . that is . . . "

Unable to finish his thought, he let it trail away. Wildrose was a nice distraction, but was he ready to commit to it?

Clearly not.

The gigantic book closed and disappeared. Taking it as permission, Remy summoned three shovels. The fire hadn't touched the back shed, which left him open to more tools than expected. They appeared, blade down, in the dirt at his feet.

Claude snored, jerked awake with a grimace, gazed around in a half-panic, and calmed. His chin dipped to his chest and eyes closed again.

Remy picked up some of the soil and let it dribble through his fingers as he scanned the field. The distant edge blurred in the growing humidity. Sunshine blazed overhead. As he crouched, he studied each nuance.

Odd, wasn't it?

The unrelenting forest, carved around what appeared to be an invisible barrier. Saplings that approached the edge grew taller, but not beyond, as if something held them back. Letum Wood, the most relentless forest in all of Alkarra, ever changing and increasing, had chosen this spot to *not* exist.

Why?

A deep-seated intuition wondered if the forest left the space open. Was it possible? Could even the ground be destined for greatness?

He deeply hoped so.

Mr. Clarke peered at Remy over tiny spectacles that drooped on his long nose, threatening to fall off the end. Sage eyebrows, fuzzy as caterpillars, lifted sky high. Gray and black sprayed them in streaks.

"Mr. Dauphin, are you ready?"

Remy didn't appreciate the upturn of judgment in Mr. Clarke's voice, knowing precisely why he asked in that tone. Remy tightened his jaw, ignoring the sparks of frustration Mr. Clarke ignited.

These days, emotions swelled high and fast.

Remy forced his tone to remain even. He wasn't here to apologize for his brother's absence, or even explain it.

"I am ready, Mr. Clarke."

Mr. Clarke's pointed glance at the empty seat next to Remy said everything.

Remy bit back a sigh. "As your time is very valuable, Mr. Clarke, we can proceed without Claude. I'm sure he'll be here soon."

A huff, and a suppressed eye roll, followed. Mr. Clarke shuffled through several papers on the table. Remy sat at the edge of his seat in the small dining room, set toward the back of the Leroy home.

Despite having nine daughters, six who still lived at home, the mansion was surprisingly quiet. At this time of day, most of the younger girls studied on the top floor, in classes with Amelie or Joyce. The maids bustled around the first floor, between the kitchen and front door. Remy and Claude stayed in two connecting guest bedrooms on the second floor, and the family lived on the third.

"Your father's estate was in good shape, Remy. The day after the fire, we were supposed to meet to discuss it."

"I remember."

Mr. Clarke's lips turned down. "He was going to appoint you the main heir." He slid a parchment to Remy.

"I'm sorry?"

"Claude has . . . struggled . . . to get his life together. It concerned your father. He felt that giving the Dauphin estate to Claude would be too great a risk. His plan was to turn it over to you entirely."

"Oh."

Father had seemed a touch nervous the night before, when he mentioned speaking to the legal witch and Claude. He hadn't wanted to broach the topic then, and no wonder.

"Unfortunately," Mr. Clarke continued, "most of your inheritance was wrapped up in the house itself. A real piece of art. Your parents took much pride in it. Currently, the land is split between you and Claude. Both of you have fifty percent share, but it means absolutely nothing now. Too bad. Any chance you recovered grimoires?"

"None."

"I see. Then you won't have anything you can sell now, will you?"

Remy shook his head. "No, but what about the business?"

Mr. Clarke's lips curled down. "I'm sorry, Remy. It's still in Claude's name. He receives all the assets. That was one change we were to discuss. Your father didn't want Claude to take everything, you see."

Remy couldn't blame his father. When the previous version of the will had been written up, Claude wasn't a functional alcoholic and Remy had just graduated from the Network school system. He couldn't have run a business if he tried.

"You do have a parcel of land, however." Mr. Clarke tapped a dull staccato on a thick sheet of paper topped by a map. The spot he tapped was the land where the Wildrose grimoire first swept him away. "It's not far from here, according to the map. He put it in your name. Apparently, there was one for Claude, as well, but Claude sold it a few years back. Not sure if you've ever seen the property?"

"Yes, just recently. Do you know why Claude sold his?"

Mr. Clarke shrugged. "I don't know why, but there you have it. Your father meant it as a gift when you handfasted."

He tutted. For all his disapproval toward Claude, Mr. Clarke demonstrated genuine mourning in his tone for Mother and Father. It drove the depth of their loss deeper. Remy nodded, but there was relief. A split inheritance didn't mean much except they either sold the land or had to build together.

It *also* meant Remy didn't have to give Claude terrible news.

Mr. Clarke passed Remy another scroll, though Remy still hadn't considered the first parchment.

"The most that you have left is the land, Remy. While your father has some investments that originate out of Ashleigh—burgeoning businesses, mostly, with a minimal profit return that I would caution you not to rely on for everyday life—and savings, there's not enough to rebuild. This is a strong neighborhood, with quality witches and large estates on either side. You could sell."

Remy perused the scroll, uncomfortable with the steady slide of Mr. Clarke's tone, marching toward something Remy would rather not see. Sell the property? How could they? It was home. Memories. He skimmed over thick paragraphs that didn't register in his tired brain.

"With your job history working for Mr. Donaldsen," Mr. Clarke continued, "you're in a powerful position to take many jobs currently on the market. Have you interviewed at all?"

"Several times."

"Any prospects?"

Remy hesitated. The interviews had been cordial, but awkward. Expending the energy to sell himself had been hard to summon. He left most interviews feeling drained and uncertain, not at all surprised that he hadn't heard back. Only his interview for the messenger paper company had gone well.

"Potentially," he said.

"At least you're trying."

The dry comment was meant to be a jab at Claude, no doubt. Remy let it slide.

"I would advise you to sell the land, use the money to build elsewhere, and get a respectable job. There's enough in savings that you'll be fine. If," Mr. Clarke lifted his pointer finger, "you can live with your brother and gain his cooperation. Should Claude request his split of the remaining inheritance, there would not be enough to build. Considering your single state . . ."

Mr. Clarke trailed off, fuzzy eyebrows raised ever higher. Much more of that and they'd leap off his face. Remy thought about what he said. His *single state* was the farthest thing from his mind, but clearly still held implications.

"But to sell our land? It's our ancestral home—"

The observation halted. It *wasn't* his ancestral home. Not anymore. At most, it was a square plot of land in a valuable neighborhood, chock full of ash and dreams. The idea made his stomach revolt. This morning's tea threatened in his throat. He struggled to swallow it back.

"It's one path, Remy," Mr. Clarke said. "Perhaps the most stable path, but of course, there will be other ideas. From a strictly business standpoint, this is what I see. I'm happy to consult with you anytime."

Remy soaked that in, lost in thoughts, until Mr. Clarke fanned several papers out and set them in front of him.

"Here are the rest of the details, but nothing to concern yourself with now. Assessment of the land, projected selling price, investment opportunities, and the profiles of the businesses your father had invested in. You'll also see the pentacles and sacran's he has set aside as a savings, I believe, for your handfasting. There is one for each of you. Not much, but enough."

"Thank you, Mr. Clarke."

Mr. Clarke stood. All papers that he arrived with lay in front of Remy. He tugged his jacket closed and fiddled with the buttons.

"Nothing needs to be decided right now. The loss of your parents is still quite fresh, and the Leroys are generous in their hospitality and support. You can take your time to decide, but at least you understand your position better."

After a mumbled thanks and an arm clasp, Remy barely noticed him leaving. One moment he stared at the mass of graphs and figures that, at one time, might have been thrilling. Father had been through his investments with Remy a year or so ago, just a brief discussion meant to catch them up after a long time apart, but it all appeared utterly foreign now.

Remy roved to the window, staring out. He clasped his hands around his elbows. The other side of the Leroy property was strangely empty. Black briquettes littered the charred ground, smudging the verdant beauty with a hole too big to fill again.

The surreal sense of everything wavering around him made

him turn, put his back to the questions. A figure stood in the doorway, swathed in shadows. Glittering eyes peered at him from the darker hallway.

"Claude?"

His brother stumbled into the room, necktie askew. The first few buttons of his shirt lay open, revealing a hairy chest beneath the white fabric. Despite his staggering movement, his eyes were totally sober.

"I just passed Mr. Clarke in the hallway."

"Did he update you?"

"He wouldn't speak to me."

"You were late."

Claude spread his hands. "Only twenty minutes!"

Remy shrugged.

Claude sized Remy up with tapered suspicion. His malevolent tone brought a chill to the room.

"Has my younger brother concluded the business of burying our parents already?"

Remy braced himself. He took his time replying.

"No."

"What did you say, little brother?"

The emphasis on *little brother* wasn't lost.

"I'm not your enemy, Claude. I don't understand why you're speaking to me as if I am. I showed up on time. Mr. Clarke reviewed the documents. Nothing was decided, signed, or assigned."

"Did he ask about how the fire happened?" Claude snapped.

Remy reared back.

"What?"

"Did he ask how it happened?" Anger flared in Claude's eyes. "That fool blames me, doesn't he? He's not going to give us the inheritance because Father's *peers* have judged me inadequate to their high-handed realm."

Remy motioned to the documents on the table. "No one

mentioned the fire or the cause of it, Claude. Mr. Clarke simply handed us all the financial information about our current inheritance position."

A hint of hesitation slowed Claude's rage.

"Oh?"

Remy used a spell to lift the papers. They soared to Claude with a gusto borne of Remy's irritation.

What was Claude getting at, anyway?

Claude skimmed the information with a gleam of brilliant intelligence that had been obvious since they were children. *That* was the brother he knew. An adept business man, with an eye for numbers and opportunity.

Not this sniveling, wallowing—

"It's worse than I thought," Claude stated. He shook his head, then put a hand onto his forehead with a wince. "I *told* Father not to invest in those companies! A waste of currency. Like the house in that blasted field you're obsessed with. Father's investment has drained our inheritance."

"No," Remy countered, "a house fire has done that. Mr. Clarke said that, as the investment stands, they have low yield. Perhaps, with time—"

"Unlikely."

Remy strove to control his tone when he said, "We'll have to see, Claude."

"Did Father switch the inheritance?"

"What do you mean?"

"Who inherits the land?" he cried.

"Both of us."

Claude paled. His eyes widened. "He didn't change it so it was just you?"

"No." Remy intentionally left out the fact that Father had planned to. "We inherit fifty-fifty."

Claude recovered enough to rasp out, "I see," and then a pale, "thank you." With a wave, he sent the papers away and lowered into a nearby chair. Elbows braced on his knees, Claude put his head in his hands. He winced and readjusted his shoulder. Despite weeks from the initial injury, it still pained him.

After a time, Claude sat up and asked, "What did Clarke suggest?"

The strained air had mostly abated, so Remy leaned against the table, hands braced on the edge. Finally! This was all he'd wanted from his brother. The opportunity to iron out wrinkles, work together, and fix their family. Weight lifted off Remy's chest, which felt as emotional as staring at the remains of their once stable world.

"We sell."

Claude's eyes narrowed.

"What?"

"We sell the land. He thinks that it's our best bet. If we take the funds and build a smaller house somewhere else, we could afford it. Assuming we both have stable jobs, of course."

Claude leaped to his feet. "That's insane!"

"Why?"

"It's our land, our ancestral land!"

"It's land. The ancestral part is rubble."

"I disagree."

"That's fine. It's one option amongst many, Claude."

"Well, it's a terrible one! What does Mr. Clarke know? He's the one that told Father to invest in the Ashleigh companies."

"I'm open to others. Do you have suggestions, or just criticisms?"

Claude paced, breathing hard. His face flushed. Every footfall brought another grimace, but he ignored it. He'd need a pain potion after this. Remy had the distinct feeling that Claude would disappear for several hours, and he'd medicate with more than just a pain potion.

Remy wanted him to fade away. Life at the Leroys' home was

easier without him haunting halls and corners like a personal poltergeist.

"We don't sell," Claude snapped. "We keep the land, and we rebuild."

"With what currency?"

"I'll find some."

"From whom?"

"Doesn't matter!" Claude cried. "I have witches that can help."

The hair on the back of Remy's neck rose. "Who?" he pressed, infusing as much pressure into his voice as he could manage. A flash of rage coursed through Claude's expression before it dissipated.

He turned away.

"Friends." The word faltered. More confidently, he added, "Witches that can loan us whatever currency we need to bring the house back to life."

"Claude, I don't think—"

"You've been gone, Remy!" Claude shouted. "Gone! And now you want to be the witch in charge? You're the younger brother and you'll do as I say. This is our plan. It doesn't matter that we're fifty-fifty split, I make the calls."

The bold violence, combined with unabashed shouting, tightened Remy from the inside out. For half a breath, the temptation to mollify his brother swept past. It's what he'd done before. Claude always had a temper, even as boys, while riding horses through the trees or playing with wooden swords.

Not this time.

"Watch yourself, Claude," Remy said carefully. "I will not contribute to your plan, and without my approval, you cannot build again. Unless you let me know exactly whom we would borrow this currency from, and under what terms, there will be no agreement. We'll split the inheritance if we sell."

Claude whipped around, slammed his hand into a vase, and

screamed. The vase toppled. Before Remy could send a spell to salvage it, it tipped onto the stone hearth. Shattering glass dissipated on the ground as Claude transported away, his bellow cut short into sheer silence.

For several long, deep breaths, Remy considered the fractured vase, the malevolence lingering in the air, and what Claude had unwittingly just revealed. They weren't on the same team.

Not by a long shot.

Bleary-eyed, Remy rubbed the heel of his hand into his eyes, blinked, and attempted to bring the numbers and figures together. No matter how hard he worked, logic wouldn't coalesce.

Shaking his head, he pressed his hands into the desk and stood. Flickering lamps illuminated the room with burnished light despite the late hour. The *shucking* sound of slippered feet moving upstairs was the only indication that life existed behind the bubble of thought in which Remy swam all day.

He went to the window and cranked it open. Cooler air drifted inside, calming his heated cheeks. He closed his eyes, leaned into it. For several long moments, he stood there, breathing deep, until a gentle rap came on the door.

He whirled around, crossed the room, and carefully pulled the door open. Amelie stood in the hallway, a shawl pulled around her shoulders. She wore a simple house dress, not quite a nightgown. Hovering behind her was a tea tray, packed with small wafers, round mints that dissolved on the tongue, and a hot pot.

"I saw your light on," she whispered, "and thought you might need a friend."

A smile tugged at his lips.

"It might have been Claude awake in here."

Too seriously, she said, "He wouldn't take the time to light lamps and be quiet. I knew it was you."

After a beat of silence, he opened the door. "Will your parents mind if their single daughter enters the room of a single male in the middle of the night while staying at their household?"

She bristled. "I'm of age, thank you very much. Just because I live at home and teach my sisters doesn't mean I can't be trusted as an adult. Also, they trust *you* implicitly. So, no."

He smiled, swept an arm inside. "Then please come in. A late drink of tea sounds just right."

Smiling slyly, she stepped past. The tea tray angled toward a coffee table next to the divan. Remy closed the door and trailed at her back, grateful to sink into a far more comfortable chair than the wooden one he endured to stay awake. She reached for the pot, tilting her eyebrow as hot water tumbled into one cup.

"You've been in your room all afternoon and evening."

"Mmm."

"Want to talk about why?"

"Not really."

"Something to do with the legal witch?"

He covered his mouth with a hand, then shook his head, but the truth was a different matter. In fact, he *did* want to talk about his day. About the options presented, Claude's rage, and Remy's deepening concerns about his brother and the company he kept.

With a spell, she sent a wafer his way. The glazed top gleamed. It hovered in front of him in blatant temptation. Smiling ruefully, he plucked it from the air. "You wicked temptress. I'll tell you anything for a wafer."

Amelie laughed. Her hair tumbled from a loose bun at the back of her neck, sliding to freedom over her shoulders. She plunked a tea sachet into her cup.

"I heard Claude yelling at you." She peered over the top of

her cup. "I'm sorry for whatever spurred your argument. It must be difficult to handle his emotions as well as your own."

Somehow, the broken ice felt easier to trod. He didn't have to wonder where weak parts existed; he could see them. Amelie had given him a gift in the asking.

"Thankfully, I rehabilitated the vase that he broke in a fit of rage and indignation worthy of a toddler."

Without looking, Amelie asked, "The rose-and-purple one?"

He nodded.

She shrugged it off. "Sophie has broken it an infinite number of times. It has been re-pieced more than it has been whole. That's why it's in here now."

Remy had a sip of tea, gratified by the instant soothing of the water. A flood of lavender slid into his tired body.

"I still felt terrible about it. Your family has been nothing but kind and giving. For him to . . ."

A touch landed on his knee.

"Remy, you are not your brother, and we know this. We would house Claude during this time no matter his atrocious behavior in honor of your parents."

He met her gaze first with shock, then a welling of something close to gratitude, but far more like appreciation.

"Thank you."

Her hand slid away.

"On that note," she continued, "I believe Claude has moved out."

"Oh?"

"The maids saw him packing his things with spells, then transporting them away. Have you not noticed?"

He glanced across the room, to Claude's closed door.

"No, I hadn't."

"Well," she said brightly, "I say good riddance and never return."

Amelie reached for her own wafer, split it in half, and appreciated the stretch of half-melted glaze before she had a bite. "So, what is it? What burden fills your eyes?"

"You really want to know?"

"Yes."

Remy struggled to find the words to explain his helpless curiosity. She provided a distraction from the real problem, which he'd eagerly take.

"But . . . why do you want to know?"

She paused, wafer halfway to her full lips. "You really don't know why I want to know?"

Remy scooted closer to the edge of his divan. "Why are you my friend, Amelie?"

"Why wouldn't I be your friend?"

"I . . . we weren't . . . that is . . ."

Understanding flooded her expression. "Ah." She lowered her treat to the plate, laying both halves around her teacup. Amelie rolled her lips, studying him, and clasped her hands together in front of her.

"You are wondering why I would care when, until your return, I was someone you . . . didn't care about. We may have grown up around each other, but I don't suppose that made us friends."

He winced, but couldn't change the truth, no matter how strongly they stung. How she managed to keep such an even expression, he couldn't imagine.

"Yes."

She chuckled breathily, rubbing her fingertips together to clear the crumbs. "I was a hopeless, romantic little girl, Remy. You were right to ignore me and my . . . fanatical attention." A hint of color rose to her cheeks. "Really, I should . . . that is . . . perhaps *I* should apologize?"

Flabbergasted, he stared.

Amelie drew in a shaky breath. "I had such a wild crush on you. This is not news to either of us."

Her bold statement cleared some of the uncertainty in the air.

He nodded.

"I . . . followed you and doted on you and . . . was horribly awkward. I'm sorry. For a young man so many years older than me, it must have been very . . . strange."

"Not *so* many years older," he mumbled.

She chuckled. "You're very gracious. Perhaps six years isn't too much older. Mother and Father are thirteen years apart."

"You weren't awkward," he tried to say without stumbling, but he couldn't. To his relief, she laughed.

"You are *very* gracious. Too gracious, Remy. Now, you're just lying to my face. I was incredibly awkward and lost in my own family and convinced that your handsome eyes were my ticket out of . . . a sea of drowning."

Her gaze went distant. He wondered what tide she battled, what waves she crested, dreaming of a way out through an impossible love story. He wanted to know. To peel deeper into those faraway layers.

"And then . . ." she began, searching for the right words, "well . . . let's just say that we all have lessons to learn, and I realized there are worse fates than a family that loves me, no matter how chaotic."

"An excellent lesson to learn."

"I agree." She softened. "Six years is a long time, Remy, and much changes. Thankfully, one of those things was my sociality. I hope we can be friends."

"Of course."

"While you were making a name for yourself, I was . . . finding my place in the family, learning how to stand on my own two feet, and by myself. Not a conglomeration of my sisters. You might not believe it," she added in a poor attempt at levity, "but it's terrible to grow up amidst nine girls."

"I literally can't imagine."

His expressive tone made her giggle, dispelling the intensity. She picked up one half of her wafer again and pointed it at him.

"You still haven't answered my question. Why do you look so haunted?"

Finding his response came much easier with that out of the way. His half-apology, disguised as a thunderstruck acknowledgement, brought to light the fact that he'd almost ignored her existence until she shone brighter than any star.

Instead of starting with Mr. Clarke, Claude's explosion, and the impossible, pressured position that Remy felt as a result, he opened both hands.

The Wildrose grimoire appeared.

"There's this book."

Amelie tilted her head, finished a bite of wafer, and held out a hand. Her fingers opened and closed in a request. He answered her wordless gesture by setting the book in her lap. The weighty thing threatened to tip off her knees at first, but she grasped it with the other hand as well. Her lips moved wordlessly as she read the cover.

"It appeared when I returned. It's . . . about an estate named Wildrose."

She reverently turned the pages, studying each. "I can see that. Very extensive, isn't it?"

"Very." He ran a hand through his hair and related everything. The way the book led him to the empty lot Father had purchased years ago, how it demanded he gather supplies, then built the beginnings of a clock. How he felt the release of a building pressure when he cleared a massive, rectangular portion of the empty field.

He hadn't returned since he left the three shovels, but had doubted work had proceeded. There was no promise between him and the magic.

Not yet.

"That's why you came home covered in dirt a while ago?" she inquired.

He nodded.

Amused, she flipped another page. "Fascinating."

"I . . . I'm considering trying to build it. Haven't decided yet," he hastened to add. "The currency requirement seems enormous and I don't think I can afford it."

"Are you capable of earning currency?"

"Yes."

"Do you have anything right now?"

"I have some savings."

"Who would build?"

"I don't know. The plans are all laid out. Another witch, perhaps? The magic started the clock, but I don't presume it would build the house. That was so small in comparison. The details of this are . . . daunting."

She hefted the grimoire, perusing each page intently. Amelie always acted intelligently, when she wasn't hiding in a bush to watch him wrestle with his brother, or deftly avoiding him during one of their neighborhood parties, but she was beyond that as an adult. Quick and agile, with a hint of humor to drive it home.

He was hopelessly charmed.

She tapped a finger on her chin, eyes still fixated on the grimoire. "It's odd, isn't it? For a grimoire, anyway."

"Aren't most grimoires odd?"

She snorted. "Perhaps each has their own . . . personality, but this is something else. Can you feel it?"

"What?"

"The . . . emotion. The energy." She gripped it with both hands. "It's almost a low hum. The kind you can't feel. It's like . . ." She chewed on the inside of her cheek, then rushed to ask, "Have you ever gone into the forest and stood there with your eyes closed?"

"Ah . . ."

"If you haven't," she said with a blithe smile, "then who are you and why are you wasting your life? If you have, then you'll know what it's like, being quiet in the out of doors. With a gasp of wind, or gentle birdsong, or wings. There's *something* in the air that you can't put your finger on until you realize it's magic. It's *in* the air. I feel that in this book."

She set her splayed hand on the cover.

"There's latent power inside. There must be. How else is it zipping you around or appearing when you summon it? It's almost burning, Remy."

"Just thought it a weird quirk of the magic."

Amelie handed it back to him. "Well, it's that, too. But this magic is different. I can feel it. I think it's trying to tell you something."

"You do?"

She smiled. "Could be a fun adventure to listen to it and see what happens. For all intents and purposes, you seem to be the magic holder. Maybe you can stop the work whenever you want."

"Maybe."

He hadn't expected her to encourage him into something as mad as building an estate that some random grimoire guided him to build. Most magic systems were easily detectable as safe, dark, evil, or useful, but others could be sneaky. What if he trusted this grimoire and something horrible resulted?

Black magic hid often enough.

"The amount of resources it requires would be most of my currency, if not all of it. Not to mention time . . ."

"You have the land, right?"

"Yes."

"Does Claude want it?"

Recalling Claude's earlier irritation with Remy, he confidently said, "I don't think so."

"The currency is yours?"

"Half of it. The currency Father had in savings is enough to get a project like this started, but not finish it. We'd need to sell the old property for me to afford Wildrose."

She made a noise deep in her throat. "Hmm . . . I see your point. Well, how do you feel about selling?"

"I don't know."

"I'm going to draw an assumption that Claude isn't happy about it, and this might be what you argued over?"

Helpless, he nodded.

"I'm sorry, Remy. It must be tough to disagree with Claude right now, of all times."

"Claude is . . . opinionated."

A frisson of pure loathing slid through her eyes, but she curbed it. Dozens of suppressed words lay behind her tight lips. He wondered again what Claude had done to cause such a stygian reaction in a woman so bright. Part of him didn't want to know.

"I imagine," she said slowly, "that with the grief that both of you face, and the physical pain he endures with his broken clavicle, that much weighs on him."

Her careful words, spoken as if she stepped daintily over a rushing creek of indignation, impressed Remy. He would have smiled had the situation been any less bleak.

"I need to do *something*," Remy concluded, veering away from the topic of his brother for both their sakes. "While your family's hospitality is appreciated, I can't and shouldn't stay here forever."

"I imagine it's nice to have something to do or think about, at any rate."

He nodded, blithely avoiding the intense surreality of Mother and Father's absence. His instinct had always been to turn to them in the conundrums. Father dealt with Claude more circumspectly than Mother, which was probably part of the problem. For whatever reason, Claude didn't respect either of their parents all that much.

"Any update from the apothecary?" she asked with another sip of tea. "Is Claude healing?"

"Seems to be."

"Did you ever find out how he broke his clavicle? It obviously happened before he found you that night."

"I haven't asked."

"Hmm. Just seems . . . odd. Where was Claude before the fire started?"

"His room?"

"Do you know?"

"Does it matter?" he asked as quickly, uncomfortable with where her silent accusation headed. "My brother didn't kill my parents."

Irritated, she snapped, "I never suggested as much, Remy. Perhaps *you* just did."

"I didn't!"

"You said it, not me."

She shot to her feet and bustled to the door. Halfway there she stopped, drew in a breath, and spun. Her face had cleared, but regret swilled in her words.

"Forgive me. This is not your emotion, but mine. I . . . Claude and I have a history of our own that I won't explain. It's better left in the past. But allow me to make it clear that I will never trust your brother, Remy. Not for as long as I draw breath. When there's something suspicious that involves him, I cannot help my inherent questions."

He met her terrible gaze, filled with pain.

"For whatever he did, I'm sorry. Claude has always been more of a heartbreaker than a love giver."

A hint of frost dampened her trying smile.

"You seem to feel pressure to leave our house, but know that you could be useful to my father. He needs help with his business, and a few home management items. He won't admit it, but his health isn't what it used to be. Work tires him, instead of reviving him. While you're figuring out what to do, help Father. My sisters love having you, and . . . so do I. Don't feel that you have to disappear so quickly. As long as you keep Claude in check," she added darkly, "then you're welcome to stay however long you want."

With that, she swiveled back around and disappeared out the door. Remy stared at the spot for a long time. Her scent faded as candles burned to goopy piles of wax that hardened again in waves.

He held out a hand and the grimoire appeared, sitting in his palm. He studied the cover. After all this thinking, ruminating, and lashing back and forth over what was *right* and what was *desired*, only one thing was blatantly clear.

He had no idea.

"I sense something special in you," he whispered, "but I'm not ready. I don't know if I have the currency. I need time. Time to say *merry part*. The memorial is this weekend, and I want to focus on them. I need time with Claude that isn't fraught with decisions. Allow me to speak to my brother. Though he is already disinclined to like you, I might be able to bring him around. Given the chance, it will be better if I create Wildrose with him, than without him."

After a final pause, he said, "Give me time."

The magic replied with a sigh.

Chapter Four

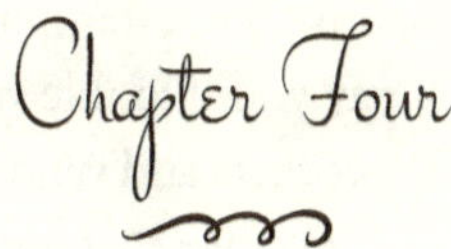

Manon and Caterina, the two youngest Leroy girls, danced beneath falling leaves under the old oak tree, delighting Remy with their happy giggles. Autumn had never been as wonderful as through their eyes.

Amelie joined them, charming him with her hair swept up in an elegant bun and a caught leaf fluttering from the top. Her sapphire gown shifted in the breeze, moving with restless music. He couldn't tear his eyes away from her. She couldn't see him through the second-story window of her father's office, which was just as well.

Sometimes, when she caught him staring at her like a lovestruck young boy, she laughed until she cried.

The irony.

"Well, my boy, you did it perfectly." James set his quill down with the announcement and beamed. "As always. That report does it. Ties the bow up. You've completed the training for the company and you're ready to go on your own."

Remy swiveled all the way around, facing his employer. While he expected James to announce as much, it was a relief to hear it.

"Thank you, James."

James tilted his head back with an observant look. "You're ready to take over, I think. Do you agree?"

He swept his hands to the side. "If you'll have me."

With a thump of his fist, James announced, "I'll have you, and more than that, I'll pay you. Double your salary, Remy, and you start tomorrow. The workers and vendors already know you, so it's simple enough to announce that you're officially transferring into my position."

Stunned, Remy blinked.

Did he say *double*?

Also, tomorrow?

James already paid Remy a generous salary. Six months ago, Remy began work at the bottom of his messenger paper factory, rotating through positions until he learned each integral step for gathering the wood, turning it to pulp, creating parchment, separating by quality, forming into correct dimensions, and imbuing with magic through a curing potion, instead of spells.

As Remy worked his way through the company, meeting each employee and learning every nuance, James hosted parties, introduced him to all his business acquaintances, and eventually ushered him here.

To his office.

From the beginning of the six-month journey, the plan had always been for Remy to step into James' position, and he was grateful to do it. The work was a thrilling challenge, and he enjoyed the familiarity.

Now the moment had arrived, and it choked him up. This is what Remy might have done for Father's business, but Claude had dissolved it into assets and closed everything down. He canceled existing contracts, burned bridges with every witch Father had formed a relationship with. Remy hadn't heard much from Claude since their argument over the land, only boring trivialities through letters. Their old life lay fallow and quiet.

"I . . . find myself at a loss for words, James," Remy admitted with a smile. "I'm so grateful."

James squeezed his arm. "I love you like a son, Remy. I always have. I could never, and would never try, to replace your father, but I'm grateful to have you here with us."

With a pat on his arm, James strolled out the door, whistling. Remy stood in the quiet of James' office and paused.

He'd done it.

He found a career that was more than tolerable—pleasant, even. A way to earn currency and create a life for himself.

As if the thought ushered it in, the Wildrose grimoire appeared. He stroked the intricate filigree on the cover, the roses twining around the title with a sharp inhale. Half a year had passed since he requested time. Not only had the moment arrived, but now the means. With double the salary, he could afford to tick off the list of supplies that the manor required in only a few months.

If he could convince Claude to sell the land.

Stomping feet, whistles, and trailing laughter echoed down the hallway as Remy pulled his thoughts together. He looked up as a flash of petticoats and dresses thundered past. Manon and Caterina must have returned inside.

Amelie peered into the office, illuminating when she saw Remy standing behind the desk.

"Merry meet!"

He smiled. "Amelie."

Sensing something awry, she gazed around and bustled inside. "Everything all right?" she drawled.

Unable to help it, he set aside the grimoire and smiled. A whirly-twirly sensation filled his head, robbing his breath.

"Yes. Yes, it's fine. Your father just . . . he turned it over to me."

Her eyes widened. "The company?"

"Yes!"

Laughing, she launched into the room and wrapped her arms around him. Remy accepted the embrace, grateful to celebrate with someone, and twirled them around. She pulled away to check his expression.

"And you're . . .?"

"Excited."

"Good! It's well earned. You'll be wonderful. None of us doubted you for a moment."

He waved to the Wildrose grimoire, but didn't take his hand off her shoulder. This was the most he'd ever touched her, and a stirring desire for more kept his fingertips glued there.

"His generous salary will be enough that I can buy supplies for the home. It will be awhile before I can amass enough, I think, but . . . it's a start."

"Even better news!"

Until she reacted so positively, he hadn't realized that he held a metaphorical breath. It *mattered* whether she believed in Wildrose. It mattered a great deal. He gently gripped her shoulders, the tips of his fingers pressing into her soft skin behind the neck, where wispy hairs danced. The last six months with Amelie had her family more firmly endeared to him, if possible.

He loved the Leroys.

Amelie, however, had him besotted.

"Do you mean that?" he asked.

"Of course."

Remy relaxed. "Good. I'm glad you think so."

A puzzled expression crossed her face. "Why wouldn't I? Wildrose looks like such a lovely manor, and it's not far from here. This part of the Network is so lovely, with all the changing seasons and the forest."

"Shall we celebrate?"

She brightened again, perhaps not noticing he'd dodged her question. "Yes! How do you want to celebrate?"

"Hmm . . . something with your sisters."

"Naturally."

"A game?"

"Of course!"

He extended his bent arm. She accepted as he escorted her into the long hallway with a well-worn rug. "Something outside, perhaps?"

Eyes twinkling, she said, "And there had better be cake."

He scoffed.

"It's hardly a party without cake."

The grimoire disappeared. He'd see it again tonight, probably on his pillow, as it waited for him every night since he asked for more time. The steady presence, but lack of insistence, was welcome.

A cacophony of voices, and a shouted, "Congratulations!" welcomed them into the dining hall.

Laughing, Amelie tugged him farther into the room, filled with her entire family, the spouses of her older sisters, a few young nephews, two dogs, a couple of neighbors, and confetti everywhere. His old chums from the Network school stood near the windows, shouting *hurray* as he entered the room.

Off to the sideboard, a giant frosted cake said, *Congratulations Remy!* Three little girls stared at it with wide eyes. Servants puttered in the background, ferrying plates and forks and spoons near a tub of cold ice cream.

Remy's mouth dropped.

"What is this?"

Across the way, James stood next to Joyce, both of them smiling wide. He had his arm around her shoulders.

"You think we'd give you the rule of our company without cake?" James cried. "Well, this man isn't as much a Leroy as I thought!"

Delighted, Remy tapped Caterina's freckled nose, swept her into his arms, and laughed. While the rest of the family plunged into a whirl of games—bean sack toss, doll dress up, and marbles, amongst others—James, Joyce, and Amelie handed out slices of cake as the servants set them onto plates.

Revelry filled the air.

In the midst of twirling girls into circles until they were dizzy, and laughing with his friends, he missed his parents. The ache ebbed more quickly than usual. Wildrose would come to pass, he secured a lovely career, and with a little luck, he rejoiced in the prospects of a future life filled with more days just like this one.

Remy stood at the treeline and stared out.

Despite being wholly and unequivocally his, he'd avoided the empty property for months. The Wildrose grimoire remained patient, which is what he felt from the land. Forbearing. Steadiness.

A willing heart.

That was silly, because it was soil, earth, tree, and sky. And yet . . . he sensed a pulse of life in the wild.

A crackle of breaking twigs drew his attention. Remy spun, expecting a chattering gnome to shriek at him, but Claude's dark eyes emerged from the forest. His hair lay askew, but not unkempt. A dark black coat graced his meaty shoulders, hanging to his knees as protection against the chill stirring from the northwest.

"Remy."

With a smile, Remy said, "Claude."

Remy opened his arms, which Claude stepped into, but the embrace was stiff, unyielding. Remy slapped his shoulder anyway and stepped back as if no time had passed at all.

"It's been too long, Claude."

The edgy diffidence faded as Claude studied him. He relaxed into something like a smile, though it didn't stretch to his eyes.

"It has."

"Where have you been?"

"Out."

"Where?"

With a near-feral smile, Claude said, "Forming my own path, Remy. Mother and Father died, the house is gone. We have to find purpose somehow. Not all of us can steal the honor of taking over the business for our Father's best friend and live in the lap of luxury."

All elation from the day before bled away. Remy stepped back, propelled by the swelling restlessness.

"*Stolen the honor of taking over the business for our Father's best friend?* You think that's what I've done?"

Claude spread his hands. "Do you see me working for the messenger paper company?"

"No, because it wasn't offered to you."

"Precisely."

The softly-spoken word dripped with disdain. Claude's upper lip twitched, as if he withheld a snarl.

"Did you apply?" Remy asked.

"Why bother?" He shrugged. "You snatched it up after the memorial, didn't you?"

"You received Father's grimoire refurbishment clients and all his stock!" Remy cried. "What more do you expect?"

"A functional inheritance, for once," Claude sniped, "but Father couldn't manage even that. Embarrassing, if you think about it. The stock of grimoires he owned amounted to almost nothing at all. I barely managed to sell them for the worth of parchment and leather."

"I thought the grimoires didn't survive?"

Claude sneered. "They did, but weren't worth much."

Fury gripped Remy. He closed his eyes, exhaled through his nose, and forced it to ebb. Disparagement—or truth—wouldn't help. Claude's relish over Remy's reaction was too obvious.

"What are you doing these days, Claude?" Remy asked, forcing a controlled tone. Less with a desire to know—his stomach ached at the thought of what dark places his brother inhabited, searching for something no one could identify—but to keep track of him. They were brothers.

Claude appeared to have forgotten that.

"Things, Remy. I've been doing things."

"What things?"

"Why should I tell you?" Claude scoffed. "Would you like to track all my doings as well, like Father? If you like, I can save all my ipsum bottles and count up how much they cost me, as Father did."

"He tracked you?"

"Oh, yes." Claude acted nonchalant, but his innate tension overrode the falsity. "He *loved* to know what schemes I got myself into. Said it was for the good of the family name, of course. *The good of all of us, Claude. This is about more than just you, you realize. Give up the ipsum, give up the taverns.*"

Remy swallowed, and it hurt. Claude and Father always locked horns. Both focused on being right in their own respective stance. They couldn't see the cliff they headed toward with every confrontation.

Claude spat to the side and conjured a bottle. Dark ipsum sloshed as he tilted his head back, chugged, and then dropped it. It crashed to the rocks below, shattering to glittering shards. Ipsum soaked the ground, permeating through the grasses and into the air. It hung, a stagnant promise.

Claude nodded to the field. "You're going to build it, aren't you?"

"I am."

"You still have that bloody grimoire?"

Reluctantly, Remy nodded once. It's not like he'd be able to hide it once construction began, anyway.

"Yes."

"It won't work." Claude sneered, kicking a loose rock into the untamed place. "I tried. The materials never went anywhere. Wasted my currency buying the first list, then letting the piles molder in the field while I waited for the magic to kick in."

Maybe that was your problem, Remy thought. *You wait for everyone else to do something.*

Remy faced out. He couldn't stand to look at Claude. All he saw was the wedge growing larger between them. An obsidian chunk of resentment, thrusting them farther and farther apart. No matter how hard Remy tried to reach around, Claude was always away.

"I'm going to try."

Claude chortled. "You're going to try to build Wildrose, and you're going to fail. Good luck. How is business, by the way? Rumor says that old man James finally gave up the mantle to a *worthy young man of breeding and repute.* You got the job *and* the company."

"Says who?" Remy asked coolly.

"James wrote to me. Invited me to a party."

"Oh." Remy blinked, taken aback. "I didn't know."

Claude said nothing.

Their parents had always been comfortable and well-off, but they hadn't been in the upper echelon. Like the Leroy family, they had space and accommodations, warmth, food, and joy, but they weren't eligible for the higher-tier sociality found in Ashleigh city, or the covens that surrounded it. Those witches had rules around who belonged, where they belonged, and why. Mother and Father, content with their lives and friends in the country, never cared.

"Doesn't matter. The Leroys aren't the right people for me, anyway," Claude muttered, and dug into a pocket. He withdrew a cheroot box, slipped one from inside, and conjured a flame. With two quick inhales, a bluish cloud puffed free.

"Still chasing society, are you?" Remy quipped.

"I'm not chasing anyone," Claude immediately countered. "I'm waiting until they see my genius."

"Why?"

Claude laughed. The smoke smelled like rancid weeds and tobacco. "If you have to ask," he drawled, "then you'd never understand. Mother and Father never cared either, which is sad, really. All those years wasted, being nothing."

Remy's shoulders swelled with righteous indignation, but before he could expunge the filthy froth, Claude flicked the edge of his cheroot on the ground. Flames sparked in the dry grass, turning to an instant blaze. It was too wet for the grass to burn on its own. The spilled ipsum surely helped, but it had to be something more. Magic, probably. Claude grinned and tipped his head toward the fire.

"That's all this place is good for, Remy. You'll never be able to afford it. Good luck, brother."

Claude turned to leave, but Remy stopped him.

"I want to sell the Dauphin land."

Claude paused.

Silence fell.

The fire crackled along the edge of a dried stick, overrun with brittle vines lashed to the ground. Greener grass stalks obscured it from view, but didn't prevent it from catching fire in a slow, dangerous burn. The scent of smoke merged with tobacco.

Claude peered at him.

"You what?"

"The land has been sitting there for six months, gathering rain. I want to sell it and give ourselves the currency we need to start again. Maybe it will give you the path to your upper echelon."

The unnatural stillness of Claude's expression worried Remy far more than his quietude. For long eternities, Remy forced himself to wait. Movement lurked in the back of Claude's eyes.

Thoughts. Roving insecurities, probably. Claude ran his tongue over his teeth, a blithely malevolent gesture, since he seemed incapable of meeting Remy's gaze.

"Sell," he murmured, sounding out each nuance and letter. "You want to sell our ancestral home."

"I don't want to, but I also didn't want Mother and Father to die. We don't always get what we want, just what we work for. Even then . . ."

Claude's cheek twitched. "Yes, yes," he said silkily, "who would want such fantastic witches to die? Look at you. Grown up Remy, enduring all the hard things that you never asked for. Poor, idiotic child."

He pulled another long drag from the cheroot, tossed it into the burgeoning flame. Remy should step on the fire before it whipped out of control, but his body wouldn't move. His thoughts locked, honed on Claude and their rising ultimatum.

By requesting the sale, Remy had officially grown the obsidian chunk between them so much the distance would never close. He understood that, just as he understood he couldn't change it. Claude was the only one holding it into place.

Claude lifted his head, met Remy's gaze. Hatred locked in his depths, swirling in darkness and pain. Quick as it revealed, it morphed into the cold stare of a man Remy hardly recognized as his childhood playmate.

"You'll have your wish, Remy. I'll speak to my business associates tomorrow, and we'll put it up for sale. Trust me. I'll get you the best deal we can find so you can move on to your . . ."

He raised a hand.

". . . better dreams. Merry part, brother."

As Claude strode away, he ground his foot on the flames. The fire puffed out in a gasp of smoke. The slag dissipated. Light vanished, as if it had never been there.

Chapter Five

"Twenty pentacles?" Remy cried. "You're joking."

The lumberman snorted.

"Lumber is no joking matter, sir. It's twenty pentacles for that much, and not a coin less. This is premium lumber. Processed, ready to use. Takes weeks to get it in this state, with loads of incantations you won't bother with, and that's it."

Before Remy could protest again, the man trundled out of sight, winding in between stacks of fallen trees, wood chips, shavings, and an amalgamation of all. Foresters appeared here and there, transporting from work sites or hauling giant logs from one side of the lumberyard to the other.

Remy considered the pile of logs at least twice his height. True enough. The lumber *was* ready to go, and the list in the grimoire was blatantly clear that Wildrose required the highest quality wood. It's not like Remy had time to figure out the incantations to take the lumber from a standing tree to this state, anyway.

He *did* want Wildrose, but it wasn't easy that the whole project would take loads more currency than he expected.

"Fine!" he shouted to the lumberman's back. "I'll take the lot."

The man spun around with a wide smile.

"I'll deliver it in the morning."

Caterina and Manon held their thin arms out to the side as they crossed a fallen log. The giant felled tree had rolled off the top of the lumber stack delivered yesterday and lay alone, in the field, ten paces from the rest.

Caterina giggled as she fell off, and Manon followed. With happy shrieks, they raced down the length and clambered on top at the other side.

"The nails arrived today." Amelie lifted a box from the ground and extended it to Remy as he approached, loosening his cravat. The silk strings hung on either side of his neck, freeing him from their trapped tightness. Afternoon sun slanted through the sky, warming the piles of lumber and sweetening the autumn breeze with a mixture of pine and sap.

"Sorry I'm a little late." He smiled sheepishly. "I had to wrap up a few loose ends at work before coming."

"The perk of being the boss," Amelie drawled, "is setting your own hours."

"Yet I would never want to do a poor job out of eagerness for my own project here." He accepted the box of nails and opened the top to inspect their length and head size. "Nor disappoint your father," he added.

There was too much solemnity in her tone when she said, "You're the best of men, Remy, and we're lucky to have you. I can't imagine Father thinking of you with anything but the highest regard."

Her *we* sent a jolt to Remy's heart. One day, he'd turn that *we* into an *I*, no matter how hard he must work. A gradual softening toward him had commenced months ago, but he had nothing certain to offer her right now. His career had finalized, but he was still a wobbly toddler on the path to his future.

Until he had a landing to keep her safe, he had no right to court a witch of Amelie's caliber.

Soon.

Hopefully *very* soon.

Until then, an unspoken expectation thrummed between them. It swelled every day with each hungry gaze—of which there were many.

Confirming that the nails met the specifications demanded by the grimoire, he set them aside. When he extended both hands toward her, she immediately set hers within.

"Thank you, Amelie, for meeting me here. I thought it would save time." He canted his gaze to the sun. "Of which we never have enough, but I'll take what's offered. The cold winter months are coming. The magic feels . . . anticipatory."

Amelie turned, surveying the piles of *stuff* he'd steadily amassed.

"It's incredible what you've scrounged up in the last three weeks since taking Father's job."

"Not enough."

"But soon."

He nodded. They awaited a few supplies from the blacksmith—door hinges, some welded brackets, and other sundries—as well as odds and ends from a quarry in the northern mountains.

After a pause, she asked, "Has Claude had any luck selling your land?"

The day after his last conversation with Claude, a white banner had appeared on their rubble mound, proclaiming it for sale. Joyce pointed out a notice in the land section of the *Chatham Chatterer* that morning. Claude had written Remy one hasty update, scribbled with nearly illegible handwriting, when it was officially listed for sale.

"Not yet."

"That will be soon, too." She squeezed his hands in a firm punctuation. "All will be well."

When the younger girls shrieked, Amelie spun into a cold autumn wind to face them. They dissolved into giggles as they petaled to the sides, frolicking on the same log. Clouds blew in from the northwest with a sinister duress in their dark underbellies. Minute by minute, their foamy mists overtook the sun and sky. Twirls of snowflakes would fall soon enough.

"First snow of the season," she said. "We better leave soon. It's only going to get colder, and of course Manon didn't bring the right cloak."

"I agree."

"Now that snow is coming," she spun toward him again, "what's next?"

He released her hands and the grimoire appeared, opened to the exact page he sought, as if the magic sensed his command.

"We could hold off building through the winter and start in the spring," he said.

"Do you want that?"

"No."

The thought of slowing progress frustrated Remy. There had been enough concessions to life and maturity the past year. Losing his parents, his home, his brother, his dream for life. He wanted this *one* thing.

"A few oddities are on the way," he said, "and then the first few lists are supplied. Except for one strange item."

"Oh?"

The tip of his finger trailed down the page, sweeping back and forth, past all the things he'd already obtained, until it landed on the bottom. The top of his index finger tapped on it. "This."

Amelie read aloud. "Fieldstones, large and small." Her voice hiked up. "Fieldstones?"

"Mmmm."

"What are those?"

"I haven't the foggiest."

"But why would the estate need stones?"

He flipped to a different chapter, his fingers taking him there by memorized rhythm. He'd perused this book so many times, he knew right where to go. "For the foundation. The plans indicate that a layer of stones will go into the ground, like bedrock."

Amelie kicked at a protuberating rock at her feet, half-covered in moss and coated with mud.

"Aren't there enough stones already?"

He shrugged. "Maybe? There might be a quarry somewhere that we could ask."

"The grimoire is normally so clear." She frowned, running a finger over her bottom lip in deeper thought. "It seems odd that it would just say *fieldstones* with two varying sizes."

"Maybe that *is* very clear and we aren't aware."

"True." Amelie pointed to a single word at the top of the page. "Did you see this? You need shovels, too. Twenty of them, to be exact."

"Oh, I didn't. Well spotted."

"We have shovels, but not twenty of them."

"How many?" he asked, eyebrow lifting.

With a spell, she summoned five shovels of varying descriptions. Rounded, spiked, and squared. They clattered near the wood piles, one of them half the length of the rest because of a broken handle.

"Hmm . . ." he said. "I have three left over from Father's shed. We'll need twelve more."

Remy shoved a hand into his pocket, extracting a handful of sacran coins. He pursed his lips and whistled. Caterina and Manon's heads whipped up, eyes wide.

"Girls, a favor?"

They hopped free of the wooden trunk and hurried over. He gave each girl four sacrans, then crouched next to them.

"Can you do a very important task on my behalf tomorrow?"

Solemnly, eyes wide, they nodded. They had Amelie's sobriety when they focused, which wasn't often.

Remy pointed to the field. "You see that big open space?"

Caterina's brown curls bobbed as she nodded. Manon tilted her head, squinting hard.

"I'm building a house there. It requires a lot of different things, like wood and axes and nails and the like." He glanced at Amelie and lowered his voice, but didn't drop her gaze. "I'm building it to impress your sister and see if she'll live there with me. Do you think it'll work?"

Amelie's lips twitched as she turned away and pretended not to hear. It was the boldest declaration of his intentions yet. When she didn't run away screaming, he took heart. Both girls giggled, dirty hands pressed to their mouths.

"Yes," Manon whispered. "She has a crush on you."

"Glad to hear it," he whispered back with dramatic gusto. "I daresay the same is returned on my part. Maybe, one day, you can help me tell her. In the meantime, I'll need your help with something tomorrow, if you're willing?"

Caterina jumped up and down on the spot. "Yes! We want to help."

"Can you purchase a few things?"

Manon nodded vigorously.

"You're learning currency in your math classes, aren't you?"

"Sacrans and pentacles," Caterina declared proudly. "Amelie is taking us to the market to practice."

"Ideal!" He grabbed her grubby hand in his, then dropped a handful of coins inside. "I have a lot of meetings tomorrow, and the market is closed for the night. While you're shopping, could you convince Amelie to let you purchase twelve shovels?"

Caterina, lips rounded with shock at such a responsible request, looked at Amelie in silent pleading.

Laughing, Amelie said, "I would love to accommodate that request. We can practice counting and exchanging currency, the way we've been learning during your math lessons. But you must keep close watch over those coins!"

Shrieking, the girls threw their arms around his legs, squeezed tight, then delicately placed the coins in their pockets. When they returned to their log, their exuberance stemmed. They tumbled around less, hands clutched greedily over their dresses. Caterina kept one fist in her pocket and walked with measured steps.

Amelie's eyes shone when she said, "Thank you for trusting them. You've made their day."

"They make my day when I see them."

"I've noticed," she said quietly. "You're always so careful to include them. It means a lot. Not everyone cares so much about energetic girls their age. You're . . . quite different, Remy."

Remy gave a rueful smile and placed a hand in his pocket. His teasing explanation to the girls hid a great deal of vulnerability.

"I love your family, and I do need their help," he mused, adding quickly, "yours, as well. If . . . if you like Wildrose."

The question was far too loaded. Wildrose wasn't truly what he offered, but in lieu of giving himself wholly to her, he left the house hanging in the air as the greatest question. They'd never expressly talked about their budding plans. The tendrils of stirring loyalty and emotion.

She pulled in a breath, lips parted as if to speak. At the last minute she paused, creases in the space between her eyebrows.

"We love you, Remy."

The wait between his response and hers stilted the sincere

words. The sentiment was true, though wobbly. Something held her back. Something fetid that sank into heart cracks and required patience and time to remove.

Remy ignored her reticence to stare at the land. His bold declaration had been enough forward movement for today. When all else felt mired in uncertainty, he could always look forward.

To Wildrose.

"We'll see what I can figure out about fieldstones tomorrow," he said quietly, sparing her the agony of hesitation. "I'll write a quarry and see how much it'll cost. I'm about to the end of my coffers for the month, so if it's too much, we'll have to wait."

Seeming relieved to return to stable ground, Amelie asked, "What will happen when you have all the supplies, do you think?"

Driving his hand through his hair, he said breathlessly, "I have no idea. I assume the grimoire will reveal the next step as soon as the resources are obtained." After a moment of consideration, he added, "We'll probably be ready to find someone to consult for building it, is my guess. *Someone* has to put it together."

A shiver slid through Amelie as she studied the incoming storm, halfway through the sky. A gust of wind breezed tendrils past her ears in a charming dance. When snowflakes freckled the air, trailing her cloak into the wind, he had to wrestle the urge to wrap his arms around her and impart his heat.

If Caterina and Manon hadn't been present, the temptation to do so might have overwhelmed him.

Desire aside, it wouldn't have been right. Not while living in her house, training under James' occasional guidance. Not fair to Amelie, her family, nor to a potential future together. If he wanted to honor his parents' legacy and make Amelie his own, he needed Wildrose.

A letter from the quarry interrupted Remy's lunch the next afternoon.

> *We have plenty of fieldstones. If you're looking to build, we have slabs or fieldstones.*

To which Remy asked, *What is the difference? I'm looking to establish a stone foundation for a new house, and the list specifically requires fieldstones.*

Thankfully, the quarry master didn't ask *what list?* Or *are you crazy?* Instead, he replied, *For that, you'll want large and small fieldstones. How big is the place?*

With relief, Remy sent the dimensions after his second cup of coffee, and had the reply before his next appointment.

> *I can send you enough large and small fieldstones to build a four pace thick foundation at those measurements for two hundred pentacles. It's a lot of stone.*
>
> *Hope you have space for it.*

Just outside his office door, Remy hesitated. Two hundred pentacles! For stones? The thought set his teeth on edge, but maybe he was too sensitive. This purchase, combined with the odds and ends that came through this morning from the blacksmith, would clear out the last of his available funds. Caterina and Manon had taken the only coins he had to rub together.

More lists existed later in the grimoire, as well. At what point would Wildrose be satisfied? Technically, it hadn't yet begun.

Remy cast an eye to the clock.

2:55.

With a frustrated growl, he opened his hands. The grimoire landed within. When he opened to the lists that the grimoire had insisted on, only one thing remained. *Fieldstones, large and small.* On the other page, the line that once said *shovels, twenty* had vanished into white.

The girls must have already completed their market trip. He couldn't wait to hear where they found twelve shovels. Remy chewed on his bottom lip until his secretary called for him.

"Mr. Dauphin?"

"Yes!" he called. "Coming in a moment!"

To the quarry master, he wrote, *I'll take the order. Expect me at 4:00 with the payment, and then I'll transport you to the delivery site. There's room.*

He spun on his heels and left his office, meeting bound. That was that. He'd officially invested his last coin into Wildrose, with no idea what result it would yield on the other side. Whatever happened next, he hoped the magic knew what it was doing.

Chapter Six

A voice raced through the office, shouting Remy's name, at six o'clock that evening.

Remy stood up from behind his desk as Amelie rushed into the room, laughing. Her hair had fallen out of her usual, loose chignon, and danced in charming waves around her neck.

"Remy!"

"What is it?"

"Come!" She held out a hand, face suffused with delight. "Come with me. You must see it."

"See what?"

She shook her head, eyes dancing. "I can't explain it! Trust me! It sent me to find you."

"Who?"

"Just come!"

Willingly, he slipped his hand into hers and allowed her to tug him away. A transportation spell swept over both of them— something *else* he hadn't known Amelie could do—until it deposited them somewhere soft, a little spongy.

On arrival, the first thing he heard was the *clink* and *chink* of shovels. An earthy smell thickened the cold, belying the brisk wind that swept past. Leaves wheeled by, cartwheeling end over end across the wet field. A brief snow storm descended last evening, then burned away under the autumn sun this afternoon.

Remy stared at *his* field.

"What is this?" he whispered.

Amelie only laughed.

James, Joyce, Celine, Caterina, and Manon stood at the edge of Wildrose's open meadow, staring in open mouthed shock. Sometime between his meeting with the quarry master at four o'clock and this moment, the fieldstones—which were little more than oblong stones of various shape, length, and heft—arrived. Dozens of enormous piles stood like sentinels near the lumber.

Where he cleared the meadow months ago, the rectangle had fallen into the ground under the influence of working shovels.

Twenty working shovels, in fact.

The tools bit into the dirt and lifted, tossing earth to the side in rudimentary, rectangular piles. Two shovels extracted rocks from the fieldstone piles and transported the rocks to the edge of the lowering foundation, while the rest of the tools bit into the ground chunk after chunk.

"But . . . what is doing it?" he asked.

"The magic!" Amelie cried. "Don't you see? Wildrose is building itself. It needed you to obtain the resources, as you said. You have the supplies, and now the magic can work. We won't have to find a witch to put it together."

The *we* delighted him as much as the relief of pressure.

The magic.

Of course. Hadn't Claude insinuated as much? *I tried. The materials never went anywhere. Wasted my currency buying the first list, then letting the piles molder in the field while I waited for the magic to kick in.*

Amelie clapped, giggling, her arms spread into the air as she spun in a circle. A long coat with rabbit fur edging kept her warm, sliding down her hips all the way to her knees. A hood lay between her shoulder blades, capturing her loose hair.

He strode past her, James, and Joyce to peer down at the edge of the growing hole. The shovels worked independently, as if an invisible crew controlled each. As expertly as professionals, too. Each stroke had purpose and intention. Each shovel dug without faltering. There was no insecurity in any movement, nor wariness. The job marched forward with astonishing speed.

A twirl of wind stirred up the grimoire, shutting it to the blank page where the lists should have been.

No.

There were no blank pages.

Frowning, he shuffled to the front, where the introductory pages remained. There had been four pages of supplies in between the introduction and the next section, which covered the first floor. The types of lumber, and different lengths had been listed there. The finish. The nails. The stones. Magic erased them as he obtained each for what felt like ages.

Those pages had vanished.

Frowning, he studied the shovels again, but they afforded no answers. Caterina and Manon ventured closer until Joyce called them back. The shovels kept their synchronized work moving steadily forward. As his shock eased, a growing realization followed.

Wildrose had begun.

Officially.

Up until this point, it felt like a vague future . . . something. Without knowing how to assemble the thing, he viewed Wildrose as a challenge yet to be uncovered. Is this what Claude had anticipated, but never experienced? Why didn't the magic move into action for Claude, but initiated for Remy?

He quelled the pang of guilt. That wasn't his fault. The magic began only after he had provided everything it asked.

Perhaps Claude had missed something.

Or maybe witches were foreordained to the lives they led.

The world bled away. As he stared at the origins of Wildrose, Remy didn't notice the cold air nipping his nose, the incoming wind, the dimming sun. Growing cold threatened, more bitter than days past.

He saw only Wildrose.

Magic filled him in a crescendo that built to the tips of his fingers. Love swelled. For Wildrose and the magic building it. For the new beginning it offered, and for all that it might be. A pleasant sensation traveled from the grimoire, through his hands, and all the way to his heart.

Something physical had changed within him because of the magic. A chamber of his heart that hadn't existed before became corporeal with ballooning affection and love. He connected with the house, and Wildrose was now part of him. As this understanding settled, he relaxed. It was unexpected, but right.

He accepted Wildrose, and all Wildrose meant, as the estate accepted him.

A gasp drew his attention higher. The tunnel of focus evaporated as all shovels paused. They hovered in the air, waiting. The flush of heat raced through his body.

He whispered, "I sense something special in you, Wildrose. I feel it. I want to be part of it. I'm ready."

As quickly as the shovels had paused, they resumed scooping dirt into neat piles, forming edges on either side of the foundation. Caterina and Manon giggled again, toes in the soil, Amelie at their side, unaware of the magic that rippled through his body.

Remy blinked into awareness as James approached with one hand in his pocket, the other clutching something oblong and leather.

"Looks like you've found yourself an interesting way to build a house, son."

"I suppose so."

"Fascinating." James clucked under his breath, regarded the shovels one last time, and lifted the leather satchel. "This is for you."

Remy studied the exterior with deepening scrutiny. A leather string wound it together. He undid the string, flipped the thin leather open, and withdrew a piece of parchment with a familiar wax stamp.

"From the sale of your parent's land," James said quietly. "Claude managed to sell it for a surprisingly high price. More than I thought you'd get. The sale went through today. That's the paperwork that his legalwitch dropped off at the house while you were at work. The currency is at the bank."

Remy glanced at the amount, eyes wide.

"So much?"

"Claude has always been a shrewd businessman, and he proved it with the sale of the plot. Rumor has it that there are already plans in progress for the buyer to build. A good thing, for you. For Claude. For the neighborhood."

The thought tightened Remy's throat. He didn't want to think about a different home on his lot. Children running on his lawn, making memories over the ghosts of his previous life.

"Close the door, my boy." James patted Remy on the shoulder. "And open another. I hope you don't torture yourself with guilt. Selling was the right move. Your parents were my best friends, and never would have wanted you to wallow or worry about it. You're building something beautiful and better. They'd be quite pleased."

Remy tucked the bundle inside his jacket pocket.

"Thank you, James."

"A pleasure."

James turned, whistled, and drew Caterina and Manon's attention. He waved his hand, calling them to his side. The five women reluctantly peeled away from the overzealous tools and headed toward them.

"You're a good man, Remy." James observed his family as they picked their way across the barren meadow, littered with the corpses of previously brilliant greenery. "Don't wait too long, eh?"

"Sir?"

"To do something with Amelie," James snapped with a hint of suppressed humor. "If you wait too much longer to court the girl, you'll have to hand her fake teeth before you manage to take her out to eat with you somewhere."

James finished his command quietly enough that the approaching group didn't hear. Remy nearly choked on his own tongue as the Leroy family departed, waving. Caterina, Celine, and Manon raced ahead while James and Joyce linked arms, walking at a more sedate pace. Amelie held onto her mother. The Leroy estate was just down the road, a thirty minute walk away. They must have come on an evening stroll.

Remy watched them go. The sense of loss and despair he might have felt at the sale of his ancestral home had dissipated in the humming connection with the magic.

With his home.

With Wildrose.

He would never be the same witch again.

Chapter Seven

Two opera tickets burned a hole in Remy's pocket.

He stared out of his work window and onto the bustling roadway of Ashleigh City, where the company kept its main office. He thought of the opera, and he thought about Claude. A month ago, their ancestral land was sold and Claude still hadn't said a word. Remy missed him.

But he also didn't.

The dregs of winter scraped at the windowpane edges, coating it in a chilly breath of air and whorls of frost. He shivered, despite a bustling fire in the hearth. On days this chilled, a fire couldn't fend off winter's tenaciously frosty fingers.

He ran his fingers along the ticket edges. This performance would be his first attempt to peel Amelie away from her house and into the forays of society. A simple evening at a musical event felt loaded with implication for her, but also for *them*. Being seen together meant something he wanted it to mean.

What about Amelie?

Though affectionate and by no means off-putting, she was also reserved and careful. Her delight in Wildrose was his main hope that she held interest in a life with him. He couldn't help but wonder if she didn't trust him because of their former history, when he'd been a brazen fool.

Remy called a farewell to his secretary, shrugged into a heavy coat, and transported. The fire would die down in the night. His secretary would move his ink bottles to the hearthstones before he left for the evening so they wouldn't freeze, and the office would close down for the weekend.

To clear his mind both of work and the fact that local vendors wanted a price decrease, Remy visited Wildrose first. This was his daily routine. Leave work, stop at Wildrose, return to the Leroy family.

Construction advanced despite the weather. Giant clouds dumped a load of wet snow overnight. The magic, oblivious to shrieking winds, pressed on with dogged energy.

"Wildrose, you never cease to stun me."

Digging the hole, laying the thick fieldstone foundation, filling it in with a liquid sort of ground stone—of an altogether different sort mixed in a cauldron and created with unfathomable potions—and building up the main walls, had taken a month. This week, the frantic activity of framing created a skeleton structure that made sense only when he studied it closely.

The pages winnowed daily. As the magic finished one aspect, the page on which it stood disappeared.

Snow creaking beneath his shoes, Remy strode around the exterior of the construction site. He paced the same trip each evening, and studied the changing nuances. He found no flaws.

Not once.

A voice called out, "It's really something."

Remy stopped short. Claude stood a few paces away, eyes bloodshot. He held no bottle. From the fifteen paces between them, Remy couldn't smell any ipsum . . . yet. Claude still appeared, for all the world, as if he'd wrestled with a devil and came out on the bottom.

"Good to see you Claude."

Claude waved an arm. "How'd you get it to work?"

"I don't know."

Claude squinted. The snowstorm left behind a pristine blue sky and a brutal cold. Clouds cleared, leaving the muted pinks and oranges of a sunrise overhead. Despite the months without speaking, Claude looked slightly better than their last meeting. He'd lost some of the gauntness that haunted him before, but hadn't gained much pep.

Claude shoved his hands in his pockets. "So . . . how have you been?"

"Fine."

"I hear good things about your takeover of James' company thus far." Claude's hands fidgeted in the coat. "I'm happy for you."

"Thanks."

An awkward pause filled the air. Remy, unsure what to say, asked, "How have *you* been Claude? I haven't heard from you."

"I received your letters. Didn't reply." Claude kicked at a chunk of ice. "I should have replied, but I'm a cad. A bastard. You know that." His voice lowered. "I'm sorry, Remy. I haven't been a very good brother. When Mother and Father died, I just . . ."

He trailed away.

"I'm sorry."

Remy, astonished at such an unforeseen event, instantly replied, "Forgiven, Claude. We're brothers."

Claude pushed his lips to one side of his face with a blithe smile. "Don't make it easy on me, Remy. You'll regret it."

"I won't."

"Doesn't matter, anyway. I've turned over a new leaf, so to speak. Have a job that I really like, and a place to stay. Plans are underway for me to do—and have—something bigger and better than our life before."

"That's wonderful, Claude. What are you doing now?"

"Mostly importing goods from other Networks. Finding suppliers for specific demands, guaranteeing they're happy, that sort of thing."

"Business."

Claude smiled. "Business."

Remy turned to continue walking, and Claude dropped into pace next to him. They stepped over snowy ground with a companionable silence for almost a full minute.

"I'm really happy to hear a positive update, Claude. I've been very worried about you."

"I know. I don't appreciate a brother like you enough."

"That's not it."

"Really," Claude insisted. He stopped walking, forcing Remy to meet his gaze. "I don't, but I'll try to."

Remy only nodded. He wanted to believe Claude—he really did. But experience held him in cautious reserve. As they continued walking, Claude said, "I've cut down on the ipsum. It was . . . a problem."

"What motivated that decision?" Remy asked carefully, though he wanted to inquire what *cut down on the ipsum* meant.

"Life."

The vague response remained that way because Claude spoke of other things. Business. Taxes. The place he rented in Chatham City with a witch he worked with. By the time Remy completed his circle of Wildrose, mapped its steady progress, and checked that all supplies remained in order, Claude's update expired.

"And that," Claude said with a hand in the air, "is that. Things are good, Remy. And I'm glad they're good."

"Thank you, Claude." He couldn't remove the stiff formality from his words. "Hearing that is a gift."

Claude glanced at a pocket watch, then stuffed it back inside. "You have plans tonight?"

Duly reminded of the awaiting date with Amelie, Remy nodded. "The opera with Amelie."

Shadows crossed Claude's eyes. He dropped his gaze.

"Amelie?"

"Yes."

"Oh."

"Why do you say *oh* like that?"

Suspicion tingled along the back of Remy's neck. Amelie's vague illusions to a dark history between Claude and herself briefly resurrected in Remy's mind.

"Amelie," Claude said slowly, "is a wonderful woman. You would be a fool to let her go, if you can handle her."

Remy frowned. "What is the history between you and Amelie, Claude?"

Surprise elevated his brow.

"She hasn't told you?"

"No."

Stunned, Claude struggled to reply. He scratched his jaw, shoulders shifting. "Then . . . it isn't mine to share." He rubbed the back of his knuckle across his cheek with a slight grimace. "She'll tell you when she's ready," then he added in a mutter, "I have little doubt." Before Remy could inquire further, Claude held up a hand. "It's my fault, brother. I behaved abominably, and she did nothing wrong. No harm was done."

"Did you love her?" Remy blurted out.

Claude laughed. An empty, hollow sound that trailed out of him like a ghost expiring. Whatever geniality he displayed had lapsed. Former shadows reappeared.

"No, Remy. No such thing as love. A heart like mine isn't capable of that emotion. Do me a favor? Don't be a fool. Lock down that family, that wife, and the beautiful life you've always deserved. All right? You deserve it, I don't, and the faster you accept that, the less pain you'll suffer."

Amelie held tight to Remy's arm as they strode through downtown Ashleigh, waited in line for their seats outside the magnificent opera house, sat down, and soaked it in. The delight in her wide eyes made the effort worth it.

"I've never been here before," she breathed. She perched on the edge of her seat, her torso twisting left and right. Candles, set in miniature sconces ringed with mirrors, glimmered from the stage. Torches illuminated the rest of the room. Incantations had been used, most likely, because the room wasn't as stuffy as he expected.

"No?"

She shook her head. He didn't need to inquire why. Opera tickets were a luxury, and with eleven mouths to feed, the Leroys managed their fun without sacrans.

"Mother brought us every year," Remy said as he draped his coat over his knees.

"Do you like it?"

"I think so."

Her eyes laughed at him, but her lips pressed together.

"You *think* so?"

"It's a good experience to have, but not one I'd replicate without someone to go with."

A couple sat in front of them, and Amelie's flood of conversation ebbed. Her initial elation flowed into sedate observation and contented enjoyment. Remy soaked in the silent affection of her hand still in his arm.

The satisfying evening passed in a wicked blur of Amelie's laugh and the grandeur of being seen with her on his arm. Halfway through the final act, she turned to whisper in his ear.

"Do you like the singing?" she asked. Her breath was a tantalizing caress across tender skin. When he turned to face her, their noses almost brushed. In the dim light, he could barely make out her features, comprehending twinkling eyes that never stopped smiling and a hesitancy he hadn't noticed in the past.

"She has an impressive range."

"I agree."

"I think your violin playing was better."

A flicker of pain registered in her eyes as she smiled. As a crescendo lifted the current soloist, chills ran up his arms.

"How many years do you think it takes to train for something like this?" she asked.

"A lifetime."

"I thought so, too."

A hiss from behind attempted to silence them, earning a giggle from Amelie. She returned her attention to the stage, but kept her arm on his. Remy ran his fingers along the inside of her forearm until they brushed her palm. Her breath hitched. She went very still.

Summoning his courage, Remy braided his fingers into hers. Their palms hovered, waiting for her approval. Out of the corner of his eyes, she smiled. She closed the distance between their hands and squeezed his fingers.

He exhaled in relief.

After that, he didn't recall a single song.

Amelie squeezed his hand as the performer, at the end of a vigorous movement, released a particularly impressive note that wound like the lazy trail of a warbling snowflake. Amelie relaxed with the music as the violins faded, like a string pulling through his heart, until all fell to silence. Tears lingered in her eyes, but he couldn't read their depths.

Despair?

Joy?

The lights dimmed.

For the span of a breath, they sat in solid black. Amelie leaned closer, breath held. Nervous tension crested through her, and her fingers tightened. Did she realize that she held onto him? He doubted it.

Quietly, he murmured, "Are you all right?"

Neck taut as a bow, she nodded.

"Fine. It's . . . hard. But . . . good. Really."

Her insistence didn't convince him. Responding to her sudden sense of fright at the unexpected darkness, Remy wrapped his arm around her shoulders. Her grip eased. A single light, created with clever mirror work, candles, and a powerful spell, sent a ray of light to a figure on the stage. The conductor.

Murmurs turned to applause. Amelie relaxed further as the conductor motioned to the orchestra, the singers, and the stage-hands. The congratulatory ovation morphed into the clatter of witches standing, discussing, and moving in a queue toward the exit. Hubbub resumed in the midst of a once pristine silence.

"We're in the exact middle." Remy gazed around. "Think we should wait?"

"I do."

She lay her head on his shoulder. The lights popped awake, shedding clarity and depth. After his calculation and watching of Wildrose, he couldn't help but wonder how *this* building had been constructed.

The moment of calm, with the whispers of retreating voices, and the tepid air after the opera, drew his thoughts down a long, long line. He turned, put a finger under her chin, and said, "Amelie?"

"Hmm?"

"Do you love me?"

She sucked in a breath. Amelie lifted her head from his shoulder, staring hard at him. "I'm sorry," she breathed, "Wh—"

He straightened, twisting in his chair to better face her. "You don't have to answer that right now. It's something I'm asking you to consider."

Amelie blinked, stunned out of the lovely spell they'd spun for the evening. Their gossamer web of enjoyment dissipated to ash. As witches retreated from the center of the room, noise followed.

"I ask," he continued conversationally, and to buy her time to breathe, "out of curiosity."

She'd released his hand and stared out. "The opera," she squeaked. "It rattled your head, Remy."

Remy laughed. "Amelie, my question has nothing to do with the opera, and everything to do with all that I feel. Maybe it wasn't fair of me to ask." He pressed a hand to her knee. "Perhaps I shouldn't have sprung it on you in this fashion, but I can't help the way that I feel. I've avoided it for so long that your father told me to get a move on it."

She tucked a piece of hair behind her ear. "Wh-what is your definition of love? That might be the wrong word."

"You know . . . I don't know? It's an excellent question."

"Love is a big word."

"Is it?"

"A big one." Her hands expanded to encompass it. "Big," she insisted. "It means . . . a lot of things."

"Like?"

"I don't know!"

"I think I do," he said helpfully. "Would you like to hear what I think love is, and why I love you?"

Amelie paled. "No."

He stifled a laugh. "No? You don't want me to tell you?"

"No, I mean . . . that is . . . I knew you cared for me. That . . . plans were in place for us to . . . *eventually* . . . but *love*? Love is so much . . . more . . . than just . . . than . . ."

Despite deepening amusement—what exactly did she think handfasting would mean?—he attempted to modulate his reaction, lest she skitter away and never return. When she stammered into silence, he gently squeezed her knee.

"Amelie, I love you."

She closed her eyes. Voice thick with emotion, she whispered, "How do you know?"

"When I'm with you, nothing else matters, and nothing feels too big."

A long, long moment passed.

"Remy?"

"Yes?"

"L-l-love," she stuttered. "You mean as friends. One family to another. You love me as a Leroy daughter and—"

His firm back-and-forth head shake stalled her.

"No, Amelie. I love *you*. Granted, I adore your family. Not trying to diminish their place in this, but they have little to do with the feelings in my heart. I think I've loved you since I returned, but I haven't felt worthy."

She scoffed, but it held little energy. Her gaze skipped away again, focusing on some distant horizon she clearly didn't see.

"Love," she repeated weakly.

The room had emptied. Two young men carrying brooms swept the floor, and the occasional squawk of a violin or trill of a closing flute sounded from the orchestra pit. One by one, the highest chandeliers snuffed out candles. The hollow reverberations of a room once filled with life reminded him of empty chambers.

Remy couldn't bring himself to regret what he said. He meant every word. The only kind thing left to do at this point was give her time. He spent the last year thinking about her every day. Sculpting an invisible life in his head. Skirting her firm boundaries. Dreaming of what they might be together. He could wait until she was ready, however long.

He held out a hand.

"Shall we return home?"

She nodded, avoiding his eyes. "Yes, please." Her hand slid into his. He side-stepped out of the velvet-clad seats and into the walkway. She kept pace at his side, though her breaths remained shaky.

Remy hid a twitch of his lips.

Amelie loved him. If she loathed him, she would have slapped him and stormed out or transported away.

She just needed time.

Remy lay awake that night, staring at his ceiling. He stacked his hands behind his head and studied the murals without comprehending their strange, gothic paintings. His chest slid from an awful squeezing near his heart to flutters of anticipation. At any given moment, he believed he'd made the biggest error of his life. Five seconds after that, he convinced himself that Amelie would run into his arms and give him a fat kiss in the morning.

In reality, nothing might happen.

The past year required only a cursory review before he easily confirmed that Amelie cared for him. Of course she did. The budding affection began the day of his homecoming party and sprouted tendrils through the most harrowing moments of his life.

She held him back from the flames, stood with him in the rain, and filled the quiet days with her calm presence. When he frowned, she smiled. If it wasn't care, then what was it?

Whatever haunted her prevented her from seeing it.

When a soft *tap-tap-tap* came on his door, it startled him out of spiraling pathways. He stared at it for a full five seconds before comprehending the noise had been real. James would have sent a message, and Joyce had never approached Remy in the middle of the night. That left one witch.

"Amelie?" he whispered.

Remy threw the covers off his legs and stood, his stomach clenched. Nervous anticipation hastened him across the room.

The cold floor chilled his toes as he crossed the rug, rousing him from the half-torpid thoughts.

He pulled the door open to find Amelie in the hallway, hair on her shoulders in a bundle of curls. She had tied a sash around her silky robe. Her round eyes held no hints of sleep, only wariness and dread.

"I'm happy you came." He widened the door. "Come, Amelie. You never need to wait in the hallway."

Wordless, she stepped into his room. He crossed to the fire, which crackled in the grate thanks to a spell. She trailed behind. The shabby armchair had a blanket across the back, several books on the floor, and the warm dishabille of daily life. He motioned her into it, but she refused with a shake of her head.

"No, thank you."

"Are you all right, Amelie?"

"Fine."

"You seem—"

"I'm fine, Remy."

Her curt reply sealed his lips. Standing, he folded his hands behind his back and waited. He didn't realize how hard he breathed until he clued into the up-and-down motion of his shoulders. Amelie wrung her hands, too distracted with her own thoughts to notice his paranoia. He forced his breath to calm. Seeing her so distressed created tension that rippled.

"You asked a question this evening at the opera," she stated. Her gaze fluttered to his stare, couldn't quite meet it, and returned to the ground.

"I did."

"Why?"

"Why did I ask you a question?"

"Why *that* question?"

"Ah." Remy lowered to the divan. "I suppose," he said slowly, "that I'm tired of tiptoeing around the obvious because of some . . . antiquated sense of propriety. Based on the way you act around me, and the energy I feel from you, I think it's fair to say that we share a genuine affection."

"But did you want to love me?"

He reared back. "What?"

"Did you *want* to love me?" she hastily asked. "You said that you did love me. Do you take it back?"

"Of course not."

Frantic, she advanced a step. "So you want to love me?"

"There's nothing I want more."

Her agitation ameliorated as she stared at him. With heightened disbelief, she whispered, "Really?"

She appeared, for all the world, like a lost child.

"Really."

Amelie sank to the chair opposite him, her breath shaky. Her fingers trembled when she swept a piece of hair out of her eyes.

"You're a handsome witch, Remy."

"My mother always thought so," he said lightly.

She folded her arms, holding onto her elbows. "All the women thought so."

"*All* the women?"

"Pershington women," she clarified with a touch of resentment. "All of them wanted to handfast Remy Dauphin. You were the talk of the village."

"You jest!"

Soberly she said, "I don't."

"You obviously felt the same way," he said with a roguish smile.

She cut him a quelling glare.

"I imagine we'd be the talk of the town," she sang, pacing. "Frumpy old Amelie lost her violin and seduced Remy Dauphin." She snorted. "No one would believe it."

Remy suppressed a laugh. Was that jealousy in her voice? Against women he'd never spoken with, and couldn't care less about?

"My adoring admirers are the grandmothers of Pershington, you mean?" he quipped, wryly.

She cut him a second hot glare.

He poorly suppressed a smile. "Is that why you always had such a powerful crush on me?"

"There were a lot of reasons."

He resisted the urge to pull her into his arms. She looked wounded and vulnerable and frightened.

"You don't know everything about me," she continued with infuriating vagueness. "We may be friends but . . . there's so little that we really tell each other and . . . I don't think . . ."

"Have you murdered someone?"

She spun to look at him.

"What?"

"It's a fairly straightforward question. Have you murdered anyone?"

"No, I haven't murdered anyone."

"As expected. Do you miss performing with the violin?"

"More than anything."

"Also as expected. Are you madly in love with another man that isn't me?"

Her lips twitched. "No."

"Progress. Are you madly in love with another woman?"

"No."

"Do you loathe the sight of me?"

Amelie canted an eyebrow. "Sometimes," she drawled.

He smiled. "Understandable. Amelie, considering that you haven't murdered anyone, I at least understand how much you love and miss your violin, you aren't in love with another witch, and you don't despise me, I believe we're on comfortable ground."

After a long pause, Remy leaned forward.

"My biggest fear in life is that I was foreordained for some great purpose, but I missed the boat, so to speak. What if I was supposed to do something epic, and I settled for ordinary?"

A leaden frown marred her brow.

"What?"

"One time, when I was ten, I filched a sacran from Father's coat pocket and kept it until we went to Ashleigh. While there, I bought myself candy and never spoke of it until this moment. Another time, I broke Mother's favorite sculpture and let Claude take the heat. It's little surprise he loathes the sight of me right now. That sculpture earned him an entire day in his room."

His sober diffidence sparked the reaction he desired. Amelie burst into laughter.

"What are you saying?" she cried.

"All my darkest secrets. If you're worried that you don't know me at all, the only way to remedy it is to dive in. Don't you think so?" He put a hand to his chin, affecting a thoughtful stare, to give her astonishment a moment to settle. "Where were we? Right. Twelve years old, and I—"

She stopped him with a hand on his wrist. "Remy, I'm only scared. Of course I know you. Of course you know me. I . . . no one besides my parents has ever said . . . well . . . *those* words to me. It's lovely and frightening."

"By *those words*, you mean *I love you*?"

With a gulp, she nodded.

He lifted a hand, caressing her cheek with the pad of his thumb. "I know how it feels to be terrified in love, Amelie. If it makes you feel better, no witch scares me more than you."

Another laugh bubbled out of her. "Well, that's a fine declaration of love."

"I have been living with your parents, and I work for your father. At the darkest time of my life, your family stepped up to save my soul and my future. If there's any witch in the Central Network that's a bigger mess than me, I haven't met him."

Her teasing smile delighted him.

"There is your brother."

Remy gathered both her hands, pressed a kiss to her knuckles. A hint of desperation thickened his words.

"I . . . I don't know *how* to court you in the romantic ways of other more eloquent men, Amelie. I have nothing to offer." He spread both hands. "My arms are empty. I have no house. My career is stabilizing into something that appears promising, but you never know how it could turn. You can't imagine how terrified I've been that I might run your family business into the ground and doom all of us. It can't be impressive that a man interested in earning your hand relies on your parents for a roof over his head."

"They love you."

He laughed, running a hand down the side of his face. When he shook his head, attempting to clear the disarming thoughts she inspired, he muttered, "They wouldn't love what I've been dreaming of doing to you for months."

Heat rose in her eyes.

"I'm an adult, Remy. They've accepted it."

The torture of such an admittance threatened to destroy his control, but propriety and a sense of obligation held his weak scaffolding together. Without the rules of sociality and all the Leroy family had given him, his feelings for Amelie would overwhelm in a crushing tide. He lifted both shoulders in a hapless shrug.

"Why would you settle for a witch like me, Amelie? Whatever I offer you, we'd have to create together. Is that an appeal you're interested in?"

Amelie linked her fingers through his outstretched hands. She drew so close that the thud of her heart beat against his breastbone. Her lips lingered above his, cascading a warm shiver down his shoulders. He closed his eyes, drawing the earthy smell of fire and flowers deep into his lungs.

"I love you too, Remy."

Emotion shuddered through him.

"The only appeal either of us can make," she murmured, the tips of her lips caressing the edges of his, "is to give the imperfect pieces of our heart we think no one will want. When, in truth, it's all any of us want. What offer could I make to you, Remy? I—"

He tightened his hold, cutting her off.

"Everything. Amelie, you give me everything."

They crashed together. His fingertips found the silky tendrils of hair he dreamt of for weeks. Her hot palms squeezed his shoulders, sizzling through the layers of his robe. When her arms curled around his neck, her thumb caressed below his earlobe.

Passion zipped like lightning as he swept her off her feet. She withdrew her kiss to stare into his eyes through sooty lashes.

"You love me, Remy, and I love you."

"Handfast me?"

She sealed the rest of their fate with a kiss and a smile. Tears sparkled in her eyes, glimmering like crystal fire. Her palm covered his cheek.

"All of my heart and soul says *yes*. Take me to bed, Remy. Let's explore those hidden dreams before we reveal our handfasting to my parents in the morning. I cannot wait to see their ecstatic faces."

Chapter Eight

When Remy held out an arm, Amelie slid inside. When his sky clouded over, her rays cut through. When rain threatened, Amelie uncovered sunshine.

The next month of life together unfolded like a series of intentionally-created cuts, forming the perfect shape. Wildrose, Amelie, the messenger paper company. Everything thrived. For the first time in his life, Remy wondered if *this* was the bliss his Father had always spoken about.

Winter descended with flurries as he studied Wildrose's expanding frame with a critical eye. The grimoire floated nearby, smaller by more than a dozen pages. The spine shrank as tasks completed, whisked away with each magical accomplishment. Wind whipped the snowflakes off the parchment as soon as they landed, protecting it from environmental damages.

"We'll need to order more marble soon," Amelie said from his side. "Looks like the slabs went into the foyer floor."

"Mmmm."

"Lumber for the next floor, too."

"I've already put the order in. They're preparing."

She pecked a kiss to his cheek.

"I had no doubts."

Her lithe waist fit perfectly in his bent elbow as they sashayed across the mostly-finished first floor of Wildrose. Glacial cold pressed with miserable force. The tip of Amelie's nose brightened to red, and she kept her hands in a furry muff while exploring. Even in frigid weather, she was a sparkling life force of her own.

"It will never cease to amaze me," Amelie tilted her head to study the soaring ceiling, "how Wildrose continues to work through wind, snow, rain, tempest, and what-have-you."

"If I could replicate the magic," he said idly, "there would be a fortune."

She frowned, disappointment marring her brow. "No! One doesn't just . . . commercialize magic like Wildrose. It's special. The uniqueness is the power. Can't you see?"

She placed her fingers on a grooved design where whittling tools and wooden hammers chipped away, forming perfect uniformity in each ivy design.

"It's not supposed to be for everyone."

He conceded with a nod. "True."

"This house has a great purpose."

He agreed, but silently. Whatever Wildrose was meant to be, it would become on its own. The foreordination and purpose of this magic had no assignment to him. He was a chosen attachment to make it happen, which made the balance of handfasting plans and Wildrose a difficult thing to achieve.

Fortunately, Amelie was a simple woman. Joyce's desire for a gargantuan wedding had been stemmed into a modest affair with friends and family at the Leroy estate, making it easier on everyone.

Meanwhile, Remy spent any free hour attempting to stay ahead of the demanding and prodigious list of requirements Wildrose assigned.

"We need more than marble and lumber, my dear." He

released her to open a cupboard beneath the main stairs. "Stones, as well. The chisels are wearing down and . . ."

He trailed away. The currency from selling the ancestral plot whittled into smaller and smaller numbers. Projections looked fair. He should be able to pay off the whole of Wildrose as long as his income remained stable.

But what happened after?

"We'll do it," she said firmly.

"I have little doubt it'll be accomplished, but what then?"

"We live in it!"

How? He longed to ask. The cost of keeping such an estate . . . He stuffed his concerns for cost and the vanishing grimoire aside. The book couldn't *entirely* fade. Plenty of pages existed that weren't lists, which circled him to the same question again.

What happened after?

Too late for questions. He'd started something he couldn't stop. They'd have to let it play out.

Amelie's voice rippled from within the confines under the stairs as she exclaimed over a hidden design in the wall. A dozen nails drifted by, hovering in a row and leading down the far hallway.

Remy studied the grimoire. As he stared, the chisels wheeled away from the crown molding at the top of the wall, collected into a pile at the bottom of the stairs, and lay next to a neat stack of hammers. The image in the grimoire that depicted the design bled away from the paper. Remy flipped the page, found it blank, and watched with growing concern as the page itself crumbled to smoke.

The next page lay unharmed.

He shook his head.

Less than thirty seconds later, hammers sprang to life and vaulted to the second floor. A flurry of boards and another cloud of nails drifted higher. Amelie emerged from her hiding spot with a smile.

"This estate is going to be the fastest creation Alkarra has ever seen."

He closed the grimoire and smiled, spelling it away to pull her close. She answered his plea for a kiss with her soft lips. Despite the crisp weather, her embrace was stalwart warmth. Contentment washed through him, then crashed a second later when she asked, "Have you heard from Claude?"

"No."

Amelie withdrew, brow wrinkled. "The handfasting is next month. You wrote him with the news, didn't you?"

"Yes, weeks ago."

"Do you think . . . is he avoiding you?"

Reservation kept her tone modulated. Amelie wouldn't care a whit if Claude didn't show up for their handfasting, except for how it would make Remy feel. Their brotherly relationship had fallen into stasis since the sale of the land. Remy hoped for greater connection after Claude's shocking apology, but Claude continued with his own life as if it never occurred. The whiplash was a confusing mess. Meanwhile, their old home lay fallow, waiting for someone to love it again.

"Claude hasn't replied to my letters. I assume he knows that we're engaged, but he hasn't mentioned it."

"Have you sent a letter recently?"

"Just last week."

"Visited?"

He shook his head. "Only once, a while ago. Claude wasn't home."

Claude's apartment in Chatham City had been nice enough, but in a rough part of the city. His roommate gave Remy a creepy sense of all not being right. Nothing motivated Remy to return.

"I'll find him, my dear. I believe Claude will come to the wedding. He might surprise us and be on his best behavior. He apologized last time, remember?"

She appeared unconvinced, but didn't press the matter. Something drew her gaze higher, and she clapped.

"Look! I believe Wildrose is framing the third floor. I suppose that makes sense, considering the second floor is moving into the next stage. Such a staggering process."

Remy's thoughts were ribbons fluttering in a breeze. So much magic. So much forward movement. So much work toward . . . something undefined, yet obvious. The house had purpose. The relentless magic made that clear.

But what?

And how did he matter in that purpose?

"Remy!" Amelie called. She'd scampered up the stairs and hovered at the edge, where flooring hadn't yet been placed. "Come see this progress!"

Spinning his thoughts to the present, he followed his betrothed up the stairs to their future home.

He decided, yet again, to trust the magic of Wildrose.

***

No news arrived from Claude that week. Nor the next, or the next.

Wintry days whittled past with pirouettes of snow, frost, and the elated giggles of Amelie's sisters as they planned their dresses. A week before the wedding, Remy fisted his latest letter—which would be the seventh he sent to Claude since Amelie selected and accepted a cord of engagement—and chucked it into the fire.

The letter had been returned.

Irritated to the point of pain, Remy spun on his heels and headed for his closet. A change of clothes, a transportation spell, and ten minutes later, the stench of rotten leaves and sewer water permeated the air. The western edge of Chatham City embraced him with all the typical frigidity of the second month of winter.

Street lamps flickered in the far distance, but not here. The city didn't keep the lanterns or torches lit this far from the main paths. One had to be certain of their own ability to handle pickpockets and thieves. A deep knot of tension Remy kept hidden welcomed them to try.

Sometimes, he understood Claude's unbound rage, and envied Claude's ability to open it wide and without guilt. Remy kept his tucked down and tried to ignore it. Claude made no excuses, and gave no apologies. Remy couldn't decide which was more dangerous.

Near a crossroads with limp street lamps, and one missing torch, several witches laughed. Their high-pitch shrieks reverberated, staining the shivering air. Remy suppressed the urge to wince. Eyes watched and discomfort was weakness and weakness invited a robbery.

A pub awaited, overflowing with patrons. The scent of ipsum thickened the air as he headed to it. Two women wandered by. One of them tripped over her loose hem, plummeted to her face, and giggled from the ground. The other doubled over with a laugh, clutching a bottle sloshing with amber liquid, and sank next to her friend in the middle of the road.

Remy paused, decided they didn't need help as they both giggled breathlessly, and pressed inside.

Navigating through the crush of bodies required patience, but gave him the opportunity to search for Claude's face. Remy might not even recognize his brother. Claude had seemed to change before his very eyes last time he saw him, and that was months ago.

Halfway across the room, Remy spotted him. Sitting in a dark corner, glowering at a young man with dirt smudged all over his cheeks, was Claude. A line of people stood behind the young lad, waiting to speak with Claude.

Remy slid to the side, gestured to the bartender for a mug of ipsum, and waited within sight. It didn't take long for Claude to register the change in the room, lock his gaze on Remy, and stare.

Remy raised one eyebrow.

Claude frowned.

The brothers had never met anywhere outside of their usual haunts before, and certainly not in a state where Claude reigned like a lord of darkness. This hideous place, with insidious shadows and dark witches, would only be sought by those that loved the nefarious side of Alkarra. Amelie wouldn't be surprised, and Remy wished he wasn't.

Remy didn't dare approach his brother too boldly, but couldn't back away, either. Others in the room appeared to have noticed the quiet, unexpected exchange, as murmurs swelled. Stares probed into Remy from all sides.

With a quick tip of his head, Claude acknowledged Remy, then looked away. A curl of two fingers brought someone to Claude's side. A young man, probably not much older than seventeen, bent halfway, listened as Claude whispered something in his ear, then nodded and took off.

Ten minutes later, the line waiting for Claude dispersed. Claude stood, crossed the room, and settled at the bar next to Remy.

"Brother," he intoned.

"Claude."

The bartender set a glass in front of Claude and filled it half full with dark ipsum. Claude acknowledged it with a flick of his fingers, put his hand on top, and rotated it in place. Long moments passed before either of them broke the quiet.

"How is life?" Claude asked.

"Good. You?"

"Booming." Claude had a sip, and set it back down. "As you can see."

"I would say congratulations, but I have no idea what any of this means. What are you doing again?"

With a deep belly laugh, Claude slapped him on the back. A boisterous energy filled the physical touch that felt entirely wrong. Remy realized why only a moment later. Claude kept a smile slapped on his face, but his glittering gaze honed onto someone across the room. An umbrous figure with a hooded gaze hidden in the depths of a dark hood.

"Get out of here," Claude muttered so only Remy could hear. "Don't be foolish enough to come back."

"But—"

"Don't come back," he hissed. "I know why you're here, and I know what you want. Trust me, Remy." Anger and concern filled Claude's voice, though his expression maintained the same hard edge. "Get out."

He grabbed Remy by the shoulder, shoved him off the stool, and tripped him as he went down. Remy sprawled on the floor, rendered dumb from a knock on his head. Pain lanced through his right shoulder, and he felt the ooze of blood staining his shirt.

"I said get out of here, maggot!" Claude thundered, standing over him. "If I see your face here again, you'll have a knife in your belly and you'll hang from the rafters."

Hands from without grabbed Remy, hauling him off the ground and tossing him out a side door. Remy stumbled into the street, grasping desperately to understand. He skidded across the cobblestone road, wincing as the pain in his shoulder flared. Scrapes dotted his shins as he rolled, ignoring the cackles of the men that hauled him out. The door slammed.

He lay on the cold road, stunned.

Ten seconds later, he sat up.

A drawling voice approached from the darker side of the building. If he hadn't just seen the young man that Claude had beckoned, Remy wouldn't have recognized him.

"From your brother." The young man handed Remy a grubby, folded piece of paper. "He means it when he says not to come back. Your kind? Not welcome here. You put us all in danger."

He tossed the piece of paper onto the ground and strolled off, whistling. He wound into the pub from the main entrance and disappeared inside.

Remy snatched the paper, stumbled to his feet, and gained his bearings. His head thudded with a sharp pain along the back, and the sticky heat of blood spread over his shoulder. Something on the ground must have cut him when Claude shoved him inside the pub.

Instead of winding through the maze of Chatham City with a burning, open wound on his back, Remy swept to the Leroy property with a spell, landing between the roots of an old oak tree.

Once there, he gasped for air. The surge of adrenalin faded, leaving him achy and confused. After several minutes, and with trembling hands, he split the paper open. A hasty message lay within.

I'll be there.

Remy tilted his head against the tree and closed his eyes. Fresh air poured over him, wrenching him from the stain of the pub, the flash of fear in Claude's eyes, and the sense that all was not right.

"Your brother is a lech, Remy." Amelie sent him a questioning stare. "That's never changed. He apologizes, then ignores. He acts like everything is fine, then has you thrown out. At this point, you have to expect him to disappoint you, so why did you go?"

He ran his bottom lip through his teeth. Blood soaked several bandages at her fingertips, staining the water basin below her to a light shade of pink. The stabbing ache in his right shoulder regressed to a mere burn after she plucked several pieces of glass out of a thumbs-length wound across the back.

Give it a week, it would be little more than a scar.

Remy carefully shrugged into a new shirt. "I don't know," he admitted. "I just . . . my parents wouldn't want me to give up on him. I keep hoping that next time will be the time that the real Claude returns."

"What if this *is* the real Claude?"

"It isn't."

With a frown, Amelie spelled all the used bandages to the fire. The bowl vanished. Supplies slipped into an orderly line within a neat, brown box, tidied themselves, and then the lid closed.

Amelie sauntered to the window, studying the view. Hints of bare skin peeked out near her clavicle as he appreciated her from a distance. He pushed to his feet to stand behind her. Carefully wrapping one arm around her, he leaned his forehead into her tousled hair. The innate warmth was a welcome reminder of what mattered most.

Her voice broke into his daydream.

"Oh, dear. I think . . . that is . . ."

She stopped.

Leaning closer to the window, she peered through ribbed windowpanes and onto what used to be his parent's property. Not seeing anything, he turned away to get dressed again. Her lashes tapered so far they nearly closed. She remained there for several minutes.

"Remy?"

"What's wrong?"

"I'm . . . not sure. Seems odd."

"What seems odd?"

He reached for a fresh pair of pants. The bloodied set lay in a heap near his laundry pile at the foot of his bed. With any luck, the maid wouldn't ask questions, and Amelie had already burned the shirt.

"Well, it's odd that someone else will occupy your old lot, for starters," she muttered. "I can't imagine another soul owning that place."

"The lot sold months ago."

"Yes," she drawled, lifting a hand to point, "but now they're walling it off. *That* is odd. Did you see the shrubs?"

Remy froze.

"Shrubs?"

"Someone planted shrubs and must have enchanted them. They're growing wildly high, well past ten paces. Thick, too. You can't see through them when you walk by. Take a look. Do you think they did it tonight?"

He stepped up behind her, finishing the final button on his pants. Shrubs lined the property. From this vantage on the second floor, he could barely see over them to the empty interior. Vines and branches opened and unfurled, climbing higher with each second that passed. The bush stood five paces thick at the thinnest. More so on the other side, near the road.

The charred interior had been scattered shortly after purchase. A team of witches had appeared on the property, raked through the remains, scattered the ash, and appeared to plant grass. In the spring, life would sprout to obscure the devastation, which led all of them to assume the new owner had no plans for this winter.

"What do you think they'll do with it?" Amelie asked.

"Who?"

She shrugged. "The new owners. Why put up hedges?"

"To hide something."

"A house?"

"I don't know. I hope they build. Start over, let life come back."

She tipped her head backward to plant a kiss on his jaw. "That's why I love you. You're a forward-moving witch. Except for when you're chasing your unwilling brother all the way to Chatham City."

He smiled weakly, not at all convinced she knew what she was getting into by handfasting him. His estate had a magical mind of its own, his brother had dark market dealings he feared to broach, and Remy's ability to communicate how he felt was still questionable. Yet, everyday, Amelie pressed onward with her plan to handfast him.

Some wild witches couldn't be taught.

"But why the bushes?" she pressed. "What need for secrecy is there? This is a quiet neighborhood."

"I guess we'll find out."

"Did you ever learn who purchased that estate?"

"No."

"Did you try?"

"I did," he said slowly, "but the name was withheld and the legal witch over the matter wouldn't divulge."

"My parents didn't hear anything either," she said, thoughtful. "They wanted to meet our new neighbors, but no one has come forward."

"Perhaps they have reason to be building up hedges if you're standing in the window during the middle of the night, staring at their property."

She giggled.

He pressed a kiss to the curve of her neck.

"Considering that we're getting handfasted in a week, there are better things to worry about than your parents' new neighbors."

She laughed as she twirled in his arms, putting a hand to his jaw. "Perhaps you're right. It doesn't matter in the slightest, as we'll move into Wildrose soon. Don't you think? Wildrose advances so systematically. It almost boggles the mind."

The idea thrilled him.

"The first floor is enclosed and the second floor framing complete. The third and fourth floor framing continues. We *could* stay there on the first floor, but it wouldn't be all that safe yet."

She twined her arms around his waist. "All I need is you. You keep me safe."

The sentiment, loaded with implication, was a gift. Many women may cast such a sentence out with little care, but not Amelie. Delighted with her trust, but mystified by it at the same time, he pressed a kiss to the top of her nose.

"Yes, my dear. Always. But when it drops to freezing temperatures and snow collects on your eyelashes, then you might have a different opinion."

Amelie rolled her eyes.

"It's enclosed! We'd be fine."

"Then I vow that we will move into Wildrose as soon as I feel it's safe to do so, and that could be right after the handfasting, though detailed work will continue after it's habitable, based on the plans."

"That's fine. We only need something safe, warm, and functional."

"Not all women are so easy to please." He yanked her close with a friendly growl. "How did I get so lucky?"

Laughing, she cried, "I have no idea! Though, to be fair, I may be as much in love with your estate as I am with you."

Enchanted by her cheeky wit, he laughed.

"Very true."

She sobered. "But I have just one other question that's been bothering me, and then we can stop talking about serious things."

He tucked a loose strand of hair behind her ear. "Whatever it is you want to ask, I will answer anything."

"Where is the counter magic?"

"Hmmm?"

Amelie extricated from his arms, crossed the room, and lowered to her knees. A blanket slipped off her shoulder, revealing her ivory nightgown that stretched from shoulder to shoulder in a wide neckline. In front of her, the grimoire perched on a table near the fireplace. She stroked the top of it. In the last several months, the page load had lessened considerably.

He leaned against the window.

"You mean *that* counter magic?"

She beckoned, and he joined her, trailing his thumb in a swirl around her shoulder. She studied the grimoire in deepening thought, a finger tapping her upper lip. How could she be so serious after being blatantly silly, this late at night?

She cocked an eyebrow at him, drumming her fingers along the spine. "What is the counter magic to Wildrose? There must be another grimoire. I've studied it cover to cover and I can't tell that the magic system provides a counter within itself."

The euphoria of being with Amelie receded slightly. The descent to reality was an agonizing one. He attempted to stave off feelings of grumpiness, but failed.

"I thought of that a few months ago, but haven't figured anything out. To be honest, I don't know."

"It's not uncommon for the grimoires to be separated," she reluctantly admitted, "but Wildrose is no simple magic system. Plus, your father *always* sold the grimoires in pairs. It's why he made so much currency from each sale."

"And also why he had so many lying around," Remy added, "almost worthless."

She shook her finger.

"Almost worthless, but not. The magic is still usable, it's just dangerous to dive deep into the system without the counter grimoire to control it in large usage, *particularly*," she tilted him a serious expression, "when it's a self-propelled magic system."

"Such as Wildrose."

She nodded her assent. Remy stuck his hands in his pockets, uncomfortable with her line of reasoning. While fair, it established questions to which he couldn't answer. He didn't like that.

"It's early yet, Amelie. Wildrose isn't even half finished, and we're still learning more about the magic. We have time."

"Maybe."

Her hesitation revealed she didn't think that very likely.

Remy pulled her close. She slid to his lap, her forehead resting in the hollow of his neck. Her eyelashes fluttered, wispy against his skin. Her heat felt as steady and radiant as the snapping, crackling fire.

"There's much about the magic we don't know," he conceded reluctantly. "But there's much we do know. Thus far, I trust Wildrose. I trust the magic. If the need for the other magic arises, I'm sure we shall discover it."

"I agree," she murmured with a sleepy cadence.

"If I can ever speak to my brother again," he added as a wry aside, "then I will ask if he knows anything about the other grimoire. He would be the most likely witch, though I can reach out to Father's legal witch in the meantime."

"Didn't Claude try to build Wildrose?"

"Yes."

She yawned. "Thank Alkarra it didn't work for him."

He ran his hand along the underside of her jaw in a rhythmic caress as she fell to sleep in his arms. Ten minutes later, she slumped against him with a gentle deadweight that he relished. Rearranging her in his arms, he stood, lay her on the bed, and tucked her in. She sighed, her profile sloped against the white pillowcase.

Remy stacked two more logs in the fire to keep the room

toasty, tossed back the rest of a pain potion she had insisted on, and followed it with a glass of water. As he stared at the fire, slumped against the divan, other questions rose.

The rules of magic clearly stated that every system had an opposite. A counter. That meant Wildrose must as well.

Instinct stirred.

Suspicions, too.

What if . . .

But then . . .

Darker thoughts of Claude, and Father, and evil men hiding in pubs haunted him. He couldn't keep a hold of each idea as it appeared, because the low hum of sleep kept intruding. He stirred in and out of dreams and half-thoughts, haunted by an unknown fear of what the answer might be.

He couldn't quite grasp the thought . . .

. . . and so he fell asleep.

The familiar *thud, thud, thud* of a hammer woke Remy.

He sat upright, confused by a dream where Mother and Father pleaded for him to find his lost brother. In the dream, Claude had wandered into the forest. Remy found him, but Claude refused to come. He banged a fist on a tree, shouting like a child. The ritual banging of Claude's fist in the dream matched that to which he'd woken up to.

Moments passed before Remy gathered his bearings, comprehending that his betrothed didn't sprawl at his side, before he realized that the noise came from outdoors. James had no plans to alter the property that he'd mentioned. The neighbors on the opposite end were on holiday.

Which left . . .

Remy jumped out of bed and rushed to the window.

He could barely see over the wall of shrubs, which crept

higher. Had they grown all night? The brambles inched for the sky in a thick wall that would overtake the Leroy estate by nightfall.

Within, witches milled. One of them was exceptionally well dressed, his back to Remy, with a black jacket and matching pants. A colored scarf draped his shoulders, fluttering in a breeze. Something vaguely familiar registered about him, but he stood too far away to be certain. Witches scurried around, hammers and other accouterments swinging from leather vests. Lumber appeared in piles, clearly summoned or transported.

Remy yanked his shirt on, tucked it into his pants, and rushed into the hallway. The distant shriek of fighting girls, Joyce's soothing response, and James huffing at something, followed Remy down the hall, the stairs, and toward the side door, which spilled onto the yard. A servant nodded to him as he hurried out in an unusually disheveled state.

The hedge lay so thick he could make out nothing on the other side. Gigantic thorns and brambles guaranteed he'd be a fool to try wading through the greenery. Impressively strong magic.

Jogging, Remy circled the outer edge of the wall. Something from within tugged his interest. The sensation was familiar, yet foreign. Like a smell on the wind, from a direction one couldn't ascertain. Or a voice one couldn't place, but heard before.

He hurried on, looping the entire perimeter. Someone might sense his presence, which might not be a bad thing. Considering these magical hedges, however, he guessed the owner didn't desire friendly neighbors seeking conversation.

Remy slowed to a panting stop at the front of the property. The thick brambles revealed nothing until a placard surprised him.

Hands on his hips, he approached a rectangular break in the hedge. His chest rose and fell. Blood thudded through his temples as he closed the distance. The placard spanned at least as long as both arms spread out, standing half as tall as himself. Black, winding script crawled across the front. Little ticks like thorns decorated each curve and letter straightaway.

Briarrose Manor.

His heart slowed.

The word bounced through his head unusually fast.

Briarrose.

He lifted a hand to the word, tracing his finger over the top. "Briarrose?" he whispered.

All thoughts swirled in a storm. Wildrose. Briarrose. The heavy feeling that tugged him out of bed and closer to the strange hedges amplified when he said the name. He *felt* this house, just like Wildrose.

Remy stumbled back, attempting to see to the top of the hedge wall. He couldn't. It extended so far it might as well have been forever. Nestled deep in the branches, particularly around the placard, gleamed brilliant black spikes. A tiny, crimson bud unfurled from the closest one, revealing the bitty petals of a blood-red briarrose.

The vines around the placard elongated, reaching for him. Stunned, he could only stare. If they lanced him, would he bleed?

Was there poison?

How could there not be?

The eternal thud of something malevolent bled through every inch of this hedge, paralyzing him. This giant wall hid a sinister promise as the tangled vines reached harder, closer, faster.

A jolt moved through Remy as the Wildrose grimoire slammed into his chest, shoving him away from the hedge by several steps, a breath before the vine would have caressed his cheek.

Remy clutched the grimoire as he blinked free from the stasis. He breathed hard still, as if he never stopped running.

"Ye gods."

Unlocked, he leaped to his feet and shuffled to the side. The growing behemoth surpassed conventional thought. Whatever —whoever—lurked within those walls wouldn't be a tribute to his parents, their legacy, or the home he lost in a rush of chance. Whatever hid inside hid secrets.

And the counter magic.

Remy's knees trembled as he returned to the Leroy estate, his brother on his mind.

Chapter Nine

"That," Remy declared two days later, "is a giant block of stone."

The quarry worker grunted, passed him a small scroll. Remy rolled it open, dusting the powder off his fingers by rubbing them along his jacket. The quarry worker exuded dust. It filled his bristly mustache, powdered his hat. When he sneezed, a cloud exploded.

"Not just one giant block of stone," the worker drawled, "but ya got three more coming."

As if to punctuate his remark, a reverberating *thud* hit the ground and sped outward as three other behemoths appeared. The earth beneath him shifted and rumbled, nearly knocking Remy off his feet. The quarry worker stood with his legs braced, as if he faced mini-earthquakes every day.

"Four," he stated. "Just as you ordered." He frowned, surveying the grounds. "You sure you wanted them this big?"

The gigantic pieces stood taller than Remy, and twice as wide. If they tipped to the side—which they appeared in no danger of—they'd squash him into the earth and snuff out his life in the space of a heartbeat.

"This is exactly what I ordered," Remy said with a sigh.

"Where ya want 'em?" The quarry worker folded beefy arms over his chest. "I can move them once, if you want, but only once. Transporting blocks like this isn't easy. Takes years of work and practice to move something so dense and heavy."

Remy held up a hand.

"A moment, please?"

The quarry worker shrugged.

Without needing a spell, Remy summoned the grimoire. It appeared in his hands, open to the page he desired. The list simply stated *four blocks of stone* and listed the diameter and circumference and requirements for the stone type.

He spun the grimoire, tapped on the list, and held it to the quarry worker for inspection.

"Can you confirm that these specifications are what you've delivered?"

The man read it, glanced at the stone bulwarks, and nodded once.

"That's it."

Remy flipped to the next page, which had nothing to do with the stone giants. It extrapolated various shingle sizes and window trim and brick dimensions for chimneys off the kitchen. He studied it again.

Shrugged.

Slammed the grimoire shut.

"I suppose here is as good as anywhere. Doesn't mention a dumping spot, which means it probably doesn't matter."

The grimoire disappeared, where it resided at various places on the first floor. Remy never knew where he'd find it. The grimoire had a mind of its own. So did the grandfather clock, apparently.

Or what little existed of it.

With the rampant speed of the magic cranking through room after room every day—not to mention staircases, expansive hearths, and decorative lintels—there was hardly time to keep up with everything except the lists. He currently sourced required items that were thirty pages ahead, but those gaps closed more readily every day.

The quarry worker tipped his head.

"Good day, then."

He departed.

Alone in the silence, Remy studied the stone behemoths. Aside from acquisition, he had no idea what the manor wanted with them. When he ran his hand over the surface, magic shimmered. Whatever reason these existed, they were destined for a powerful purpose. Protective, too. The surge of ferocity and loyalty stirred from the deep heart that was Wildrose.

"Whatever you will be," he said, gliding past, "you will be fierce. I welcome your presence, and look forward to learning more."

He left them behind at the top of a circular drive that solidified with each carriage, delivery, and day that passed. Movement out of the corner of his eyes drew his attention. A small army of chisels and hammers raced across the yard, flocking the stone structures in a cloud of tools.

Amused, Remy pressed on to inspect the interior. With any luck, the future nursery had finished and he could let Amelie know.

***

"Mother!" Amelie shouted from the third floor of the Leroy manor. Her call echoed down the stairs, speeding past where James and Remy stood at the window, watching the same section of hedge they'd stared at for days.

"Strange." James clucked and shook his head. "So strange."

As one, they spun away from the sight. The nefarious hedge

blocked out sunlight, casting a pall over the Leroy home. James' attempts to contact the owner failed. Protests from neighbors arose.

All was in vain.

"I'm coming, Amelie!" Joyce called. She bustled past, holding the front of her skirt so her feet could pitter-patter up the stairs without restriction. Under her breath, she muttered, "She better fix that tone! The seamstress is on the way over and I won't have it."

Remy fought the reflex to run.

Last time the seamstress came and attempted to fit all the Leroy girls in the same session—to avoid duplicate charges—all had descended into tears, snapping voices, and chaos.

"Well!" James cried in an unusually loud tone. He slapped Remy on the back. "Guess we better go to Wildrose so I can answer that question, then. Shall we head over there now, Remy?"

"What—"

"That question." James tipped his head toward his wife, halfway up the stairs, with widened eyes. "The question about the . . . thing . . . at Wildrose." More insistently, James said. "You *needed me to check on that thing at Wildrose.*"

Catching on, Remy cried too loudly, "Oh yes! Thank you very much. Now is an excellent time to fix that, er, problem at Wildrose. Yes. Naturally."

"Nice try James!" Joyce called over her shoulder as she stepped on the landing. "I see what you're doing. Probably better if you're gone, anyway. Just don't be late for dinner! We're welcoming family from out of town for the handfasting tomorrow evening, and I won't be able to speak to everyone at once, James Leroy!"

"It's impressive, my boy." James tapped the end of his walking cane on a recently-finished wall. A firm *thud* responded. "Solid construction. It would take fire and magic and some other catastrophe to destroy this place."

Remy smiled as they moseyed down the fourth floor hallway. A set of finished walls and floor occupied half this level. The other half was in the process of framing. A flurry of tools descended on the lumber and barren spaces like a crowd. The synchronized motion was an impressive clockwork.

Despite the plethora of hammers and tools, none ran into each other. They worked as one, yet alone.

"Your father found this grimoire in an old bookstore, you know?"

"I didn't."

"Yes, yes. He thought it interesting, like all the others he collected, but didn't purchase it at first. He left, but it haunted him. He returned the next day and bought it."

"The counter magic too?"

"I believe so." James frowned, his bristly eyebrows low. "I remember two grimoires in his arms, but he didn't say anything about the other. Just this one. He wanted to see if he could make it happen."

"That's why he bought this land?"

"Yes."

They fell into mutual thought. A pang of sadness rose in Remy. Tomorrow, he would handfast Amelie without his mother simpering over clothes, her love of Amelie Leroy, or his father's impossible taste in fashion.

He'd miss them.

"Whatever happened to Father's grimoires, do you think?" Remy asked to distract himself from the melancholy. "I forgot to look for them and assumed they were destroyed."

"Lost in the fire, I imagine."

"Most grimoires aren't affected by fire, I thought?"

"Depends. Some grimoires are copies, and those can burn. Just the originals retain the protective magic. At least, none of the ones that I've encountered."

"Father rarely sold copies."

"Not rarely." James shook his head. He rapped a doorframe, studied it, and pressed on. "Never. He *never* sold a copy of a grimoire. Nelson dealt strictly in originals. It's why he made such a powerful reputation. Anyway, we eventually searched through the ashes for his grimoire collection, Joyce and I. We figured he'd want them to be part of your inheritance, as it seemed only right. All were lost."

"All?"

He nodded. "And quite the collection to lose."

"Or taken?" Remy ventured.

James shrugged. "It's one of the many mysteries that surround your parents' death. How did the fire start? Where did the grimoires go? He had enough rare discoveries that you might have been able to sell them and make a small fortune. There's a market for that. Though," he added conversationally, "there's a market for everything, isn't there? Oh! What's this?"

James paused at the end of the hall, peering into a half finished room. The floor had been established, but only a portion of the walls and the ceiling. In the middle of the room stood a tall, oblong box.

"The grandfather clock," Remy said, regarding the structure. "It's come a little ways, though the construction isn't finished yet. Funny little guy. Not even fully created yet it wanders around."

They ventured inside, the sound of their feet echoing in the cavernous space, and approached the box. Remy stared in curiosity until something drew his attention. He lowered.

"How interesting."

"What is it?"

"That little box, you see?" Remy motioned toward a rectangular, wooden box. "It was the first piece of magic that the grimoire revealed. It assembled itself before my eyes. A . . . premonition, if you will, of what was to come."

Touching it would be inappropriate, he felt. He didn't understand his instinctual hesitation until something flew over from the hallway. A long panel of wood, recently stained. Another followed. The wood settled on the ground next to these pieces. Other odds and ends flowed behind them, creating piles.

James watched with deepening interest. "Very thorough magic."

"Indeed."

"Looks like it'll start to assemble the inside of the clock." James smiled with reminiscent warmth. "Your father and I used to tinker with clocks. Fun little thing to do on our days off. We had a good friend who was a clockmaker." He cleared his throat. "That's the inside of a box, part of the cogs. Have you had any clock supplies on your list?"

Scraps of metal soared over and settled near the treated wood. The amalgamation made little sense, though Remy understood what the magic strove to become.

"Probably."

"Hmm . . . best leave it be," James said, echoing Remy's thoughts. "The work is sometimes delicate. Whatever it is, the magic is at play, probably drawing pieces from all over the house. See that little piece? Appears magically rendered, or altered, if you ask me. Might be integral. Quite interesting."

They backed out of the room, leaving the mystery alone, and ventured down the main staircase. While solid and weight bearing, the unfinished stairs still creaked under their weight. Dust shifted from the seams and cracks and dribbled to the ground.

"Your building on this lot has stirred up the local neighborhood," James mused, glancing at him. "Did you know?"

Remy brightened. "I didn't know."

"Witches are asking us questions."

The thought vastly amused him. "Really?"

"Gossip," James admitted. "Nothing mean-spirited. Now that Briarrose popped up next door, they've turned their attention to *it*. Still, I felt you should know."

"They don't like Wildrose?"

"This far outside of Ashleigh, our little village of Pershington is a quiet place, and witches need something to gossip over. I doubt it's little more than that. Most residents are worried at the speed in which this house is being built, and the . . . unnaturalness of it."

"Are you serious?"

James shrugged, his white hairs fluffed in a breeze from an open window. Nails slid inside through the open square and whirled down the hallway. James motioned to them with a thumb.

"Estate building doesn't happen like this, you must admit. I see it from start to finish, so it's easy for me to understand. But the rest of them? They don't know anything except that it's going really fast."

"But . . . unnatural?"

"They're worried that the magic isn't good."

"It's not *bad*."

James paused mid-stride. His questioning brow perched with eagerness. "Do you know that?"

"I . . . well . . ."

Remy fumbled over his explanation. Nothing about Wildrose felt dangerous, though it was *strange* it assembled so quickly. He couldn't apply words to sufficiently explain. With a shake of his head, Remy continued walking. James trailed him.

"It's too late to stop it, at any rate."

James pawed a hand through the air. "*Stopping* isn't necessary. I merely wanted to impart some awareness. After Wildrose is finished, you could invite the community inside. Seeing it, and understanding, will remove any fear. There are neighborhoods in this part of the countryside with family-driven manors, like ours, but not giant estates like this. Wildrose will be a boon for the local village."

"True."

Tentatively, James inquired, "What is it, exactly?"

"What?"

"Wildrose!"

"What do you mean?" Remy asked, incredulous. "Wildrose is an estate."

"No, no. Why . . . that is . . . why is Wildrose . . . building like *this*? It's one thing for a magic system to exist that creates itself, but it's another thing to have purpose behind it. There must be a reason for Wildrose to scramble together with all haste, as if something important depended on it."

"Oh. That. I'm not sure yet."

"Mmm. It'll be revealed."

For the rest of their tour of the fourth floor, neither spoke. Remy didn't enjoy the idea of Wildrose as a root of speculation amongst gossip mongers in the village, but didn't experience much surprise, either. The magic was an enigma, to put it mildly. An enigma he bonded with through inexplicable means.

"What do you think of it, James?"

"I like it."

"Does it concern you?"

"No." He shook his head. "No, I don't think it's bad magic, I think it's new magic. Witches need more understanding, that's all. You're a wise man, Remy. Motivated and smart. A chip off your father's shoulder, as they say." James clapped him on the hand, and it felt like a father's blessing. "If you trust it, so do I."

"Thank you."

"Are you ready for tomorrow? A handfasting is a big deal."

Laughing, he admitted, "Not in the slightest."

"Good. That means you're paying attention. Do the best you can, Remy. Take care of her. Such a bond will serve you, and your family, for lifetimes. That love ripples through generations."

Chapter Ten

Remy leaned back in his chair, stared at the ceiling, and closed his eyes. His secretary continued to speak, but for some reason, it was easier to track the flow of problems when he had nothing to look at.

"Thus," his secretary finished, "the delivery failed on the side of the vendor. We had already released the crate of messenger paper into their care. As our delivery wagon drove off, the vendor's worker dropped them into the puddle. We estimate that, with the average depth of a puddle, only a few sheaths of the paper could have been ruined, at best. The vendor is asking for a full load replacement."

Remy sighed.

Of course.

"Thank you, Seb." He opened his eyes, withdrew his feet from where he propped them on the desk, and straightened. "It's clear what's happening here, and I appreciate your thorough research and reporting. Please set an appointment for me to speak personally with the vendor, and I'll work this out."

Seb blinked, hand paused into position above his page.

"Sir?"

"Yes, Seb?"

"You will speak with him . . . directly?"

"Yes."

"But this vendor is attempting to wheedle messenger paper!" Growing outrage tightened his voice. "He's a cheap man. He's lying to take advantage of his mistake."

"Correct."

"If you give him your time, as the Head Witch of The Messenger Paper Company, it will only encourage him, and other witches, to do more of the same."

Blithely, Remy stated, "I hear you, but I disagree."

"James would not—"

"I'm not James."

His curt reply cut Seb's protest short. Months had passed since Remy accepted responsibility over the business, and occasional growing pains manifested. One of them happened to be Seb's opinions on vendor management. Seb pressed his lips together and curled the paper closer to his chest.

"I appreciate your thoughts, Seb, and agree with you on many points. I don't plan to capitulate to the vendor or allow him to get away with blatant manipulation. Most witches have a harder time with subterfuge face-to-face. In a way, the vendors see *us* as the problem. They believe we price gouge for our own profit. If we educate, it will reveal that we're on their side."

The building tension in Seb wound down.

"Oh."

"James is a wonderful man. I happen to be handfasting his daughter tonight," Remy said with a quick smile, "but he and I operate the business differently. That's a good thing. Times change, and so do markets. This will allow us to press forward in the best way possible."

Seb opened his mouth, closed it again, and croaked with some difficulty, "Forgive me. I didn't understand."

Remy waved it off. "No apology needed. We'll see how this

goes. I don't know if it will work, but it did when I worked with Mr. Jameson and a particularly difficult customer in the Eastern Network."

After a slight delay, Seb asked, "Might I ask one further question?"

"Please."

"Why *are* you working today? It is your . . . that is . . ."

With a huff, Remy laughed. "My handfasting day, you mean?"

"Yes."

"I'd really rather not be at my in-law's house right now. It's pandemonium. My bride wants to surprise me with her appearance, I have no family to speak of, and we don't handfast for another . . ." he glanced at his pocket watch . . . "Seven hours. If I can keep myself occupied and out of the way of their . . . female plans . . . all the better."

"It makes sense, sir."

After Seb left, a *plink* came from the window. Remy spun, frowned, and stepped up to the window panes as another *plink* sounded. A tiny stone someone threw from below made the smallest scratch on the bottom pane.

His eyes widened.

The young man he'd seen working with Claude last month at the pub stood in the street below. Seeing Remy, he waved an arm, mouthing something. Remy twisted the metal handle and shoved, forcing the window open with a groan.

"Need ta see ya!" he shouted. "Can I come up?"

***

The young man arrived at Remy's office with a hooded witch leaning heavily on his too-skinny frame. Seb glared disapprovingly as they scurried past his desk with barely a cordial nod. Remy closed the door behind them.

"I'm Chase," the young man said. "Claude's assistant. Good ta see ya again."

He had a bright, jovial voice, for a young man carting around a witch that appeared to be half dead. Chase sat the figure on a wooden chair with a grunt. The hood slipped off, revealing a disfigured visage. A swollen eye, split lip, bloody nose, and torn hairline. Remy recoiled.

"Claude?"

"Got in a bit of a tiff just now." Chase nudged Claude toward the middle of the chair so he didn't fall to the side. "Wasn't sure where to take him, as his roommate was the person he fought with. Thought of you. Boss said something about your business here in Ashleigh, once. Can't believe I found ya without a Guardian harassing me. They're brutal up here in Ashleigh, eh? Ya look wrong and they nab ya!"

Remy ignored the pedantics and crouched at Claude's side. "Claude?"

Claude moaned, his right eye barely open. The left had swollen shut entirely. Remy reached into his pocket, extracted a few coins, and passed them higher. Chase collected them in his fingers with a second's hesitation.

"Go to the market on the corner," Remy commanded. "Buy two steaks from the butcher, and tell him you want it from the icebox. Cold as he can get."

"You're feeding him steak? The man bloody lost a tooth! He won't be chewing anything for days."

"For his eyes," Remy snapped. "Do as I said. While you leave, send Seb in."

Chase accepted the coins and slunk toward the door, mumbling under his breath about *wasting a good steak* and *these uppities don't know anything about fighting*. As Remy poured a glass of water for Claude, Seb appeared. He didn't try very hard to hide his disapproval.

"Yes, Mr. Remy?"

"Please go to an Apothecary. We need an antiseptic potion and fresh bandages." Remy glanced down, saw a swollen and disjointed knuckle on Claude's hand, and chewed his bottom lip. "Nevermind, just bring the Apothecary. Tell him to bring his sewing kit. Claude will need . . . quite a bit of help. I think one of his knuckles is broken."

Seb faded to the main office with the closing of the door. Claude lifted his head and tried to whisper. A streak of blood oozed from the corner of his fat lip. He probably *had* lost some teeth. Remy put a hand on Claude's shoulder, not sure where to touch that wouldn't be wildly painful.

"Take it easy, Claude. We'll have you stitched up and talking in no time. Might as well close your eyes and rest. You're in for it when the Apothecary arrives."

Claude's right eye closed. His head lolled forward onto his chest, and he fell into a light doze.

"He probably won't eat anything solid for a couple of weeks." The Apothecary toweled her hands off, using her left hand to scrub blood free from her right fingers. She cast Claude a wary look. "He's likely cracked his jaw bone, in addition to losing a tooth and loosening another."

Remy nodded. "We'll start with milk."

"Be careful with that right hand, too. It's going to swell between those two knuckles. That's what happens when you use metal bars to drive a punch."

The idea of Claude using metal knuckles in a fistfight that might have killed him—or the other guy—was hard to reconcile. Remy kept his composure through sheer willpower.

"Thank you. I appreciate your quick response."

Was Claude the same witch with whom Remy grappled with in the grass during hot summers as a boy? The witch that taught him to sneak out of school without Mother finding out? No, he wasn't. That undeniable truth still packed a punch.

Chase lingered in the corner, listening with keen ears, hands in his pockets, and a bored affectation. His gaze was too intent for someone who didn't care what happened, but Remy let Chase think he had him fooled.

The Apothecary handed Remy a leather bag filled with tiny glass bottles. "These are pain potions. They aren't very strong, but they'll take the edge off. Avoid ipsum while on these." She twirled her fingers above her head. "Gives them weird dreams."

He nodded.

Her attention darted to Claude, who slept on the ground. He looked less roughed up with the blood removed and his hair out of his face, but the black stitches on his hands, hairline, and the extensive bruising didn't do him any favors. As Seb escorted her to the door, Chase advanced.

"Ya keeping him here?"

"Not here."

He certainly wouldn't take him to the Leroys, though he had no doubt they would welcome Claude in. Carefully, of course. With boundaries. But they wouldn't refuse.

"Then where?"

"I'll . . . take him home."

"Where's home?" Chase asked.

Wildrose, he thought.

Amelie would be upset when she found out. She'd been daydreaming of their first night at Wildrose together for months. Knowing Claude had interrupted her dream to be the first one there would irritate her. She'd have to know. Remy wouldn't keep a secret from her, considering their handfasting would happen in less than five hours from this moment. Yet, she didn't need to know tonight.

"Sounds good to me," Chase said. "I'll head out, see where they're putting the body."

As he strolled by, Remy stopped him with a hand on his arm. Quick as a cat, Chase smacked him in the wrist, wheeled around, and shouted. He crouched in a defensive position, eyes on fire.

"Calm down," Remy snapped. "What did you mean, *the body*?"

Warily, Chase straightened again.

"The other guy. His roommate? Claude killed him, of course."

"Of course?"

"No one wins against the boss. Everybody knows that."

"What spurred this fight?"

Chase's entire demeanor changed. His loose joviality and general amusement with everything—no matter how strange or bleak or dire—instantly ended. His expression tightened like a buttoned-up dress.

"Can't tell ya that."

"Why not?"

"Boss's business. He'd use the metal knuckles on me next, and once you're blessed, ya don't escape."

"Blessed?"

Chase ran a finger along his knuckles. "One hit from Claude and the metal knuckles—we call it blessed—and most witches are gone. The killing part comes from the rest of the beating, but Claude does that while they're passed out. Some call him soft, but . . ."

Chase shrugged, as if to say, *What can you do?*

Remy locked his horror deep in his chest. What world in Alkarra had Claude sunk into to associate with such strange practices? Not just be part of them, but *drive* them, lead them, guide them? Only the power of their shared blood kept Remy from shoving Claude back into Chase's arms and the brotherhood of the streets.

Claude could have one night at Wildrose.

That was it.

"I'll take him tonight," Remy muttered.

"Sure. Tell boss I'll see him soon. Hey, where do you live?"

"Doesn't matter."

"But how will I find him?"

"He'll find you."

Chase considered that, shrugged again, and strolled out, one hand in his pocket while he whistled a bright ditty. Remy, staring at his brother's prostrate form, rubbed a hand over his face.

"Claude, what do I do with you now?"

He stepped to Claude's side, convinced his brother truly slept. Chase's departure didn't stir motion from Claude. The Apothecary had given him a drink of powder mixed with water that helped him drop into deep sleep. Remy clutched Claude's less tattered arm.

"Hope you stay asleep, because I'm transporting you away, and I think it's going to hurt."

A room awaited at Wildrose.

A *prepared* room.

Remy stared, open-mouthed, at an array of unexpected supplies sitting on a table next to a bed, with the covers turned down, and a crackling fire in the hearth.

When did that bed arrive?

The pillows?

Firewood stacked along the wall. Who brought firewood for a fireplace that, as of yesterday, had not finalized?

His astonishment over Claude's unexpected insertion into his day was instantly overshadowed by the tightly-bundled and anticipatory room. Remy expected an empty space with a window and little else. They transported into a ready home.

Claude lay sprawled on the bed, limbs wide, snoring lightly.

He hadn't woken, but twitched now and then and mumbled under his breath. The swelling stabilized, hiding his eyelashes. He couldn't open one eye. He'd appear grotesque for a week or two.

With difficulty, Remy peeled Claude's shoes and socks off, cut through a pair of pants that should have been washed days ago, and managed to gently remove Claude's shirt. Before he could conjure a bucket of hot sudsy water, one appeared at his elbow, accompanied by several washcloths.

Carefully, he touched the top of the pile. The washcloths pressed down, then bounced up in spongy appeal. They were real enough; this wasn't a dream. The smell of clean cotton cut through the cloying stink of the streets.

Claude didn't stir as Remy bathed him, changed him, stripped the now-filthy sheets—not surprised to find clean, ready ones underneath—and put the laundry in a pile near the door. When he checked seconds later, the laundry had disappeared.

Remy regarded the walls.

"Are . . . are *you* doing this?" he asked a painting. As expected, the bouquet of flowers had nothing to say. Remy pulled the covers higher over Claude's shoulders. His brother slept more deeply after the bath. The sun inched toward the horizon as Remy checked his pocket watch.

Three hours to the handfasting.

He needed to return to the Leroy estate, lest they suspect something wrong. The day of their handfasting was not a good time to stress out his future wife.

Rising to his feet, he said to Wildrose, "Thank you for . . . your help. I'll be back in a few hours to check on him."

Again, nothing replied. He didn't expect it to. But the fact that a well-stocked pile of firewood sat near a merry hearth, herbs, tinctures, potions, new bandages, another fresh change of clothes, and a water pitcher all arrived without him, he understood that Claude didn't need him.

Remy could find his betrothed, soothe any problems, prepare for his handfasting, and return to check on Claude without alerting anyone.

Wildrose had arrived.

Chapter Eleven

Joyce's silver-backed mirror had tarnished near the bottom, no matter how much polish and cleaner the maids attacked it with. Joyce fretted over it as a sign of their *dwindling prosperity*. Nevermind that the mirror was tucked in Remy's room, where no judgmental visitors ever trod. She sighed whenever someone mentioned it.

Today, Remy stared into that mirror with a startled surreality.

If he had peered into the future, to this exact moment, two years ago, he wouldn't have recognized himself.

At that time, he walked unknown roads each morning while Mr. Donaldsen slept and met witches from every Network in Alkarra. Remy didn't think much about the future, currency, construction costs, vendor relations, or these adult responsibilities.

Not once would he have guessed that he'd return home, discover his awkward, gangly neighbor had blossomed into a true gift. Nor did he imagine that he would lose his parents, and his brother would turn to deals with wicked men.

All the while, Remy lost everything right after he found a grimoire that took over his future.

He shook his head.

Life.

He straightened his cravat for the tenth time, then gave up with a huff. With half an hour to the handfasting ceremony, a crooked cravat would have to suffice.

When he whirled around, he faced an empty room. All his belongings had been packed away and transported to Wildrose early that morning. Before escaping to work, he'd stashed them in a bedroom in the corner of the second floor, which had been finalized days ago. There would be a good amount of privacy there.

Far from Claude.

Amelie still didn't know Claude slept at Wildrose, and he'd leave it that way until after they returned from a newlywed holiday in the Northern Network. He hadn't seen his soon-to-be-wife yet, and couldn't wait to hold her in his arms. Amelie had gone to great lengths to hide all day.

He missed her.

The sensation of rushing waves sloshed around his stomach, making it impossible to think. The door slotted open. Joyce called into the room.

"Remy? Are you decent?"

"Yes. Come in!"

She hurried inside, lovely with a pearl necklace, a dress that rustled as she moved, and a broad smile. Joyce, a genuinely happy woman despite the nine chaos tornadoes that surrounded her, carried tears in her eyes.

"Joyce, is—"

"Fine." She waved a hand. "Everything is fine. I came to check on you."

"On me?"

With a fluttering hand, she tugged at his cravat, brushed off his lapel, and clucked over him. In less than ten seconds, she had the crooked problem set to rest.

"It's your handfasting day, Remy. This is a big day. Hopefully, one of the best of your life. Until you hold your first child in your arms, of course. Nothing beats that day."

He couldn't fathom.

But he wanted to.

"Are you nervous?" she asked.

"Knowing Amelie awaits? Not at all."

A smile graced her features. "Of course not. Of all of our daughters, you've chosen the most spirited. I admit that, for years, your mother and I plotted ways to convince one of you boys to marry one of our daughters. I never expected it to be you and Amelie. Your mother would be . . ." She choked up. ". . . pleased beyond all measure."

She patted his chest. He soaked up the maternal touch. Words stalled in his throat.

"You're a good witch," she concluded tearfully. "You'll be happy with her. If you can handle her!" she added in a watery laugh. "My goodness, but that woman has opinions, and good luck stopping her if you go against them!"

One tear chased another down her cheek when Remy leaned closer and wrapped his arms around her. She returned the embrace, patting his back several times before peeling away. Tears sparkled on her lashes as she swiped them with a bent knuckle.

"I know you'll take good care of her," she squeezed his wrist, "and that means everything to me. I'm sorry that your parents aren't here, but I know how proud they are."

Emotion rose in a haze to his eyes. He banished the tears, smiled to satisfy her, and watched her stride across the room. With every step, she gained a little more verve. At the door, she turned, waved, and called out to a distant voice beckoning her. The door closed behind her with a little *thud*.

Remy braced himself for the ceremony and the soiree ahead. His parents wouldn't be there, and neither would Claude. But Amelie would, and his new family. The Leroys had given nothing but love and support. At the end of the day, Wildrose awaited. Wildrose, and the rest of his life.

That thought spurred him to the next.

He squared his shoulders and strode into the hallway.

Amelie was a dream. His dream.

An ivory-and-mint dress, suffused with layers of lace and a fluffy material, cradled her shoulders, arms, and back. The rest swooped down her elegant waist, past her legs, forming a train behind her. Her hair lay loose, with riotous curls around her shoulders.

"I can't take my eyes off of you," he whispered. "You are beautiful, my dear."

Amelie grinned through her tears.

Before the brief handfasting ceremony that the Pershington High Witch would conduct, all eight of her sisters circled Remy and Amelie, hands clasped. They danced to the right, laughing and singing, voices echoing as they chanted a handfasting blessing.

Blessed goddess
On this day
Grant our loved ones
Lovers' pay
May their hands
Forever clasp
This handfasting promise,
From first to last.

Amelie grinned so wide her eyes nearly closed. The cord of engagement had been swept off her wrist and hung from her neck in a long chain. After the ceremony, they would bury it beneath a tree, or within the confines of a family chest, to grace the land or their future children.

Once the sisters completed the chant, they separated in half, four peeling to one side, four to the other. Amelie and Remy stood together, at the top of a crowd of witches. An open walkway separated the amassed group into two sections. The High Witch of Pershington waited at the end of the walkway.

Remy took Amelie's hand. They strode down the path amidst cheers and calls. He skimmed the crowd as they passed, smiling broadly to the known and unknown faces. Remy stopped, halfway down the aisle, in awe.

Claude stood at the far edge of the crowd, dressed in his finest—a great deal shabbier than the other attendees—and his hands clasped in front of him. The fingers trembled. His face, which had been a lump of swollen and bruised flesh only a few hours ago, appeared as clear as a sky. No mark.

No bruises.

Amelie paused to follow his gaze. When Remy turned and met her curious stare in mute astonishment, there was genuine relief in her tentative smile. Somehow, Claude had dragged himself out of bed, dressed in different clothes, used magic to transform his appearance to avoid stares, and brought himself to the handfasting.

She didn't know about Claude's attack, and clearly couldn't tell he must have transformed himself, but she was glad he came all the same.

"I'll be right back," he whispered.

With a nod, she let go.

Remy parted the crowd, heading straight for his brother. Once he stood in front of him, signs of sloppy transformative magic were apparent. Gingerly, Remy clasped him in a hug.

"Brother."

Claude's voice shook, husky and thick. "Congrats."

The effort of holding such demanding magic while half dead, amongst witches he hated, meant Claude might not last long. Remy didn't expect it. The gesture was more than enough. As they withdrew, a collected sigh emitted from the crowd.

Remy fought back tears.

"Thank you." He gently grasped Claude's shoulder. "I love you."

Claude met his eyes.

Nodded.

Understanding the silent command, Remy whirled around, and returned to his bride. Amelie beamed as he joined her side.

They approached the High Witch of Pershington, and the ceremony commenced. When it finished, and Remy kissed her for the first time as his wife, they turned to face their family and friends together. The crowd stood, throwing flower petals and seeds. Their bright shouts filled the air.

Claude had already vanished.

Remy watched him go, heart in his throat, and gratitude whirring through his body like new blood in his veins.

A giggle escaped Amelie when Remy snaked an arm under her shoulders and attempted to tickle her side. She flicked him in the chin with her pointer finger, chortled when he recoiled in shock, and melted to his shoulder with another laugh.

"You can't take a sip of your own potion," she taunted with her charming and infectious confidence. "I fight back. You tickle, I flick."

"A good life rule, in general."

He growled, gathered her wrists, and kissed her soundly. When he pulled away, she peered deep into his eyes. Her smile sank all the way into his soul as she reached up, drawing her fingers through his accrued stubble. Hair dropped in a drape around her face as she pushed away, studying him as if she'd never seen him before.

"You're a handsome man, Remy."

"I've heard that before."

"You're *my* handsome man."

"I rather like the sound of that."

Tenderly, she caressed a hand down the side of his face. "I love you."

He captured her fingers, pressed a kiss onto them.

"I love you, my dear."

"Is this surreal?"

"Very."

"Are you happy?"

He held onto her arms above the elbows and pulled her close. "I expect we'll forever be this happy."

To his amusement, a blush colored her cheeks. She attempted to squirm free, but he flipped her back to the mattress with a roguish laugh and pinned her until she yielded to his kiss.

With a sigh, she gave in. Her fingers wound through his hair, her heart slammed against him, and Remy lost himself.

He forgot everything.

Except for Amelie.

His wife.

Chapter Twelve

The fire snapped days later as Remy hovered on the edge of sleep.

Darkness colored slanted window panes that hid the vast mountain vistas beyond their northern alpine chalet. The charming house in the Northern Network hid behind mountains and vales. One of James' contacts loaned it to Remy and Amelie for the week after their handfasting, and Remy never wanted to leave. The thick evergreen scents, the thin air, fluffy snowfall, and vast views were a needed reprieve.

The caress of a silk garment brushed his cheek, his neck, rousing him from sleepy layers. Remy blinked awake, emerging from a doze. He lay with his head on Amelie's lap, his arms looped lazily around her waist. She sat upright, reading a book, running her fingertips idly through his hair. She stopped to turn a page, and the caress renewed. Her eyes raced back and forth, deftly taking all the information in.

Remy rolled over, eyeing the title.

"What is that?"

Amused at his sleepy question, she canted an eyebrow. "A book."

"On?"

"Household charms."

"For Wildrose?"

"Yes."

Recalling the way the room had provided everything Claude required for his stay, Remy said, "We may not need household charms."

She lowered the book to peer over the top.

"Oh?"

"Wildrose is . . . special. What if it provided everything we required?"

"Then I would call it a magical manor, indeed. Everything?"

"Most things?"

The book slid back up. From behind it, she said, "If that was true, we would be very, very lucky."

He opened his mouth to explain. It would necessitate telling her about Claude, which he was loath to do. Now was better than later, considering the past four days of bliss and silence they'd experienced.

She turned the page and continued, removing his chance. "These are not very complicated charms," she continued, "but I've found them quite useful. In fact, I haven't slept a single night without them since . . ."

She trailed away.

Her hesitation darkened the air. He felt the change like a shift in temperature or a sweep of the wind. He propped his head on his hand, pressed a finger to the spine, and lowered the book.

Uneasily, her gaze met his. Her lids shuttered, as if she realized she'd said something wrong.

Gently, he asked, "Since?"

She swallowed, her throat bobbing. "I don't want to tell you."

"Tell me what?"

"What happened."

"What is it?"

She gazed around. "This is so happy. I . . . I don't want to ruin it with those memories. They're . . . ."

She shuddered.

More concerned than ever, Remy pushed to his hands, head tilting. Whatever she hid in those shadows all these months—or years—it wouldn't be good. The thought instantly riled his protective instincts.

"Amelie?"

With a heavy breath, she set aside the book and drew her knees into her chest. They removed his cushion, giving him space to rearrange next to her. He mentally braced himself.

Eyes lowered, she said into her knees, "Claude."

The back of his neck prickled.

"Claude?"

Quick as a mortega, she lifted her eyes to his, dropped them again. Her arms tightened their hold around her legs. He could barely hear her as she whispered into them again.

"I keep protective charms around me whenever I sleep because of Claude."

His spine clenched. Instant heat leaped to life.

"What did he do?"

Amelie shoved off the bed. She paced next to it, arms folded tightly over her chest, her brow low, words harried and tight.

"It was late one night, maybe a year or two after you left. I was in the garden, watching for a flower that Louise swore bloomed in the moonlight. Lucia was supposed to go with me, but she fell asleep and I couldn't wake her up. I didn't want to miss it, so I went out anyway."

Remy edged to the side of the bed. He kept his hands propped beneath him, ready to grab her if she stumbled. Her eyes grew so distant, her motions so frenetic and sharp and panicked, she wasn't really *here*.

"There was a noise from next door. It was loud, sounded like someone was hurt. I worried it was your father, so I left the garden and rushed through the arbor. When I got to the other side, Claude stood there."

She stopped, shivered, and fell silent, staring hard in the distance. Remy stood up and slowly reached to touch her. When his fingers grazed her arm, she jumped. Her gaze elevated, hardening with each word.

"He was drunk, but then, since you had left, he was always drunk. He babbled about an argument, laughed over something about your father. The way he spoke reminded me of a toddler. A giant, drunk child, prattling on, connecting thoughts in his head but not reality. I couldn't . . . I couldn't make sense of it."

She turned away, but didn't take herself out of his touch. He pressed his palm to her arm, holding her just above the elbow.

"When he saw me, he went oddly still. Stared at me. Said I was a beautiful girl and that . . ." She swallowed again. Her eyes closed. "That he had noticed."

An oily feeling crawled up Remy's back. He tightened his other hand into a fist until the fingers threatened to crush each other.

What had Claude said to him? *It's my fault, brother. I behaved abominably, and she did nothing wrong. No harm was done.* After viewing the underworld in which Claude dealt, and his half-dead face only a few days ago, Remy didn't question the depths to which his brother might plunge in the name of desperation.

Amelie curled close to Remy. Relieved that she didn't try to avoid him, he wrapped his arms as far around her as they would go, cradling her.

"Then he just . . . attacked. He lunged, grabbed my arm. I tried to scream, but he covered my mouth with his hand. He was drunk, but strong. When I tried to run, we both tripped. He landed on top of me, and his weight was too big for me to budge. I tried to scream again, but he hit me across the face."

Remy held his breath. He tightened around her, he couldn't stop it. The rage swelled. Amelie leaned back. The distance had dissipated from her gaze as she reached up, touching his face. The sweet touch, so tender, dispelled the locked rage.

She whispered, "Remy, it's all right. He didn't succeed," and he melted. She pressed her forehead to his.

"The hit dazed me, but I didn't give up. I fought like a cat, screeching, until I somehow managed to wiggle away. He fought back, very powerfully, too, but he was too drunk to keep a hold on me. I can't remember all the details, but I eventually managed to knee him in the groin, he rolled off."

Remy attempted to breathe through the red cloud of rage gathering in his mind's eye. Only understanding that Amelie was safe with him in this moment calmed the tempest.

"I ran, hid in the house. I irrationally thought he might follow me to my bedroom and finish it there. I know, it doesn't make sense, but I wasn't thinking straight. So I hid under the bottom cupboard in the kitchen pantry until morning. Louise found me, teased me about eating cookies in the middle of the night, and I let her think that's what happened. But," she added softly, lifting her left hand, "once the rush of attempting to save myself ebbed, I realized that, in the scuffle, I'd seriously hurt my hand."

Remy sucked in a sharp breath. She regarded the bones in her hand with a tilted head.

"How?"

"I don't know." Her hand lowered to her side again. "It's all a blur. I believe I tried to hit him several times. There was . . . pain." Her face scrunched slightly. "Might have popped him good in the jaw, but . . . I don't know. I didn't want to tell anyone what happened, so I hesitated. By the time I worked up the gumption to lie about the injury and see an Apothecary, the swelling had worsened. They couldn't reset the bones in a way that would be the same as what they used to be. After I fully healed, playing the violin was painful. I could only manage a few minutes at a time."

"Claude," Remy hissed, overwhelmed with a flow of deepening love for his wife, and a plague of revulsion for his brother.

No harm was done?

What a fool.

With a hand on his cheek, she directed Remy's focus to her. "He must have remembered some of the altercation, Remy, because he's left me alone ever since. For the most part," she added. "At first, he went out of his way to avoid me. Stopped coming to shared dinners entirely, seemed to disappear, that sort of thing. I believe he thought I'd tell on him, but when Father didn't confront him, we seemed to have an unspoken truth. He was so drunk, I don't know what he remembers."

Remy braced both hands around her face. The pads of his thumbs swept her cheekbones.

"Why didn't you tell your parents?"

She shrugged. "I don't know. I was young, and frightened. By the time I realized something was wrong with my hand, the injury traumatized me as much as what he *almost* accomplished."

"They didn't ask how you did it?"

"I lied."

"Your parents would have stopped at nothing to defend you, Amelie."

Amelie closed her eyes and exhaled. "I know. That's exactly right. They loved your family, and I didn't want to ask that of them. Father and Nelson. And then . . . Mother and Marguerite? How could I tear their friendship apart?"

"My father—"

"Please," she whispered, "I've already battled these what-ifs out myself. I did what I did, and I can't take it back. The Amelie of today would. But that Amelie? She was young. Frightened. Terrified. By the time I gathered myself together emotionally, months had passed. Claude attacked, my bones broke, I lost my violin career . . . it was too much. Besides, I didn't want your parents to leave. What if they moved away? That would mean . . ."

She trailed off.

He frowned.

"Mean what?"

Despite her traumatic retelling, the first hint of true emotion appeared in her eyes. Tears filled them. "It would have meant that I'd never see you again, and I couldn't bear that. You didn't know that I existed, Remy, but I still held some hope for you to wake up and *see* me. I couldn't give that up."

Shock rooted deep, growing wide tendrils from his heart and out. He breathed in and out, deep and slow.

"You . . ."

With a rueful smile, she braided her fingers between his and finished the sentiment for him. "Cared so much?"

Weakly, he nodded.

"Yes, my Remy. I cared that much. In retrospect," she said with a bit more vigor, "I can say that Claude gave me a great gift. He taught me the power of assertiveness and being prepared. At the time, I was tired of being the mousy girl that disappeared into the hedges or the wallpaper or behind her sisters. From that point on, I was different. I found the real Amelie. I discovered that she's a girl unlike any of her sisters. She's daring, and bold, and won't let witches treat her that way. I may have lost my violin career, but I can still play. For shorter periods of time, but still . . . I did not let him take everything from me."

She pressed his palm to her heart. The dull, reassuring thud hit with a gentle kiss every other second. He curled his hand around her nightgown and pulled her into his chest, closing the distance between them.

"Amelie, my life, my soul, my love. I will never deserve you."

She smiled, hovering her lips over the top of his. "You didn't come back for years, my dear, but I never gave up. Not once. I've always known, even when you didn't, what we were meant to be. And now, here we are."

Remy crushed her into his arms. Amelie had been right—she would always be right, in all ways. This wasn't the time and place to dwell on it. She'd told him the truth, aired the festering wounds that he had suspected, but never found on his own. Now, he had unresolved business with his brother.

He tucked it away, burying it deep. Late that night, while Amelie slept, he spelled Claude a message.

Do not be there when I return.

Claude had answers to give.

Chapter Thirteen

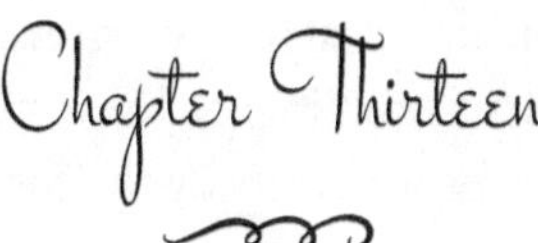

When they returned to Wildrose after a week in vertiginous heights, nothing had changed.

Except for everything.

Four sprawling stone giants stood atop Wildrose. He gaped, mouth open, at the twisted faces.

Gargoyles.

Giant gargoyles.

Their stone exterior had been chiseled to artistic perfection. From where he stood on the graveled drive—suddenly, the shipment of tiny pebbles and rock chips from the quarry made too much sense—he could see details in the gargoyle's broad grimaces. Each one had a hole in their mouth.

As he stepped onto the stairs, flames erupted from the gargoyles. They unfurled heat banners that stretched into undulating crimson and orange ribbons. It felt like a statement. A return. Heat radiated from their message.

"Ye gods," Amelie whispered at his side. "They are fierce."

"Come, my dear." He tugged her higher. "Let us see inside."

They hurried up the stone stairs, through the double doors, and into the main reception hall. When they left for the North, the exterior walls along the third and fourth floor were just starting as the magic finished interior framing. Today, the exterior appeared complete.

The smells of fresh wood and stain filled his nostrils. Amelie entered behind him, dazed at the progress. He paused at the bottom of the stairs, straining to hear the usual bustle of construction. Silence, broken only by the rustle of Amelie's dress from behind, answered.

Utter stillness.

"It's so quiet," she whispered. "No hammers or clattering boards."

Remy nodded absently. He hadn't heard such quiet in so long, he didn't know what to make of it. Amelie shuffled forward another step, her fine brow pulled over her eyes. She twisted to meet his gaze, head cocked.

"*Such* silence," she said. "Is the estate . . . complete?"

"It . . . it can't be."

"Can't it?" she drawled. "You plan to source lumber and other things for the rest of your life? At this rate, Wildrose would overtake the entire Central Network in a few years."

The magic created a cadence and song that would be utterly impossible for witches to exemplify. It worked tirelessly, without inefficiencies. Of course it could build such a complicated estate in a short time.

Even so, the thought of Wildrose finishing unsettled and thrilled him. He'd spent so much of his thought power the past several months trying to keep ahead of the magical hunger, the resources, everything Wildrose needed to appear in the world. He couldn't fathom that the relationship might . . . finalize.

"It could be," he said.

"What list are you working on?"

Blinking, he realized he didn't know. Was there another list? "I can't remember."

When they left for the chalet, stonework was settling into

place one careful stone and mortar-filled shovel at a time, sealing the third and fourth floors.

Did it dry by magic, as well?

Two at a time, he took the stairs to the second floor, standing at a junction of right, left, or straight. The smaller hallway cut ahead, leading to doors on either side. At the far end, window panes glimmered as sunlight cut through in glowing ribbons.

Amelie followed far more sedately. "I don't remember those stained glass windows when we left. The rose color is lovely, set with the green ivy design."

"It's only been a week," he whispered, dazed. He shook his head. "A week. How is it—"

He broke the thought off mid-sentence to travel to the right. More windows suffused light into the long hallway, decorated by a carpet that ran the length of the gleaming wooden floor. All that lumber turned into . . . this. The lumber mills and sanders and shovels had worked tirelessly for days, scrubbing the grimoire free of—

He gasped.

The grimoire!

A staircase on the left, at the end of the hallway, led to the third floor. The passage was narrow and cramped. Skinny walls brushed his shoulders, and the whole space had an unfinished feel, but it did the job. Clearly, the house didn't plan for many witches to be aware of this access. He spilled onto the third floor.

The hallway and rooms resembled the second floor in structure. Doors, a main hallway running the length of the building, and a rug. The aesthetic was entirely different. The second floor had a coziness, decorated with a soft hue of rose or lime green and plenty of places to sit, admire artwork, or enjoy the sunshine. Up here, yellows and reds predominated the landscape, like vibrant summer sunlight and crimson flower petals swirling in the wind.

Remy's heart raced as he opened doors, searching for a room

that he couldn't remember. Despite having the blueprints almost memorized, seeing them in real life had always been a juxtaposition. He struggled to align the real Wildrose to the one that built in his mind.

The library waited ahead with mostly empty shelves. The magic had created the infrastructure, including a hardwood desk that took up much of the left side of the library, near tall windows, but left the shelves barren.

He skidded to a stop, twirling around. Floor to ceiling, gleaming bookshelves, the color of pecan, filled every available space that wasn't occupied by windows. They filled the areas beneath the windows and overhead, too. Cubbies perched over a small door thin enough to be a closet, but might be a disguised entrance to the room next door.

So many mysteries.

He rushed to the desk, hearing Amelie's approaching feet hurry from the side stairs, her breath fast.

"Remy?"

He yanked the drawer open that was closest to him, and relief stole his breath. There, in the bottom of the drawer, awaited the grimoire. Carefully, he pulled it out just as Amelie hurried into the room.

"Remy? What's wrong?"

"The grimoire," he murmured. "I thought . . ." He swallowed hard. "But it's fine. The book is fine."

She pressed her cheek into his shoulder, her breaths evening out.

"You thought the grimoire might disappear?"

"I worried so, yes."

Her fingers trailed over the top. "It looks fine. So thin! Can you imagine? When it was the full size . . . it almost seems like a dream."

The book had shrunk to a tenth of its original size. He shimmied through the papers. No plans or blueprints or lists remained. Mostly blank pages at the back, some containing information on resource finding that he'd long ago read again and again. Nothing shockingly new.

All the magic had bled free. Overall, it had a deflated appearance, as if the breath had been knocked out of the grimoire. The buzzing, vibrant energy had winnowed, and Remy felt as if he missed a friend.

A sound like crackling fire drew his gaze upward. He peered outside.

"What's that?"

Amelie shook her head, laughing. "I have no idea. All of this is new to me!"

He hurried to the window in time to see a banner of fire surging overhead. It came from the direction of the behemoth gargoyle statues perched atop the roof.

"The gargoyles."

"Throwing fire again?"

"It appears so."

He withdrew from the window, dazed, feeling as if holding the grimoire, and being in Wildrose, had something to do with their activity.

"Wonder what it means?" she asked. "There weren't any char marks on them before. Do you think this is the first time they've thrown fire?"

He could only shrug.

Who knew what to think?

He had a feeling something else lurked within. A protective, closely-held magic. *The Guardians of Wildrose* came to mind, but from where, he didn't know. Remy closed the grimoire and pressed it to his chest. He stared around, wonderingly, at all the shelves left to fill. It would take a lifetime to do it, but he couldn't help his excitement at the thought.

"I'm going to go upstairs," she said, drawing away. "I want to see the master bedroom at the very top. I haven't been in that room at all."

Aimlessly, he drifted into the hallway. Amelie climbed toward the fourth floor, heading to the final half-level, right in the middle of the building, that would be their room for the rest of eternity, if he had anything to say about it.

He'd join his wife in a moment, but he wanted to enjoy the quiet while he had it to himself. A feeling of preparation welled up within. A sense that something grand and extraordinary had just begun. A sense of beginnings.

New beginnings.

For the first time since his parents had died—and maybe before then—Remy felt as if he'd finally come home.

Remy put his hand on the wall, his fingers caressing the intricate design along the edge of a gilded frame.

"We did it," he whispered.

A sizzle of energy through his fingertips replied, echoed by the sound of a grandfather clock tolling in the distance.

He glanced higher.

Wildrose.

"Now," he whispered with a slightly faltering smile, "what are we supposed to do?"

While late-season snow swirled from a grumpy sky, a gentle *clink* startled Remy early one morning. He glanced up from his coffee mug and *Chatterer* scroll to find an entire breakfast spread on the table. He peered suspiciously at the fresh bread, hot tea, churned butter, and three plates.

Were they expecting guests?

"Thank you, but only coffee for me for breakfast."

He returned to his *Chatterer* scroll.

A *rap-rap-rap* on the main doors brought his attention from the news. He set the scroll aside, drawing his coat on as he studied the fare. A pot of sugar, and one of cream, settled in the middle of the table.

Odd.

He hurried down the main hall as he adjusted his collar, chuckling to himself as he rounded the corner into the main foyer. His sleepy wife wouldn't be up. It was only eight o'clock in the morning, and work beckoned him not for another hour.

He pulled open the door to find a woman with two female children huddled around her. The youngsters clung to her legs. Twins, apparently. The emaciated woman had wide eyes and a pale face. Dirt smudged the bridge of her nose and swiped around sharp cheekbones, leading to droopy ears.

"Merry meet," he said.

"P-please," she whispered, shivering, "d-do you have a well?"

"A well?"

"We need water. We can't find a stream." She gestured to the forest. "Just water. That's all. We'll leave, I promise."

A tickle of understanding awoke a glimmer of thought to invite them in. Didn't a lavish breakfast await?

Ah.

Now he understood.

Remy pushed the door open. "I have more than water, miss. I have a warm kitchen and plenty of food. You look hungry. Would you and your daughters like some hot tea with bread and butter?"

The girls let out ecstatic cries and pushed forward. Weakly, she tugged on their ravaged clothes to pull them back. She lifted a stout chin with an air of stubbornness, mixed with hope.

"We haven't any currency."

Remy smiled softly. "None required."

She blinked.

"Pardon?"

He beckoned them further. "Come in. I'll take you to the kitchen. Let's start there."

A shuffling of noise from behind drew the woman's gaze higher. If possible, her buggy eyes widened. Amelie walked down the main stairs with a smile, her hair pulled into her usual loose bun, and a fresh dress.

"Merry meet," Amelie said with a kind smile as she stepped down the final stairs. She carried a bundle of linens with her. "I heard something about hungry stomachs?"

The girl on the right squeaked, looking desperate. The other clutched her tummy, though she appeared more wary. Thorns tangled the ends of her hair.

"We didn't mean to impose," the woman insisted, close to tears. "We just need some water, and I didn't want to take it from your well without permission. We're thirsty."

Amelie put a hand on the woman's shoulders and gestured to the pile of linens in her arms.

"These are for you, I believe. They appeared upstairs while I was preparing for the day. Which means that you're most welcome."

"Breakfast in the kitchen,' Remy said with a meaningful smile.

Amelie beamed her response, then turned to the woman and her daughters. "Will you join me? I haven't eaten yet and would appreciate the company. This big estate is quiet when Remy goes to work."

The woman, glancing between them, eased a little.

"You're in earnest?" Her disbelieving tone held a touch of awe. "You'll really let us eat breakfast without paying?"

"Of course!"

The girl on the right began to cry. The other leaned into her mother. Amelie put an arm around the threadbare woman that smelled as if she'd spent too many nights in the forest.

"Come with me. We'll start with breakfast while the hot

water is preparing for your baths. Once you're warm and well-fed, we'll discuss a plan from there."

That evening, Remy canted his head.

He observed the two girls playing with wooden toys on the ornate rug of a room on the second floor, not far from the stairs. Their mother, Bertha, stood on his left. Amelie stood on the other side of Bertha, watchful. Because Wildrose provided dolls and blocks and puzzles, the girls were wholly enthralled.

"It's strange," Bertha said carefully.

She kept a wary eye on Remy, but when he didn't react to her opinion, she released a held breath.

"It is a bit odd," Remy agreed. "Such a manor as this. Magic, and all that."

"That too," Bertha said, "but I meant that these are their favorite toys. When the house burned, we lost everything. For the magic to know . . ."

The girl on the left, Bree, and the girl on the right, Ann, giggled when Bree knocked down a pile of painted, straight sticks that once stood in various formations. The wooden ball they rolled was perfectly smooth and polished, spiriting across the room to pummel the sticks with ease.

"Though," Bertha added, "our sticks weren't as nice as those. These are beautiful and colorful."

Amelie smiled. "Certainly, a nice touch."

Amelie and Bertha slipped into discussion of their lost house and a chaotic life before their arrival here. A complicated story he received pieces of in snatches since his return home from work. An injured, drunken father. Something about a fire, stumbling through the forest.

Remy, distantly aware of the slow, but steady, conversation maintained between Bertha and Amelie, swirled in his thoughts.

After a full day at work, he'd returned home to find utter transformation in place of the desperate witches on his porch that morning. Bertha, with a good scrubbing, several meals, some sleep, and new clothes, was unrecognizable. The two girls, with bright smiles and thorn-free braids, had revived.

Amelie had clearly earned Bertha's trust and admiration. The mousy woman followed his wife everywhere, racing to do anything she could to prevent Amelie from working. Wildrose was the same way with his wife, and with Bertha. At every turn, the estate strove to surprise and delight their visitors.

Astonishing magic.

And from where? With the grimoire whittled down to mere pages as the details finalized, he didn't know the source.

How did it manage?

From *where* did it manage?

Bertha asked in a tentative question that drew him out of his reveries, "This estate is really new to you, too?"

Amelie met his gaze over the top of Bertha's head, which wasn't difficult. She was a bitty thing. Amusement, and a half smile, shone from his wife's lovely visage.

"Yes," Remy admitted with a bit of a sheepish laugh. "Has Amelie told you that we only just moved in a week ago?"

Bertha nodded, delighted at the confidence.

"Yes, over lunch."

"We're learning as much as you, Bertha."

"I did mention to Bertha," Amelie admitted, "that all attempts to find a housekeeper have failed thus far. If she were interested, we'd be delighted to host them with room and board in exchange for help."

Certainty trickled through him, confirming the rightness of this plan. It was as if the magic had planned it all along.

Remy smiled. "I agree. Your daughters are delightful. They'll bring some life to these quiet halls, and Amelie can use help managing this much house."

Bertha illuminated like a bank of candles.

"You approve?"

"My wife is the real heart of this household." He sent Amelie an adoring look. "Whatever she says, goes. She never seeks approval from me."

Amelie sent him a look of unfettered adoration.

Bertha's hands fluttered to her face and tears gathered in her eyes. Bree, the older of the twins, instantly snapped her head up, arms rigid as she checked on her mother. Seeing a smile, Bree slowly relaxed.

Once the girls resumed play, and Bertha's chattering elation ebbed, Remy said, "I'll inquire to the High Witch in Pershington to see if there's room in the local school for the girls, if you'd like that."

Bertha's jubilee died a quick death. She swallowed audibly, gaze cast down, and mumbled something. Amelie leaned in, her hand hovering over Bertha's shoulder.

"I'm sorry, Bertha, what did you say?"

Bertha whispered, "They've never been to school, and would be so behind. I don't want to send them for all the kids to tease."

She broke off with a sob. Unbothered by the display—Remy could only assume this had happened many times throughout the day—Amelie pulled Bertha close, rubbing her back with a soothing noise.

"It's all right, Bertha. We'll figure it out. We will. There are tutors we could hire to catch them up, then send them to school slowly. Maybe first to meet the other children their age?"

If possible, Bertha's caterwauling increased. The two girls had ceased playing to watch their mother, fear in their eyes. Seeing her concerned children, Bertha waved at them in between sobs.

"Fine . . ." she gasped. "So good . . . too good . . . don't deserve it!"

Amelie calmed the woman with a patience and persistence Remy couldn't help but admire.

What a mother she would make!

A tray of tea, scones, and cream appeared, drawing the twins' attention with the smell of fresh baked goodies. The delightful scent of warm pastries and butter swirled as the tray settled on the table.

Within minutes, Bertha gave Remy a wobbly smile filled with quiet gratitude, and sat with her daughters for a snack before bedtime.

Remy disappeared into the hallway, leaving them to it, and strode down the hall. As he walked, the grimoire appeared in front of him near the main foyer. He stopped below the wide spiral stairs that vaulted to the next floor and studied the cover, which altered before his very eyes.

Words appeared, scrawling out.

Wildrose, a grimoire.

The magical system, plans, and structure for the enchanted service manor. A refuge for witches seeking assistance.

Enchanted service manor?

Hold on.

He swiped his thumb across the words. "That is not what you told me before," he said, frowning. "An enchanted service manor?"

It hardly made sense, such an elegant and lavish house to serve *witches seeking assistance*? From whom? And to what end? Where did the power to maintain this originate? The plans had faded and disappeared as they accomplished . . . and why?

Did the pages hold the magic?

The questions didn't stop.

"There are many places in this estate in which I might find

you," Amelie said from just behind, "but I confess that this random spot below the stairs is not where I expected you to be."

He shook his head, lifting his gaze to hers with a sheepish smile.

"What's wrong?"

"Nothing." He shook his head. "It's just . . . this has appeared."

He motioned to the cover, watching her eyes shift over the subtitle and title. With amusement she said, "Huh."

"That's it?"

Amelie wound an arm through his and tugged him toward the stairs. Darkness drenched the lower floors. He would have gone to check the locks on the doors, but he knew they'd already be secured.

"Well, yes. What do you want me to say?"

"That you're surprised."

She eyed him. "Are *you* surprised?"

"That this house is suddenly a compilation of a," he turned the book to better see the writing, "*magical system, plans, and structure for the enchanted service manor. A refuge for witches seeking assistance*? I'm not surprised. I'm shocked."

Amelie gestured toward Bertha and her daughters' shared room behind them. She guided him to the left, toward the front side of the stairs. "Isn't that exactly what happened today?"

"Well, yes."

"So?"

He frowned. "There are . . . implications."

"Such as?"

"Strangers coming into our house, for one."

"And?"

"That may not be safe for you."

A noise in her throat indicated deeper thought, not to mention her tapered eyelashes. "I see what you mean. But don't you think the magic will help us select out those that are a problem?"

"I don't know!"

"I think it will."

"But we don't *know* that."

"Not yet. We've only just met the first witch—three witches, really—that Wildrose wanted to assist. We'll need to give it a chance, don't you think?"

"I suppose. Are you all right with this?"

She didn't think long before saying a simple, "Of course. We have so much. Why wouldn't we give?"

He stewed as they mounted the stairs leading to the third floor.

"How amusing," she said, clearly delighted, "that you, of all witches, are questioning Wildrose. You have fought so relentlessly for its creation, have experienced all the nuances of the magic so deeply, yet it reveals its purpose to you and you balk?"

He felt her observation like a mallet to the heart. Did he betray himself? The magic? The feelings he felt around it?

That wasn't his intent.

Not at all.

"I'm not *balking*," he muttered.

She laughed as they continued up the staircase. "Besides," she continued, "why poke fingers at it? Wildrose is what it is. Why shouldn't all witches have lovely places in which to escape? Us included. I'm rather fond of an estate that will set out breakfast in my stead. I love to sleep in."

Remy chuckled, unable to help it. Only Amelie's generally optimistic attitude toward the world and all its rifts and rills could find allegiance through such simple means. He envied her.

As she mounted the final set of stairs leading to the master bedroom, he heard the familiar crackle of fire outside. He'd almost forgotten about the gargoyles, and felt a moment of reassurance to hear their imposing bellow of flames.

"Do you trust the magic?" she asked.

"I believe I do." He hated his own hesitation. "I do trust the magic," he quickly added, lest it be heard, "but there are many witches to think about and take care of. Caring for needy witches is admirable, and something we would both enjoy. But what of *our* safety and health?"

"Perhaps that is part of the magic."

They climbed to the top floor in silence. He stopped her just inside the master suite, holding both of her hands. Torches and candles sprang to life. An already established fire roared in the hearth, likely started by Wildrose as they headed toward their room.

"I won't put you in jeopardy, Amelie."

She pulled him close, laying an arm around one shoulder. "You won't, Remy. Wildrose is here for a purpose, and it has chosen us to see it through. It did not choose Claude, though he tried. The magic brought Bertha, who will be a wonderful addition. She needs assistance getting back on her feet and keeping her daughters safe. I have no doubt Wildrose will provide whatever else is needed for them, us, and whomever else may wander through. Mark my words—I wouldn't be a bit surprised if Wildrose pulled in a needy tutor to teach the girls."

Remy sighed. Something in her implicit, bright faith touched the darkness of his doubts. How deeply he loved Wildrose, but how difficult it felt to trust, even after all these expositions of power, love, and resource. Claude had once been affable and safe.

And now?

Remy nuzzled her neck.

She brushed his lips with hers. "*This* is our purpose, Remy. You are running father's company, yes, but as a means to an end. Our real purpose lies in the walls of this home. Your family, and your manor. This is where we will make our change in the world, my dear. Wait and see."

Chapter Fourteen

A month into life at Wildrose, and all was a blur. The work of going into each room, ascertaining its value, its purpose, cataloging each nuance, then returning later to find it had shifted ever-so-slightly and in subtle ways, nearly drove Remy mad.

Not to mention the grandfather clock.

An adroit, problematic little thing.

Issues with the grandfather clock began with the odd feeling that something followed Remy. While he stood on the landing of the fourth floor staircase, at the south end of the manor, and paused, the sensation of being watched renewed. He'd felt it before, but ignored it as sheer paranoia.

The premonition came again.

Below, three visitors had just disappeared into Letum Wood after staying the night on the first floor. Wildrose had filled them with a scrumptious breakfast, and then Remy saw them on their way. He'd watched them fade into the forest, so it couldn't be *them* that stirred his suspicions.

A shuffle of sound came from behind.

He spun.

The completed grandfather clock stood there, as tall as him, with an elegant face, stained cherry wood, and a gleaming silver knocker that swung back and forth with unusual zeal. When it finalized, he couldn't be sure, but hints of the estate sparkled within. As James predicted, it seemed the magic used pieces left-over from other construction to put the clock together.

A sort of culmination point.

"Did you just arrive there?"

Of course the clock didn't answer Remy, but he couldn't help feeling as if it wanted to. Sentience infused Wildrose. Though it felt as if the magic could speak, it never did. Not with words. It moved things, created aid, cleaned rooms, infused tools, produced food, amongst other toils.

Never spoke.

Remy shook his head. "No." He wagged a finger at it. "You weren't right there a few minutes ago. I don't know where you *were*, or where you have been for the past month, but you weren't right there."

The clock ticked away.

Peculiar, but nothing strange enough to stop his momentum. Curiosity regarding the clock compelled Remy to study it before he turned around and headed the opposite direction. The feeling of being watched chased him across the fourth floor, toward the staircase. He paused, whirled around, and startled.

The clock stood ten paces away.

"Are you following me?"

The clock hands ticked to a new minute with a sleepy sound. Remy held his breath, considered what this might mean, if anything at all, and stepped backward twice. The clock hurried forward the length of two strides.

No matter which way he moved, the clock kept a certain distance between them. Remy headed down the stairs with deepening inquiry, but the clock floated down each one without difficulty.

At the second floor, halfway across the manor, Remy stopped. The clock paused also.

"Do you need something?"

When no obvious response followed, Remy continued his course toward the office. Once inside, the clock joined, as expected. It settled on the other side of the room and seemed to root in, as if a clock could sigh.

"The puppy of Wildrose." Remy chuckled. "What a bizarre place this is."

"I think," Amelie said from where she sat on a divan, "we need to accept that we are not in charge of this manor, the way most witches might be for their own home. We are . . . stewards. The magic is the boss, not us."

She peered at Remy from over the top of her tea cup. The smell of ginger wafted into the air, and she appeared a bit piqued. All the exertion of running round the estate. She insisted on inspecting the fields, spying the space for a future stable, amongst other things.

Assuming Wildrose *wanted* stables.

Remy sat across from her. This time, the clock did not follow him. It ticked away, content on the first floor, looking out the main doors like a puppy.

"You're right, my dear. I might be wasting my time, trying to make sense of each room."

She set her teacup down.

"You're agitated tonight, Remy."

He bounced to his feet again and paced across the room, unable to hold still. The temptation to slam a quick sip of dark ipsum stole over him, but he stifled it as quickly as it came. No, he didn't do that. Claude started ipsum with such innocent means, and he wouldn't follow.

Remy shoved another log onto the fire. The library was large enough to contain his bad mood, but not for long. This was Amelie's favorite room, and he wouldn't cloud her enjoyment with his temper.

"Why are you agitated?" she asked.

He hesitated to tell her. Deciding there was nothing for it, he spun to face her again, hands clasped behind his back.

"Claude is coming over tonight."

Her eyes widened.

"What?"

"I invited him."

She gained her feet, tottered, and slowly lowered. He rushed to her side, concerned by the pasty color stealing over her face and neck. She had already returned to the divan by the time he joined her.

"Amelie?"

"Fine." She waved a hand. "I'm fine. I just . . . stood too quickly."

He drew in a shaky breath. "I invited Claude after we returned. With all you've told me about your shared history, I . . . need to speak with him directly. I must. It's been swelling inside me until I can't wait any longer."

Amelie's reproachful glare said everything her lips did not.

"I know," he insisted, gripping the back of the divan to keep himself contained. "You don't want Claude to come here, and I agree."

She really didn't appear well. Unbidden, another cup of tea appeared on the tray. This smelled strongly of peppermint. She murmured her thanks to Wildrose, which took better care of her than he ever could.

Wordless, Amelie questioned him with her eyes. A little color restored with the tea.

"I must set my boundary with Claude in person, Amelie. Now that I know what your history is together, I will not allow him to come to Wildrose after this evening. He is not allowed to drop over. He is not allowed to be alone with you."

She put a hand on his wrist. "I understand, Remy, but I'm worried about your response to this. It's in the past. He hasn't been a problem to me since that night."

"That might be luck."

"It might," she countered, "or it might not. I don't know. I'm not defending him because I don't feel the need to. He attacked me and took something that I can't receive again. But I am worried about *you*, and what a conflict between you and your brother might mean."

Remy paused, having already thought of this several times. In the end, he only felt greater strength to his conviction.

"I must, Amelie." He lifted the back of his hand to her cheek, caressing it with his knuckles. "You are my wife, this is my home. He has to understand that I know your history, and I won't stand for it. He's not welcome here."

She leaned her face into his palm and whispered, "Thank you. That does bring some sense of safety and relief, but . . . I'm afraid that choosing between us—"

"He made that choice."

Relieved, she pressed a kiss to his palm. "Then I shall leave you to it, my dear. If you need me, I'll be in our room, resting."

Bags thickened the skin beneath Claude's eyes, giving him the appearance of a tired old man. He didn't look much like the Claude that Remy remembered. A shrunken version of him, perhaps. Remy pondered the possibility that this *wasn't* Claude.

Was there some horrible misunderstanding Remy could call out?

His brother might emerge from the folds of this imposter and reveal a cruel and odd joke.

No such rending occurred.

Claude entered the formal dining room with a stiff back and a wary smile. His eyes roved in constant assessment of the estate. The uncertainty set Remy on edge, more than he already felt.

Words had built in preparation all day, pressurizing each moment. With Claude in his sight, Remy had no idea what to say. After a thickening silence, during which Claude stood near the door, Remy attempted to croak out a single word. His voice didn't work. A gasping growl came out instead.

"Remy," Claude said, with a wash of what appeared to be apprehension and understanding. A gravelly, scratched tone had overtaken his voice. He didn't sound much like Claude, either. "Good to see you."

Remy's nose twitched.

"Claude," he growled.

Claude stood near the door, arms at his side. He had clearly taken pains to clean himself up. His skin was clean, his hair brushed, but he couldn't, or didn't, hide the shabby state of his clothes. While they weren't threadbare, like his assistant's had once been, they seemed to have endured a lifetime of use.

Claude spread his arms. "Wildrose, from what little I've seen of it, is a dream. You did what I could not. Congratulations, brother."

No triumph or gloating lingered in the words. If anything, a sense of glittering malevolence darkened them, but Remy couldn't be sure. He might assign any nefarious deed to his brother, these days.

"Thank you. It was never about doing what you didn't."

"I know," Claude said, so lightly it had to be a lie. He spun on his heel, eyeing the soaring windows and elegant sconces along the walls. Each windowpane sparkled, clear as a crystal. "Have you hired any help to help you run it?"

"Yes. Amelie is in charge of that."

Remy studied Claude's face for any hint of a reaction to

Amelie's name, but Claude betrayed nothing. He meandered from seat to seat, trailing his fingers along the backs of the chairs, humming.

"I see."

"You're well," Remy said. The statement held nuance and layers.

Claude's gaze flicked to him, then back.

"Yes, thanks to you, I hear. To be honest, I remember very little of the hours after my fight with . . . what's his name."

His casual dismissal of his previous roommate, a witch he killed, struck Remy as horribly sad.

"Do you remember coming to the handfasting?" Remy asked.

"Mmm." Claude frowned. "Vaguely."

A lie, too.

But why?

"I was glad to see you there," Remy said. Such a pathetic sentence hardly contained the joy and hope Claude's attendance had inspired. Until he learned the truth of what happened to Amelie, Remy thought some reconciliation with Claude might be possible.

"I'm sure you were glad to see any family there on your handfasting day," Claude said, vaguely. "You have the dream, Remy. The house. The wife. The in-laws. The career. Everything so . . . neatly packaged."

Claude smiled, and it appeared feral. His voice was tight, barely controlled. He turned to face Remy again, hands folded in front of him. Claude continued to speak, perhaps to fill the expanseless void between them.

"As you said previously, I am well. Thank you for noticing. This is the best I've been in my entire life."

Strangled, Remy said, "Oh?"

Claude leaned forward, brow high. "I've found a home. Or,

rather, a place to live, to exist, and to run my business." He raised a hand. "A lot like this, as you might imagine. As grand, really, once it finishes."

A low churn in his gut told Remy he wouldn't like whatever came next. The foreboding felt oddly familiar.

"I'm pleased for you, Claude."

Claude laughed. The belly-deep sound was rich with disbelief and suppressed hostility.

"Claude—"

"Live your high life," Claude snapped. "Have your dream, Remy. Allow me to tell you exactly how happy I am that you usurped my inheritance, took everything that belonged to me, and can rub it in my face the way you always did."

"What are you talking about?"

Claude laughed again, a reverberating angst within. "Don't you see? We've always been the opposite, you and me. Now, I've solidified it."

Claude paced closer, narrowing the gap. Remy forced himself to hold his ground as Claude's dark form, barreling toward him, made him want to throw fists.

"Solidified what?" Remy asked.

"Prosperity," Claude hissed. "You see, I'm going to live the life meant for me. The one taken away. The one you so willingly sold. If we can't have our ancestral home to inherit, I'm building my own. One that matches yours. Nay, exceeds it. Everything you are, Remy, I will be . . . and more."

The final words, whispered with hasty vitriol, sent a chill down Remy's back. He knew, without Claude saying it, what he meant.

"Briarrose. You're the one that bought the land. You found the grimoire. You're building Briarrose."

Claude sneered, "I found it in the ashes with the rest of the grimoires the fire left behind. Everything you have here, Remy, I will have there. On *my* land. I will be the son that our parents would be so proud of after all. Isn't the irony divine?"

He stood so close his rank breath caressed like a cold embrace. Remy held himself tight, lest Claude see the revulsion. The burning hatred that accompanied Claude everywhere stained the air. Whatever regret and sadness Remy felt by drawing a line against his brother melted in the face of such adroit bitterness.

Remy didn't know this person.

This was not his brother.

"She told me," Remy whispered.

Claude paused, jarred out of his irritation. His face slackened. Claude opened his mouth, but Remy didn't give him the space to protest.

"Don't try to defend yourself, or disprove her. I know the whole story, and while I'm willing to hear your side of it, I can guarantee I'm not going to believe the version that came from the drunk fool who ruined her life. You realize that *you* are the reason she lost her ability to play the violin? In the fight of her life, you broke her hand. It didn't heal well, and she can only play for a few minutes at a time. You took everything from her, Claude."

Claude's lips compressed. His entire body tightened, as if he could tuck himself into a dark star and explode. For several seconds, he trembled, his breaths pointedly steady and elongated.

Remy let out a shaky breath. "I don't know where this leaves us, I only know that I won't welcome you into Wildrose ever again. You may visit me anytime you like at work, but not here. I won't have you near Amelie."

Claude's pungent disdain took on new power. What had once been bitterness turned to venom.

"That's it?" Claude demanded. "You'll dismiss your brother so completely out of your life on the word of a hussy?"

The simmering rage exploded. No sooner had the words escaped Claude's mouth than Remy's knuckles impacted flesh. Pain rippled through his hand, his wrist. The electrifying jolt shocked his shoulder.

Claude's face crumpled as Remy's fist slammed into his cheek. He staggered, one arm wheeling, the other clutching his face. He stumbled over a chair and fell on his rump with a curse word. Flailing, Claude stood up. Red suffused his face. His eyes dilated.

"You bastard!" he screamed.

Remy held up both fists. His right hand shook. He might have broken the knuckle. A distant pulse of pain that he barely felt indicated something wasn't right, but it didn't matter.

"You call my wife a hussy one more time," Remy promised, "and it'll be the last thing you ever say."

Years ago, Claude, the larger of them, had easily defeated Remy in their boyhood wrestling games. Beneath the veneer of an ideal older brother had been a tempestuous soul. In an outright match, and under any other circumstances, Claude could beat him.

Not today.

A world of emotions twirled through Claude's eyes, most of them rage-bound. A darker, restless spirit infused him. Claude remained immobile, one hand clutching the chair he'd tripped over, the other cupping his face. The slightest hint of swelling appeared near his left cheek bone.

"That's it then?" Claude spat. "This is how we'll part?"

"You chose your path. You didn't have to call her names. You could have taken my boundary, offered an apology for ruining her life, and gone on your way. There was hope, Claude, but you insulted my wife, in my home, to my face."

"This was supposed to be mine!" Claude shouted, advancing. "This house, on our land, was supposed to be mine. Everything Father had—mine! If you hadn't come home. If—"

Claude broke off and spun around. Something was written in his eyes. Impassable and hard as granite. For a moment, Claude appeared frightened. Remy lowered his hands and waited. Claude, gathering himself together, said nothing for a long time.

"You've made your choice, Remy. I'll respect it." Claude clenched his jaw, cold, stony, and utterly unreadable. "Merry part."

With a whirl of magic, Claude transported away. Remy paused, feeling out the intrepid air left behind. While not all that adept at sensing magical systems, he ascertained that Claude *had* left. He hadn't made himself invisible in an attempt to surprise attack.

Minutes passed before Remy could relax through the shoulders. Several more ticked by while he stood there, eyes on the tumbled chair, and breathed.

Claude.

Gone.

Firmly gone.

Remy had all but dismissed him out of his life, and rightfully so. In protection of himself, his family, and his property. Still, it didn't come easily. Doubts and regret washed through him. Remy sank to a chair, head in his hands. The words, *what have I done?* formed on his lips, but didn't cross. He couldn't ask.

This had been the right thing.

The softest pressure came to his shoulder. "Remy," Amelie whispered, "it *was* the right thing."

He lifted his head, surprised to see her there. He must have been speaking out loud without realizing it. Tears sparkled in her eyes as she braced both hands on his cheeks.

"I'm sorry," she whispered. "I'm so sorry, Remy."

Remy grabbed her, burying his face against her dress, as the locked, heaving cries finally vented. She gathered him close, running her thin fingers through his hair. When his emotion calmed, she tilted his head back with a nudge of his chin. Tears coursed like rivers down her cheeks.

"My dear, you have lost so much. I'm sorry."

"You heard?"

"Only part of it. I was concerned when I heard shouts . . . I'm sorry if you didn't want me to listen, but—"

He shook his head. "No. It was yours to hear as well, only from a safe place." Remy stood, clasping his arms around her. His hand caressed her cheek. "It's me that's sorry for what he's done. For—"

She cut off his apology with a firm frown. "It's not yours to apologize for, Remy. I'm only worried that resentment will grow. You cut your brother out of our lives for my sake. Will you—"

"For us." He pressed their foreheads together. "I did it for *us*. Claude is not safe, and with what he's done to you, I will not take any risks. You are worth it. Eternally worth it, Amelie."

She drew his hand down, pressing it on her stomach.

"For the *three* of us," she whispered.

He went very still.

The word *three* raced through his mind, sprinting like galloping horses. He withdrew to stare at his hand on her soft abdomen.

"Three?" he whispered, husky.

A slow, watery smile appeared on her lips. Amelie giggled, as if she told a great secret.

"Three."

"Three?"

"Three! What you did today will protect our child, Remy. Our *child*."

He swallowed hard. Tears misted the sight of her, and goose-bumps washed down his arms.

"Child?"

Amelie grabbed his face with both her hands, her lips a whisper against his.

"Your *child*, Remy. The next Dauphin. Today, you have protected not only your wife, your home, and yourself, but your child. We are to be parents, Remy Dauphin. The legacy of your family lives on through us."

Chapter Fifteen

Amelie's bunched lips and arch brows indicated an emotion adjacent to displeasure, but not quite as powerful.

She sat at the kitchen table, elbows propped, hands clasping a glass of water, as she stared at the bouncing fire in the hearth. A fresh stack of firewood and boot tracks on the floor meant she'd restocked it herself, which also meant she'd felt something.

Amelie moved her body when she experienced deep emotions. The more difficult the movement, the better for her mental regulation. He'd once found her scaling a tree when she was anxious over choosing a High Witch for their handfasting ceremony.

"Evening, my dear." Remy bent to kiss her cheek, migrating toward a plate of food off to the side, not far from the hearth. "Busy day at work today, but all is sleeping at the shop for the night. Saw your parents. They're coming over for dinner tomorrow. How are you?"

She arranged her tight lips into a smile as Remy collected the plate and brought it to the table. He gave her another kiss, then sat across from her. Before he realized he needed it, a fork appeared.

"Thank you," he said.

Carefully, he studied Amelie, who hadn't moved.

"Busy day at Wildrose?"

"Yes." She cut a glance toward the doorway. "Are Bertha or the girls in the hallway?"

He shook his head.

Amelie slumped forward onto the table, head on her stacked fists, and moaned. Alarmed, he reached a hand out.

"Amelie?"

She waved him off. "I'm fine. Just . . . worried. Frustrated, but only a little. It's certainly not the girls' fault, and not really Bertha's. One can't assign blame in situations like this. I mean, they're *foresters* and—"

"I cannot follow a single word."

She lifted her head. "The twins? They're completely uneducated. Between them, they understand about three letters in the alphabet, and I had a feeling those were guesses. They can count to twenty, but that's it. They don't know anything of Alkarran history, except ridiculous stories about nymphs and selkies, and their attention spans are about five minutes long."

His expression sank. "Oh."

Amelie put her head in her hands. "They've been here two months, and I feel . . . frustrated. Bertha isn't motivated to work, but she will if I coordinate her daily tasks. She struggles to see them on her own. She's . . . emotional, but won't talk to me about why. The girls are delights, but loud. They run across the hallway on the third floor and it drives a headache right into my head."

Remy opened his mouth to suggest something, but closed it as quickly when she straightened, hair mussed.

"I'm emotional," she declared, her voice wobbly. "That's all. I hear pregnancy is wild that way. Also, I thought this life with Wildrose would be a bit easier, what with the estate supplying so much of what we need. Another person came yesterday for a quick meal. A male. Older gentleman," she quickly added when alarm widened his eyes, "a grandfather of sorts. He stayed only for lunch, regaled us with a few stories, entertained the girls, and then returned on his way."

"So quickly?"

She shrugged, then began to sob. "I suppose? I don't know, Remy! There are so many comings and goings . . . I can't keep up! It's all so . . . exhausting."

Stymied by the rapid change of emotion, he abandoned his food, sat next to her on the bench, and held her close. Amelie cried in his arms, babbling incomprehensible tidbits about fear of labor and her mother stopping by and Wildrose being so kind. He didn't try to make sense of any of it, but rubbed a hand over her back until the big emotions decompressed.

She straightened, wiping tears free with her fingers.

"Can we afford a tutor?"

The rapid change of topic—she'd just been whispering something about being behind on baby clothes—startled him further. Before he could wrap his mind around the request, she shook her hand.

"No, never mind. I can teach the girls. It's . . . overwhelming to think about, but I can manage their education until the baby comes. There's no prayer of getting them where they need to be with students their age before I deliver, but we can get them on the path . . ."

Amelie stood, sounding determined, if not miserable.

"Do you want to tutor them?" he asked.

She sighed.

"No."

"Then we'll find a tutor."

"Can we afford one?"

He hesitated. Wildrose supplied many things. They existed

from somewhere, and nowhere, at the same time. The ready-made-food still came from the larder that his income supplied. A closet full of linens and sewing supplies sometimes arranged themselves into necessary clothing. Toys for the girls seemed to come from nowhere, that he could tell. In a word, he had no idea.

For the past several months, he'd kept close track of expenditures and budget, and made little sense of it. They seemed to have enough, but not an abundance. In all his attempts, he couldn't quite pin down *how* Wildrose worked.

"I think so?" he said.

She mopped the tears off of her face with the back of her wrist. "I'll teach them until we find the right one. These are all just growing pains, Remy." Her tone adopted a slightly chiding tone, as if *he* had been the one with an issue. "This will pass. I admit, it's a bit harder than I expected, having witches in and out of our lives, driving my day into unexpected twists and turns. It'll be a real mess when the baby arrives!"

A wail threatened her already-fragile composure again.

He took her hand in his. "Lean on my faith in the magic, my dear, while yours is wobbly. It's what we do. Things will be all right."

She tried to smile through her tears, but they caught her in a new flood. With a cry, she returned to his arms and vented her emotions again. Before he could firmly grasp all that had just happened, she shoved away.

"Thank you. I'm done." Her high-pitched insistence climbed octaves as she stepped toward the hallway with another round of sobs strangling her voice. "Just need a minute, please. Leave me alone!"

Amelie climbed the side staircase across the hallway, leaving Remy staring at his cold food and the empty kitchen with a head full of questions.

A knock rang on the door the next day, reverberating sound through Wildrose like the footfalls of a troll. Remy commanded the doors open before he reached them. By the time both swung into the room, he blithely slipped into the foyer.

A young man stood on the porch. He clutched a tattered valise, wore a torn rimmed hat, and an old frock coat graced his shoulders. The lapels cut sharp angles across his chest, where patches of velvet rubbed free. An overall shabby look accompanied his frizzy hair and a full beard. His broad shoulders and full torso gave him the appearance of a tired teddy bear.

"Merry meet." He spoke with a calm, rolling tone. "My name is Xavier."

Remy extended a hand. "Xavier, good to meet you. I'm Remy. Would you like to come inside?"

Xavier clasped Remy's arm, then hesitated. His canny gaze darted around, taking in Wildrose' extravagant foyer, where an elaborate chandelier glimmered, and spiral stairs extended several floors up.

"Thank you," Xavier said slowly, "but I'm not sure. To be honest, I'm not certain why I knocked on this door. I just . . . felt . . ."

"Compelled?" Remy supplied.

Xavier grimaced. "Perhaps, as uncomfortable as that sentiment can be in a magical world. There was no ill feeling around the house, but I still felt as if I should stop."

Was that how the magic worked? Gentle persuasion?

A sense of instinct?

"You weren't forced here, were you?"

Xavier recoiled, then laughed heartily. "Do you think a man like me could be forced to do anything?"

Remy snapped two fingers.

"An excellent point."

"Your estate is quite beautiful. Very . . . drawing. Is it a spell? Do you lure passing witches in with an enchantment?"

"No! But I can see why you'd be concerned. This is Wildrose, a manor that exists to help those who need it."

"Oh?"

"Magical," Remy added.

Xavier nodded with wide-eyed understanding. "Then that partially explains the feeling, perhaps, that destiny waits here. It was too powerful to refuse." Xavier gave a short, barky laugh. "Does that sound insane?"

"Not at all. You're in good company. Others have said something similar. You came because, perhaps, you need whatever the estate has to offer."

Xavier's obvious interest deepened. With a welcoming gesture from Remy, Xavier stepped across the threshold and into the manor. Remy made a mental note to mention the purpose of Wildrose to their guests sooner. It might create a sense of safety, and engage the interested parties quicker.

Not to mention prevent cold drafts from whispering into the halls during the winter. Fuel wasn't cheap.

As the doors closed behind him, Xavier said, "I'm always on the way to meet fate. Aren't we all, don't you think?"

"I do."

"You wouldn't happen to have any need for a tutor, would you? I just lost my position, and I'm looking for another one that offers room and board in exchange for education. At least until I can figure out what might be next for me. I've just recovered from a months-long illness, and I don't have a lot of strength for travel or building."

Remy froze.

He half-spun.

"Tutor, did you say?"

Xavier slipped his hat off. "Yes, a tutor. Is that a problem?"

A grin slipped across Remy's face. He shook his head,

snorting in amusement. "Not a problem at all. Come with me, Xavier, I have two young girls for you to meet, and a bedroom for you to approve, if you want it. We have room, board, and hungry students. After this," Remy added with a chuckle, "my wife will never be wrong again."

Chapter Sixteen

Pregnancy struck slowly, and then all at once. The calm days of spring passed in occasional bouts of sickness, long mornings in bed, and nights at the pantry, with a candle, and complaints of *being famished*.

Remy lived it all with untold enamor. Business was stable, details finished within Wildrose. It wasn't at all unusual for tools to zip through the estate, duty-bound who-knew-where, and then return an hour later. He couldn't keep up with the details, but he didn't need to.

Wildrose knew.

It was enough.

During the first week of summer, a wee dog scampered ahead of Remy as they strolled down a long dirt road together. The canine pranced with dainty feet, a rope tied around his neck that Remy held. Nose in the air, the little chap investigated the budding flowers, nodding grasses, and patches of sunshine.

Twenty minutes before, Bertha had thrust the rope and the dog into Remy's arms, saying, "Your missus wants you to take the dog for a walk so it stops chewing on the banister," and disappeared into a room where an Apothecary attended a wounded man who appeared an hour before that.

Meanwhile, Amelie settled the two young teenage boys passing through, requesting a place to stay for the night and a warm meal to eat. In exchange, she led them to their firewood pile. When he left, they chopped each piece with the zeal of youth. In the midst of that commotion, a family of twelve witches occupied the entirety of the second floor until their father, who recently lost his job, settled debt issues.

The blessed pandemonium of Wildrose.

With the sun warm on Remy's arms, and fresh breath filling his lungs, the chaos and clutter of Wildrose faded. Ye gods, but he hadn't expected so much noise in so little time.

"You know," he said conversationally to the pup, "your owners have a rather large family. Ten children! How do you manage not to be trod on with your tiny legs and little body?"

The dancing dog sneezed into a flower, spraying pollen. While the pup scampered through pillows of pine needles on the side of the road, Remy gazed overhead. Pristine sky. Descending heat. Finally, winter dissipated. The pup sniffed at a pinecone, barked, startled himself, and leaped away.

Remy continued on his way down the road, grateful for a momentary reprieve from his office and library. Pregnant or not, Amelie commanded the manor with all the grace and calmness of a woman that grew up with eight sisters. She commanded Joyce's better traits in all the most impressive ways, and Wildrose purred with few hitches.

"Oy!" a voice shouted from off to the side. "Not there!"

Startled out of his thoughts, Remy paused. The dog, at the end of the lead, glanced back with a huff of irritation. To the left, a hedge of briarroses loomed like a giant specter. His breath caught.

Gads, had he strolled so far?

Amelie teased him about getting lost in his own head too often while puzzling over issues with the company. Apparently, he'd done so today. He'd walked far enough down the road to Pershington that he'd arrive at his previous neighborhood. The titanic screen of briarrose hedges encompassed the entirety of his former estate, swamping all in shadows.

In that shadow, his heart pounded.

He thought of Claude.

Claude, who claimed the land. Who built something within that would be like Wildrose, but the opposite. The sister magic, for certain. Or counter, as one might refer to it. Remy could only guess what it would look like, though the questions had long occupied his nights and his thoughts.

Drawn closer, he continued down the road, then cut to the left. No carriages raced by on this sleepy weekend morning as he strolled into his old neighborhood. At the top of the land, where the hedges met the road, was the same sign as before.

Briarrose.

Remy studied it. The hedge had deepened over the last several months, growing over the placard and into the bush. Much more time, and the length between the hedge and the placard would be as thick as his arm. He reached past his elbow to touch it now.

Tiny petals, blood-red in presentation, swayed toward him. He caressed one with the top of his finger, then recoiled with a sharp intake of breath. It cut him! A drop of crimson welled up on his finger. He swiped it off on his coat as the dog issued a warning growl.

A voice called out from behind the hedges, and another answered. From just behind Remy spoke a third.

"Next week."

Remy whirled around, half expecting to see James back there, but his father-in-law wasn't anywhere in sight. An older gentleman awaited with dust on his pants and hands. Wood chips scattered his shoulders, and his aged face had the hard-won look of a lifetime of labor.

"Sir?"

The man nodded to the hedge wall. "Next week, we're burning the hedges down. The house is done."

His eyebrows rose.

"So quickly?"

The stupid question didn't surprise the witch, though. He shrugged. "It's easy to build a house when magic does all the work. You wouldn't believe this thing! Building itself. Never seen the like."

Remy's heart turned thready. "Really?" he managed, though weakly. "A house that builds itself?"

The man nodded, lips pursed in thought. A slight frown marred his brow. "Neat to see, really. The owner hired me to keep track of all the supplies the magic needed to make it happen, and it hasn't stopped since. That was hard enough, even with two other blokes helping." He nodded toward it again. "You hear them talking in there?"

A crawling suspicion stole over Remy.

"Yes, I do hear them. Sounds like a management nightmare. Did you acquire lumber? Stones?"

"Scads of both, and then some." The man hooked his thumbs in two straps running from his back to his front pants. "Went to a quarry up near the north for the fieldstones. You know the one?"

"I do."

"Lots of deliveries from them, but they said they'd had another purchaser requesting the same. Isn't it odd? It was the only place that had everything we needed available right now. Lumber was tricky to find too," he added, as if any random stranger would be this invested in how to source materials.

"You used the quarry out of Scadbury?"

"I did!" the man cried. His gaze tapered. "How'd you guess?"

Remy forced a smile. "Luck, I suppose. I do a lot of material sourcing for my work, and they're the best."

"Right on."

Remy glanced back to Briarrose. Without realizing it he'd been slowly edging away. The dog stood at the end of his leash, as far from Briarrose as he could be. The top lip snarled back every now and then, but he didn't attack.

"Burning the hedge next week, you say?" Remy asked, finally circling back to what the man first said.

The man tossed a flippant hand toward the gigantic beast of a plant. "You got any other ideas on getting rid of so many bushes?"

"Not really."

"Me neither. Magic grew them, I suppose," the man reasoned, tilting his head this way and that, "so maybe it could take it down. Just as easy to burn them, should the neighbors be comfortable with it."

"Hmmm."

"Guess I better check with the neighbors, eh?"

"Please do," Remy said.

The man patted his pockets, then spelled a piece of parchment and pencil to his hand. He jotted the idea down. Remy couldn't fathom what James and Joyce would say.

The neighborhood had been as curious as Remy for the past several months, wondering what would reveal when the bushes decreased. Only James, Joyce, Remy and Amelie knew the true owner, as Remy didn't have the heart to tell anyone else, and Amelie avoided saying Claude's name whenever possible.

"Well," the man waved once, "have a good walk! Nice to meet you. Can't wait to see the unveiling. The owner wants to make a big production of it, so tell all your friends!"

He headed toward the side of the bushes. As he approached, they split, then sealed together before Remy could steal a glance inside. With a twisted stomach and weak knees, Remy continued on his stroll. The dog trailed behind, following him to the main road, which eventually led back to Wildrose through up-and-down country hills. He should talk to James and Joyce about this development.

Should warn them . . .

Remy kept walking.

None of them needed to see what lay behind the briars. They knew what the bushes held. The foreman had only confirmed Remy's deepest questions and greatest fears: Briarrose was Wildrose's twin.

Perhaps in everything.

Except one thing.

Purpose.

No magic could exist without a counter, and the darkness that clung to Claude would surely manifest through his home. Blackness swelled from the hedges. Hadn't the foremen seemed to sense it also? While a sense of pride filled his tone, wariness abounded.

A manor that large would take up all the estate space and intrude on James and Joyce. Briarrose would affect everything.

He could feel it.

Dear Remy,

Last time we met, we left on a strained note. Accept my apology for my part. I respect the boundary you set and have abided by it. I will continue to do so.

In three days, I will unveil my new home. Our ancestral land. My inheritance. Briarrose is completed and ready to be seen by the world, and I would like you to be there.

From what I hear, many witches in the neighborhood plan to be in attendance.

News of Amelie's pregnancy has reached me. Congratulations. I hope she's doing well.

Yours,

Claude

Chapter Seventeen

The day of Briarrose's unveiling dawned with pristine clarity and the whetted angles of hoar frost.

A crowd of witches, mostly local neighbors, stood before the giant bushes they stared at for months. James, hands in his pockets, lingered at the back with Remy. Joyce watched from a window that overlooked Remy's old home grounds.

Remy long ago said his *merry part* to his childhood. The memories of a home he couldn't reclaim were bound up in the past. No one could take them from him but time. Details of those days scrubbed away daily, replaced by the nuances and intricacies of life at Wildrose. He released what didn't matter in the past to make space for what did matter in the future.

Time, an ever-moving wheel.

"What do you think?" James glanced at Remy through fluffy white eyebrows. "Will Briarrose look just like Wildrose?"

Remy shook his head. "I don't know what to think."

"You indicated it might."

"According to the foreman, there's a good chance."

"I think it makes sense. According to Amelie, you've long suspected that there's a counter grimoire floating around. I knew there was, but didn't think it survived the fire. Might be better that it survived, so you can learn the full weight of the magic."

"Father's grimoires were all missing," Remy added, "because Claude took them. He confessed as much to me."

James frowned. "That's too bad."

"Is it?"

"Some of those grimoires shouldn't fall into the wrong hands, if you know what I mean."

Remy wished this whole day could be over with. The built up and dramatic crescendo was unnecessary. He eyed a *Chatterer* journalist that transported a few paces away, quill poised. The journalist mumbled, dictating to an enchanted quill that wrote his words as quickly as he spoke them. He paced around the edge of the crowd, eyes darting, lips recording every detail and nuance.

Remy was grateful when he moved out of earshot.

"I'm more concerned what this might mean for you, James." Remy admitted. "Living next door to Briarrose might be a mess for you and Joyce to navigate. So many witches coming and going at all hours of the night. It could disrupt your peaceful neighborhood. Father was wise to buy Wildrose a lot of land at the far end of the road, away from Pershington. But here?"

He shook his head.

As they spoke, more witches popped into place from transportation spells. A surprising majority had the low, gangly, underfed appearance of city orphans, like Claude's assistant Chase. They congregated around the periphery, farther away than Remy or James. James circled intermittently, taking the situation in.

"I want to support and love Claude," James said, sounding tired, "but all attempts to reach him have been thwarted or in vain. He wants nothing to do with us, and I don't want anything to do with the witches he keeps company with. I'm hopeful that this manor will give him renewed purpose, but . . ."

He trailed away. No need to finish the thought.

The sound of rustling bushes, and a voice shouting from within, caused a hush to fall on the crowd. Witches transported into place with greater urgency. They were a range of the oddest types. Stuffy business witches, an obvious politician based on the regalia of his clothes, and then a few scholarly characters with poised glasses and ink-riddled fingertips. Men, all of them. Not a single lady in the crowd.

Remy checked his pocket watch, not surprised to find it one minute to the hour. Claude had never been on time a day in his life. Not the Claude he remembered. Would this also start late?

At precisely the hour, the shuffling bushes belched a familiar man. Claude emerged from beneath the Briarrose placard. The hedges had grown to such thickness that a twisting tunnel had formed, completely blocking off a view of the interior. Tension thickened.

Run-down Claude had utterly disappeared. He looked hale, hearty, and bright. The excess weight had transformed into a muscular stance that brooked no weakness. He stood powerfully strong.

Claude emerged with an elegant walking stick, topped by a piece of amber studded with yellow diamonds along the base. He wore a lavish black silk shirt beneath a pristine white vest, freshly-ironed pants, and the gold chain of a pocket watch looping out of a breast pocket. He grinned, teeth altered to an unnatural shade of white, and spread his arms.

"Friends, neighbors, customers, and business partners. Welcome to Briarrose. It is my deepest pleasure to admit you through my doors today. What an honor to have you."

He bowed.

Remy ignored the fact that Claude didn't mention *family* in that odd list.

While Claude extrapolated on the benefits of Briarrose on the community, the Coven, and the Network, Remy asked

James under his breath, "Can you sense any transformative magic around him?"

"No."

"Me either."

"He appears healthy. Healthier than I have seen him in quite awhile." More quietly, James asked, "Do you think it's possible that he gave up ipsum?"

A voice inside Remy said, *no, this must all be a trick,* but the proof lay before him. Claude had certainly turned his life around, even momentarily, and tentative hope sprouted as a result. He wanted to believe it was possible, despite how unlikely. The strain their relationship had gone through the past few years meant they'd never be *very* close again, but he wanted better than cordial and impassive strangers.

"I hope so," Remy said.

"Have you spoken with him since your last confrontation?"

Remy shook his head.

"Probably for the best," James said.

Per Amelie's request, Remy had not betrayed her secret or her story to her parents, though he struggled to contain it. Being part of a family of eight girls made her ability to become invisible nearly unparalleled. Joyce, her attention constantly pulled elsewhere, lacked the ability to notice.

Claude elevated an arm.

"Please join me as we welcome Briarrose into the community, the Coven, and the Central Network."

Fire sprouted along the top of the hedge, bouncing in bright flames. Witches scuttled away as the flames dropped like falling candles. Orange licks of color crawled toward the ground, borne on a spell. They chewed through the briarroses, conjuring black smoke, in minutes.

A screen of smoke lingered until the last twig and petal succumbed to flames. Wind swept past, conjuring a collective sound from the crowd that was neither gasp, nor scream.

Briarrose revealed in hints through a choking black smoke. Dark glory surrounded a magnificent structure like noxious fog, which stood almost too large for the land space. It dominated the neighborhood, commanding attention with dingy stones, four stories, and wraith-like creatures guarding the top. Not gargoyles, but some other hellish amalgamation. They sprawled giant wings and roared, talons clutching the stone as if that's all that held them.

In almost every plane, window, and square, Briarrose mimicked Wildrose. The structure, cadence of the architecture, flowing movement of the stones and wood and design . . . except for the hesitating air.

The sense of misplaced magic.

The sinister challenge from within.

A driveway cut through the lush grass starting at Claude's feet, heading straight to the main entrance of two double doors. Black stones doubled as gravel, leading the way to the foundation of similarly torrid walls. No pleasant fountain curled around the end of this drive, as it did in Wildrose. Instead, a giant sculpture of an attacking beast stood there, neither real creature or witch. Remy tried not to recoil from the horrid features—ten eyes, bared teeth, feral talons out of its three arms.

Briarroses lead the way to the manor, thorns gleaming with poison and promise. It was elegant, beautiful, and terrible.

"Ye gods," James whispered.

Witches pressed up the drive and toward the estate in one motivated body, whispering amongst themselves. Claude allowed them to slip by, greeting each witch as they passed with a nod, a murmur, a wide, almost maniacal smile. James and Remy waited until the very end, when all other witches had already passed.

Claude, seeing them linger, smiled all the more broadly. The corners of his mouth appeared pained. As they closed the distance, Claude strode towards them to close the gap.

"Remy and James. Thank you for coming." He bowed to James. "Good to see you, neighbor."

"A masterpiece," James admitted with a hesitating smile. "Truly, Claude. You've made a beautiful building."

Claude, his smile fixed, cast a glance to Briarrose.

"She is magnificent. But Remy knows all about that, doesn't he? Our manors are practically twins. Isn't that perfect? Unfortunate that only one of us could claim the ancestral land, but then, it went to the right person." Claude tapped Remy on the shoulder with his cane. "As you always used to say, brother. Things work out as they should. Come. For the two of you, I shall give a personal tour."

Remy avoided looking at James as he followed Claude inside, because he wasn't sure he would go through with the tour if he saw the same apprehension on his father-in-law's features as he felt himself. Remy braced himself as they mounted the steps, feeling an odd sense of deja vu.

This is not my estate, he silently chanted to himself.

Of course it wasn't.

Yet, it was.

Briarrose unfolded like a low dream filled with foggy alleys. The entryway and foyer matched Wildrose exactly, except for the decor. Black, tangled vines formed a stunning chandelier overhead. An elegant onyx marble, cut through with streaks of gold, lay on the floor and climbed the stairs. Gleaming metal with hints of red sculpted each sconce, while murals adorned the wall, painted to display obvious gluttony and naked revelries.

James averted his gaze.

Remy couldn't peel his attention away.

Claude led them up the broad stairs to the right of the entryway, just like Wildrose.

"Unlike what you have at Wildrose, Remy, I will not be hosting the needy or infirm. I will be hosting those with greatest *motivations*. Instead of ragamuffins that can't keep currency in their pockets, I have agreements with some of the wealthiest witches in the Central Network to work here. We plan to fill Briarrose with power, might, and change."

The ominous words sent a shiver through Remy, but it was the disdain of their delivery that made him the most upset. Claude, who had never been the beggar thanks to the parent that he scorned, could conjure no tolerance for those who had.

They passed a sculpture of a nymph with swollen breasts and snarling lips. Crimson liquid appeared to drip from her bared, sharp teeth, but it was only paint. The gleam of red that ran through the metal shone in the nymph, an allusion to blood.

Remy gratefully passed her.

"No bedrooms for the weary." Claude tapped on open doors as they passed. "You can see that each room is outfitted with desks, tables, chairs, plenty of light—or dark options—for whatever my patrons need."

"Patrons?" James asked.

"Business men, James." Claude smiled over his shoulder. "They are renting office space from me in order to work, hold meetings, the like. Thanks to these same business partners that contributed capital, a little currency that came from selling Father's lackadaisical grimoire collection, and a lot of luck at the gambling tables, we managed to pull together enough currency to buy the supplies for this place."

Claude sent Remy a smarmy smile that set all his hackles on end. No matter how far Remy wanted to run from here, he refused to budge. If this was the relationship they were going to have, and the disparate lives they would lead, Remy desired to understand as much as possible.

At the end of the hall, a thin doorway opened to a staircase that led to the next floor. The layers of Briarrose mimicked

Wildrose to a shocking degree. Remy felt he could navigate this house with his eyes closed, only he didn't dare. One false move, and the very devils of Alkarra would have him.

Claude led them to the third floor, which was as dark as the second. No decorations here, only bland walls, closed doors. When James reached out and touched a doorknob, all remained locked.

Claude tutted.

"No, no. These are . . . other . . . work rooms. They're reserved for our most important customers."

The word *customers* sent a sense of apprehension through Remy that he didn't like. Nor did the dwindling tone in *work rooms*.

"What do you offer?" Remy managed to ask.

Claude only smiled. "That's nothing for you to worry about."

The stack of horrific rooms continued all the way down the hall. Somedays, Wildrose seemed too big. Others, too small. Depending on how many witches came and went on any given day—they'd had as many as twenty for meals, and thirteen staying overnight—Wildrose was never too little or too much.

Briarrose, on the other hand, was an exposition of *too much*. Similar to navigating an endless nightmare. No matter where they turned, the shadows continued. The unending rooms, the lack of levity. The breathings of the underworld thrived within, whispering through the walls. Briarrose had been built on top of the ghosts of their old life, and the sinister tint in the air forced Remy to wonder if his parents weren't trying to tell him something.

"Is Chase still your assistant?" Remy asked as they passed a painting of three witches burning another witch in a fire. The twisted, shrieking face sent a silent scream through the air.

James shuddered.

Claude scoffed. "Why don't you ask what you really mean to

ask, Remy?" The sheer decorum and modulation of his voice slipped away for a breath, so quick that Remy might have imagined it. "Am I still associating with *those* witches?"

"I didn't ask that."

The smile returned, and mocking came with it. "Sure you didn't, perfect little Remy. Yes, Chase is still my assistant. You see, when your family gives up on you and forbids you entrance into their life, you have to find your own family."

Claude twirled, and Remy realized that they were at the main staircase on the fourth floor. The garish, nightmarish decorations reached a fever pitch as he glanced toward the master suite, perched on top of Briarrose like a cake topper, above the fourth floor. Murals graced the walls again, violently offensive, with depictions of bared chests, screaming women, and dismembered body parts.

The mirth in Claude's eyes deepened. "Don't you like it? The darker side of witches? This is where they come to satisfy the needs that good witches like you could never understand. The root of all evil, you might call it. Reality, says the rest of us. We plan all manner of debauchery here. Gambling. Games. Fights. Sex. You name it, Remy, you'll find it."

James stumbled back a step. Through building layers of disgust, Remy held onto his composure and reached for his father-in-law. The disappointment he felt meant there had been a small measure of hope for Claude to have brought them because of a desire for reconciliation, though such felt impossible with the history at their backs.

His smug smile revealed all. The more uncomfortable they felt, the greater his enjoyment. Claude invited Remy and James here so he could brag.

"Have at it, Claude," Remy said. "I hope, somewhere in all this, you find your way."

With that, he led James down the stairs, out the door, and away from Briarrose's smoky bushes and haunting perimeter.

Only Amelie could shake away his shadows.

He clung to her that night, his fingers trailing her bare arm, across her softly rounding belly, and then higher again. The soft velvet of her skin soothed him. He pressed his forehead to the back of her head, kept his arms around her, and thought of everything good in the world.

"Boy or girl?" she asked, holding onto the wrist of his arm that lay beneath her. His lips twitched into a smile. She asked the question on purpose, and he loved her for it.

"Boy."

She scoffed. "Girl."

"We'll name her Grogda, shall we?"

Amelie burst into a peal of laughter, banishing earlier nightmares. "Grogda, the troll of legends?" she asked, tears in her eyes from laughing. She spun in his arms to face him, and he tucked a piece of hair out of her eyes.

"You really want to name your daughter after Grogda, the troll from the north that came out of the mountains, into the forest, and wreaked such havoc that her tall tales have been told to children for centuries?"

He schooled his expression. "Yes, of course. Don't you expect any child to do the same to our comfortable, stable life?"

"Rampage into it like a troll?"

"Absolutely. Look at what Bree and Ann have done to the place."

She hooted. "You have me there. Though, thankfully, Wildrose repairs each little ding and knick." Amelie propped her head on her hand, her gaze tapering with a hidden smile. "But do you really think our life here is stable? Witches coming and going. Dinners packed with strangers, or no one at all. Apothecaries in and out. I never thought I'd be best friends with an

Apothecary, or five. We see them so often. It's amazing how many sick witches require help."

Her question forced a moment of introspection Remy hadn't planned for. More seriously, he asked, "Don't *you* think life here is stable? The details might change, but the manor remains constant."

Amelie seemed to respond more to the lines in his brow than his words. She scooted closer.

"Well . . . I suppose it is stable."

He arched a questioning brow. She laughed, pressed their lips together in a too-quick kiss, and withdrew as fast. He almost chased her for a deeper one, but held back because he wanted to know what she'd say.

"Our life at Wildrose is wild," she admitted, "and unpredictable and erratic, but isn't that everything I always wanted? My own home? A place to give back to the world because I have received so much?"

Her innate goodness drew Remy's thoughts to Claude, deepening his frustration. Naturally, Amelie sought only to make the world a better place, while his brother swam in nefarious cess pits. Amelie, who had so many reasons to hold resentment. Claude, who had so few.

"Yes," he finally said. "It is stable. We have a roof, food, magic, and friends. I'd call that the definition of stable."

A slow smile crawled over her lips, but faded as quickly as it came. She swiped her thumb across his bottom lip.

"You are so serious tonight."

He looked down, unable to peer into her trusting eyes. He slipped his fingers through hers, enjoying the firm grip of her strong fingers. Maybe stability in Wildrose was an utter lie. Maybe the only true stability he had was this.

"I saw Claude today."

She brightened with interest.

"Oh?"

"I went to visit with your father this morning, do you remember?"

"Yes, but you see Father most weekend mornings. I sometimes think he likes you better than he likes me."

Remy managed a struggling smile. "No, never. You're the better part of all of us. At any rate, we saw Claude together."

"Not surprising. Father is always trying to help Claude."

"James is a good man. I was glad to have him with me when we saw Claude, at least at first. We went because Claude invited your father and myself to the unveiling of Briarrose."

Her eyes turned to saucers.

"What?"

A frisson of guilt niggled him for half a breath. Like the rest of the Coven, she had been as curious as everyone else to know what Briarrose would eventually be when the hedges disappeared. Not for the first time, Remy was absurdly grateful for Wildrose's position, hidden down the road, away from Pershington and their old neighborhood, blissfully unaware of the toils outside the estate.

Remy swallowed. "Claude revealed Briarrose today. It was all a bit more dramatic than I thought was required, with fire and some pomp but . . . reveal it he did. There were no women there," he added as quickly, sensing a rising fire in her eyes. He shuddered. "I wouldn't desire you near there at all if your parents didn't reside next door."

Curiosity won out over irritation. Her sharp gaze faded into an open-mouthed shock.

"Tell me everything!" she cried.

Somewhat reluctantly, he replayed each moment and detail he could remember, from her father's reaction to the revealing house, their conversation before they saw Claude, right down to accurate descriptions of the horrifying murals and artwork.

Unlike Joyce, Amelie hadn't kept herself *so* isolated from the world that she couldn't understand the depths of depravity that some witches enjoyed descending. Still, he didn't like saying them aloud. She had rolled onto her back and stared at the ceiling while he spoke. She closed her eyes.

"My goodness."

"There are few words adequate in our language to cover such an experience," he said with a wry sigh. "I find myself having a hard time articulating it as well."

Amelie pushed up again.

"Briarrose truly is Wildrose's antithesis?"

He nodded.

"But . . . those kinds of witches in the neighborhood . . . my parents live next door!"

"I know."

"It's not fair. This is not your parents' legacy."

"Agreed."

"Don't you think something else is driving Claude?" She leaned closer, grasping one of his hands. "It must be, don't you think?"

"What do you mean?"

"How could you, the best witch I've ever known, come from the exact same upbringing and family as Claude?"

Remy shrugged. "Choices?"

Or foreordination, a silent voice suggested. His silent voice. He pondered far too much over purpose and fate.

Amelie chewed on her bottom lip. "Maybe," she drawled. "Or maybe there's something else bothering Claude, telling him that he must prove himself. Guilt, perhaps. It's a terrible motivator."

"Guilt over what?"

She hesitated. "Your parents death?"

He reared back.

"What?"

Soothingly, she put a hand on his shoulder. "Remy, think about it. Everything you told me about the night your parents died was horrible, but some of it was plain confusing. Claude's behavior afterwards, too, was suspicious. From the starting of the fire, the lateness of him waking you up, to their death. It just . . . it doesn't add up."

The thought propelled Remy out of the bed, chasing him back and forth, so horrible to consider.

Furious, he cried, "You're accusing my brother of killing my parents!"

"No," Amelie said carefully, "I'm saying it's possible that the fire might have started with Claude, but he won't admit it. I'm not saying he *meant* to kill them. The whole thing might be an accident, Remy. Maybe Claude read, fell asleep, and the curtains caught to flame from his candle. But he can't admit it because he's so ashamed, and it's eating away at him."

Remy sank into his memories, replaying that night over and over again. The scent of smoke and the sense of horror knowing his parents twirled away in ash drove most of the memories. He didn't like to think of that day.

In the end, he shook his head, exhausted from the effort. He didn't appreciate considering a murderous slant on an already terrifying brother, but he couldn't deny that she might be right.

Which hurt most of all.

He collapsed on the bed again. She snaked an arm round his shoulders, pulling him close to her side.

"I'm sorry," she whispered against his back. "Maybe I shouldn't have—"

He put a hand over hers. "No, it's fair. There's obviously a chance that their death was a result of something Claude did, and he knows it. There's also a chance that's not true at all. It's a question we may never be able to answer in this life."

"Do you think Claude would admit it if you asked?"

"No."

"Do you need that kind of closure?"

He thought for a long time before saying, "No."

She sighed.

"As to your question of how we could come from the same household?" Remy continued, "I have no answer. I can only think that, along the way, we chose very different paths, and that's resulted in where we are now. Unless this whole life is some cosmic joke, decided upon by a being that is not us, and all is predetermined."

"I don't believe that."

He said nothing.

Amelie sighed, a quiet expiration of air that cut to the bone. He didn't want her worrying about Claude or Briarrose. Not with a baby on the way and an estate to care for. Their life must move forward.

For good or ill, Wildrose required it.

Chapter Eighteen

Summer whittled to autumn.

The warm days of fall whispered by, busy with a pumpkin harvest—thanks to a passer-by that created and planted a garden which various wanderers helped Amelie maintain as a thank you —and preparations for the new baby.

Amelie's belly swelled, and so did her joy.

One frosty winter day, the sound of Manon and Caterina giggling from outside his office drew Remy's gaze away from his desk. Were his in-laws here? A mess of cogs, two arms, bolts, a few nuts, and other knickknacks littered the small table.

Remy studied the amalgamation of once-moving clock parts with a stymied sense of uncertainty. He had no idea how to put the grandfather clock together again, though this wasn't his first attempt to understand the sometimes radical contraption. He lifted both hands toward it, speaking to Wildrose, as he often did.

"Have at it, then. It's your clock, but thank you for letting me try."

Usually, Wildrose would pick up the pieces in the same methodical and organized fashion in which it built the manor.

Everything would click together until the whirring motions and restoration thrilled him. When everything else felt wild, Wildrose made sense.

Today?

No such push.

A deepening dread filled him. Ye gods, would he have to figure the clock out on his own? Perhaps the ease of living in Wildrose *hadn't* been a good thing. Challenges used to delight Remy, but now he'd rather let magic deal with intricacies. He was a thoroughly spoiled master of a magical manor.

Which may not be a good thing.

A sound from the hall drew his gaze higher, accompanied by a quick rap on the door. Joyce called in through the crack in the door.

"Remy?"

"In here!"

James and Joyce slipped inside. Though Joyce smiled, it appeared weary and struggling. James nodded his droll greeting, eyes sagging at the ends. In the last several months, either age had snuck up on his in-laws, or Briarrose's swamping effect on the entire community had caught up to them.

Either way, both were older and less hale.

"Welcome." Remy stood. "What a pleasant surprise."

Joyce peered at the knickknacks on the desk while Remy wiped oil and dust from his fingers.

"Have we interrupted something?" she asked.

"Nothing wildly important. Just fixing the clock."

Intrigue crossed James' features. "Mind if I take a look? I'd be happy to help piece it together. Nelson and I used to work on clocks, you know."

Remy waved a hand. "Please do. Wildrose normally fixes these things itself, but the clock has been pestering me more than usual lately, the hands going wild. I think it might have broken something—"

James dove into work, murmuring, nodding, and exclaiming under his breath. He showed more vivacity than Remy had seen in awhile, so he stepped away to leave him to it. Maybe *he* was why Wildrose didn't fix it.

"Celine and Manon and Caterina are downstairs. Agatha and Sofie are occupied for a day or two, so you won't see them this time." Joyce gave a wobbly, worried smile. "Are you sure it's all right that we come without invitation or announcement? We'd like to stay the night, if it's okay with you. It's just . . . that is . . ."

Guessing the source of her anxiety, Remy said, "Claude is hosting another gambling tournament?"

She nodded, lips pinched.

"They are so loud." She wrung her hands together with a shake of her head. "Despite calling the Guardians and having extra patrols through the neighborhood, I don't feel our girls are safe. You know we put that big fence up? Well, someone broke through it and wandered into our backyard. Horrible." She shook her head with distress. "The Turners next door have put their house up for sale, did you hear?"

"I didn't."

Another shake of her head. "They can't handle Briarrose and her occupants anymore. Dissolute witches, a terrible pall over the neighborhood. Just awful."

Remy put a hand on her shoulder. "Joyce, Wildrose will always have you, no questions asked. If you check your favorite rooms on the fourth floor, I imagine you'll find them prepared, just the way you like."

Relief suffused her smile, which was less wobbly this time. "Thank you, Remy. We have been blessed to have you in our lives."

"I feel the same."

"Where is my daughter?"

"Resting upstairs. She was tired after lunch. I'll go check on her, bring her down."

Joyce clucked at him. "No need for her to entertain me. We know Wildrose like the back of our hands. I'll track down Bertha and see if I can help with anything. Celine is helping Caterina and Manon finish some studies in the kitchen. That Xavier!" She fawned. "Handsome witch and an excellent tutor. So grateful you introduced us."

Another voice floated down the stairs from the master suite.

"Remy?"

"Yes, my dear."

"Please," Amelie called. "I need you."

Remy took the stairs two at a time, moving crisply, but sedate. He loosened a button at his neck, thinking of Claude's latest gambling soiree. He hadn't thought of his brother much the last several months. Thoughts of the baby, tasks at Wildrose, kept him occupied. The Claude door had closed after Remy toured Briarrose. When he thought of Claude now it was mostly due to issues.

Shaking those thoughts free, he hurried up the final stairs to the master suite and slipped inside.

"Yes, my dear?"

The room, kept warm by a fire, cast a long view over a frosty forest. Rain had moved in overnight, gracing them with a muted slate sky and the general feeling of oppression. Frost graced the leaves, heralding an early fall.

"I think my water has broken," Amelie said from within the drawn curtains of the four-poster bed. "We better call for the midwife, or my mother. My back aches something fierce, and quite methodically."

He froze.

In theory, her words made sense. They'd spoken to the midwife several times, read books aloud, and prepared for the reality of the delivery. However, he wasn't sure what to do now that the actual moment had arrived.

How could she sound so calm?

"I'm sorry?"

"Remy, this is hardly the time to joke."

Remy hurried to the bed, pushed aside the heavy damask curtains, and peered within. Amelie lay on her side with a pinched expression. Her swollen belly was propped on a pillow. She grimaced, pressed one hand on the small of her back.

"Truly?" he whispered.

Weakly, she smiled. Flitters of primal fear colored the depths. Yet, he saw resolution. The path had started. The most dangerous path she'd likely ever walk, and not a power in Alkarra could stop it. He couldn't remove the next several hours from her, but oh, how he wished he could.

Remy's mouth opened and closed. He didn't know what to say to impart courage to his wife. To bolster her for the task ahead that only she could complete.

"What . . . do you . . . that is . . ."

Calmly, she repeated, "Please fetch the midwife, Remy. At the very least, send her a message to come to Wildrose." With a little moan, she added, "Better find Mother, too. I might need some help."

Ah! *That* he could deliver.

"Joyce is here."

"She is?"

"Your father and sisters, too. They just arrived."

"Oh."

"I'll just . . . I'll go for her?"

"Yes." She moaned again. "Yes please!"

Remy swallowed rising emotion before he scuttled away from the four-poster bed. Many times over the last year, he'd contemplated what this moment of change might feel like. Would he be frantic? Would the baby come amidst chaos and upheaval? Or would it experience a quiet slide into the world? A gentle transition from one existence to the next, like sleeping and waking up somewhere else.

He put a hand on her cheek.

"If I could take the weight of this burden from you, I would, Amelie. I would take it all, and then more, but I cannot. I know you can do this."

Tears brimmed in her eyes. "I don't know if I can."

He smiled. "I *know* that you can."

A tear dropped down her cheek as Amelie nodded. Her hand covered his and squeezed. The corners of her eyes tightened in a grimace. He removed his touch, though leaving her was the last thing he wanted.

"I'll be right back."

James and the grandfather clock kept Remy company.

The completed clock stood off to the side of the hallway, ticking away. The friendly tock of its moving hands had a soothing rhythm, as if it wanted to impart comfort. For a long while, Amelie's voice came through the master suite door as normal as ever. Gradually, she quieted.

The air in Wildrose thickened as Celine, Caterina, Manon, and occasionally Amelie's older sisters, Mathilde and Katriona, trotted up and down stairs. Women's voices clucked and gabbled in whispers and occasional giggles.

After half an hour in the office, listening to James drone on about something to do with the business, developments in the market, and a potential new vendor to clinch down, Remy returned to the hallway outside the master suite. He leaned against the wall and sank to the ground.

There, he stayed.

Sometime around midnight, James approached with a yawn and patted Remy on the shoulder.

"It'll be all right, Remy. These Leroy women are hearty. Went through this ten times with Joyce—we lost our first at birth, you know. Come, let's go to the library. No sense waiting in the hallway."

Remy couldn't tear himself away, so James eventually left without him. An hour later, he found James asleep in a chair near the library fireplace. Remy covered him with a blanket and returned to his vigil.

While the women bustled and tutted and settled Amelie, summoned items sped past Remy's spot on the fourth floor hallway. Teapots, then cups. Sachets, and a bowl of sugar. The clock ticked away at his side, as if its dedication could move time along her restless path.

Remy paced the floor around three in the morning, tried not to think about how many ways this could go wrong, or how much agony Amelie might endure, or had endured already. The intensity of Wildrose shifted when hot water steamed by, followed by fresh linens and branches of witch hazel and then ice. He couldn't fathom what it might mean.

Amelie cried out once.

Thrice.

The midwife sang something in a cheery tone, and Joyce spoke next. Her steady, soothing cadence calmed Remy as he plastered himself to the double doors.

A final cry.

Not Amelie, Joyce, or the midwife.

A baby.

Remy choked. His hands wouldn't work fast enough to throw the doors open and race inside. Amelie sat on the edge of a chair, towels and blankets all over. Blood stained each of them. The midwife, crouching in front of his wife, held a squalling mass of red, purple, and blue. Skinny limbs flailed, and a wet face released a lusty bellow of disapproval.

Amelie, panting, sobbed his name.

"Remy!"

He rushed to her side, folding his arms around her. She melted into him, crying, as Joyce wrapped the squalling child into a blanket and settled it in Amelie's arms.

"A boy," Joyce whispered, her eyes sparkling. "You have a son, Amelie, Remy. A beautiful son."

The world faded as Remy used one finger to gently pull down the blanket. A wet, dark-eyed, plastered-hair face peered at them, mouth bobbing open and closed. The dazed expression made him laugh, and then cry. Tears dotted his cheeks.

"Amelie." He pressed a kiss to her sweaty hair. "Oh, Amelie. Look what a beautiful baby we have been given."

She turned into his neck and sobbed. The soothing hums and directions of the midwife, as well as Joyce puttering around the room, setting everything to right, lay a reverent hush on the master suite.

All of Wildrose held its breath. The estate seemed to understand that an heir had been born.

Amelie smiled through her tears.

"Isn't he perfect?"

"Perfect." He spirited a gentle finger down the side of his son's downy cheek. "He is perfect, Amelie."

The midwife spoke calmly about breastfeeding and walking and drinking water and witch hazel baths and sitting on ice. After a long family snuggle, Remy accepted the precious bundle while Amelie gingerly toddled to a waiting bath.

Carefully, he crossed the room to stand at the window while studying every contour of his son's face. Outside, a new dawn rose. Brilliant light sparked the sky.

"You've changed my life," he whispered to his son, "and I cannot wait to see the world with you in it every day."

Two days later, Remy stepped into crisp air and closed his eyes. Wildrose felt stuffy and overcrowded, despite an utter lack of visitors and plentiful fires keeping the necessary parts of the house warm.

While Amelie recovered from labor, and their son, Quinten, found a flow with breastfeeding and sleeping, Wildrose accepted no visitors. None came to their door. Only Bertha, who moved into her own place in late summer and daily transported to the manor to work. The Leroys returned to their home the next day, after Claude's most recent dissolution finished and the sunshine brightened their walls again.

Remy sank into the cool moment outside by himself, appreciating the wispy fog on his face. It settled his nerves as well as his soul. Overwhelm plagued him. Part of him longed to be in the bedroom, rocking his son, watching over Amelie to make sure she rested. Another part, perhaps too large a part, wanted to stay in the silence, where change wasn't inevitable, and everything made sense.

The crackle of wheels over stone dragged his exhausted eyes open. A carriage rolled down the road, the horse slowing as it neared their drive. Remy stiffened as it stopped, turned to the left, and jangled down the crushed gravel.

Who would visit today, of all days?

The black-swathed exterior, and a familiar crest—a B with thorny vines winding around it—was all-too familiar.

Remy's exhausted mind was too tired to draw assumptions. Chase, Claude's assistant, leaped from the front of the carriage. Wearing a finery he'd surely never possessed before, with his hair pomaded and slicked back, Chase approached with a devil-may-care grin. Remy must look a mess, because the closer Chase walked, the wider his smile.

"Mr. Dauphin." Chase bowed and extended a letter. "From my master."

The word *master* rang in the back of Remy's mind as he accepted the missive. *Master* not *boss.*

Remy dismissed the observation as a hearty amount of skepticism piled inside him. His suspicion might be born from sheer exhaustion. Days with an infant, a recovering wife, and the normal machinations of work and Wildrose would exhaust anyone.

"Thank you."

Chase gripped his hands behind his back, inclining his head in a respectful nod.

"As you've established a firm boundary against my master coming onto your property, you'll forgive him for not extending direct congratulations." Chase touched his fingertips to his forehead in a salute. "Best of health to you and the family, sir."

Chase spun on his heel, climbed to the top of the carriage next to the driver, and waved once in a farewell.

Remy watched him go, considering. Had he imagined it as part of a hallucinogenic, waking dream? As he studied the front of the letter, he decided it wasn't. Dreams didn't produce letters.

It might be a nightmare.

With a yawn, he tore through the wax seal, which directly mimicked the elegant B on the carriage, and flipped the pages open. Claude's familiar handwriting filled the interior.

Brother,

Congratulations on your heir. The good news has just met my ears. Accept my profound and heartfelt wishes for his health and yours.

Remy tightened, then forced himself to breathe. Claude had intentionally left Amelie out of that sentence. Nothing would ever convince him that it was an accident. He forced himself to keep reading.

If you are open to it, I would love to one day meet my nephew.

Yours,

Claude

Remy shoved the letter inside the envelope and stared hard at the misty, soupy sky. Dank clouds hung low over the forest, obscuring sunshine. Wetness filled the air. Letum Wood never appeared more haunted and bleak than foggy days, when the wood was almost obscured by the clouds, but not quite.

He spelled the letter to the upstairs fire and ran a hand over his face. Exactly what game was Claude playing? Assuredly, there was a game, or an angle, to which he strove. Otherwise, he would have included Amelie in his well wishes and extrapolated on his smarmy *congratulations* that didn't have a sincere curve to any letter.

Claude could have ignored them.

Remy preferred the latter.

There wasn't a hint of drunkenness in the handwriting that would explain why Claude sent the letter, either. Was there some reason Claude wanted to meet his nephew?

Would he harm him?

Remy's immediate revulsion to the idea led to deepening curiosity. As much as he wanted to believe his brother had kindness and goodness rooted in his darkening soul, Remy harbored no hope. The devilish landscape of Briarrose, and the nefarious deeds Claude allowed in his home to gain whatever Claude sought, prevented belief.

Why had he written?

Why couldn't they let each other go?

Quinten Dauphin may never know his uncle, unless Claude worked hard over time to prove that he had no motivation to disparage their boy. Remy would have to keep the boundaries drawn, and avoid his brother.

He wouldn't answer the letter.

"I'm not proud of it as a plan, Claude," Remy whispered, as if his brother could hear, "but ignoring you is the only choice you've given me. The influences in your life are poison, and I won't allow them here."

Remy scrubbed his hands over his eyes to wake himself up and wheeled around. As he straightened, a mug of coffee appeared, colored to a pale shade of brown that indicated his favorite amount of cream.

Smiling, he had a sip.

"Thank you. I believe you're right. I'll need the liquid courage this provides. Wildrose, you always care for me."

Despite his better sense, a feeling that someone or something watched him from the trees followed him through the double doors. He ignored it, certain it was exhausted paranoia, and returned inside.

Chapter Nineteen

Quinten's old soul peered out from serious eyes. In many ways, the three-month-old resembled his mother. In others, his father. He had a stubborn streak that spoke to the Leroy side, and an inability to focus that spoke more to the Dauphins.

"You," Remy touched the tip of Quinten's nose one bright morning in early spring, "will change Alkarra for the better, and be the steward of Wildrose. May you uphold your inheritance and responsibilities well."

While Amelie napped in the master suite, Quinten accompanied Remy on his rounds of the estate. Bertha spoke with two gentlemen who had stayed overnight—one of them had been here for a week, recovering from a bad fall through a weak spot in his roof—and the other was passing through. The antiseptic smell of lemon tinged the air. The Apothecary must have just left.

Bertha, seeing Quinten and Remy approach, grinned and waved. She carried a mop and empty bucket. "There's our wee lad," she crooned. "So good to see you both this morning!"

Quinten blew a spit bubble, staring in wide-eyed appreciation as he clutched her finger. Bertha made exaggerated faces and noises and he kicked his legs in response. The two gentlemen bled away with nods and farewells, disappearing together.

"Anyone else here, Bertha?" he asked.

"No one left, sir. Mr. Nakamura finished recovering and gives his hearty thanks, but he's on his way back home. The other gentleman, Mr. Petrov, is seeing him there. They became good friends last night."

"Glad to hear it."

"The estate might be quiet for a bit, sir."

Bertha reluctantly extracted her finger from Quinten's grip and picked the mop back up. With a departing smile, she headed down the hallway. Anne towed behind, carrying several feather dusters. Bree would be somewhere in the kitchen, probably, attempting a new scone recipe. The girl had proven to be a whiz with food, now that Xavier had taught her fractions.

Proof that hope always existed.

A rap on the doors drew Remy's attention. He marched down the stairs, speaking to Quinten the whole way, and pulled it open. A well-dressed, middle-aged man stood outside with a spreading nose, dark black stubble, and inquisitive eyes. He studied Remy for a full five seconds, eyes lingering on Quinten.

"Is this the Wildrose estate?" he asked.

Something in his brusque manner set Remy's hair on edge. He readjusted his grip on Quinten and stepped forward, occluding the open space in the doorway with his body.

"It is."

"Are you Remy Dauphin?"

"I am."

The man pressed his lips and made a humming noise in his throat. He tilted his head back, studying the underside of Wildrose's main awning, held up by columns that marched across the front porch and toward the long stairs that led to the driveway. At the foot of the stairs, a lone horse stood tethered to one of the horse rails.

"Can I help you with something?" Remy asked.

"I'm curious about your estate, if you don't mind me asking." The man shuffled away a few steps, and Remy appreciated the gap. He breathed a little easier with the probing stare off of Quinten.

"I do mind."

"That's fair," the man said, nonplussed. He stopped his perusal, held out a hand, and met Remy's eyes. "My name is SJ. I'm a part of the local coven and live on the outskirts of Pershington, on the western edge. We haven't had a reason to meet before, but I heard about your parents and their untimely death a while ago. I'm sorry that happened."

The initial distrust tempered ever so slightly as Remy accepted his forearm, clasped, and released him. Quinten fidgeted, drawing SJ's attention for a brief moment.

"Do you mind," SJ asked, "if you and I walk around the outside of Wildrose? It's a warm morning, and I have some questions about this manor. I think you're the only one that can answer them."

Bertha, too happy to ignore mopping and take Quinten, whisked the baby away to the nursery. Remy and SJ stepped onto the wet grass of Wildrose and began a slow saunter around the edge of the manor.

Remy couldn't explain the source of his curiosity—it made far more sense to refuse SJ and send him on his way—but he had a feeling that a simple refusal wouldn't stop this witch.

Persistence lined his smile. Witches like SJ carried themselves with confidence and power. They didn't leave simply because cooperation wasn't easy.

In a word, Remy was attentive.

"I come," SJ said, "at the behest of others. The building of Wildrose created a stir amongst the residents in this coven."

"It's been over a year."

"Yes." SJ continued, as if the observation hadn't been made. "The questions and rumors about its origins aren't surprising. Small populations spread great gossip. But the chatter increased when Briarrose was built. The two estates are shockingly similar."

Remy tensed; he couldn't help it. He was all but blind to the goings-on at Briarrose, except for what he observed when he visited his in-laws, which was less and less often. They stayed at Wildrose with increasing frequency instead. The dark effect of Briarrose seeped into their home, driving them farther away. Caterina, Celeste, and Manon had transitioned to daily lessons here, with Bree, Ann, and Xavier.

SJ's canny focus missed nothing.

"Your brother owns that property," SJ continued, "according to records and what I hear from other neighbors. It's not hard to find witches willing to talk about Briarrose," he added with a little huff.

"My brother, Claude, owns Briarrose."

"Your parents owned the land before that?"

"Yes."

"Did he inherit it as the eldest son?"

"Partially. We both owned it, then sold it. He purchased it."

Unbeknownst to me, he silently added, but felt no reason to add family drama to the conversation.

"Logic follows, I suppose," SJ mused.

Something about SJ's barrage of questions struck Remy as odd. If SJ were truly part of this coven, he would have already known all these answers. Anyone that had been here more than five years knew his parents, the tragedy of the lost estate, and the drama of Briarrose's opening day.

SJ spoke as if he was part of the coven, yet not quite.

Remy extracted from the suspicious thoughts before SJ caught onto his line of reasoning. He struck Remy as the sort of witch that could anticipate most problems in their infancy. If SJ hoped for Remy to extrapolate more details, he offered none. He had a feeling he didn't need to, and that SJ tested him, which only made his heedfulness double.

Remy stopped.

"Why are you really here, SJ?"

SJ drew alongside him. After a moment's hesitation, he said, "I'm here to figure out what's going on with these strange houses. Two of them pop up within months of each other, they're built by magic. Both appear to have witches coming in and out at all hours of the day, without any rhythm or routine, and are run by brothers who are, by all appearance, estranged."

The words, coming from a stranger, pierced deeper than Remy might have expected. He forced himself to hold his expression, just in case. Might SJ work for Claude? He couldn't see how it would matter, or what Claude might be attempting to learn, but he couldn't trust his brother.

Not to mention how strange it was to comprehend Wildrose from without. Remy knew that nothing evil lurked in here, but would others?

Remy gave the same explanation he gave to the witches that came to Wildrose. "All of this is run by the same magic."

"Oh?"

"The two grimoires, together, make a full system, I suppose. One house is focused on doing good," he gestured above him, "and the other . . ."

Remy shrugged.

SJ took that in without surprise. "And how am I to tell which is good and which is bad that doesn't rely on you telling me? Claude has the same opinion, by the way. He thinks he's doing the world a favor with that strange place."

Remy scoffed. "Do you really need to ask?"

"Do I?"

Equal parts irritated and amused, Remy snapped, "Apparently, you do. I'll let you answer that question however you want. If you'd like to come in and tour Wildrose, it's open to you. You can make your own deductions then. I'll be eating breakfast soon, and you're welcome to join."

SJ shook his head. "Not necessary yet, but the offer is appreciated. I suppose I wanted to meet you. I'm good at reading witches, and I get a much more positive energy from you than your brother."

"You've met Claude?"

SJ laughed, but didn't answer.

Remy continued the stroll, not surprised when, this time, SJ didn't match his stride. He remained behind, standing in the same spot.

"Witches are uneasy about both estates," SJ called to Remy's retreating form. "We'll keep watching."

"Feel free."

"I'll return!" he called.

"See you then!"

With a wave, Remy disappeared around the corner. But his heart pounded in his throat, unduly nervous by the hidden warning in SJ's words. He couldn't fault SJ—or SJ's employers, if that were the case—their concern. But Wildrose wasn't the problem. It wouldn't take long for SJ to ascertain that. Remy drifted toward the back door into the kitchen, wondering if Claude thought the very same thing.

Chapter Twenty

Remy's new assistant, a woman named Kate, narrowed her focus as she attempted to discern a letter.

"I'm sorry, sir." She handed it over. "I don't know what it says. I've attempted to read each line five times, but without much success."

He accepted it, smiled when he saw his wife's atrocious attempt at a note, and said, "That is from my wife, Kate. Her handwriting is nothing to brag about. Based on the general appearance of the letters, I believe she's telling me when dinner will be ready. Thank you. I'll take care of it from here."

Relieved, Kate backed out of his office, closing the door behind her. They'd spent the last three hours going through project plans, his upcoming schedule, and three new vendor proposals. If they could start stocking messenger paper in a small store within Chatham Castle, there would be a definite increase in sales.

James had done all the hard work of establishing messenger paper and its necessity in the Central Network, so they always had stable sales, but Remy had to maintain those relationships and build more.

They'd been lucky, so far.

No competition rose to create their own version of the paper —not that it had much variation, being enchanted paper. He had ideas for expanding their offerings. Whether those ideas would sell, he couldn't wait to test.

Thick-headed from thinking and talking for so many hours, he strolled to the window and peered down. The bustle of downtown Ashleigh, which hosted a lazier traffic compared with Chatham City, prattled by with carriages, the shouts of children, and fluffy clouds passing in the sky.

Dinner wasn't until six, and they'd be entertaining a new vendor, which meant he'd return home by five. Most of the work was wrapped up here. There were still four hours left in the work day and then the weekend beckoned. Surely, leaving a few hours early wouldn't impact any important machinations . . .

As he flirted with the temptation to return home and play with Quinten on the eve of his first birthday, an unexpected sight caught his attention below. Remy leaned forward. Was that . . . Chase, Claude's assistant?

The very witch stood in the middle of the narrow, downward slanting cobblestone road. He lifted a hand in salute, then pointed toward the basement.

Remy shoved the window open.

Chase tipped a quick bow.

"Good to see you again, sir. My master has just approached your interior, hoping to visit with you."

A cold rush filled Remy from the inside out. Ye gods, he hadn't seen Claude in well over a year, and didn't wish to see him for many more. No, that wasn't entirely true. He did long for any rational and intentional reason to see his brother. He never found one. He doubted Claude felt the same drive.

The sound of feet climbing the stairs slipped below the door. Remy frowned, closed the window, and left Chase standing in the street. The only reason Chase would stand in the streets while Claude approached from within would be to make sure Remy didn't attempt to leave. Remy could transport away, of course. Or lock the door, attempt to act as if he wasn't there. Chase was meant to help Claude understand how Remy reacted.

Either way, Remy didn't like it.

The boots outside his office drew closer, then stopped at Kate's desk. Before she could ask Claude what he wanted, Remy commanded the door open with a spell. Claude stood at her desk, regaled in simpering high fashion. Despite the expensive clothing, he looked decrepit, half-drunk, and a general mess. The stinking confidence from before attempted to rise, but something like fear quelled it.

"You can let him in, Kate," Remy said. "He's my brother."

Claude stood in the middle of Remy's office, arms loose at his side. Remy hadn't left the window. Standing at his desk felt too pompous, and approaching Claude too unsafe. He rooted to the spot.

"Claude."

"Remy."

Remy conjured two cups of coffee and sent one to his brother. "Have it," he said in an attempt to break the skein of anxiety filling the room. "I know you like it black. Or you used to, anyway."

Claude accepted the cup, elevated it in a silent toast, and had several hearty swallows. The offering seemed to ground him. When he spoke, he had an unusually gravelly tone, as if he'd used his voice too much for too long.

"How are you, Remy?"

"Good."

"And your son?"

He managed a half smile. "Healthy. Smart, too. Has a bit of a rebellious streak."

"He's a year?"

Remy nodded, hiding his surprise that Claude bothered to remember. Until this moment, Remy hadn't realized that he still had some desire for Claude to meet Quinten tucked deep, deep inside. Remy braced his hands on the windowsill behind him and leaned on his palms. His coffee mug hovered at his side.

"How is business?" he asked.

A flash of panic crossed Claude's expression, then disappeared. He motioned to a chair across from Remy's desk with an upturned brow, and Remy waved his permission. Claude sipped his coffee as he sat.

"Business is . . . well . . . I don't know."

"Oh?"

Claude shrugged. "It's hard to tell. You know how slippery currency is. Here one day, gone the next. You live high, and then you live low."

No, Remy wanted to say, *that's not my experience at all.*

The opposition would only inflame Claude, who always had a sensitive side regarding currency. By his brother's pained expression, a vast amount of desperation or humility must have driven him here. Claude fidgeted with his mug, running his thumb along the handle.

"What's wrong, Claude?"

"We didn't part well, Remy," he blurted out. "Not well at all, and it's eaten at me over the last year. I sent you a letter."

Remy bit his bottom lip. "I received it. Thank you for writing."

Pained, Claude said, "You didn't write back." His voice vibrated, as if he struggled to keep an accusation out of it. Confusion swelled back up through Remy. One minute, Claude looked ready to rip him in half. The next minute, he wanted to be a happy family.

Where was the truth?

Remy had a large swallow of coffee, then sat in the chair across from his brother. When he lounged, one foot crossed at his ankle, he dismissed his hope for an early escape from the office to prepare for the vendor's dinner. His gut told him he'd deal with this development for several hours.

"Based on our previous meeting and the undertones of hostility in it," Remy said carefully, "I thought it best if we allowed Quinten time to grow up before he met his uncle."

Claude seemed to take that in with little effect. Eventually, he shrugged. "Your kid, your rules."

"What do you need, Claude?"

He scoffed, a hint of the expected bitterness wafted from it. "You think I always come when I need something."

Remy said nothing.

Claude, not meeting his gaze, admitted, "You're right. I do come when I need help, and I'm sorry about that. The truth is that I have nowhere else to go. It's . . . not easy saying it."

He set aside his coffee mug and smashed one hand into the other, popping his knuckles in a nervous gesture.

"Currency troubles?" Remy asked.

"Amongst others."

"Others?"

"I had enough currency, Remy. I really did. The currency was there, hidden in Briarrose, and then it was gone. I tried to find it again, but it's like it disappeared."

"Stolen?"

"I believe so."

"I'm sorry, Claude."

"Not as sorry as myself," he muttered. "All that work . . . gone!"

"You have witches coming and going all the time, I hear. Could one of them be responsible for taking it?"

Claude shook his head. "Not in there. It was my office,

which Briarrose keeps locked. It serves me, you know. Wildrose must do the same for you?"

The plaintive query felt like solid, common ground. Remy couldn't help a little thrill when he nodded.

"Yes, in its way."

"Is it . . . protective?"

"How so?"

Claude shook his head again. "Nevermind that. Anyway, the currency was meant to pay off a debt to one of the Briarrose investors. He had been waiting for payment for some time, and I had to move . . . assets . . . and give those assets, ah, a chance to work . . . before the currency could be ready. When it was, it disappeared."

His fingers splayed outward, mimicking an explosion. Remy ignored the vague details. Who knew what kind of *assets* or *time* the nefarious underworld of Briarrose would need in order to create currency.

"How does that much currency disappear?"

"I can't fathom."

"Did you explain this event to the investor?"

"Of course."

"And?"

Claude swallowed so hard his throat bobbed. "And," he drawled, "it obviously didn't go well. This witch is the only investor that hasn't been paid yet, and he hasn't been happy about waiting this long. These investors aren't merry witches, Remy. They're hardened men of the world that don't take *no* for an answer. It's . . . it's not done. When they ask, you supply. I didn't supply."

A dozen other questions came with each revelation, and the tiresome work of biting them back and attempting to ignore the details would exhaust Remy before Claude's rotating emotions could finish the job. The prickling fear in Claude's voice kept him riveted.

"What is the result?" Remy asked.

"Nothing good," Claude retorted hotly.

"Are you in danger?"

He rolled his eyes. "Always, Remy. Most of us are *always* in danger. Very few witches lead the sedate, stable life of a man in a magical estate that does the dishes for him and his wife."

Once again, Remy bit the inside of his cheek with disagreement. No, that didn't sound right either. Had Claude achieved this strange view on the world from Briarrose, or had he always been this cynical?

"It's almost like the house took it," Claude mumbled, eyes jerking from side to side, as if afraid Briarrose would hear.

"Is it possible for the manor to steal currency?"

He couldn't fathom the same from Wildrose.

"I don't know! I just know nothing is safe in Briarrose now. The house, it . . . it's like it has a personality. When it has a vendetta against a witch, it'll act on it. Plenty of witches have been forcibly removed from the manor. One of them almost died because of it. They're blaming it on me," he hissed, and the growing panic manifested again.

Remy almost asked, *Can you explain to these witches that the manor is doing it?* but stalled the query. It would mark Claude as insane. Very few would understand. Besides, an underlying fear bubbled in Claude. He didn't say it outright, but he gave the impression of one living in abject terror.

Claude shook his head, as if irritated with the whole affair. He threw his hands up. "The wild thing is this: I think the manor doesn't *want* me to be out of debt. I think it wants me desperate."

"Why would the manor care?"

"I don't know. That's why I came to you. I wanted to see if . . . if you could tell me about Wildrose. Does your manor do this too? Is the magic bound with some other purpose?"

"No."

"What does it do?"

"Not that," Remy countered. "Wildrose gives, freely. So freely that sometimes it's surprising. I'm not sure how it conjures some resources, and then others it clearly uses at our cost, such as food."

"Does it speak to you?"

"Not with words. Does Briarrose?"

Claude shook his head. "No, not with words, as you said. But . . . it's like there is an . . . understanding."

"Understanding?"

Claude put a hand to his head and grimaced, as if he had a headache. "In my mind. It's like I can sense when the magic is angry. It seems angry all the time. It takes my energy, my time. Well, now that it's taken all that currency, *I'm* angry. When I return, it's . . . it might be explosive."

"Your relationship, you mean?"

He nodded.

Remy scooted to the edge of his chair, quelling an outward expression of curiosity or concern. Just like the random stranger, SJ, that showed up almost a year ago, he didn't understand if underpinnings existed. Claude might be making all this up, though Remy smelled no sign of ipsum.

For all intents and purposes, Claude acted dead sober.

And frightened.

"What do you mean when you say *it might be explosive?*" he asked. "Is that literal?"

"I hope not," Claude said as quickly. "Briarrose wants something from me, I can feel it. I've put off answering its silent queries, but I don't think I can do that much longer. I'm not paranoid," he added with a snap. "I'm not."

"I never suggested it."

The distrust shining from Claude's eyes showed he didn't believe Remy. In fact, Remy had considered that with these odd houses, such could happen. The presence of the magic might form a personality. A sense of ownership, control? Whether it was possible, Remy wasn't certain. Claude's description made Briarrose sound like an entity. A growing malefaction and monster.

Wildrose lacked all those properties except magical presence.

A crawling sensation raced up Remy's back as Claude's words replayed through his mind. *Briarrose wants something from me.*

"What's going on at Wildrose?" Claude rasped. "Is it the same?"

"Not at all."

Irritation flashed across his features. "Of course not," he muttered. "Remy always gets the easy path."

"Claude, I—"

Claude waved it off, his affect morphing back to one of long suffering weariness. "Nevermind that, I'll deal with Briarrose. Sounds like you're not having the same issue, which is . . . interesting. I think I can make all of this go away if I come up with the currency to pay off the last investor."

Claude gave a far more pointed stare.

Remy's stomach churned. The purpose of this conversation finally dwindled to its inevitable end.

His job was stable and steady, with an income that allowed them to live comfortably in Wildrose, but there wasn't an abundance of currency. What he'd managed to save had come out of some level of sacrifice, and the savings wasn't much. Without new product ideas growing, they were destined to middle-class highs and lows. That wouldn't be so bad, if they didn't plan to have a family, and expect costs to rise.

"Say it, Claude," Remy commanded. "What do you want from me?"

"Currency."

"How much?"

Claude drew in a deep breath through his nose. "A thousand pentacles."

Remy blanched. "A thousand?"

"Yes."

Claude's unchanging stare startled Remy more than the amount. No apology lived in such a gaze, as if Claude willed all his emotion away and approached his life with the cool hauteur of business.

"Claude, I couldn't manage to give you half the amount."

"I'd take that. Half would help."

"I just said I couldn't."

"Then what can you give me?" Claude bit out desperately. "What can you do for me, brother? These men are not witches to cross. They're not witches to hold a debt with. If they can't get the currency from me, they'll come to you."

The last words shuddered out of him with great emotion.

Remy froze.

"What?"

"They're unforgiving!" Claude cried. "Ruthless, too. They don't care how they get their payment, just that they receive it. They know of the success of Wildrose, that it's a twin to Briarrose, and they would not be ashamed to extort you for the sum." Claude's pleading reached a frantic pitch. "In fact, they have already made allusions to such happening. It's why I came! The *only* reason I came. There's a chance we can fend this off your family before it begins."

Fury bubbled within.

"You would bring this to my doorstep," Remy hissed, "after all that you've done?"

Claude buried his face in his hands. "I'm sorry, Remy! I didn't ask for them to come after you, and I didn't tell them *about* you. They're smart. They know how to extort and make currency."

"Claude! I have a child!"

"I know!" he shrieked. "I know, Remy! But the dominoes are falling. I can't stop them. You can be as angry as you want, but there's nothing you can say that I haven't accused myself of. I'm in too deep, and you're in danger as well."

Remy shot to his feet to pace. Is this where SJ came into the situation? Had *he* scouted out Wildrose so many months ago, hoping to learn more about its potential? Disgust welled up within. He'd invited that witch into his home, so freely.

"This has nothing to do with me," Remy muttered, clenching his fists. "Nothing at all."

"I know!" Claude wailed. "I know! But I can't lose Briarrose."

"Sell it," Remy demanded. "Sell Briarrose to whomever you're indebted to. It's only right."

Shock filled Claude's face. He recoiled.

"Sell it?"

"Have you never considered that? You could bring utter barbarians to my doorstep, endanger my one-year-old son, my wife, myself. Yet, you wouldn't stop that venom by selling the manor?"

With a pale whisper, Claude said, "Not once."

"Give Briarrose to your investor if you have to, but don't bring my family into this!" Remy insisted. "You played with fire, brother. Now you're getting burned. I'm sorry that it had to happen this way, but it's not my fight. I won't save you."

Claude lost all color as he mouthed the words *sell Briarrose*. Had he heard a single word since then? Unlikely. Claude's abject confusion stirred alarm bells. Why would Claude react with such savage shock and fear?

If Claude felt sorrow for creating a dangerous problem, how had he *not* considered it? Claude's explanation played through Remy's mind again. The allusions that Briarrose had taken on an evil bent and personality, in particular.

Was it possible?

Could the estates themselves gain greater power?

It had been months since Remy last read the grimoire. It changed, sometimes, according to what the manor needed. Wildrose had a lovely routine and rotation of life. It required little deviation.

Briarrose had nothing *but* change.

Claude jumped from his chair, folded his arms over his chest, and stood at the window. Barren, he said, "I cannot sell, Remy. It's all that I have in the world. The only . . . the only proof of a life. The fulfillment of all I have done and sacrificed. The sins on my shoulders . . ."

Remy rolled his eyes.

"Mother and Father don't expect you to prove your life, Claude! They'd want better than you endangering innocent witches! Your *nephew*, nonetheless."

"I can't, Remy. I cannot let it go. The price has already been too high."

Remy ran a hand through his hair with a shocked, disbelieving laugh. Just half an hour ago, he contemplated returning home to Wildrose to play with his son in the rosy glow of a life he worked desperately hard to maintain. Claude reappeared with danger in his wings.

Yet again.

"Surely, to save yourself from this witch, if not others?" he inquired.

"Selling Briarrose would be far more frightening. Far more . . ."

Claude shuddered.

Remy forced himself to reconcile with the ugly truth: Claude wouldn't stop this monster from banging on Remy's door. His passive, spooked brother, half the physical witch he used to be, had no real fight.

Remy closed his eyes, loathing the situation, his brother, the vile witches behind this insidious plot.

But there was a path.

"I can come up with the sum," Remy croaked. It would require a great deal of trust on James' part, some selling of assets for the company, and all their life savings, but he *could* do it.

Claude spun. His bloodshot eyes blinked quickly, as if holding back tears. "What?"

"On one condition." Remy held up a finger. "You give me the Briarrose grimoire."

Claude's mouth went slack.

"You want Briarrose?"

"If you give me the Briarrose grimoire to study and compare with Wildrose, then I'll get you the currency."

Claude pulled his shoulders back. His eyebrows crashed together in real astonishment.

"Remy, I can't."

"Why?"

"You're not the owner of the magic. It's *mine*."

"Not if I loan you the currency. You'll make me the owner of the magic. It's my only stipulation."

Fury distorted Claude's too-thin features. "I won't do it. You just want to destroy Briarrose. You're judgmental, like the rest of them, and think it's an evil place."

"Briarrose might change if the same witch holds both manors. We could make it more functional, perhaps. If Briarrose is truly as . . . difficult . . . as you're describing, something must be done, Claude. For my family's sake."

"I won't give you the grimoire!" Claude shouted, his eyes maniacally wide. "This is my inheritance, my legacy. I earned the currency to pay for the land and I found the currency to build the manor. I won't let you take it from me, you greedy bastard."

"I don't want the manor, Claude! I want safety for my family."

"You'll sell Briarrose."

"I don't know what I'll do, but—"

Remy saw the swinging fist before he comprehended what it meant. At the last second, he turned his head to lessen the blow. Claude's fist grazed his cheek, minimizing the impact. Remy stumbled into his chair, hand gripping his throbbing skin. The blow stunned him, rather than knocking him out.

"You can't have Briarrose, Remy. You can't have *everything*." Claude growled, tears in his eyes. "I'll figure out this problem without your interference. I should have known that coming here was a mistake." In a cutting tone reminiscent of the cold Claude that Remy recalled from years past, he added, "You're a bigger disappointment than Father."

Claude transported as he strode across the floor. Half-dazed, Remy stumbled to the window. Chase leaned against the building opposite the factory, hands in his pockets. Something down the road grabbed his attention. He leaned forward. Remy couldn't see, but assumed that Claude called for Chase, because the young man disappeared, leaving the road empty again.

A foamy storm swirled into the sky that afternoon, heralding an early winter darkness. Colder weather entered with alluringly warm days and calm skies, only to froth at the lips as snow advanced.

Remy considered the approaching storm, broiling fast and dark over Letum Wood, as he hid behind a tree. The quiet of his old neighborhood made no sound, leaving an eerie silence. Wind gusts skittered pebbles and leaves across his ankles as he leaned against the trunk and studied the view.

Across the way, Briarrose filled the sky with a bulkiness like land clouds. The manor seemed to have doubled in size. He counted the windowed rooms. The manor hadn't grown, only the sinister energy.

They visited the Leroys so rarely that he hadn't seen it in

months. Briarrose cast a pall over the whole neighborhood. Three families left in the last year alone, abandoning their homes because no one would buy. The effect was haunting.

From the shadowy copse of trees where he stood, Remy comprehended a few of Briarrose's details. Muted glows hinted at witches within, doing who-knew-what, near tepid flames. Briarroses had grown across the property line, swirling around Amelie's old house and threatening to overtake the structure. Scorch marks from gardeners attempting to burn them back littered the grass, but couldn't stem the flow. Briarrose wasn't beholden to boundaries, either.

How perfect that Claude and Briarrose should have found each other.

Despite an hour sitting at his office desk, a cold slab of meat pressed to his cheek as he stared morosely at the fire, his face still hurt. He ignored the urge to probe the tender area. Claude used to wrestle with Remy. A stray fist, knee, or elbow to the face wasn't rare. Remy had been slugged in the eye more than once, and accepted it just fine.

The shock of *this* hit came more from disbelief than ailment. Claude's fist to the cheek had been a bold flash of violence, born from rage.

A sign of dwindling control.

Forgotten love.

Amelie would notice once he returned home, and he'd have to tell her.

Remy's cheek throbbed as he pondered Claude's desperation, sense of fear, rapidly-changing emotions, and defense of the manor. What if Claude had accepted Remy's offer? Remy would have approached James for a sum he couldn't explain. It could have destroyed their relationship.

Besides, what would Remy have done with the grimoire, with Briarrose? Could such a sinister estate be used for good?

Unlikely.

What a confusing mess.

Remy fought with the urge to rush into Briarrose and demand to know more about the magic that frightened Claude, one of the most recklessly fearless witches he had ever known. The thought of such darkness encroaching on Wildrose, his safe haven, the place he maintained with dedication, sacrifice, and compassion, wouldn't form.

He couldn't.

The feeling emanating from within was so malignant, he couldn't bring himself any nearer to Briarrose, or his brother.

Steeling himself for Amelie's questions, her willful rage, and a vendor's dinner he couldn't put off, Remy set off down the road. He needed a walk to clear his head, and the impending storm to match his mood.

After a successful, if not quiet, dinner with his potential new vender, Quinten fell asleep in Remy's arms later that night. The grind of the rocking chair on the wooden floor, the whisper of breath on his arm, and Quinten's heavy body bundled up in his arms, soothed Remy.

He didn't need to continue rocking. Quinten had been dead asleep for almost twenty minutes, yet he couldn't stop. The motion moved his thoughts.

He hardly remembered a time before his son gripped his heartstrings in a chubby fist. Before requirements and necessities didn't pack his day with undue drama and responsibility. He couldn't fathom a life without Quinten, and Amelie desired many more children.

The gentle patter of slippered feet, and a familiar tired smile, entered the room. Amelie sank into a rocking chair next to them. She closed her eyes, folded her hands in her lap, and yawned. Remy stood, carefully laid Quinten in his crib, and returned to the rocking chair. Wildrose shared their sigh as they settled into the quiet.

"As far as vendor dinners go," she drawled, "that might have been the best we've hosted thus far."

Remy smiled. Mrs. Zimmerman, a business witch from the Eastern Network that dealt more with companies outside of her home Network than within, had been a charming woman. White hair, a belly laugh, and an endless number of jokes endeared her to Amelie immediately.

"Stocking messenger paper in the East would be a huge boon." Remy poorly hid a yawn. "More than I might have expected."

"They have some versions already, it sounds like."

"Not as reliable."

"That's something." Her lashes parted, eyes fluttered. "Do you know . . . I think the house has somehow soundproofed this room?"

"Why?"

"When Quinten is sleeping, I can't hear anything out there."

"We're on the fourth floor, right by the master suite," he pointed out, agitated by the thought that Wildrose could be *that* thorough. It shouldn't have surprised him. The estate had done far more detailed, shocking things than soundproofing a room. Something in the suggestion made him feel brittle.

"There's still plenty of sound it might pick up," she continued, nonplussed by his defensive edge. "It's amusing and wonderful. Don't you think? Can you imagine living without Wildrose?"

He felt sick to his stomach at the thought. No, he couldn't. And why did that seem like a problem?

"Do you think we're destined to live a certain life?" he blurted out.

At his question, her eyes widened.

"What?"

"Do you think we're meant to do what we do? That there's some . . . foreordination . . . or something?"

Her brow furrowed into a puzzled smile. "What brought that thought forward?"

Remy debated all day whether he should tell her about Claude's confrontation, deciding that she must know. With safety on the line, she deserved full understanding, but he loathed telling it.

"Claude came to see me at work today."

Fatigue scrubbed free, fading into surprise as she straightened. Her fingers curled around the ends of the armrests.

"Claude?" Her gaze landed on his cheek. Understanding clicked. "When you returned home from work, you said you ran into something at the office!"

"I did. Claude's fist."

Outraged flushed her cheeks.

"What happened?"

He gave a vague sketch of their conversation, avoiding the harrowing details, such as the lifelessness in Claude's eyes, and the bitter taste of his repugnance to the idea of offloading Briarrose. Seeing his brother in such a state was unnatural. No matter how hard he tried, he couldn't stop seeing the little boy he once loved and revered.

The candlelight flickering over Amelie's features did nothing to soften her fear as the weight of what he revealed sank in.

She asked, "Are we safe?"

"For now," he said swiftly, "yes, I think so. I believe Wildrose will protect us."

"Can it protect us from a force as wicked as Claude? From its *counter* magic? Perhaps Claude or Briarrose are the only ones that could break through the magic. They're sister magicks, Remy."

Remy's heart curled up. "I hear you, my dear, and I don't

know how to answer. The truth is, I don't think *anyone* knows what it means."

"Of all the tricks to pull," she snapped, rocking with greater gusto. "Drawing us into this . . . and you putting a boundary down! What are they doing over there? Don't answer that . . . I don't want to know." She clenched her hands, tipped her head back, and growled. "Oh, I hate him!"

Remy reached for her. With a quiet sob, she left her chair, sat on his lap, and curled into his arms. He let her emotions vent. When she chose to pull away, he used his thumbs to swipe the tears off of her cheeks. Quinten snoozed in his crib, oblivious to his parents distress.

"Does Wildrose have the same grip on you?" she asked with a darling hiccup that reminded him of a little girl. "Are we destined to the same fate as Claude?"

"The magic has some hold on both of us," Remy mused, though the wording made him cringe. He wouldn't take it back. *Couldn't*, really. Wildrose had a hold on him, and he'd be a fool to deny it.

"I love and trust Wildrose," he continued, "but there's a shadow side to everything, isn't there?"

Her face had wrinkled into a frown as she returned to her own rocking chair. "Briarrose is the shadow side."

"Is it?" he asked quietly. "Because maybe Claude thinks *we* are the shadow side. And if it's true, why does one brother receive the good, and the other receive the bad? What if Claude had been truly earnest and eager for Wildrose to build itself under his tutelage? He might have been a good witch as a result. Better, at any rate."

"There's no comparison, Remy."

Amelie reached over, put her hand on his arm. "Your thoughts are so heavy, I can feel them."

"Why did I get the good magic?"

"What do you mean?"

"Why did Wildrose choose me? It certainly did. That day, in the house, it slammed into me. Flew me here." Remy shook his head, frustrated by the unanswerable. "Claude said he tried and it didn't work. He was . . . angry about it. Wildrose came to me. Why?"

Amelie's hand slipped free as she blew a light raspberry.

"Claude and Wildrose didn't connect in the same way as you. Isn't it obvious? He is not a good witch, Remy. The magic couldn't have worked for him. Obviously," she added with a little frown. "Look at what called to him: Briarrose!"

Her easy dismissal wasn't so easy. There would always be parts of Claude he would love. Memories he clung to. Until he could remove the younger version of his older brother, he would never understand *this* version, nor forget the memories.

Thus, Remy had locked himself into a position of constant uncertainty and wariness around a witch he used to love.

"He wasn't always this way, Amelie. It's impossible for me to let go of who Claude once was and accept who he's become. Not when I know that he's capable of better, because I've *seen* better in him."

Amelie's head turned to the side to more fully face him.

"I'm sorry, Remy. Claude is a hard topic, and I'm sad that you have so much to mourn with him. However, you shouldn't torture yourself with guilt that Wildrose worked for you when it didn't work from Claude. That is nothing you control."

"So you don't think we're foreordained for the lives we lead?"

She drew in a deep breath, shrugged. "I think witches choose, and witches receive. It's as simple as that."

He passed a hand over his eyes, exhausted to the bone. "We're going to figure out how to keep us safe from Claude and his cronies. I promise, Amelie. Wildrose won't fall to Claude. Remember, the houses are the other's antithesis? Briarrose's evil is Wildrose's goodness and strength. There might be safety measures built into the manor that we aren't aware of. And, if we must, you and Quinten could leave for Mathilde's house in the Western Covens until we're sure."

She nodded. The bubbling frustration cleared with her tears. He managed a smile that he didn't feel. "Plus," he added, "Wildrose has continued to pull in new witches that need help. We have two sleeping in the guest bedrooms on the first floor, don't we?"

"Yes."

"The magic wouldn't put witches in danger, so we must be safe."

That seemed to settle her the most. With relief, she nodded. "True. I hadn't thought of that."

"Nor do I think Wildrose will put *us* in danger." He pressed a kiss to her forehead. "We'll be fine, my dear. Just fine. Tomorrow, I will peruse the grimoire and the library. Bertha said books have appeared there lately, none of which she can find a source for. Perhaps they're meant to help. With any luck, Claude will take care of his ugly business on his own. We'll be prepared and come through all right."

Chapter Twenty-One

Quinten, bouncing on Remy's knee, gurgled a spit bubble, then let out a bright peal of laughter. Remy shook his knee up and down in a jiggle that further amused his son, and turned his page in the grimoire.

Nothing there.

The Wildrose grimoire lay open on his desk, just out of reach of Quinten's grubby, grasping hands. Amelie slept upstairs. A new, second pregnancy wrought all the energy from her these days. Meanwhile, Remy contemplated pages he'd long ago memorized. Details about the manor. Facts. Basic layout and measurements. Anything that one might need to know to understand Wildrose.

"One day," Remy said, sliding Quinten to the other knee while he continued his perusal, "this will be yours. Will you love Wildrose as much as your father? We could always grant it to your sister, you know, if that's what your mother is having next."

Quinten patted his hands on the desk in a failed attempt to ravage a quill. Remy turned the next page.

He did his best to keep Quinten away from the ink bottle while loosely scanning the words. He'd read all this dozens of times. In the past, he could remember occasional and very rare changes to the text. How to repair a specific window pane that broke from an errant bird, information about soil type while preparing a garden. When a room altered, the changes were tracked in the overall map near the back.

Something unexpected caught Remy's attention.

He paused.

There.

He hadn't noticed *that* before.

A clause, halfway down the page, snagged his focus.

Wildrose is inherently tied with its sister, Briarrose. In order for each to remain, both must exist. The fate of both manors is connected.

He sucked on his front teeth.

"Well, demmet."

Quinten babbled a fast, "Duh duh duh duh."

Laughing under his breath, Remy said, "Don't tell your mother I'm teaching you curse words already. We have long enough to get in trouble with her as it is; we shouldn't start too soon."

He read the words again.

And again.

Claude's uneasy truth came back to him, but in a different way. The hope that Remy could save Claude as well as his family had been a selfish one, bound up with an evil witch that would destroy Remy because of Claude's promise. Claude might have been more right about Briarrose and Wildrose than he knew.

Suddenly, Remy's suggestion to sell Briarrose seemed like the *worst* possible idea.

If the two manors were tied together through the magic, and

reality nearly proved it, for both had risen at the same time and appeared to fulfill magical identities, for better or worse, then a new owner of Briarrose could undo Wildrose entirely.

Nor could Claude take Remy's other, unstated suggestion and burn the entire thing to the ground before the wickedness grew too powerful.

What of Wildrose?

What then?

If Briarrose fell, would Wildrose immediately follow?

Did the magic actually *bind* them?

He perused farther into the grimoire, but found no answers. No new revelations manifested for him to better understand. The implications continued to spiral through Remy's mind with deepening dread.

Tied together.

Ye gods.

He *had* to save Claude if he were to save himself, and how was that fair? How was it possible?

Of greater discomfort was yet another truth: in some capacity, he understood, in a deeply intimate way, Claude's terror at the thought of selling Briarrose. Remy could no sooner part with Wildrose than he could his own soul. There had been an integration.

A tangling.

Together, they merged into a unit that could not be, so why should he have gotten the good magic? Claude the vile?

Was there a sense of preordination? Did the magic know its masters before they arrived? As if it sought their father, knowing they would come along. Or could fate be such a fickle mistress as to flow through two brothers who once loved each other, and allow them to destroy their only ties through mutual devices?

Love and life were such impossibilities.

Remy flipped the grimoire shut, then opened it again. He

reached for the closest quill, sitting on top of a blotting page, with just enough ink to finish his goal.

"My boy." Remy straightened Quinten on his lap. "I have an idea. Let's put you in the grimoire, eh? Our family line and genealogy may continue forever as the Dauphins of Wildrose. For we belong to the magic. We do. Like my brother," he added under his breath.

As he finished the final stroke of Quinten's name, a call from without drew his gaze higher. Bertha rapped on the door.

"A new family just arrived, sir. They've lost their home to a flood and came to Letum Wood to try to scratch out a life while they rebuild. They found Wildrose."

Grateful to extract himself from the depressing thoughts of his brother, he stood. Quinten came with him, but deftly snatched the quill on his way up. Remy removed the inky feather before Quinten gummed it down his throat.

"Do we have room?" Remy asked. "I thought we were almost full. The manor was unaccountably busy yesterday."

"One witch left this morning, opening a room." Her cheeks flushed bright, as if she'd been scurrying around. "It's been busy."

A reassuring sign.

Or so he hoped.

"Thank you, Bertha. I'll be down to welcome them. I'm sure Wildrose is already preparing their room. Will you check on the kitchen?" His gaze lifted to the clock. "It's almost dinnertime, and last I checked something delicious baked over the fire."

"Joyce is already on it." Bertha smiled sheepishly. "It's nice to have your in-laws here. They're very handy, and Wildrose seems to like them."

Remy smiled an agreement. James and Joyce had been staying on the fourth floor, where they only allowed family to sleep, for the past week. Briarrose's dark affect extended into their home, enveloping them in deep depression, inability to think, and general unwillingness to return.

It all but drove them out.

Amelie insisted they stay, her four youngest sisters amongst them, until they could figure something out. Thus far, no plans had formed. No obvious path to removing Briarrose or the problem of Briarrose manifested.

"Glad to hear it," Remy said. "James and Joyce are excellent witches. Now, it'll be a job and a half getting all these people fed, if you ask me. I'll introduce myself to the family, you commandeer the food with Joyce. Might as well get started."

—

Despite a packed house, Wildrose's visitors settled in with little drama that evening. Most witches, stumbling from a place of deep need or abject fear, had little emotional space for drama. They volunteered to clean up dinner, the house, gather firewood, or draw water from the well. As a system, these good witches were a consistent lot.

That meant something, too.

The effort must please the magic, for it didn't attempt the jobs these witches offered, and populated their needs with eagerness. Another sign of safety and inherent goodness, to Remy's way of thinking.

Amelie awoke after several hours of sleep, refreshed and less nauseous, and swept Quinten away, leaving Remy alone in the office. He paced in front of the bookshelves, uncertain what to do with the heavy thoughts of Claude and Wildrose and Briarrose occupying his mind.

Frowning, he turned to the window, considered going to Briarrose, thought better of it, and turned around. James might be up for a game of Networks, or another discussion on dealing with the Briarrose issue. In fact, he should tell his father-in-law about recent developments with Claude.

Might be—

"Remy?" Amelie pushed into the office, alarm in her eyes. "Remy? Someone is here for you."

A uniformed Captain of the Guard stood behind her, one hand on a sword at his right hip, the other holding a hat he'd clearly taken off when he entered the house. Behind the Captain was a familiar face.

SJ.

For some reason, Remy didn't feel all that surprised to see them there. He braced himself.

"Come in, gentlemen."

Amelie questioned him with her wide gaze, but he only shook his head, pressed a kiss to her cheek, and whispered, "I don't know what they want, but I know who they are. Everything is fine."

Some of her anxiety peeled away as she stepped out of the office, casting one last, uncertain glance over her shoulder before she closed the door. SJ gave Remy a nod in greeting. More than a year had passed since their initial meeting, and Remy's theories about SJ had ranged wildly.

Unlike the Captain, SJ wore nothing out of the usual. A pair of worn brown breeches, a white shirt, and a half smile that looked more wary than welcoming. "Good to see you again, Remy," he said.

Wryly, Remy replied, "Wish I could say the same." He extended his hand to the Captain of the Guards, who accepted the clasp.

"Ralph," the Captain said. "I came on SJ's bidding."

SJ stepped closer. "My name is Saul. Saul Joseph to those who know me well."

"SJ," Remy said.

"SJ," he affirmed. "I'm not a neighbor."

"I already guessed that."

Amused, SJ continued. "Who do you think I am?"

"For a while, I thought you were a paid mercenary. Then I considered that you might work for my brother, or on your own. Ideas have ranged broadly. I figured I'd know eventually. You didn't strike me as the kind of witch to come by only once."

A sense of hilarity danced in SJ's dark eyes. "It's been awhile since I introduced myself."

"Some witches are memorable."

"I think I'm flattered. None of those guesses are correct, Remy. I'm a Protector."

He withdrew the sleeve over his wrist, revealing a mark in black ink. Remy couldn't make sense of the design before SJ covered it up again.

"I'm sorry, what?"

"A Protector." SJ motioned with a tilt of his head to Ralph. "I brought him here to help us out, because there's a developing situation that I've been tracking for a year and a half and it's about to turn ugly. This . . . situation . . . involves you."

"And Claude?"

SJ nodded. "We need to talk about Briarrose and your brother, Remy. He's in grave danger, and so are you."

"I know."

"You know?"

Remy nodded. "Claude came to my office yesterday, asking for help."

SJ and Ralph exchanged surprised glances. "Oh?" SJ asked, brow elevating. "What kind of help?"

"Currency. He owes someone."

"Did he say who?"

"No."

"Did you say yes?"

Remy paused, thought it over, and finally said, "I offered a solution he didn't like. We didn't part well. Not that we ever do," he added drily.

If possible, SJ's frown deepened. He folded his hands in front of him, rolled his lips. "It's more important that we talk than ever before. Please, Remy. If you will, tell us everything."

SJ and Ralph filled the office with a tenuous presence. Remy waved a window open, canting it a palm-span to bring fresh autumn air into the stuffy room. As soon as Remy motioned them into chairs, SJ began to speak.

"Tell us about your brother, Remy."

"Sure." Remy leaned against his desk. "I don't know where to start. What information are you searching for?"

"Tell us more about yesterday, which is when you last saw him?" Ralph asked. A scroll and enchanted quill, spelled so that it didn't require ink from a well, popped into the air and poised brightly, awaiting Remy's reply.

"Yes, that was the last time. He came to me at work because I've asked him not to come to my house. Years ago, while drunk, he attacked the woman who is now my wife. He might have raped her if she hadn't managed to escape. Thus, he isn't allowed here."

Gravely, SJ said, "I'm sorry. I wish I could say that I was surprised."

"Me too."

"What did Claude want?" Ralph asked.

"First, tell me why you're asking."

After an exchanged glance with Ralph that Remy couldn't hope to read, SJ sighed.

"Claude has been dealing with unsavory types for a long time. *Dangerous* unsavory types. He first caught our attention years ago with some underground businesses. Purchasing stolen goods and reselling, that sort of thing. We haven't had proof against his dealings until recently, when Ralph stumbled upon a problem."

Ralph, picking up SJ's subtle handover, said with some hesitation, "I have four witnesses, three women and one male, that have come forward about what's happening at Briarrose."

A building dread pooled in Remy's belly. "What is it?"

"Prostitution," Ralph said, "and slavery. Together," he added, as if the picture hadn't been clear enough. "According to all four, who approached independently from each other, and I don't believe crossed paths at all, Claude has been dealing in prostitution for years. It was his main source of income, though he's created other dealings."

"Gambling," SJ supplied. "Amongst others. Extortion, I would imagine, but we don't have solid proof yet."

Shock made it difficult to breathe. For five eternal seconds, Remy absorbed their revelations. His chest seized, his heart cracked. Physical pain tightened him in a grip that held time still for an interminable length. Recalling the dark shadows in Briarrose, the desperation that tainted the air, Remy hated that he couldn't even doubt their report.

"Claude?" he whispered, hoarse.

Ralph nodded once. "The witnesses were victims, all four. Since they came forward, we've been watching the house. Rather," Ralph tipped his head toward SJ, "*they* have been watching the house."

"The witnesses gave us names of witches who are purchasing time with these enslaved witches," SJ said. "We've observed all of the witches that the witnesses spoke about coming in and out of Briarrose. I've gone in myself," he added, "and confirmed all they've said."

"You couldn't stop it then?"

SJ snorted. "No. The level of illegal practices in that estate were far too advanced for one Protector on a scouting mission to do alone. Not with enough evidence to satisfy the High Priest and Council. Infiltration was extremely difficult, and I had to revise my plan seven times before it finally worked."

A hint of annoyance colored his tone.

"That's why we're helping," Ralph supplied. "We'll need an entire contingent to secure and clear the Briarrose manor. Rumor has it that your estate is a replica of Briarrose." His eyes flickered around. "Reportedly, less evil. I can confidently say that I agree. This seems a perfect antithesis."

"Similar to the structural detail," SJ confirmed, then added, "I stayed a night or two in Wildrose a few months ago. Transformed, of course. It settled questions of whether you and your brother were in business together. Clearly, not the case."

Remy groped for a chair and sat down. He ignored the fact that SJ had stayed in Wildrose under a different persona to do his research. An uncomfortable thought, certainly. He forced himself to focus on the matter at hand. To think, he'd almost loaned Claude the currency to save that awful place.

"Claude said he was in danger," Remy said quickly, thinking of anything that might help. "As I mentioned already, he owes someone currency and doesn't have enough to pay them. Said that he *did* have it, but it disappeared."

The quill scribbled away.

"Theft?" Ralph asked.

Remy shrugged and stammered through a harried explanation. He told them about Claude's visit, his frustration, his deepening tie to the magic of Briarrose. Neither gentleman said a word until after Remy finished his halting summary.

SJ sent Ralph a knowing glance. "Claude knows who is after him," he concluded. To Remy, he added, "We weren't sure if Claude realized what enemies he'd made. Another Protector has overheard plans out of the Tate Covens for retribution against Claude."

"He knows," Remy whispered.

"There's another problem," Ralph said. "Well, there are several other problems with Briarrose, including prostitution, slavery, illegal gambling, and a potential black market poison ring that we haven't confirmed."

The list sickened Remy. "What's the problem?"

"We can't get close to it."

"What?"

"Hedge walls have grown around the exterior," SJ added. "Every time we try to breach them, the four wraiths on the top spew molten fire—aimed at us, I might add. Myself, and another Protector, have tried every spell we can think of, but we can't get in. Either the hedge stops us or some other form of protective magic."

"Tried digging." Ralph added.

"Even tried flying." SJ rubbed an elbow with a grimace, as if remembering a pain. "Didn't work to lower down, either. The wraiths have . . . surprising force."

"I didn't know," Remy admitted.

SJ shook his head. "Doesn't matter. In the end, we can't break the perimeter. Two Guardians are injured after approaching what used to be the walking path. Vines with long barbs attacked them. They're recovering with an Apothecary, who's had to pull each barb out of their skin." SJ's fingers moved a span apart, indicating the length of Remy's two thumb knuckles. "The barbs were that long, and covered in a hallucinogenic poison. The two lads almost went stark-raving mad."

"Will they recover?" Remy asked, aghast.

"Yes, but it'll take awhile."

The thought of Wildrose doing such heinous acts horrified Remy. How could Claude allow it?

Did Claude allow it?

His brother's allusions to the house becoming a monster hadn't left Remy's mind.

"If these issues hadn't cropped up," Ralph continued, "we

wouldn't have involved you, Remy. We would have cleaned Briarrose out already and all of them would be in the dungeons at Chatham Castle."

"It gets worse." SJ grimaced. "There's been a known plot circulating amongst well-known thieves in the lower Central Network Covens to kill the High Priest. We have an inside witch and are tracking it. However, the witch whom Claude owes is heavily involved in the plot to kill our leader. We're . . . concerned . . . that Claude may know something about it, or may be supportive."

Ralph added, "Worse, we think the plot might have been planned at Briarrose. Our inside witch hasn't been able to discover where the actual planning meetings take place, despite integrating in high circles."

Remy rubbed a finger over his lips, shaking his head. While Claude was obviously in over his head, Remy hadn't expected *this*.

"It's hard to think Claude capable of such a thing as plotting to kill the High Priest," Remy admitted, "but I can tell you that he hasn't mentioned it to me."

"We assumed not."

"When we spoke," Remy continued, "what surprised me most was how defensive he became over the manor. He was as possessive as he was frightened. If you were trying to enter, he must have holed up inside to keep it safe."

"Hence the hedges?" Ralph asked.

Remy nodded.

"Can you get in?" SJ asked.

"I don't know."

"Would you be willing to try?" Ralph asked.

"Yes."

SJ released a breath that loosened his tense neck ever-so-slightly. He cast his gaze around, as if he could encompass all of Wildrose in a glance.

"I know your estates are magical twins, or whatever. We were hoping that you might have some ideas. A weakness, perhaps, or insight into the structure of the house."

"I-I don't know," Remy admitted, hands spread. "I know Wildrose, at least a little. The manor has its own magic. We live here, but the magic is really in charge. There's the grimoire." He motioned to the desk with a nod. "I was reading it earlier today, to see if it mentioned Briarrose. It does, but only once. Nothing that would help you gain entry or defeat Claude."

The words nearly choked him. Stated like that, and under this malevolent context, he couldn't help but wonder what they must think of this magic. Wildrose was not Briarrose . . .

. . . or was it?

Did his magic hide wicked schemes? Was it possible that the magical system wasn't supposed to be balanced and Wildrose would turn on them and possess their souls? The repellent thought sent shivers through him. He attempted to force them back, but they lingered like wraiths.

"Is anyone in Briarrose with Claude that you know of?" Remy asked, gaining his feet again. He felt dizzy when he stood, but that might be the ballooning disgust. Or the way it felt when one lost all hope for a loved one.

Ralph shrugged. "We're not sure who's there."

"His assistant is a man named Chase," Remy offered. "Is he inside?"

"We know Chase," SJ said, "and yes. I believe so."

"Briarrose is a busy place." Ralph glanced from Remy to SJ. "It would be odd if some of his business partners or investors or customers weren't able to enter through a different route."

"They must," SJ said. "They conducted a new round of what they call *gathering* last week. We found out too late."

When Remy frowned in question, SJ continued. "Slave gathering. Not just sexual slaves for their prostitution ring, but workers as well. The witches have to swear themselves to the manor for a certain length of time. Some of them are working off debts to Claude. Others are enemies that they're removing from the streets to watch more closely. Many are innocent, plucked from the cities."

Remy fought the urge to vomit.

"Do you communicate with Claude regularly?" Ralph asked.

"No."

"Are the houses . . . connected . . . at all?"

Remy held up two hands. "I don't think so, but I'm not sure. The magic must be, somehow. As quickly as Wildrose was built, so was Briarrose. I believe the magic of each manor relies on the other. There's still much I don't know," he added.

Until this moment, Remy hadn't realized how much they trusted Wildrose. How stupid it might have been for him to do so.

"We can look at Wildrose's grimoire for the blueprints." He used a spell to open it to the right page. Snatches of memory surfaced from when he toured through Briarrose what felt like years ago. "The structure is the same. I've only been inside Briarrose once, when he first announced it, but their similarities were clear."

Remy's gut clenched as his eyes gripped the one sentence he didn't want to see.

Wildrose is inherently tied with its sister, Briarrose. In order for each to remain, both must exist. The fates of both manors are connected.

"It only mentions Briarrose once in here." He swallowed rising panic. "It doesn't say anything about whether the magic will let me access Briarrose because of Wildrose or not. I really don't think so. They're too . . . different."

Disappointment flashed through Ralph's eyes, but he said nothing.

A message appeared in front of SJ. He skimmed it, handed it to Ralph, and said, "Another Brother at the scene says that a few witches arrived through the back hedge. It parted to allow them in. Either Claude is watching from somewhere and sending the magic to allow them, or the house knows these witches."

"It might be the magic," Remy said. "Claude acted as if the magic of Briarrose impacted him. Frightened him, even. If we can get rid of the magic, maybe we can clear this up?"

SJ and Ralph's dubious expressions gave him little hope. Remy flipped through the pages of the Wildrose grimoire, headed toward the middle. Small sketches of the house, shown through a map, revealed the layout of Wildrose. SJ and Ralph remained quiet while Remy thought through a growing idea, bit by bit. Once a rudimentary sketch developed, Remy lifted his head.

"I'll get into Briarrose," he said. "I'll speak to Claude. I can approach my brother, see if I can somehow . . . I don't know . . . remove the magic. Maybe help him understand what Briarrose is doing."

SJ tilted his head back, considered something with a purse of his lips. "Remy, do you understand that Briarrose might not be the problem?"

"Yes," he said, a little too quickly.

Clearly unconvinced, but unwilling to push the issue, SJ shrugged. "If you're willing to enter Briarrose and find a way to let us inside, we'll be there to support you. You'll have Protectors and Guardians available. The goal is to find a way to bring us in, or Claude out."

Remy closed the grimoire.

There is no foreordination, he thought. *Only choices.*

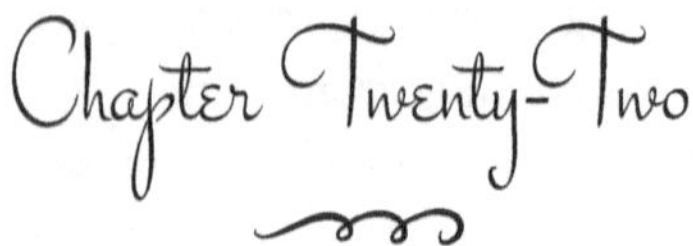

Chapter Twenty-Two

An hour later, Remy approached Briarrose alone.

Gravel ground under his shoes as he walked the drive, toward the hedges. His heart slammed, his hands sweated.

SJ, Ralph, and who-knew-how-many-other Guardians hid somewhere in the neighborhood. While Remy changed his clothes and prepared to leave Wildrose, SJ and Ralph sought out James. He gave them information, a tour of his house, and instructions on where they might use his property to access Briarrose.

Meanwhile, Joyce, Bertha, and Amelie refused to pack and leave. In Amelie's words, *Wildrose is goodness, Remy. We're safe here, or it never would have allowed all these witches to seek assistance. I believe in the inherent goodness of the manor. You must, as well.*

He gave no response to that, but repeated in his mind, *I trust Wildrose,* in an insecure loop.

The reminder didn't help.

Remy turned his focus to Briarrose again. He didn't think about the contingent of Guardians waiting to storm the estate, or the Protectors aiding them. They had plans that hinged on

Remy's inside information. None of their machinations meant anything without him figuring out how to breach Briarrose.

If he could.

As he converged on the giant hedges, their size stymied him yet again. They grew as thick and wide as the days before Briarrose revealed. The sense of wafting evil had intensified. The immoral aura reached out and shook his bones, gripping him in chilly claws. He fought off a shudder and straightened his shoulders.

He had no idea if this would work.

Briarroses shifted in a late evening breeze, their crimson heads darkened along the tips. Their petals were dank, limp, bobbing uselessly, not immune to the gross evil within. Their once-sweet perfume had turned cloying. It burned along his nasal passages.

He paused at the hedge.

If he reached out, he'd touch the thorns and briars. Would the magic reveal something? When Claude disrobed Briarrose, he had emerged from a tunnel. The hedge had been wide enough to burrow into and snake around.

"Claude?" he called. "It's me, Remy. I'm alone. I want to talk to you."

Movement shifted the branches in front of him. They curled, twisting like a mat, to reveal a thin passage that would admit him through if he turned to the side. The short walking space ended in darkness. Vague hints of lighter sky appeared on the other side, but he wasn't certain. He resisted the urge to seek out SJ, doubtful the hedge would allow anyone unseen slide by.

Not worth the risk.

With Amelie and Quinten bright in his mind, Remy pressed onward.

As he stepped into the hedge, it folded behind him, braiding together. If he retreated, he felt relatively certain there would be no visible seam. No break. This claustrophobic space barely admitted him. The bush pressed on each side, littered with menacing thorns.

Panic threatened to distract him when he allowed himself to comprehend that he might have stepped into his death. A living thing this titanic could easily crush him, grinding his bones to dust that would eventually become filthy, poisonous briarroses.

Remy lifted an arm like a wing in front of his face and shuffled into the blackness, refusing to give into those thoughts. Briars clung to his hair, scraped his jacket, as he worked through the wedge. Odors filled the air. Foul, metallic scents that he feared might be the hallucinogenic poison from the barbs. He held his breath.

A hint of fresh air gave way ahead. He stumbled into a clearing, ejected from behind as the hedge closed. On the lawn of Briarrose, Remy drew a gasping breath.

Moonlight irradiated a haunting scene. Briarrose loomed higher than ever, filling the sky with dark shapes and torrid shadows. A lumpy form flickered with a candle on the lower floor, otherwise hidden by nighttime.

The oppressive evil engulfed the evening. Had it always been this strong? Certainly not. The intensity of Briarrose's mighty presence had increased. The hair on the back of his arms stood. He didn't have the greatest interest in sensing magic as a skill, but he couldn't help it here. The ignoble impression overcame him, oppressive and overbearing, at the same time. He endured the rigor as it escorted him to the manor.

Despite instinct urging him to escape through the hedge before it was too late, Remy pressed on. For the brother he once loved.

For answers.

For the sake of his family, and for Wildrose.

Besides, he had a feeling Briarrose kept him here for a reason.

Remy crossed the lush lawn. The thick carpet had a spongy, healthy texture, the emerald so brilliant it was garish. Moonlight brightened black-petaled flowers bobbing along the edge of the walking path. He saw vague blurs in the manor, no details, as he strode through more briarrose bushes and their gleaming, crimson vines.

No break in the hedges.

No obvious weakness.

Briarrose hedges grew tall enough to blanket two estates, stacked on top to bottom, and still not reach the zenith.

Tough luck for SJ, thus far.

Remy turned his attention forward. The interior of Briarrose appeared abandoned. No movement shuffled past the windows. Curtains had been drawn on every floor except the very bottom. The wide-open windows revealed two stationary candles and one torch, which cast a weak glow. As he climbed the stairs leading to the main porch, a rustling movement shifted near the upper floor windows. Remy studied it until he moved out of sight.

At the double-door entrance, Remy stalled. His heart thudded so hard it might have knocked for him. He drew in a stabilizing breath. Whatever happened after this, there would be no return.

He knocked.

The reverberating sound echoed like an old man's groan.

Footsteps approached.

Quick.

Quicker.

A shadowy figure appeared through the dark stained glass mural on the double doors. The image portrayed was a hideous creature with tentacles and claws, beckoning him inside. Remy ignored the gnarled imagery, a Briarrose specialty, and focused on the movement within.

Locks slid free and the door swung open.

Chase stared out.

"How'd you get in here?" he asked.

"The hedge admitted me."

Chase glanced past his shoulder, then around the yard, up to the ceiling of the porch awning, and back to Remy. With great reluctance, he widened the door opening.

"Quick, then. C'mon."

The door closed as briskly as it opened, and the prickle of tightening shadows wrapped Remy from without. He shuddered as Chase led him away from the open windows. They entered the main hallway. It branched right or left in a T junction. Thus far, no other obvious entry points, except breaking through the windows.

If they could breach the hedges.

Once they were under the stairs that wound up the foyer, Chase stopped. "You really shouldn't be here, Remy."

"I know."

"So why are you?"

"Claude came to me asking for help. I want to talk to him about it."

"And?"

"And what?"

"What do you want to talk to him about?"

"Help."

Chase scowled. "He needs currency, not conversation. Give me the coins or the details and I'll send them to him."

Cooly, Remy replied, "I'm not granting one thousand pentacles to my brother's Assistant, thank you very much. He's my brother. I'm . . . worried. I want to help."

The intent was real enough, even if the *help* that he would offer wasn't what Claude wanted.

Chase shoved a hand in his pocket and fidgeted with something inside. He drew out a cheroot, lighting the rolled tip with a spell. The unnerving joviality of Chase's other interactions was lacking.

"There's no helping the boss anymore. Even if you had the currency," Chase eyed his clothes, his empty hands, and added, "which I doubt. Currency isn't enough."

Ah, Remy thought. *Back to boss now, are we?*

"Things with Claude are that bad?"

Chase grimaced, smoke streaming from partially split ips. "Worse. Downright dangerous. It's why the hedges reappeared. The witches he owes currency? They're angry. Quite angry. He expects them to attack at any minute."

Remy motioned around. "If it's such a bleak and dangerous outlook, why are you still here?"

"You think we can escape?"

"Can't *you*? Leave Claude to his own punishments."

Chase scoffed. "At some point, every good ruffian has to accept that sometimes you go down with the ship, eh? No changing that. We all take risks, and we all die."

With a tap of a finger, he flicked ashes onto the rug, covered them with his heel, and ground them into the carpet fibers.

"If you really want to see the boss, you'll have to go in on your own. I won't have any part of your arrival, 'cause no one is supposed to be here and I'm not getting in trouble for you."

Remy staved off the helpless terror that such sentiments might inspire. The chance that he'd escape Briarrose grew more bleak with every passing second.

Ignoring those instructions, Remy asked, "You can't transport out?"

Chase laughed again. Hollow, loud, and long. "Not a chance! The magic has a better grip on this place than that."

"So it is the magic that's made Briarrose so . . . sinister?"

"What do you think?" Chase shot back as quickly. "Which is more evil? Man or magic?"

Remy pressed his lips.

How to answer?

"Someone admitted me just now. Was it Briarrose, or Claude? Your response matters!"

"Don't know. Other witches keep trying to come in, but it's pointless. They'll never be stronger than Briarrose, and we don't know why it admits some witches and not others."

Remy couldn't help wondering if *we* really meant *Chase*. Did Chase and Claude know everything together?

Chase lifted his arm, motioning down the hallway to their right. "Told you, I'm done with this. You want to make a bigger mess of things, he's down there. Good luck."

Chase made himself scarce.

Alone in the heart of Briarrose, Remy drew in his surroundings. It smelled musty and left a metallic taste in his dry mouth. A quick scan revealed no candles, and attempts to conjure one led to failure. With all the curtains drawn and doors closed, the path to Claude resembled heading into the blackest fog. Not a single light cast illumination for depth or texture.

Bleak miasmas awaited.

Remy pressed into the dark. His tentative steps made no sound, muffled by carpet. As he reached his arms to the side, feeling the edge of the wall, the breaks in the doorframes, and counted his way to the end, he pondered exactly what he meant to do once he found Claude.

Where did his brother hide?

In what state?

Remy tried a doorknob, but it didn't give way. He attempted another, but it was locked, too. Only a growing, impending sense of evil drew him farther down the corridor. If he truly wanted to find Claude, he'd follow the trail. The dire, filthy, horrific, magical trail that beckoned with vibrant malalignment.

At the last door on the right, he stopped.

He could sense it.

Remy glanced over his shoulder. Vague shadows illuminated furniture outlines near the foyer, distantly lit with moonlight. Society felt thousands of worlds away. Courage fled. Good sense drove him to leave Briarrose and return to relative comfort and safety before it was too late. The urge fizzled fast.

He grasped the doorknob, which gave way beneath his touch. The door creaked open. Remy pressed against the wood, swinging it inward. A pace at a time, a room revealed.

Light bounced on a gothic display of terror, revealing collections of knickknacks and oddities. Gaudy curtains hid shelves, while others remained open for perusal. A disembodied hand floated in a glass jar to his right. Ice slid through Remy's veins. He froze when a chilly voice greeted him.

"Brother," Claude called. "Please, enter."

Claude sat on a throne in the middle of a room, elevated off the floor on a dais. Sculpted black clouds swirled around the tops and sides of the throne, studded with screaming skulls, hollow eyes, and the capes of swirling wraiths. Bones formed the chair legs, and black silk cushions puffed up the sides in giant wings.

Claude's leering smile and bright eyes illuminated something terrible and bleak. He sat there as a living manifestation of Briarrose.

"Remy, Remy, Remy." Claude beckoned with a curl of his fingers. "How delightful to have you in our throne room."

Remy swallowed, startling when the door slammed shut behind him. A lock drove home, sealing him inside.

"Our?"

Claude straightened his spine off the chair. His smile didn't sway. He drummed his fingertips along the armrest.

"We, Remy. The magic, and me. *Our* home. We're glad to have you. Always. Always glad to welcome my brother in bone and magic. Isn't it wonderful, our double ties? We haven't seen eye-to-eye in quite awhile, not since you left. Since mother and father died. But now, we share this lovely magic. We're twins, Remy."

His maniacal ramblings reminded Remy of a deep delusion. The radiation of such soul-darkness came from Claude as much as it came from the room. Whatever wasn't right in this house couldn't be just the magic.

Magic infected him.

Or did Claude infect the magic?

Remy's heart bottomed out. He had felt so certain the path would be clear. He'd see his brother, extract the source of the problem, and all would come to ends. Claude's sinister sneer, his hooded gaze, muddied the water. Remy's frightened brother existed no more.

In his place stood *this* man.

Briarrose was not a controlling, lurid entity, it was a stone-and-mortar estate. A building, imbued with magic, at the mercy of its owner. The title of controlling, lurid entity belonged to Claude.

Claude maintained the house, the hedge.

The evil.

The confirmation of Remy's greatest fear sank through him like a hefty stone. The erasure of hope was not a surprise, but regrettable. Devastating. Remy swallowed his rising despair, shoving the responsibility of brotherly love as far out of mind as he could.

Claude plucked something with his fingertips, in a soothing gesture. Like a child. Only after a few moments of study did Remy realize it was the Briarrose grimoire. Claude cradled it to his chest like a beloved toy. More than that. A black sash strapped the grimoire to his torso in a crossed pattern.

"I know about the Protectors and the Guardians outside, Remy. They're invisible, but not really."

"I didn't see any."

Claude smiled. "Sure you didn't. There's loads of them,

hiding themselves, piled next door at the Leroy's. Inside, it too. We're not stupid, you know."

The unnerving plural set Remy's hair on edge. He shuffled back a step, but his shoulders collided with the wall.

"I love Briarrose, Remy," Claude sang, "as I know you love Wildrose. You must, or else the magic would not have admitted you. Certainly, I didn't want you in here, but what can one do? Like recognizes like."

"My love for Wildrose is nothing like what you have with Briarrose. This is . . . vile."

Claude ignored the insult and flicked one hand.

"Say what you want about it, it's the same magic. Balance, you understand. This magic *is* an experiment, you realize? What happens when one half of a constructed magic utterly stabilizes the other? When a system has to be whole, it requires all working parts. Magic like this, which appears so powerful and independent, is a lie. Just like me. Just like you. All of it. Lies."

Claude tipped his head to his shoulders and began to caterwaul a horrible, warbling melody that extrapolated his adoration of Briarrose.

Was he drunk?

Raving mad?

The agony of watching Claude unravel was infinitely worse than anything they'd experienced together.

"It's magic doing this to you, Claude. Let it go."

Claude laughed, a gurgling, loose noise that reminded Remy of blowing wind. Claude propped a leg up on the side of his throne-like chair, draping his head off the other. One arm hung limp off the other side. He didn't *sound* drunk. No bottles littered the floor, no stench of ipsum in the air.

"Let it go," Claude sang, then laughed again. He crossed his arms over his stomach, laughing so hard he doubled up, curling like a dead roach. "It's magic," Claude said in mocking mimicry. "Oh, Remy, you child. You naive, idiotic, child."

"We'll destroy it together, Claude. You and me. We'll get rid of the estate and the grimoire."

Claude leaped to his feet with a snarl. "Don't you see, fool? Destroying Briarrose will destroy Wildrose! We are tied to these estates, you and I. Irrevocably. One cannot survive without the other. Are you willing to destroy your precious Wildrose just to have lordship over what is mine? Wholly mine?"

Emotion rose in Remy's throat at the thought.

Destroy his manor?

He couldn't.

And yet . . . such was true.

It had to be.

Wildrose had warned him through the sentence in the grimoire, but he didn't want to believe it. The helplessness was an overwhelming force. Remy refused to succumb to it. Not yet. There was still time for despair. Later. When he didn't have to think this fast.

"Do you remember when we were ten?" Remy asked as Claude staggered into the throne again. Once he flung himself back into the oversized chair, he hung his sweaty head, chin to chest, as if he gave up. "Do you remember when we found Father's stash of darker grimoires? The ones that he kept until they could sell, or he donated to the Great Library of Burke?"

Slowly, Claude lifted his head.

"Yes."

"Do you remember how the house changed after the dark grimoires were cleared out? We always felt better. It's why he never kept them for very long. If they wouldn't sell, he didn't like having them. Said it *altered our emotions to be too near the darkness.*"

Claude scoffed. "You prove your innocence, fool. You told yourself a story about dark magic. You told yourself a story that you *believed*. A story about magic costing something, demanding something, but you made it up. Dark magic doesn't create an aura. It's *you* that creates the aura. Your judgment and disparagement against the noble darker arts and their pursuit of power."

As Claude stood, Remy spoke louder.

"Father told us that dark magic settled in the bones if you left it in one place too long, that it could seep out of the grimoires and into the house around it. That's why Father never left them in the house."

Claude peered at Remy through a slack expression and slotted eyes. "Why does it matter?

"Because Father was right. You've been swimming in awful magic, Claude. You can't see it, either. You're too . . . ingrained. Enmeshed. You need to get out from under the magic. Once it doesn't have power over you, then you'll understand. Everything will improve."

With each panting breath Claude sucked in, the edges of his lips lifted until something like a smile stretched across his face. He shoved away from the dais and closed the distance between them. A vinegary smell accompanied him.

"Remy, you hopeful mess. You don't get it, do you?" Claude leaned close to whisper in Remy's ear. His breath was a hot roll of steam. "The magic isn't keeping *me* here. I'm keeping *it* here."

Claude thumped the cover of the grimoire with his fisted hand. A hollow *thunk* sang in reply. He shoved past Remy, slamming a hand into Remy's shoulder and nearly knocking him over.

He laughed.

"Roam around, Remy! See whatever you want. Partake in the delights of the flesh you've probably always denied yourself. Heroes like you are always gratingly perfect, but no need to pretend such goodness here. Briarrose is the place you go when being the *good guy* doesn't feel good anymore. Slake your lust. Partake of delights your wife would never grant you . . . just don't expect to leave. No one will get out of here alive. Too bad you walked into your own death."

———

Messages went nowhere.

All windows remained locked.

Doors were enchanted closed.

Not a hint of broachable space anywhere.

No witches lurked in the first-floor rooms, most of which were locked. The few Remy managed to peer into made him want to vomit, so he recoiled. Everywhere, darkness. Fog lingered on the manor, removing the chance of escape. He couldn't see outside the hedges. The sun might burn bright overhead. He'd never feel it. Claude had created a sinister cocoon that sucked up goodness, light, and time.

Claude's gibberish about being stuck in Briarrose didn't strike fear in Remy's heart yet. There was room to bargain, to assess, to test. He had a chance to return home because somewhere, locked in those layers, existed his brother. The question was how to save Wildrose in the meantime.

Remy wandered Briarrose until he found what he sought.

The library.

It wasn't situated in the same place as the Wildrose library. At least, not that he could tell. The debauched decorations and infernal lighting made it impossible to know exactly where he stood at any given moment. He wasted too much time constantly reorienting himself.

When Remy stepped inside the library, he thought he heard screams. Distant, ghoulish sounds that no human could make. He froze, an ear cocked. After listening for a minute, the sound didn't repeat.

If books could cry, they would make that sound.

He strolled along the periphery of the room, viewing the titles on the spines, and attempted a mental inventory.

No books existed here that he'd bother with. Occult topics with demented titles, such as *Soul Sucking Spells* and *The Worst of It Is Yet to Come* and *Madam Yancy's Guide to Beheading*. If ghouls had a library, this would be their favorite. All the worst topics festered in silence. Had Briarrose created them? Had Claude called to them? Both, probably.

Wildrose hadn't populated her own library. If the two estates were truly opposites in all ways, logic followed that Briarrose would arrive complete, instead of with space that allowed growth and autonomy, like Wildrose.

To Remy's deepening frustration, nothing in the library helped. No obvious grimoires, no insights to the manor. Nothing that spoke about Briarrose, like ledgers, records, a receipt. He doubted Claude would be that organized.

The scuffle of a foot drew his gaze high. Remy pushed away from the shelf where he slouched as Chase entered the room. As before, a sense of tired resignation filled him. They stared at each other.

"So," Chase drawled. "You survived."

"Here I stand."

"I thought he'd kill ya," Chase admitted.

"Thanks for letting me walk into that alone," Remy muttered.

Overhead, a reverberating *bang* and the crash of shattering glass broke the air.

"Things must not have gone well with Claude," Chase drawled. He nodded to the ceiling. "He's throwing things and shouting. Only does that when he's really mad."

Remy ran a hand through his hair. "No." He shook his head. "It didn't go well."

"Better you than me."

Remy fought not to roll his eyes. The callousness of Claude's minions would never cease to annoy him.

A new thought occurred to Remy as Chase dug in his pockets, no doubt seeking another cheroot. Perhaps Remy didn't need the library to tell him about the manor. He might need *Chase*.

"How long have you worked for Claude?" Remy asked, striving for a bored, conversational tone.

Chase, not seeming all that surprised that Remy broke the conversation barrier first, said, "As long as I got memories."

"How long is that?"

"I don't remember anything before I was eight."

"Oh?"

Chase gently knocked a palm against the side of his head. "Carriage accident. My pap was driving. Slammed into another carriage one night. Drunk, like he always was. I went flying out of the back, slammed into a tree. Guardians came. Apothecaries. Didn't see me, hidden in a shrub." Chase shoved his hands into a pocket, abandoning the search for a cheroot. "Who knows how long I lay there?"

"Who found you?"

"Claude."

Remy tilted his head. "Really?"

"Claude found me," he asserted. "Not sure how. Maybe I was groaning. I only remember waking up in a room in a pub. Claude was smoking a pipe, speaking with someone through the door. He wouldn't let them in. Didn't understand until later why not."

"Why?"

Chase flashed a dark smile. "Slavers. I reckon it's when he first met them, learned what they did. Ironic, right? Wouldn't let them have *me*, but . . ."

Remy's upper lip curled. Chase waved it off. "I can't remember what they said, my brain didn't work right for ages after slamming so hard into the tree, but I think he bargained for my freedom."

"Paid for you?"

Chase shrugged again. "Hard to tell, and he won't talk about it. I only tried asking once, but he cuffed me on the side of the head and told me to never ask again."

The irony almost drove Remy to laughter. It didn't make sense. Closing his eyes didn't stave off the growing headache.

"I'm sorry, Chase."

Dumbfounded, Chase stared at him.

"Sorry?"

"About my brother."

"You're sorry that he saved me?"

"No. I'm glad he saved you. I'm just sorry about everything else. His . . . behavior, I mean. You deserve better than what he's given you, even if it was a second chance at life."

Chase reared back, pressed his lips together, and said nothing. For a dazed ten seconds, neither spoke. Clearing his throat, Chase said, "No one has ever told me that I deserve anything before."

"That's too bad.'

A rolling *thud-thud-thud* spiraled over the floor, as if something heavy and round had just been thrown. Chase motioned to the ceiling with his head.

"He wasn't always like this, you know. In terms of bosses, I could have it far worse. He feeds me. Gives me a little currency. Work my legs off, sometimes, but what else would I be doing?"

Sounds like slavery to me, Remy almost said, but withheld. Chase wouldn't give him any information if Remy pushed him to a defensive state. Whatever Chase was or wasn't, he held loyalty to Claude.

"My brother was once a good man. It's . . . hard to see him like this."

"It was the fire that broke him."

"Fire?"

Chase hummed in his throat. "Your parents? That fire. That's what changed for him. I knew him before, and I've known him after. Wasn't pretty."

Remy frowned. "I know *what* fire, but I don't know what you mean. The loss of my parents broke him?"

"No. Starting the fire."

Remy sucked in a breath. "He started the fire?"

Chase leaned back, suddenly aware that he might have said something he shouldn't. When Chase tensed, gaze sliding to the door, Remy clamped a hand on his skinny arm.

"What did you say?"

"I don't know for sure!" Chase rushed to say, hands held high. His long fingers quaked. "I only know what I've heard when he's been drunk. Really drunk. Sometimes, he gets stupid drunk and he doesn't know what he's saying. Those times, he's blubbered about starting a fire. About deaths on his shoulders. Stuff like that. It makes sense! After the fire, Claude was different. Meaner. It's when he started to really get dark, you know?"

"Tell me everything."

"There had been a fight. That's all I really know. A fight between Claude and someone else?"

"My father?"

"Maybe. After it happened, Claude only explained a few things. When drunk, he never rambled about *who*. Just said that he had been angry and they fought. Swung something, maybe? I think he blacked out, because he spoke about waking up to smoke. He crawled out, found blood on his hands. Found you, I think?"

The night of his parents death replayed through Remy's mind in shades. The nightmare. The screams in his dreams. The sense of blurred reality, and waking up to the smell of smoke.

Claude had been . . . blunted. Shock did that to a witch,

though. By the time Remy escaped the flames, the house was ablaze and too far gone to save. The timeline certainly was fuzzy.

Amelie had voiced suspicions over Claude starting the inferno, even on accident, hadn't she?

"They fought," Remy whispered, "about the house. The night before, Father said he wanted to speak to his legal witch about the house. He meant to give it to me instead of Claude . . ."

The memory whispered from the depths of his most deeply suppressed horrors. How right that Briarrose would help him reclaim the sordid nightmares he intentionally locked in the darkest spaces.

Chase, head slightly down, listened without interruption.

"Claude had been drunk and a little angry since my return," Remy continued with rote focus, "but he'd always been angry. That wasn't new. Father and Claude always had tiffs. That also wasn't new, but . . . I hadn't . . ."

Remy shook his head, weakened by grief. Could their argument have driven Claude to this desperate state?

Underneath Claude's diabolical exterior, did he once love Father?

"When?" Remy demanded. "When did he tell you this?"

"Loads of times. Told you, whenever he's truly sotted. He sobs like a child, too. Apologizes. Says he doesn't deserve them, or the ancestral land. That you're the better man. It's why I came to you that one time, when I thought he'd die. Figured that, if he thought you were a good witch, it was worth a try. And, if he died, you'd need to know eventually, anyway. Better to die with a brother than without, to my way of thinking."

Remy ignored the strange logic of the underworld and rubbed a hand over his eyes. James had advised him to let go of the questions and not put himself through the agony of wondering whether his parents could have or should have lived. Somehow, Remy had been able to dismiss it from his mind.

Claude had not.

"Ye gods," Remy muttered. Right when he thought he understood the depths of depravity he dealt with, more information arrived.

When would it stop?

A thud crashed overhead, so loud Remy startled. He winced when a second bang resulted in a distant spray of broken glass.

Chase grimaced. "He's throwing a fit again. Does that, you know? Stalks around, breaks stuff. Briarrose fixes it, so he breaks it again. It's his way. Well, if you say something to Claude about the fire, don't mention me, all right?"

"Any chance we can get the grimoire off of him?"

"No."

"Have you tried?"

Chase laughed.

Taking that as a negative, Remy lifted his eyebrow. "Is he serious when he says that no one can leave Briarrose?"

"Yes."

"What about letting others in? Could we do that without Claude?"

Chase mimicked his lifted brow. "Like the Guardians?"

"Yes."

"Not a prayer."

"Why?"

"He won't allow it. The hedge will eat anyone that tries."

"Has it actually eaten a witch?"

"Sure has."

Remy hid a wince. What a horrific death.

"Does Claude or Briarrose control the perimeter?"

The question startled Chase, because he stared at Remy for a long minute. "Is there a difference between them?"

"There has to be."

"Let's hope, eh?"

Remy shifted, running his bottom teeth through his lip

before he asked, "Do you see that you're enslaved by Claude also?"

With little change in expression, Chase asked, "Whatcha mean?"

"Claude might have saved you years ago, but he kept you as much a slave as any others. Your life is not tied into Claude's, no matter what debt he's manipulated you into believing. You can go."

Chase shifted, clearly uncomfortable. "That doesn't sound right. Claude says I'd die without him."

"You wouldn't."

"But—" Chase's lips sealed. He scowled. "I . . . I don't think . . . if he heard . . ." Chase glowered, arms tight across his chest. His livid expression gave Remy a thrill of hope.

He pressed harder.

"If I gave you the chance to escape without Claude finding you, would you take it?"

After a long moment of searching thought, Chase unwound. His arms hung at his sides again.

"Yes."

"Would you leave the streets to create a better life away from Claude?"

Wary, Chase nodded.

"I can give you that."

"You're lying."

"Why? You know Wildrose, right? It's what we do."

"He'd find me!"

"Not from the dungeons."

After another eternal scrutiny, Chase tilted his nose into the air and peered at Remy with slotted, suspicious eyes.

"How?"

"First, we need to distract Claude long enough to send a message outside of Briarrose. Can we?"

Disbelieving, Chase asked again, "The Guardians?"

"Yes."

He held up both hands. "I'm not doing it! Boss'll slaughter me if I betray him while I'm in the same house."

"Not if he couldn't reach you. I'll be with Claude, not you."

After another too-long pause, Chase asked, "You're serious?"

"Dead serious."

"You could really keep me safe from him?"

"Really."

A hint of interest flickered in his eyes. Taking his only advantage, Remy quickly asked, "Are the hedges enchanted?"

"Yes."

"Controlled by Claude?"

Chase nodded.

"Does Claude watch them constantly?"

"Guess so?"

Another reverberative bang smashed upstairs. "How is he controlling the perimeter while also throwing a tantrum?" Remy asked with increasing exasperation. "He has to be exhausted. It won't last forever, right?"

Chase held up both hands in a placating gesture. "I'm not the brains, sir. I just do what he tells me to do, sleep under his roof, and eat everyday . . . for the most part."

Remy ignored the affectation of innocence for now.

"Are there still witches in Briarrose?"

Incredulous, Chase cried, "Of course there are witches in Briarrose! Where else would they go? It's not like they can just leave, can they?"

Remy gritted his teeth.

"Where are they?"

"Third floor work rooms." Chase jerked a thumb down the hallway. "Locked inside."

"How many?"

"Ah . . . fifteen?"

Ye gods, the filth of this operation. By sheer willpower, Remy forced his voice to moderate.

"Do you know the spells to free them?"

"Sure. Claude had me lead customers to the rooms all the time. Quick enchantment, not all that strong. Why?"

"Let's assume that Claude doesn't have constant control over the hedge boundary," Remy said, pacing. "Which means we could get a note or two outside. We can get *you* outside, which means we could also escort *them* free."

"Better not try. It'll only make him angry."

"That," Remy said hoarsely, "is exactly what I want. It would make our job a little easier, believe it or not."

Chase appeared dubious. "You want to tick him off?"

"You bet I do."

Tapping his teeth together, Remy fell into thought. His initial plan had already fallen to pieces, but another one cobbled together in its place. He spun to face Chase again, infusing eagerness and confidence into his voice. Chase would never agree if he knew how much Remy quaked.

"I've got it," he announced. "A plan. It's wild, and might not work."

"Sold me," Chase muttered darkly, shoving his hands into his pockets.

Remy held out an arm.

"Are you choosing freedom? Or are you choosing slavery?"

For a full minute, Chase stood in the same spot. An internal debate roved behind glassy eyes. If Chase had true allegiance to Claude—given their history, it was a fair bet—then he might reveal Remy's motivations instead of taking the message.

All would be over.

But if Chase believed in something better . . .

Chase said, "I'll only do it if you guarantee that I don't have to see him ever again."

"I'll vow it."

"You will?"

Remy wiggled his fingers. Chase immediately clasped his arm. Magic coursed through Remy's elbow, to his heart center, as he stated the vow. When it finished, Chase gaped. "You're bloody mad."

"I'll have to be, for this to work."

With less certainty, Chase asked, "Exactly what am I doing?"

"Delivering a message."

Remy held out a hand. With silent magic, he conjured a blue-white wisp. The liquid spell commanded quite simply, obeying each unspoken direction. The cloudy spell navigated like a fog, sliding over his knuckles, fingers, and wrist in a swirl, and then gathering above. A familiar face formed then, drawn from deep memories.

Father, as Remy remembered him. Remy observed the loving smile, joyful expression, and held back tears.

The smoke dissipated.

"Briarrose doesn't suppress all magic," he concluded. "At least, not in this room. Does any suppression exist elsewhere?"

"Just the slave rooms. So they can't escape," Chase added helpfully. "There's no currency in runaways, or so the boss always said."

Remy's gut twisted.

"Right," he muttered. "C'mere. I'll show you what I mean to do. Expect the Guardians to arrest you, but I'll plead on your behalf when this is all over. Let's face it, your options are bleak either way. Die with Briarrose, or hazard a chance with the Guardians and Protectors waiting outside. Claude isn't going to come out of this unscathed. It'll be the prison, or death. Let's hope for the former."

Chapter Twenty-Three

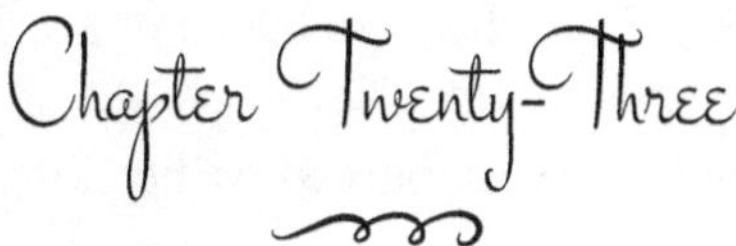

Twenty minutes later, Remy approached the room directly over the library.

When he pressed an ear to the door, no sound stirred. With any luck, Claude had accidentally knocked himself out during his frenzy. The fact that this entire plan hinged on Chase executing his commands with exactness only made the situation feel more fraught. He'd succumbed too quickly. Or, perhaps, Chase actually recognized his chance at freedom.

Would it work?

It must.

After Chase released the workers, he agreed, under a magical vow, to take them and two envelopes to the back hedge, out of sight of Claude's current windows. If Remy did his job correctly, Claude would be distracted, allowing Chase to destroy a small part of the hedge with a spell. The workers and Chase would slide free. The envelopes would race to SJ and Ralph, who should be waiting somewhere on the other side.

Meanwhile, Remy would deal with Claude.

Remy stared at his hands, attempting to draw courage for the confrontation. Amelie would be at home, on edge with tension, but blissfully unaware of how precarious his position. It's what he wanted.

She shouldn't know this terror existed.

"Amelie, my dear, I'm sorry. I don't know what will happen to our home when I put this plan into motion, but forgive me, whatever it is."

The back of his throat burned as he closed his eyes. He squeezed both tight. There was one answer to the Briarrose problem. He didn't know what the solution would mean for Wildrose, but he knew the path.

"Wildrose," he whispered, "forgive me. But I think that it's possible you were never meant to exist in your full power forever. I see it. Such strength, in a balanced system . . . you're not long for *this* world. This was always your destiny."

Lashes wet, he opened his eyes. An unnerving silence swelled through Briarrose, setting his hair on end. He set his attention on the door.

His brother waited inside.

Remy had to bargain with a madman, draw him to the edge of sanity, and tip him over. In the chaos, he must also obtain a grimoire that might resist his touch. Briarrose may not have the sentience Claude attributed to it, but it may not desire Remy close. If he accomplished those fraught tasks, he had to figure out how to destroy said grimoire.

"All in a day's work," Remy muttered.

He knocked.

At first, nothing happened. He waited so long that his knuckles lifted again, his lips parted to speak, when the door flung open. Claude, hair wild, clothes askew, loured from within. The grimoire remained lashed to his chest.

"What?" he sneered. "The delights of Briarrose not to your high-handed enjoyment, Remy?"

To Remy's greatest relief, ipsum stained Claude's breath. Inebriation would make this easier.

With a trembling voice, Remy said, "Nevermind that. Claude, is Briarrose haunted?"

Claude's eyebrows crashed together.

"What?"

"Let me in, please," Remy whispered, hurriedly, and then with greater fervor. "Please let me into the room! There's a bloody ghost coming after me."

Dazed, Claude stepped back. Remy raced inside, whipped around, slammed the door shut. He sprawled against it, arms spread, breathing fast.

"Don't go out there!" he hissed.

"Why?"

Remy sucked in a breath, closed his eyes. His shoulders lifted and fell. "A ghost followed me here."

"What?"

"A ghost!" he cried. "I swear, it looked like Father."

Claude paled.

"Father?"

"He said something." Remy pressed a hand to his forehead. "I couldn't really tell. He shouted. You know how he shouted?"

Mute, Claude nodded.

"Yelling about fire and murder and Mother and—"

Claude shuddered and separated himself, staring at the door in horror. Remy forced his hands to shake as he joined Claude's side, mimicking his terror. Swallowing audibly, Remy continued.

"Father said . . . they were murdered, Claude. He said he'd come to face their murderer. Said that Briarrose has conjured them, called them here. The house *wants* them to chase us. I . . . I don't know what it means."

"No!" Claude shouted. "No!" He whirled around, slammed his palm into the wall. It shivered, then cracked. Remy's eyes darted to a clock over the door. The minute and hour hands inched forward.

In one minute, Chase should have all the workers free.

In five, they should be at the back door.

In seven, at the hedge.

In ten, they'd vanish.

Remy initiated a spell that wasn't complicated, but required precision. A blue-white wisp dropped to the floor and swirled in rotating circles. It slid underneath the door. Remy finished the first layer of the spell. Light flashed.

Claude, stumbling toward a desk on the other side of the room, blubbered about currency and fairness. He didn't notice the whitish fog.

Remy trailed behind his brother, wrenching his face into confusion. "Who was it, Claude? Who murdered Father? Was it someone you know? You knew his business associates better than me. Did a deal go wrong? If we're to get rid of his ghost, we must—"

Remy broke off with a gasp. He shouted in terror, and rushed behind Claude. A coil of smoke glided into the room. As he initiated the second layer of the spell, a percussive *bang-bang-bang* rattled the door. The gauzy substance gathered ballast.

Claude screamed.

From behind Claude, Remy began the third layer, lips moving soundlessly. A thunderous voice bellowed from where the wisp ballooned.

"I have come for the truth!" it shouted. The imitation of Father's voice wasn't perfect. A bit too trilling and high. Clearly, a voice wrought from memory. Claude's face had gone two shades paler.

The clock said tick-tick-tick. Chase should be approaching the hedge. A fourth layer of magic.

"The truth!" Father's ghoul cried.

Remy snatched Claude before he dropped into a faint. In the lurid, strange place between consciousness and reality, Claude mumbled.

"Say it again, Claude," Remy urged. "I can't hear you over Father!"

For dramatic effect, a second round of banging rattled the door. Claude's head fell onto his chest, bobbing stupidly. He stuttered a few incomprehensible words. The blue-white apparition hovered, requiring another repetition, and a fifth layer, to advance further into the room.

Claude gave a strangled cry.

"Father!"

Remy longed for Claude to clear the accusation. The fire could have been an accident or a terrible combination of moments. It could have been *anything*.

"Father," Claude gasped. "I'm sorry. I'm sorry!"

"The truth," the ghoul pleaded. "Tell Remy the truth!"

Claude breathed raggedly. He lifted his lolling head with a sluggish daze, as if he arrived from a hollow tunnel. Bloodshot spiderwebs crawled through his sclera. He hesitated.

"Remy?"

"Yes?"

Claude shook his head.

Desperate, Remy applied another repetition of the fifth layer. The specter advanced in a cloud-like pool. Shrill, likely from Remy's emotion, Father shrieked, "I shall avenge our deaths!"

"Me!" Claude shouted, sobbing. "Father, it was me! I killed you. Your disappointing son!"

Though Remy expected it, the shock hit with stunning force.

"Claude?"

Claude threw himself out of Remy's arms. Remy scrambled to catch him, but Claude slammed to the floor and caught himself with his forearms. Greasy hair spilled in rigid clumps onto his torn, stained shirt.

"I killed them, Remy!" He sobbed. "Mother, I'm sorry. I'm

so sorry! Father and I fought. I was drunk. I don't remember everything. Only . . . only the rage. Father . . . you yelled, too!" Claude tilted his head back, glowering at the ghost. "You told me you were disappointed. That Remy deserved the house, and I wasn't good enough."

A cold fist held Remy's throat captive. Had he the ability to conjure words, he would have nothing to say. His mind felt slow. Numb. Stuck underwater.

Claude flopped to his back with a wail. "I forget the rest, Father. I forget! There was movement, and then pain. I remember a candlestick in my hands and darkness. Fire." He keened. "I remember flames! Putting papers in the flames, then to your beloved, precious books. The desk, engulfed."

The vaporous amalgam dissipated. Claude's ringing sobs filled the silence left in the hollow of Father's falsely-constructed voice. The agonized shouts echoed, spreading the foul breath of Briarrose.

Remy sank to the floor. Shock left him dazed. His hand on Claude's shaking shoulder. Claude, sprawled on the ground, faced Remy. Tears and snot glistened on his upper lip. His ruddy cheek pressed to the cool floor. He squeezed his eyes so tight it forced tears free.

"We fought, Remy. We always fought."

Tears filled Remy's throat.

"I know, Claude."

"I wanted to be better, Remy. I wanted to be like you. Good. Kind."

"I know, Claude."

Claude whispered, "This was all I could be, Remy. I could never be you."

He wept like a wounded child, his body wracked in spasms from the force of his grief. When the paroxysms calmed, the muscles in his face slackened. A glaze covered his eyes. Claude straightened, exhaling.

"I remember," he whispered. "Remy, I *remember*."

Gaining strength and momentum, Claude pushed to his knees. Remy shifted away. In place of his regret, wrath swelled.

"Father and I stood in front of each other," he whispered. "I remember . . . swinging, but was too drunk to land the fist. Father ducked." Claude's lips tightened. His voice dropped. "He hit me in the stomach. On my way down, I . . . I grabbed something."

A cry split his face.

"The candle?" Remy asked.

"Yes." Claude's nostrils flared. His cheeks drew in, shoulders expanded. "I clutched that candle. The wax . . . it burned."

Remy battled rising, terrible emotions when he studied Claude's lightly scarred fingers.

"The fire didn't burn you, Claude."

"No," he breathed. "It was the candle. I swung that candlestick as hard as I could. Father toppled, so weak." Claude slammed a hand into the wall and shouted. "I swung it at Father's head! The candlestick fell on top of contracts Father once promised to put in my name, but he now planned to put in *yours*. Said you were the responsible son. The one who would take the business and the manor."

Claude's shouts distorted to a livid hiss. He shoved off the ground. Remy rose with him, backing up. The dark air in Briarrose gathered around Claude like a collapsing heart. Claude swung, pointing.

"You!" he thundered. "You stole my inheritance! If you'd only stayed away another year, or a few months, I would have had everything I deserved. But it didn't matter that I stayed, that I was the obedient son. Father was going to sign it all over to you. I couldn't let him."

Claude's body contracted like a bull ready to charge. Remy braced himself. In a blow-to-blow battle, he wouldn't win. Not with Claude's ballooning rage. But he wouldn't run, either.

"I hit Father with that candlestick," Claude growled, "and he fell. The blow to his head knocked him out, and he lay on the ground. When the contracts caught fire, I didn't stop them. In fact, I helped them along."

Disgust welled up in Remy. He wanted to vomit. Attempts to breathe were almost futile. The fetid air sickened. The evil in Claude intensified. Neither madness nor magic primed Claude.

Only undisguised hatred.

A brother wronged.

A witch who refused to forgive.

Claude couldn't hide in the refuge of insanity or black magic. What he'd blamed on Briarrose had been his own failure, and wasn't that Claude? He'd spent his life blaming everyone and everything else. Claude pressed a hand to his chest. The grimoire hadn't moved.

"I let that fire build around Father and all his demmed papers until it carried a good flame," he continued, maniacal. "I threw books on top. He didn't stir, Remy. Like he knew his time was over and a new heir arose. I ran to the bookshelves, grabbed the grimoires, and transported them. The contracts to sell them could be re-written, and they were," he added with a lecherous smile.

He lifted both hands and laughed. A belly-deep sound to resurrect undead wraiths. Claude calmed in a breath, one hand lifted to his lips, locked in recollection. A shade of mourning crossed his face.

"But the fire spread. It spread beyond what I meant, Remy. It grew out of control. The fault was mine. I should have let it burn until Father died and then put it out, but . . . the grimoires."

He trailed away, shaking his head. His lips turned down. "I regret Mother's death. I don't know what happened to her. She must have been asleep in their room . . . her injured knee, perhaps?"

Acid stung the back of Remy's throat. He couldn't think about Mother and what she endured. He had to finish *this*. When he glanced at the clock, he could barely comprehend how much time must have passed.

What of the enslaved witches?

Chase?

A strange expression crossed Claude's face. He twisted, half-looking over his shoulder, to the far wall. With a cry of outrage, Claude spun on his heel and raced to the window.

"What," he shouted, "is happening at my hedge?"

Remy sprinted across the room and launched himself onto Claude's back. They tumbled to the ground, heads conking. The impact sent lightning spikes of pain spider webbing through his skull. He groaned.

Unfazed, Claude shoved Remy off, rolled on top, and pinned him with his burly arms.

"Those blasted Guardians are in my hedge, aren't they? I can feel the magic changing. This is *your* fault. I won't give up Briarrose, so you'll pay for this and every death that results," he shouted. "You always received the best of everything. The inheritance was going to you. Amelie. Wildrose! What I was denied, you scooped up. When you leave Alkarra, I shall finally find peace."

Claude grasped Remy's throat. His meaty fingers squeezed. The sheer force of pain took Remy aback, swirling with panic. His mouth popped open.

He slammed his hand up.

Claude dodged it.

Remy tilted his hips to the side, but Claude trapped him with his legs. The unrelenting pressure drove deeper.

He fought harder.

Slamming fists, wheezing gasps, bucking chest. All remained futile. Claude's apoplectic face loomed overhead, twisted in fury.

Remy's heart would vault out of his chest. He couldn't over-power Claude. He never had.

Nothing gave.

Claude's scream blurred into the background. Dull thuds filled Remy's ears. A shadowy tunnel encroached from the sides. With dying hope, Remy said a quick spell.

A ball of light zipped into the air, broke through the window, and hurtled outside. It exploded in a spray, illuminating the dimly lit, and closely-held room. The distraction provided a chance for Remy to swing a weak arm. He cuffed Claude in the cheek, momentarily weakening his grip.

Remy gasped in a fast breath.

Claude doubled down.

Ropes appeared, lashing Remy's flailing arms. Despite the desperate rush of air, oblivion threatened again. Amelie and Quinten whispered to the front of his thoughts. Wildrose would care for them.

And the baby.

Oh, the new baby.

Remy's struggle against the enchanted ropes slowed. He dredged up the edges of his reserves, shoved his life force out of the corners, and cast his final spell.

Light shimmered behind Remy. He sensed it, more than saw. Claude choked, screaming out unfathomable things, as Father's ghostly apparition charged toward Claude in a vengeful swoop. Claude toppled to the side with a shriek.

The ghoulish apparition dissipated the moment it touched Claude. The five seconds of confusion bought Remy time to whip onto his side, gulp air, wheeze, and shoot another blazing shot of light at the door. This slammed into it with a weak *thud*, then scooted underneath.

Claude screamed. "It wasn't Father's ghost. It was *you*!"

Rushing voices came from without. "See the light?" SJ shouted. "Head up there!"

Claude's head snapped up.

He glowered.

"Who," he hissed, "are they?"

Weakened by the death-throes, Remy spelled away the enchanted ropes and shoved to his feet. He struggled to a stop, head whirling. Feet thundered up the stairs, closing in, as Claude threw himself at Remy. A knife glinted in his right hand, swinging for Remy's heart.

Remy crouched, grabbed Claude's wrist mid-air, and twisted. Bones cracked as he shoved Claude's arm away. The tip of the knife scraped Remy's chest, slashing his shirt, biting muscle and sinew, as they plummeted to the ground together.

They landed with an *oomph*.

Remy's spine slammed into the floor first, then his head. His teeth jarred. A headache thundered from back to front and back again.

For a dazed moment, all was silent.

He conducted a rapid and frightened assessment of his body. Toes moved. Fingers, too. Breath entered and left. Heart pounded. Everything hurt. His throat whistled and wheezed with each breath. His legs ached. A sharp pain pressed into his left knee. Tingling assaulted his hip, which is when he realized that Claude's heavy frame pinned Remy's legs. Heat trickled across Remy's knee.

Confused voices shouted, calling his name.

"Remy?"

"Open the door!"

The knob rattled.

SJ beat it with a fist. "Remy, now!"

The floor began to shake. A steady tremor crept toward the middle of the room. At the same time, a metallic smell filled his nose. The spreading warmth on his legs increased. Blood.

The panic of nearly dying sloughed into a new concern. Remy lifted his head, staring at the side of Claude's limp face.

"Claude?"

Books shivered off the wall, pelting to the ground. The windows cracked as a surge wrenched the bottom of Briarrose, as if someone had taken it by the sides and shook it. Smoke drifted through the air, accenting the crackling window panes that shattered.

SJ shouted through the thick wood.

"Remy!"

Remy sat up. The movement jarred Claude. He slipped to the side without resistance and a vague *thud*.

Time stilled.

Claude's slack face, half open eyes, answered Remy's unspoken question. Blood spread across his white shirt beneath the grimoire. The gigantic knife gleamed from where it stuck through the book and into Claude's chest.

Right through the heart.

Remy recoiled. A shelf fell. Dust and paper plumed into the air. The door blew open, forced by a spell. SJ spilled inside. He paused in the doorway, taking stock, before darting over and sliding to a stop in front of Remy.

SJ shouted, but Remy couldn't hear. Plaster dropped from the ceiling. The world shivered beneath his hands.

He comprehended only Claude.

The grimoire.

Claude's weapon sliced through the pages of the book, through the heart. Blood stained the pages pink. Gray ash formed around the edge of the knife and crumpled, turning each page and the leather cover to powder.

The grimoire disintegrated.

"Come on!" SJ screamed, one arm under Remy's. He pushed Claude off Remy's legs. Blood smeared his pants, his knee. "We gotta go! The whole demmed thing is caving in. Those bloody monsters outside are spraying molten lava all over the place."

A terrific crash from the hallway punctuated the command. Remy tripped to his feet as a chunk of ceiling impacted the floor. Beryl flames illuminated from cracks in the ceiling, spilling a deviant light. The grotesque wraiths sang in high-pitched screams. Their shrill sound rocked the air. Remy attempted to stand.

His legs gave way.

SJ gripped him around the shoulders, yanking him away from a chandelier that plummeted. Remy held on, attention locked on his brother. His dead brother. The ceiling collapsed, burying Claude in plaster and wood and dust.

Remy departed with the tingle of a transportation spell.

Chapter Twenty-Four

SJ braided his fingers together, looped them around his bent knee, and leaned back.

"Must say, Remy," he sang, "Chase delivering your letter, marching with those haggard looking witches, and then having him surrender as we broke through the bushes was a twist I didn't anticipate. Nice touch. Dangerous, but nice."

Three days after Briarrose's inevitable demise, Remy stood at the hearth in Wildrose's library, which remained utterly unscathed, despite Briarrose being nothing more than a heap of rubble. The singing wraiths burned until the very end, their lime fire consuming the entire estate. The haze had only just cleared.

A final protest before Briarrose released herself.

"I didn't know if it would work," Remy whispered. His voice hadn't fully returned after being half-strangled to death. His throat ached with each attempt to speak. At least it didn't hurt with each pulse of his heart anymore.

"It did work." SJ whistled. "But goodness, was it close."

Remy recalled very little of the final moments in Briarrose except SJ appearing, Claude's pale face, the grimoire crumbling to ash. The string of moments in between remained vague. It felt as if he lived in a snow globe. He could only touch one or two flakes at a time. The rest cluttered his head, but he didn't see them.

The soothing, steady grounds of Wildrose eased the agitation of what he'd endured, but slowly.

"Where is Chase?" he asked.

"In the dungeons."

"For how long?"

"If he survives the interrogation by the Council and the High Priest?" SJ shrugged. "Not sure."

"Did the High Priest read my testimony?"

"Yes."

Remy spun to face SJ for the first time in minutes.

"And?"

"And what?" SJ held up his hands. "What do you want me to say, Remy? Chase made his choices. He aligned with your brother, who wasn't a good witch. No amount of compassion for his start in life will change what happened."

A bitter taste filled Remy's mouth. "I would have died if Chase hadn't betrayed his boss and done what I asked. He wants something better. He was as much a slave as the rest of them. When the opportunity arose to do the right thing, he did."

"You would have died," SJ countered, "if you hadn't taken a risk and distracted your brother while Chase sent the messages through the shrub, and then tried to open a path for us. I don't feel all that much compassion toward Chase."

"I do."

SJ held up his hands. "It's up to the High Priest and the Council. They'll decide what to do. Your letter and explanation was read to them. It will help, I think," he quietly added.

Despite the truth about Remy saving his own life by risking everything on a ghost and a few spells, the observation didn't sit well. Flirting with death wasn't a situation he wanted to discuss. He wasn't a Protector, but a businessman. A father.

He wanted to talk about *that*.

"Still doesn't seem fair," Remy said as a final protest. "But I see there's not much else I can do. I'll visit Chase later."

SJ agreed with a sigh.

"What about the other witches inside?" he asked with a sudden rush of anxiety. All the locked doors might have hidden so many witches. Briarrose, once broken, toppled in minutes, according to bystanders.

"Fine."

"Really?"

"They have a long road ahead now that freedom is in their grasp," SJ said carefully. His gaze tapered. "Couple of them were wanted witches, so the Guardians are happy. One of them was a co-conspirator in the plot to assassinate the High Priest, so my boss is happy."

"Really?"

SJ nodded. "Claude was bold, that's for sure. Briarrose too, for that matter. Did you see that strange fire?" SJ shook his head. "Really weird. Greenish flames, sometimes pink. Had to be magic, because I've seen nothing like it before."

"It was magic."

"Huh. Well. No one else was inside that we're aware of," SJ replied. "Chase claimed to have freed them all, which is fortunate. Might help his case."

"It appeared mostly empty when I was there."

"Chase confirmed the same." SJ glanced at Remy's neck, a bruised mess of a place. "How are you?"

His pointed question didn't go unnoticed.

Remy turned away.

"Fine."

SJ scoffed. "Liar. He almost got you. How did you stop him?"

Saying *the ghost of my father* sounded too strange. The whole plan had been a wild attempt. A last prayer. Looking back, he couldn't believe it worked.

"Lucky magic."

"Very lucky. Claude was a big man. Based on the bruises around your neck, you had a pretty close brush with death."

"Too close."

"It's not easy," SJ said quietly.

All the energy left Remy. He'd replayed the scenario with Ralph, too, after it happened. When an apothecary cleared him to try to speak, he said what he could. A spell wrote the rest, preventing him from having to state everything.

Days later, and he still didn't want to discuss it.

He wanted it gone.

After a contemplative pause, SJ stood up. He brushed his hands off on his pants and kept his distance.

"You're a hero, Remy. I know you don't feel like it, but you removed the Briarrose problem without loss of innocent life, and you've kept your family safe. You freed the captive witches, helped prevent a plot against our High Priest, and removed a place riddled with evil. The estate is gone, and that's a good thing."

Is it? he wanted to ask, but the question would be pointless. It *was* a good thing, and he knew that. He didn't want it to be true because it would mean something for Wildrose. Something he hadn't deduced yet.

"Thanks."

SJ's eyes roved the room, which remained blessedly unchanged despite the loss of its sister magic. "That house is gone, so what about this one?"

SJ so casually voiced Remy greatest concern. What would happen to Wildrose with an unbalanced magic?

"I don't know."

"Sturdy construction," SJ mused, fingers rolling down a wall, "and an absolutely beautiful rendering of architecture.

Makes sense that magic put it together, because it would take witches a lifetime to mimic it. A piece of art, really."

"I agree."

"For all our sakes, I hope it sticks around. Could be really good for this Coven, you know? Anyway, thank you, Remy. Appreciate your help. Know you can reach out to me anytime you need it."

Quinten managed to squirm out of Amelie's arms and onto the grass with a hysterical giggle. His chubby fingers gripped stalks and pulled. He laughed when the fading green blades slid through his hands.

Remy chuckled.

Amelie threaded her arm through Remy's and leaned her head on his shoulder. He wrapped his arm around her waist, pulling tight. An autumn breeze warbled by, tinted with hints of incoming winter and snow. The crisp fall day had been warm and lovely at high noon, but tapered toward cooler edges. The end of her nose flared a charming red.

"How are you, Remy?"

He pressed a kiss to her forehead.

"Fine, my dear."

Not far from where they stood, Briarrose had disappeared utterly. Where charred remains once existed, trees sprang up. The unnervingly fast degradation set the whole neighborhood on edge, even as they felt a collective relief that the eyesore was gone. It really had been a garish thing.

Amelie's parent's house remained as stolid as ever. If houses could talk, it would also be relieved. The gardener had washed the exterior after the fire, scrubbing the strange ash free. With magic, it removed easily enough, restoring her old home to its original peaceful splendor.

A baptism and renewal, of sorts.

At Remy's insistence, James purchased the land for a pentacle coin, ensuring that no hideous monster of a home would spring up from a stranger ever again. When his in-laws died, Remy and Amelie would own both their ancestral properties together. They'd never leave Wildrose, but the holdings would support the ancestral estate.

A beautifully tied knot.

Life returned to the imperfectly peaceful place it had been before. The great evil no longer breathed down their necks.

"It was Claude, all this time," Remy whispered with a shake of his head. "His actions led to the death of my parents, and *he* brought great evil to Briarrose. A whole month later and I . . . I've had a hard time wrapping my head around it. Believing he's gone."

She held him tighter.

"I'm sorry, Remy."

Her lack of defense was another affirmation. Claude had been a troubled man with a history of terrible decisions. Remy didn't like that it ended with that truth, instead of others, but he accepted it.

"Choices," she observed calmly, "not foreordination."

"Choices," he agreed.

"What do you think Father will do with the land next?"

"Let it run wild."

"What do you mean?"

He pointed to the manor shell, which crumbled farther into the earth every passing hour. Growth sprouted as quickly as it vanished.

"The forest is already overtaking it. Like it was always meant to be the master. We're going to let it grow. It'll provide a protective screen for your parents house and the neighborhood."

"After what they've been through, they've certainly earned it."

With a weak smile, Remy agreed. The briarroses and thorns that had crawled along the neighborhood, infecting other houses, spreading their poison, had disappeared. Repairing grass sprang up. New ivy, too. The place looked, for all the world, as if nothing horrible had ever touched it.

Quinten pushed unsteadily to his feet, managed a few steps, and collapsed again. His flailing arms obliterated a pile of leaves. Amelie stepped in front of Remy, forcing him to meet her gaze.

"Are you truly all right, Remy?"

Remy ran the tips of his knuckles down her cheek and smiled.

"I am. I'm sad at what Claude became, and I'm sad for the choices he made, but I am happy with you. I have the life he secretly craved, but never worked for, and it is more than enough."

Tears filled her eyes as they pressed their foreheads together. "I confess," she said with tears on her cheeks, "that I am partially relieved. I feared for our son as Claude's jealousy grew. For Wildrose."

"We have nothing to fear anymore."

"What of Wildrose, do you think?"

The magic, though so obvious and straightforward in some ways, continued to surprise him in others.

"I think it will remain," he admitted. "Eventually, the lacking balance in the magic will weaken its power and it will break down as a casualty to time . . . but not yet."

"Think our son will enjoy it?"

"And his," Remy whispered. "And *his*. At least, I hope. Despite all that's happened, I can't help but wonder if this was the path of the magic all along. Maybe it was supposed to be this way. The evil stamped out before it gained real root, but the legacy and power of the magic will allow Wildrose to forge a good impression on the world."

A gust of wind blew past, stirring her hair. Amelie turned her face into it, an eye on Quinten, who played with a sapling.

"Isn't that what magic is?" he asked. "Our attempt to make things a little better and easier than we found them?"

Amelie snuggled close. She cradled their next child in her womb. They would carry a brighter legacy to their children, and so on. Like Wildrose, none of them were meant to stay forever.

They were only meant to be here awhile, and do good while they were at it.

Remy gathered her more tightly in his grasp, pressed a kiss to her hair, and released her. He picked up Quinten, who squealed with airborne delight, and settled him in the crook of his arm.

Together, they strolled over his ancestral land, past the growing buds, and away from the final remnants of Briarrose.

"Wildrose awaits," he whispered to Quinten, "and we shall always be here for it."

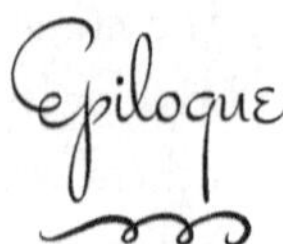

Epilogue

The scritch of ink on paper was a soothing sound. Remy barely heard it, as he barely heard anything these days. Unlike Quinten, he didn't take great delight in writing out his thoughts.

He did, however, love a pedigree.

As he crossed the final t, ensured a dot on the last i, Remy leaned into his chair. Sixty years old, and such life to show! The Wildrose grimoire contained more than the magic of his legacy, but his legacy itself.

His family.

The branching pedigree had a great deal more movement and power than he'd ever dreamed when first starting out with Amelie. When Wildrose whipped him to this hallowed spot and all but commanded him to build it, he had no idea the results. That, on a lovely spring day decades later, he would hand the grimoire to his second son, the established Dauphin inheritor.

"Take good care of her while you have Wildrose, my dear. For she was everything to me."

Solemnly, Baron said, "I will, Father."

For how old the paper must be, the power endured. The grimoire gave Remy hope that Wildrose had years in her, yet.

Oh, sure. The magic changed. Meals didn't sporadically appear in the same way. Rooms cleaned and rearranged, but not so often. He sensed the gradual dwindling power, but she held reserves.

Wildrose was not destined to fail yet.

Remy shuffled to the window. Long had his sons and daughters taken care of the manor, accepted the strangers that roved through, and the odd tweaks and things that came with living here, but now it was truly theirs. He wasn't long for this world.

Time wore on him.

He felt it.

Amelie tugged at him from the lands and lives beyond, beckoning him back to her side. Five years alone, and he missed her. Wildrose wasn't the same without Amelie bustling around, laughing all the time.

From the window, he said to Baron, "The magic will fade, son. Entirely. It must," he waved a hand, "and you already know this, but it bears repeating. With the counter magic vanished, it will not actively maintain forever."

"Yes, Father."

"This was the way," Remy whispered, tears in his eyes.

And oh, what a way!

What a beautiful life.

"It was never meant to be forever." Remy cleared his throat. "But for now. One day, Wildrose will find its final master. I can feel it."

Baron's response faltered, though he tried to hide it. Baron loved Wildrose, but not like Remy. No one had attached to the estate in the same hopeless fashion. Perhaps because Wildrose found Remy at the same time as the greatest loss of his life. Wisdom dictated that the magic chose the witch, and not the other way around.

Foreordination might be true, after all.

"That final master," Remy continued, "will love Wildrose

out of the world, as I loved Wildrose into it. Such is the degradation of unbalanced magic, but the power of goodness. In the end, it's worth it. We all make choices. We all live with them. That is the real beauty of what we're doing here, Baron. The real beauty is often the quality of the life, and not the way it began."

The Sisterhood

BOOK 9 IN THE NETWORK SERIES

Oh, my reader friends. The adventure does NOT stop here.

Click on the book to purchase your copy of THE SISTER-
HOOD, the ninth novel in the Network Series.

Yours in magic,

Katie Cross

About the Author

Katie Cross is ALL ABOUT writing epic magic and wild places. Creating new fantasy worlds is her jam.

When she's not hiking or chasing her two littles through the Montana mountains, you can find her curled up reading a book or arguing with her husband over the best kind of sushi.

Visit her at www.katiecrossbooks.com for free short stories, extra savings on all her books (and some you can't buy on the retailers), and so much more.